CW01507842

Contents

The Duke Takes a Wife.............................5
Three Times A Lady...............................157
The Bride of MacKenzie Black..............311

DR

Not Just Royals

DAHLIA ROSE

Not Just Royals

The Duke Takes a Wife

Chapter One

"Jasper McTavish, Tenth Duke of Northumberland, twenty-third cousin to her majesty the Queen…"

"Sod it all, must they go on and on with that bloody long-winded title?" Jasper muttered.

He winced as the person called out his title, and Jasper pulled at the tuxedo tie at his neck. Looking at the people that milled about the sunken ballroom of the hotel while he stood at the top of the stairs, Jasper could tell he was going to have a horrible night. All eyes had turned to where he and his uncle stood while they were announced. His uncle, Brewster McTavish, looked proud, and they weren't even calling his name.

His uncle was there to make sure he behaved and to offer his opinion on another matter: a wife. His family, in their wisdom, had decided it was time for him to marry as per his father's will, and he hated the whole fucking title nonsense. He wasn't willing to give up his manor, because it was where he found peace. But if they thought he would be a quiet church mouse and let them set him up with some pinch-nosed uppity bitch, they were sadly mistaken. Jasper grinned wickedly at the thought while the guests clapped. His uncle leaned over and spoke quietly in his ear as they descended the ballroom steps.

"I can't allow you to go off the script for tonight, my boy. I can see the wheels turning in your head," Uncle Brewster said.

"What ever do you mean, Uncle?" Jasper said innocently as he snagged a glass of champagne from a passing waiter.

Uncle Brewster grunted. "Just be happy I convinced your mum it should be me travelling with you, not her."

"You mean it's good for her. I'd have thrown her out of the plane without a parachute," Jasper said mildly.

Uncle Brewster chuckled. "My sister is... never mind, I'd of probably let you."

There was no love lost between him and his dear old mum. He became Duke when his father died, and Jasper had no doubt his father had jumped in the grave to get away from Cornelia McTavish.

He caught a glimpse of a red dress moving quickly through the crowd but before he could see the face, the person was gone. Ebony skin and a satin red dress was all he saw. But he could feel the eyes of other women on him as he walked through the crowd at the gala. He nodded and smiled like a good diplomat before he took a sip from his glass. They were to be in Washington, D.C. for only five days before he returned back to Northumberland and normalcy. Uncle Brewster hoped that at the elite gala where politicians who ran the country wheeled and dealt out favors over cocktails and expensive food, Jasper would find a woman worthy of being the new Duchess and attraction would bloom. He was hoping he could find a sodding good beer and a room to hide out in for the night.

"Just look at them. If their eyes were any hungrier, I'd be picked to bones by now," Jasper said.

"Come now, Jas, there are some very beautiful women here," Uncle Brewster said. "Give it a chance, you never know what may happen."

Jasper caught sight of that red dress again in the crowd and was intrigued. He handed his uncle the champagne glass. "You may be right, Uncle. I'll find you in a bit. Go act British or whatever."

"Jasper, where are you…"

He was gone before his uncle could finish the frustrated sentence. Each time he caught a glimpse of the dress, he followed. In between bites of canapés, he tried to fend off flighty women that stopped him at every turn. They laughed too loud and asked the same question each time. "Oh my God, what's it like to be a Duke?" How did one answer that exactly? Jasper was starting to get impatient because they were deflecting him from his task, finding the red dress and the woman who was wearing it. He finally took a breather by the bar and hoped they would stop talking to him for at least a few minutes.

The bartender came over and Jasper practically begged him for a beer. He had to settle for American lager. Compared to European beer it was weak, and he grimaced. *At least it's something,* he thought. He took another swig of the beer straight from the bottle and leaned over the bar.

"Gin and tonic, please. More gin, less tonic," a husky feminine voice said from beside him. "It's been a piss poor night."

Jasper saw the hem of the red dress by his feet and smiled. He'd been chasing her all night, and when he stopped moving she'd come to him. If that wasn't some kind of destiny intervention he didn't know what was.

"Well hallo there," Jasper said smoothly. "I've been searching for you since this thing began."

"Can it, buddy. I don't want to be hit on," she said coldly.

"No, seriously." Jasper smiled. "I have been barreling through all these snooty people each time I caught sight of your dress."

The bartender placed her drink on the bar, and his dream in red took a long sip. "Now why would you be doing that? Let me guess. In D.C, I'm a jewel and you can do so much for me in this town."

"Actually no, I don't live here. Catch the accent?" he teased.

She raised an eyebrow. "Oh honey, you are not the only European accent here. I had two Germans who live in the city ask me to be the meat holder for their sausage."

He choked on his sip of beer. "Well, that's disgusting."

"You're telling me. After I threatened to rip their throats out with my teeth, they got the picture, so excuse me while I don't fall under the British charm," she muttered and took another sip of her drink. "If I was in uniform this wouldn't happen, but no, my boss made me wear this dress. Oh Zeva, you can look feminine, show me how pretty you are, and that's an order. Chauvinistic son of a bitch…"

Jasper kept silent and let her temper simmer down. If he'd learned anything it was don't interrupt a woman venting her frustration, and it seemed she had a lot to be angry about. He assessed her. She was a beauty, from the long dark hair that flowed down her back to the tapered eyebrows she had arched in his direction which he wanted to trace with his fingers. Her lips were deliciously coral pink, and he wanted to give her plump bottom lip a nibble. Her body was curvaceous and the ebony leg that peeked through the slit in her dress was tempting.

"I shall challenge all who have offended you to a

duel," Jasper said smoothly. "I'm pretty good in a bar fight, too. Let's take them all on."

She sputtered a laugh. "Thanks, but I think we shouldn't cause a political-slash-international incident."

"That's no fun at all," he murmured. He held out his hand. "Jasper McTavish, at your service."

"Oh, you're that guy they announced. All they needed was trumpets to herald your arrival," she teased. "Duke this and that of the third kind, the one who will rule them all or something. Man, that's some title."

"I cannot stand it, but apparently it must be done," Jasper laughed at her description of his title. He liked her already. She didn't give a flying fuck about who he was. "And you are Zeva…"

"Sargent Zeva Troy of the United States Army, but treated like a secretary and concubine at the whims of my commanding officer, who is a D.C. blowhard with a wife and grown children." She raised her glass in his direction then sighed. "I'm sorry for venting to you, strange man with the accent."

"Not a problem at all, the bar fight is still on the table," Jasper teased. She was genuinely unhappy and somehow he wanted to fix it. "God, this beer is awful."

Zeva downed the rest of her gin. "Want an adventure?"

"Where are we going?" Jasper asked, instantly intrigued.

She arched her eyebrow at him again and leaned forward devilishly. "Come with me if you want to find out and before my asshole commander finds me."

"Let's go," Jasper said instantly. Hell, for all he cared he would follow her into traffic.

They didn't go up the ballroom stairs. Instead, she led him to the far side of the room and out a decorative side door that was hidden into the wallpaper. He guessed by the tables stacked with tray after tray that it was how the waiters were replenishing hors d'oeuvres to go back to the guests.

"Grab a tray of those, will you?" Zeva said from in front of him.

"The nibbles?" he asked.

She laughed. "The nibbles, that's so cute. Yes, grab those, I'm starving." Jasper grinned and did as she asked while she led him to a room. "Okay, wait here for me."

"Are you sure?" he asked, looking around in the darkness. "I'm not being what you Americans call 'punked,' am I?"

She laughed and flicked on a light revealing a kind of green room with lounge chairs, a TV, and a large coffee table. "You're not being punked, and that's a stupid show that has been cancelled for years, stop watching it. I've been at this hotel before for conventions and a few other things. I know its secrets." She took a crab canapé from the tray and popped it in her mouth. "Mmm, yummy. Now trust me and wait here. I'll be right back."

She closed the door before he could say a word, and he was left alone. Jasper put the tray on the table and picked up a remote. He flicked on the TV and he could see the ballroom they just left and a few other rooms for that matter. He smiled as he sat down and loosed his tie. It seemed to be a bonus to know an insider to this place. Zeva came back soon after, sliding through the door she cracked just enough to get in and closing it gently before she locked it behind her.

"Look what I got you." She held up an ice bucket and pulled out a bottle of Newcastle.

"Bloody hell yes." He sat up as she came over and sat next to him and handed him a bottle.

"Crap, I forgot the bottle opener," she muttered.

He felt along the edge of the table. "No problem, I have a trick."

Jasper positioned the cap of the beer bottle along the sharp corner of the table and used the ball of his hand to smack it hard. His trick snapped the bottle cap off easily, and he repeated the action with her beer as well.

"That's pretty cool," Zeva said and ran her finger

along the top of the bottle before putting it to her lips. "I had to make sure you didn't break the tip."

He found a sexual suggestion in her finger on the rim of the bottle and in her words, but didn't take it any further than his mind. She'd had enough of men perving on her for the night. She didn't need him to add to it.

"So what's this room used for?" Jasper asked. "Why would they need to see the ballroom?"

"Sometimes when they are meeting or having some other type of event here, people use this set-up to read the room. Say it's a convention and they're pushing a new product, they can put out different swag bags or brochures and read the people in the room to see if they'd be receptive and pattern the presentation to suit," Zeva said. "Politicians use it but to push their agendas, who would be in favor, who would not."

"Yeah, I can get that, but why the other little nooks and crannies we are seeing on the side?" he asked.

"That's the sordid side of this place. This is D.C., secrets and knowledge are power." Zeva's voice went grim. "If they can use it to gain an advantage, they will. Not many people know this is here. I found it by happenstance last year and now you know to not get caught on camera."

"Sounds like politics and royal titles can go hand-in-hand," Jasper said. "Well, look at that, two people canoodling in one of those little crannies."

"She's married to a senator and he's bisexual plus married." Zeva grabbed the tray and put it on her lap before sitting back and starting to eat the finger food.

Jasper grabbed three. "The behind the scenes is much more fun. By the way, won't you get in trouble for leaving the gala?"

"Won't you?" she countered.

"Touché, but my uncle won't fire me, not that I care much in the least," he answered.

"Well, my commander could get mad, and I could also get mad and file a harassment case against him, but that's trouble I don't need," she explained. "I'm just going to get these last few months in and my time in the military is up. I'm going to leave this town and find a job someplace quiet and away from politics. Being a military attaché to the White House with that man is the worst position I ever had."

"You should file for some kind of sexual harassment. Don't let him get away with it," Jasper countered. "No man should ever be allowed to use their authority like that."

Zeva gave in a sidelong glance. "That's sweet but naïve. In this town they would eat me alive and spit me out. I've never shirked away from a fight, but I don't set myself up to lose my credentials or my pay. I managed it for two years, ninety more days won't make a difference. Besides, I set up my replacement as my revenge."

"How so?" Jasper questioned.

"My replacement is a six-two sergeant who was injured on deployment. He can no longer serve in that capacity but he is a hell of a soldier and admin." Zeva smiled. "I'd love to see him try to hit on or grab ass with Mike."

"Oh, you are wicked," Jasper laughed.

She placed her finger on his lips. "Shush, not too loud."

"Okay." He smiled slowly and was disappointed when she moved her hand away.

"What about you, Duke? What do you do to pass the days across the pond?" Zeva asked.

"The Duke thing is just a requirement," Jasper said. "I like to work with my hands. I craft furniture, and it's sold from the stable I converted beside my manor house."

"You're kidding, you don't sit around eating kippers and playing polo or hunting with your dogs?" Zeva asked teasingly.

"You're reading one too many romance novels," Jasper joked. "We actually have to work for a living, at least I like to. Some of the rest of my family not so much."

"Want me to kick their asses for you? I am pretty good in a bar fight," Zeva teased, using his own words.

"I may take you up on that," Jasper said. He smiled when she laughed but the wheels in his mind were already turning.

They hid out in the private green room, eating canapés and watching the crowd until they started to slowly mill away.

"I think it's time we head back," Zeva said as she stood. She kicked off her heels, and from his seat he averaged her to be around five four in height. "The crowd is emptying out, but we can still sneak in unseen and pretend we were there all along."

"Listen, I'd like to take you out to dinner," he said and added quickly while she put on her heels. "As a thank you for saving me for tonight."

"You don't have to do that," she said with a smile.

"I know, but I want to. There has to be a good pub in Washington you can recommend. Let me treat you to some fish and chips," Jasper cajoled. "You can't send me home after one night of fun and leave me with my stuffy old uncle for five days."

"And what would you have done if you hadn't met me?"

"Searched for you until I did find you," he said putting on the charm. "Come on, be a good egg, take me to a pub and let's have Guinness this time."

"Fine, you convinced me with Guinness." Zeva walked over to a desk, grabbed a pen and a small notebook, and wrote quickly. "That's my cell and where you can meet me tomorrow at eight. Don't be late, Duke Jasper McTavish, I'm not one of your wenches. I won't wait."

He took the paper with a smile. "Again, luv, too many romance novels. I gave up all my serving wenches long ago."

This time it was Zeva who laughed too loud, and he put one lone finger on her lips with a "ssshh." She grinned and went to the door and unlocked it before taking a peek outside. They took the tray and placed it, empty, back on the table. Zeva hid the ice bucket with the beer bottles under the long tablecloth of one of the tables.

"This was fun. See you tomorrow, Jasper," she said before sneaking through the way they came in.

"Bye," he said quickly before she was out the door.

He counted to thirty before going out the same way. No one had even noticed them. He barely caught a glimpse of that red dress before she blended into the crowd. He found his uncle easily. He was animated, talking to two older women, and when he caught sight of Jasper he excused himself quickly and came over.

"Where have you been all evening?" Uncle Brewster blustered. "I had several women rather interested in meeting you."

"And I was not interested in meeting any of them," Jasper said smoothly. "I was meeting someone on my own."

"Jasper, remember what your mother said. Someone with income who can help sustain the lifestyle of the family…" Uncle Brewster started to stammer.

"I don't gave one flying fuck about their income, they can go work like the rest of us do," Jasper practically snarled. "I will choose whom I marry and you should choose to have a backbone sometimes when it comes to my mother and your two spoiled daughters."

Uncle Brewster sighed. "You are right on some points, but one can only judge from the outside."

"One can see what's been going on from the time I was a child, Uncle." Jasper sighed. "I never held it against you nor will I ever, but you do know I will not be dictated to by the family."

"You always marched to your beat, son," Uncle Brewster said and clapped him on the shoulder. "So, where is this woman who is going to be part of the McTavish family?"

Jasper spotted her going up the stairs and said softly, "Her."

His uncle followed Jasper's gaze and she looked back and caught the both staring. Zeva gave him a wink before continuing her assent out of the ballroom.

"Oh dear," Jasper heard his Uncle Brewster murmur with worry in his voice.

He didn't care, he already knew that the McTavish clan would revolt at his choice, but he wasn't worried. He could tell from their conversation she would be able to handle her own. Title or not, none of them could hold a candle to Zeva. Her strength and beauty enamored him. This wasn't about what they wanted but who he wanted. Zeva would be his wife.

Chapter Two

"This looks like a nice thing to wear," Zeva murmured to herself.

She looked in the mirror at her choice of clothes and wondered if she should change. She has having dinner—well, fish and chips with a duke. *Screw it, I'm not changing,* she thought as she looked at her jeans and the soft pink sweater she wore. The wide neck sloped off the shoulder revealing the black wide strap of the camisole top she paired with it, revealed her smooth skin. He had asked her out, not the other way around, and she wasn't in the habit of changing for anyone. After making sure her ponytail was high and smooth, Zeva slipped on her boots and stepped from her apartment onto the stone steps.

She locked up and headed out into the D.C. night to meet Jasper. The Four Carriages Irish Pub was in her neighborhood and it was an easy walk. Jasper was standing outside right at eight o'clock as she walked up. He leaned casually against the stone doorway with his hands in his pockets. He was talking to the bouncer at the door and Zeva took the time to assess the duke. His hair was dark as a raven's wing. While it was longer than the military cuts she was accustomed to seeing, it suited his angular jaw. He was tall. She was at least five four without heels and he was at least six two. Jasper had broad shoulders, and he was wearing a black evening jacket, the kind with light brown leather at the elbows.

His slacks were the color of the leather patches on his coat. He was definitely handsome, but his motives were still unclear and because of her last few years in D.C. she trusted very few people. He looked towards her and met her gaze. As she walked up a slow smile crossed his face. Zeva's heart gave a little jump in her chest and she wondered what the heck that was about. She wasn't one to get flutters of excitement, she was too damn jaded about this world.

"Hello Sargent, you look simply smashing as usual," Jasper said warmly.

Zeva gave him a smile. "You'd reverse that thought quickly if you saw me in uniform."

"I doubt that very much," Jasper said and turned, extending the crook of his arm to her. "Shall I escort you inside?"

"Are you always this formal?" she asked, linking her arm through his.

"I could say my mum taught me good manners,

but that's not the case," he commented mildly. "Let's just chalk it up to me having a respect for women."

"Okay, let's do that," Zeva said. She wanted to ask more about his life but they had just met and it wasn't her place.

She always liked the inside of the pub she chose. The Four Carriages emblem was made of bronze and attached over the bar. It was always shining, as if Ralph the bartender and owner got up every day and polished it until it gleamed. The pub was mahogany throughout and kept immaculately cleaned, not a speck of dust in sight. The red suede booth had no stains or anything and the food was amazing. Zeva would know because sometimes when she came home late and had no inclination to cook, Ralph's wife Joan's shepherd's pie and chicken was comfort food and gave her life.

The older bartender was short and bald at the top, with the rest of his scraggly white hair combed as neatly as possible. He had worn a white shirt and tie for as long as she remembered. In fact, all his staff wore black pants and white shirts with ties. Ralph once told her if they respected how they looked, they would respect his business and the customers. Since she'd never had a problem, Zeva would say his assessment was correct. His wife Joan was plump and just a bit taller than her husband, and Zeva adored them both.

"Sargent, look at you, and on a Sunday no less," Ralph said warmly. His gray mustache waggled as he smiled.

"I know, I know, my uniform is much better," Zeva teased. She stood on the brass rail that wrapped around the lower part of the bar and leaned over to kiss his bald head.

"Careful now, if Joan sees you she may find out about our secret love affair," Ralph teased.

"I already told her and she says I can keep you because you snore," Zeva replied with a wide grin.

Joan, with her hair in a bun and wearing the same uniform covered with an apron, came out of the kitchen just as Zeva was speaking.

"She's right, I told her she can have you. I'll import a fine Irish stud from home," Joan said and gave Zeva a wink. She looked from Zeva to Jasper. "I may not have to, I see you've brought me one."

Zeva laughed. "Ralph, Joan, this is Duke Jasper McTavish."

"Aye, I know who he is. I saw him on the news last night," Joan said. "Plus, I worked for your grandmother long ago, a very long time ago before we moved to America."'

Jasper looked surprised. "Gran? You mean when she still lived in Kildare?"

"Aye, before they married her off in forty-two I was her maid on the estate," Joan answered. "I wasn't willing to travel to England and leave my Ralph so I paid my severance and along with what he saved we moved here."

"Small world," Jasper mused. "It's lovely to meet you. I would have loved to know Gran in her younger years. Mum wasn't the nicest to her near the end…"

"You have your grandmother's eyes, kind eyes," Joan said. "But enough of that, let's get you two a table and some of our amazing food into you, not to toot my own horn. Ralph, you pour them a pint of Guinness each, will you?"

"Yes, task master," Ralph groaned and Joan swatted at him with her white towel. He grabbed her in a big hug and kissed her cheek amidst her girlish giggling.

"Come on, Jasper, let's get to a booth before they get any friskier." Zeva's voice held humor as she took his hand and led him away.

They found a booth and slid in across from each other, and Jasper looked back to the still playful older couple.

'They are what it's all about," he said. "I would love to have that forty years from now, looking at the same face and having that connection each day I wake up."

"They amaze me. When I moved here, the first day I came in in my uniform, they treated me like I was their child," Zeva said. "It is such a coincidence, she knew your grandmother."

Jasper nodded. "Yes, it is. I would love to hear more. I hope I can pop back around to this place before I leave and bend her ear a bit."

"You have five days. You know where it is now and you can come visit anytime." Zeva smiled. "Oh, and your accent became thicker with a bit of Irish when you spoke to them."

"Really, you were listening to my accent," Jasper drawled. A waitress came over and brought their Guinness and two menus with a smile.

"Don't get a big head about it." Zeva pulled her drink over. "It's nice, that's all."

"Your voice is nice too, it's like a good Scotch with a bit of an after bite." Jasper took a sip of his own drink. "That's a bloody good pint."

"This is the best place ever," she replied. "Are you saying that my voice is harsh?"

Jasper shook his head. "By no means, let me explain. There is this whiskey from Belgium, it's called prickly peach, it starts out sweet and you catch a hint of peach Saison…"

"What's a Saison?" Zeva asked.

"It's a fruity pale ale and it's added to the whiskey," Jasper explained. "You take a sip after it's been aged and you get this burst of fruit and whiskey flavor and then a tart bite at the end. That's your voice—sweet with a hint of a bite to let people know you're not to be crossed."

She inclined her head. "Okay, I'll give you that as a compliment."

"It was meant to be one," Jasper answered.

As they sipped their drinks, they scanned the menus and chose their dinner order. She convinced Jasper to share an order of Buffalo wings with her as an appetizer. He decided on the shepherd's pie due to her raving about it, and Zeva picked the lobster ravioli. Their food came out quickly and piping hot, and as they ate they chatted about nothing and everything. Zeva found herself loving the simple conversation, but in the back of her mind she sensed an agenda. She chalked it up to her wariness of men in the political mecca of the United States. By the end of the night and after a few pints and great conversation, she looked at the time and it was past ten. Looking around she saw many of the patrons were already gone.

"We should get going. Ralph and Joan won't rush us but they close around ten-thirty, and I've got to be at work for eight in the morning," Zeva said.

"I didn't even notice how late it was," Jasper said. "I should check in with my uncle, make sure he actually ate and didn't drink his meal."

"He's an alcoholic?" Zeva asked pulling out her wallet.

"No, yes, kinda, well, it's a long story," he answered and covered her hand with his. "The tab is mine to pay. I invited you out tonight."

"I have no problem sharing the cost," Zeva said.

"Certainly not." His voice held a hint of outrage, and he pulled money from his pocket. From what Zeva could tell he left a substantial tip.

She held up her hand. "Fine, you win, thank you for a lovely evening."

"I shall walk you home," Jasper announced as they stood.

"I just live down the street a bit, I'll be okay. I can wait with you while you get a cab," she offered. "I can protect myself if necessary."

"It's dark and I wouldn't feel right letting you walk alone," he insisted. "We can call me a taxi from in front of your place."

"Deal." She took his hand and shook it briskly.

When he laughed, she found she liked the rich sound that came from his lips. In fact, Zeva found she liked many things about Duke Jasper McTavish. He was the most down to earth person she'd ever met.

"One second, I would like to speak to Joan before we leave," Jasper requested.

"Sure thing," Zeva said easily as they passed the bar. "Hey Ralph, is Joan still around or has she gone upstairs?"

"You leaving so soon," Ralph teased. "She is in the back."

"May I speak with her please," Jasper said politely.

"Sure thing," Ralph answered as he went into the back of the pub to get his wife. Joan came out wiping her hands with a towel and smiled at them both.

"How can I be of service?" Joan asked.

"I was hoping I could come back and talk to you about my Gran," Jasper asked tentatively. "You seemed to have a good relationship with her, and I was hoping you could tell me more about her life. My mother doesn't speak of her. To be honest, my mother is nothing like Gran and by the time I came along… well, she wasn't a good mum. Gran was my world, and she left me the manor I live in now where I craft my wood pieces."

"So you carve like your great uncle?" Joan beamed.

Jasper leaned against the bar. "I had an uncle who carved? Please tell me I can come back. It's like I was meant to be here and know you. Our paths crossed for a reason."

Joan gave him a gentle smile. "Come see me tomorrow afternoon around one, we can go for a walk and talk."

"That would be perfect, thank you," Jasper said gratefully.

"Just don't be stealing my woman, son," Ralph said severely but gave a wink.

Jasper put his hand over his heart. "Her honor shall be protected, sir. Besides, I think my interests lie elsewhere."

On those words, he gave Zeva a look. Again the damn butterflies invaded her body and she cursed them silently. Joan and Ralph shared a secret look and a smile.

"Well, on that note, time to walk me home," she said quickly.

"Good. She thinks she is a badass and we worry about her walking home alone," Joan said. "Night to you both, see you tomorrow Jasper."

"Goodnight and thank you, Joan," Jasper said.

"Night guys," Zeva said and gave a small wave.

Ralph's bouncer, who also happened to be his cousin's son, was going inside as they left and held the door open for them. Walking back the way she came she was definitely aware of the man next to her as they strolled through the September night.

"Seems they have a lot going on with your family," Zeva said curiously.

"I'll tell you about it sometime," Jasper said, and she heard the reservation in his voice.

"You sound like you think if you tell me I'm going to run screaming into the night," she said in a quiet tone.

"I'm hoping you won't," he replied.

"I'm curious to what your end game is and why you are interested in me?" She stopped outside the steps and turned around. "This is my place."

"See me tomorrow night, after work," he said.

"Don't you have any diplomatic stuff to do?" Zeva asked.

"No, I apparently was given the invitation and my mother accepted on my behalf." Jasper cupped her cheek and looked down at her. "I think I am very glad she did."

"What do you want from me, Jasper?" Zeva asked. His touch was warm against her skin, and she noted how big his hand was framing her cheek.

A smile spread across his face before he asked, "Right now, would a kiss be too much to request?"

"Not at all," Zeva murmured and lifted her head.

She'd be lying if she said she hadn't been wondering what it would feel like to have his lips on hers. Zeva was not disappointed. When his lips touched hers, she felt not a simmer of attraction but an instant flare of pure heat. She opened her mouth beneath his, inviting, daring him to taste her. Jasper groaned and moved his hands down to her waist and pulled her closer as he dipped his tongue into her mouth. Zeva echoed his moan, completely amazed that she felt such an immediate desire for a man she hardly knew. But her body acted like it had known him all her life, and by God she wanted him. He pulled away reluctantly and she sighed in disappointment, wanting the kiss to go on.

"I'll guess I'll see you tomorrow," Zeva said with a smile.

"I'm glad you will, we can talk more then," Jasper said.

"Going to tell me what you and Joan talk about?" she teased.

"You can come with us if you want," Jasper replied and the offer floored her.

"I was kidding, Jasper, you don't have to tell me your family business," she said quickly.

"I want you to know." Jasper gave her a hard kiss. "So tomorrow then?"

"I'll be home at eight, I'll make you dinner," Zeva invited and pointed to the doorway "It's a three level duplex apartment. My bell is the one on the bottom and my apartment entrance is private."

"I've never had someone make me dinner before," Jasper said.

She raised an eyebrow at him. "What about the servant wenches at the manor?"

"Again, too many romance novels. I live alone, I don't have a staff nor do I want any."

"I'll make you an American feast." Zeva smiled. This time it was she who kissed him long and deep until they were both breathing heavy. "See you tomorrow, duke."

He grinned at her before walking to the curb. Jasper hailed a passing cab and soon he was inside and looking at her through the rear window of the yellow car. The kiss and the attraction they shared was an interesting development. He wasn't like the cocky assholes she'd dated since being in D.C., that was for sure. Zeva walked up the steps to her apartment door, unlocked it, and went inside. She was still curious about his motives, but Zeva had never backed away from anything in her life. If Jasper turned out to be an asshole with some dark intention she would fix it in her way. Till then, she was willing to see where it went.

Jasper could feel Uncle Brewster's worried gaze as he moved around the hotel suite. It wasn't that his uncle was concerned about him, per se. No matter what, Uncle Brewster was deathly afraid of his sister and not completing what she wanted. No matter how much bravery he showed, it was like his uncle wore a metal collar made of his sister's domineering intentions. Jasper shook his head sadly, knowing that this woman was his mother and in a way she had trapped his uncle into an existence of servitude.

Jasper had refused to be bullied by her from the time he understood she was toxic.

"Stop looking like the world is coming to an end, Uncle Brewster," Jasper said calmly.

He was dressed and ready to go meet Joan for a walk to the park and later see Zeva. He wouldn't tell his uncle too much, because if his mother called, his dear uncle would spill the beans.

"I just think you could be spending time looking for a suitable Duchess," Uncle Brewster stammered.

"Who said I wasn't?" Jasper asked mildly. He took a sip of the tea that was on the breakfast tray sent by room service.

"Jasper, please consider what your mother is saying," Uncle Brewster pleaded. "We need the income to sustain the family."

Jasper gave him a direct stare. "No. Cornelia wants the income you can and have sustained, Uncle. You let her destroy your life and turn your daughters into clones of herself."

"Your mother needs money. She called this morning." Uncle Brewster sighed. "There is to be a gala in London and she needs to buy dresses for her and the girls."

"Why in the bloody hell are you telling me?" Jasper asked angrily. "Let me be clear, Uncle, they are not getting a penny of my hard earned money. They can live quite nicely on the stipend left after my father's death. I even forfeited my share so she would shut up with the whining about it being such a dreadful pittance. She called you to have you ask me, didn't she?"

"Just a few thousand is all she needs, and she wanted to check on how the wife search was going," Uncle Brewster answered.

"It's none of her business. I am doing it because it's required of my title as per my father's will, not to garner her money. Somehow she got that warped, but then it is my mother," Jasper pointed out. "And I'm not sending her or the bitch cousins any money."

"Those are my daughters, Jas," Uncle Brewster said coldly, showing a small spurt of anger on behalf of his daughters.

"And if you loved them so much, you wouldn't have let my mother drive your wife away and turn them into what they are now. Grow a backbone, man, and stand up for yourself to all of them!"

"You are on the outside looking in, your mother and I have been through a lot..." Uncle Brewster said.

Jasper leaned forward. "No, she is jealous of anything that isn't about her, that's why she ruined you and Lillian and so much so the woman ran and left her daughters. She hated the life you showed your wife, and no matter how much my dad loved her it was never enough. Now you are her lackey, jumping to do her bidding and so very much alone that I can see it weighing on your shoulders." He sighed and added sorrowfully, "I hope you break free of her, Uncle. I love you that much I want to see you away of this mess. I want you to find Lillian, live in a seaside cottage, and be happy for the rest of your life in your gardens with a woman who truly loves you."

"It sounds like a good dream, but I doubt it will happen," Uncle Brewster replied.

Jasper looked at his watch and stood up. "It will if you fight for what you want. You've got to stop waffling between wanting to be free and letting me go my own way to falling under Cornelia's whims. In any case, I've got plans that I can't be late for. I'll check in on you later and then I have dinner with a friend."

"Your schedule is pretty booked, it seems, while I'm here in the suite alone," his uncle joked.

"Go out, have fun, do something for you," Jasper said. "Explore, uncle. You don't have to sit in the hotel for five days."

Uncle Brewster looked at him. "In all honesty, I'm rather enjoying the peace and quiet. I have a good book and room service at my beck and call."

"Well then, I'll see you later." Jasper gave his uncle a quick pat on the shoulder as he left.

Sometimes all he wanted to do was to hug the man and then help him escape from the will of his daughters and Jasper's mother. But he couldn't save the older man, Uncle Brewster had to break that manipulative cycle all on his own. In any case, he wasn't going to be deterred. Zeva was perfect, strong, sexy, and independent. His mother would have one hell of a time trying to run roughshod over her, and he had no doubt that Zeva could give as good as she got. All he could think about while he lay in bed that night was how it felt to kiss her, and he wanted more in the worst way. He stepped out into the sunshine and hailed a cab to take him back to the pub. In less than twenty minutes Jasper was promising Ralph that he would bring his wife back in the same condition she left in.

Joan tucked her hand into the crook of his when he offered her his arm. "I do miss the old gentlemanly ways of Europe."

"I'll be as chivalrous as you need." Jasper took her hand and kissed it soundly, loving when the old woman laughed.

"Now, what do you want to know about your grandmother?" Joan asked as they walked.

"Everything," Jasper said automatically. "You said I craft like my great uncle. I didn't even know I had one. I feel like my mother has hidden a lot of my family history from me."

"She's not proud of where she came from, that's a certainty," Joan said. "Your gran married Lord Edwards and became lady of the manor house that you now own. That was where your mother and uncle were born. Your gran wrote me when she had the twins, and as the years went by she wrote of the affection of your uncle and her worry about Cornelia. She said it was like something was missing from her—empathy—her happiness only seemed to come from material things."

"She's that way now," Jasper murmured.

"She used your uncle as a gopher, and when she couldn't have her way he was her favorite person to take out her rage." Joan shook her head. "Your mother almost sent her away to a convent, but your grandfather married her off to Duke McTavish and then you were born. She'd hoped it would help your mother to become a mum, but she was cold to you as ever, only showing affection when her husband was around."

"I was the apple of her eye when she hosted parties or her league of friends were around," Jasper explained. "Dad figured her out eventually and started taking me with him on his trips abroad and sending me away to school. If she didn't have her way she made him miserable. When he died I became duke, and she said I was to take care of her now. By that time we well and truly hated each other, and I told her I would never be that person who gave in to her callous needs."

"And well you shouldn't," Joan said as they

entered the park. "I'm a bit parched, how about you get us two iced drinks from the cart over there and we can sit on this bench under the shade."

"Certainly, what would you like?" Jasper asked graciously.

"An iced coffee please. Don't tell Ralph, he says it makes me hyper," Joan laughed.

"Your secret will go with me to the grave," Jasper promised. "I'll be right back with your drink."

He walked the short distance to the cart that sold drinks, sandwiches, hot dogs, and pretzels. He got them both two vanilla iced coffees and two warm cinnamon pretzels. Jasper came back to where Joan was sitting and handed her a drink and the pretzel, much to her delight. She nibbled at the large warm treat and drank deeply from the cup before speaking again.

"So your mum is still..."

"A bitch, yes," Jasper answered. "My father's will states I should be married to keep the title. She saw it as 'get married to a wealthy woman' so she could have more money. We rarely speak, so she put Uncle Brewster up to going with me so he could keep an eye on whom I may choose."

"And you have chosen Zeva," Joan said knowingly. "Does she know yet?"

"There is no hiding anything from you, is there? I plan to tell her tonight," Jasper admitted with a laugh. "Any ideas on how I should broach the subject?"

Joan took a sip of her drink and said bluntly, "Take the bull by the horns and tell her. One of two things will happen: she will punch you in the face and kick you out or hear what you have to say. But your mother will try to make her life hell."

He nodded. "I know, and I think Zeva would give as good as she gets. It not just about the title, I've only known her for two days and I cannot stop thinking about her."

"There is no time limit on love or attraction," Joan said. "I was dancing with another boy when I met Ralph at a social in Kildare. I went for a glass of punch and he told me he was going to marry me and to come away for a walk with him. A week later we were in love and saving money for our marriage. When I left the service of your grandmother we did just that. Our heart knows way before our mind does."

"I think it does as well,'" Jasper said. "I want what you and Ralph have. I have never seen it in my life but I know I want the kind of love that will last a lifetime."

"If that's what you want, then you grab it with both hands and never let go," Joan said and then warned him. "Your mum will make Zeva's life a living hell if you let her, and she will be vicious, cruel, and I have no doubt dangerous. Don't let her ruin any life you are trying to have with her."

Jasper met her gaze and vowed, "I won't. I'll stand for her, I swear it."

"I have no doubt," Joan replied and put her drink down to dig into her purse. "I think you walked into our pub for a reason. I have no doubt your Gran is looking out for you from above. Here is a letter from her, actually there are two letters in one. These are for the time you may need ammunition to shut her up. I would suggest hiding them away until you get home. Don't let your uncle see them, it affects him too. Keep them safe, Jasper."

"Are you sure you want me to have these?" Jasper said, doubtfully looking at the envelope that was brown with age.

"Yes," Joan said firmly. "These I feel were meant for you and to finally bring you peace from your mother when the time comes."

Jasper took the package. The paper was well preserved and felt firm in his hands, speaking to the old, thick paper it was made with. Joan also added another layer of protection by putting them in a baggie to protect from water or the elements.

"Thank you," Jasper said almost reverently. "I am so very glad I met you. You and Ralph must come visit the manor. Make it a family trip, bring everyone, your kids and grandchildren, there is plenty of room."

"We may take you up on that, because we are trying to take an extended trip to Ireland sometime soon," Joan said with a smile.

They talked about how Ireland and England had changed from when she was there to now, and Jasper enjoyed whiling away the hours with the older woman. It reminded him of how his gran used to be. A great big smile, loving personality, and blunt as a hammer. In a few hours he was walking her home and returned her to Ralph who looked at his wife with pure love on his weathered face. *Yes, I definitely want that,* Jasper thought as he hailed a cab to take him back to the hotel. When he got there, he found his uncle snookered drunk, almost passed out. Jasper sighed, defeated, and knew this was another thing he wanted to fix with all his heart but couldn't. It was one of the ways Uncle Brewster escaped the reality of his life.

"I love you my boy, always have. Only connection in this world that keeps me going," Uncle Brewster said as Jasper helped him to the second bedroom of the hotel suite.

"I know, Uncle, I love you too," Jasper answered and got him settled.

He ordered room service for lunch and another meal to be sent up, along with Tylenol and two bottles of water before he left for the night. He'd make sure there was a meal in the little kitchen area of the suite that his uncle could warm up when he finally woke, and the water was for him to hydrate. The Tylenol would be for the headache he'd have to deal with after his afternoon foray into the bottle.

Jasper looked at the letters before he hid them in in his locked case. For the longest time his gran was the only connection he had after his father died, and when his mother pushed her away from the home and Gran passed he'd felt lost. Joan gave him back part of his foundation with those letters, and maybe it would be a way to not only free himself from his mother but to save his uncle as well.

Chapter Three

Zeva looked around her neat apartment and wondered if she should vacuum the rug on the hardwood floor where her coffee table sat. She decided against it and checked the potatoes roasting in the oven. The steaks she had in the broiler smelled delicious. When she left work at six-thirty to come home and cook a meal for him, she caught fresh hell from her chauvinistic commander.

"Sir, I've done the last of your paperwork and I'm heading home," she said when she knocked and poked her head into his office on Capitol Hill.

"That includes the packet for the meeting with the Secretary of Defense?" Commander Brighton asked.

"Yes sir," she said politely and wanted to actually scream because when had she ever not done her job concisely.

He looked up and sighed. "Why don't you ever wear your hair down from that severe bun? You are not a school teacher from the sixties, Sergeant Troy, you can look feminine."

"That is not part of my job requirement, sir, and per military guidelines my hair meets specification to be neat and off my shoulders." Zeva's voice was polite but cold.

"Well, you work for me, and I say you can wear your hair down, let it frame your face and look like a woman," he replied. "I still have the image of you at the gala in my head, you were so very delicious."

'That is inappropriate, sir, may I leave?" Zeva had to remind herself that she was almost done working with this pig and not to be court marshaled for kicking his junk into his throat.

"What if I wanted you to stay late and work closely with me at this desk," he teased and licked his lips.

Zeva wanted to gag. "I would say my boyfriend would take issue with that and possibly make a diplomatic case of it. He's the Duke of Northumberland." She watched gleefully as her commander's face turned red.

"Since when—you never mentioned being in a relationship with some duke before," he blustered.

Zeva's resting bitch face was on point because her expression never changed. "We are not girlfriends at lunch gossiping, sir. I would never assume the commander would want to know about my personal relationships outside the office. Again sir, I have done all the requested work for the day, may I leave?"

"Fine, go home to the pansy-ass fancy pants man," Commander Brighton said.

Zeva saluted smartly. "Thank you, sir. Good evening, sir."

When she closed the door a grin split her face and she had to keep the dance out of her step as she walked away from the commander's office to her small work area that she called the closet.

Jasper worked in her favor today, and maybe for the rest of the time she was there Commander Brighton would keep his sexual innuendos down to a minimum. For that alone, Zeva figured she owed Jasper a delicious meal. Along with the kiss that seared her down to her toes, she'd even rustle up some dessert. He rang the buzzer to her apartment promptly at eight. Zeva had to admit she loved a man who was on time as she crossed the room to open the door. Jasper stood there looking elegant as ever in casual jeans, a polo shirt, and black leather jacket.

"Look at you, someone may think you're a native dressed like that," Zeva teased and stepped aside. "Come on in, probably not as fancy as your manor house but welcome to my home."

"It's very inviting, especially with the person who lives here being in my thoughts all day," Jasper said, and his baritone voice was like a caress along her skin. She closed the door and he pulled her into his arms. "How about a kiss of welcome?"

"Sure, why not," Zeva murmured.

She gave in to the need because she was thinking about kissing him too. Zeva sighed in delight because nothing felt more perfect than when his lips touched hers. The kiss wasn't too long, but it was enough to make her warm and aching in all the right places. Jasper pulled away almost reluctantly and looked down at her as if mapping her face for his memory.

"I hate that I have to leave in a few days," he said huskily. "Getting to know you has been the best thing to happen to me in a very long time."

"You could always stay longer," Zeva hinted.

Jasper shook his head. "Unfortunately no, I have work and my business. I want to talk to you about something."

"We can talk over dinner. I would like to hear what Joan told you about your family if you'd like to share," Zeva said and took his hand to lead him into her eat-in kitchen.

"I would, but I'd rather talk before dinner if we could," Jasper said. "You may decide to kick me out before feeding me."

"That doesn't sound good," Zeva murmured and her stomach lurched. "Let me just turn on the warmer on the stove so the steaks don't dry out. I'll grab us some beers, in case I need to hit you over the head with the bottle after our conversation."

Jasper smiled. "It won't come to that, I hope."

"If you say you're betrothed to someone and you want me as a side piece it just might," Zeva warned.

"A side piece?" he questioned.

"A mistress," she elaborated. "I'll be right back."

Zeva moved quickly to make sure dinner wasn't ruined and grabbed the cold drinks from the fridge. On impulse, she reached into the freezer, took out her bottle of gin, and poured a shot in one of her glasses. She swigged it down to help calm the nerves that were now aflutter at his wanting to talk. Nothing good came from a statement like that, and it would be her luck to be attracted to a guy that wasn't available or a liar. Her defenses went up, because it seemed no matter where they were from men were all the same. Zeva uncapped the beers and went back to the living room to hear the down and dirty of what Jasper had to say. He was still standing by her burgundy sofa when she returned.

She placed his drink on the coffee table and sat before saying two simple words. "Sit, talk."

"You seem perturbed," Jasper said as he sat down.

"I'm not. Just waiting to hear what skeletons you are dragging out of your closet," she replied.

Jasper took a deep breath and said, "Marry me."

She was taking a swig of her beer and almost choked. Zeva fanned her face. "Excuse me, what?"

"Be my wife," Jasper repeated with a smile. "You weren't expecting that, were you?"

"Not at all," Zeva admitted. "Jasper, we've known each other for three days."

"Let me explain. Part of my father's will to retain my title was to marry, and the time has come for me to do so," he began. "My mother is a witch from hell who thinks I'm to marry to help bring money into the family for her and my cousins to spend. I refuse to be a part of that, and I will marry whom I chose. You intrigued me from the first time I caught sight of you moving through the crowd, and then you took me on an adventure. I want to marry you."

"Ummm." Zeva honestly didn't know what to say so she focused on part of what he said. "Your cousins and your mom?"

"Uncle Brewster's daughters. My mom efficiently ran off her twin brother's wife and then took the twins under her wing. They are twenty-eight year old versions of the wicked queen herself. She molded them in her image, to replace the son who wouldn't fall in line I suppose," Jasper explained. "Uncle Brewster is a kind man, but rather weak, so now he is basically pushed and pulled around by those three and no matter what I do to help he can't seem to break free of it. Hence his propensity to favor the drink to compensate."

"So you want me to marry into the chaos?" Zeva

laughed unbelievingly. "And here I thought you liked me."

Jasper took her hand. "I do like you, very much so. They would not be able to run roughshod over you. You would give as good as you got and we could have a good life together. I know we can't say we love each other now, but the attraction we have is magnetic. I think I can find my forever with you, like Ralph and Joan. Unless you don't feel the connection like I do…"

"No, no, I feel it," Zeva agreed. Her mind was still reeling from everything he said. "There is tons more we have to discuss. I still have three months on my duties with Commander Brighton. What if we don't work out, would I want to be married and then in essence be sentenced to a relationship that I don't want? I'd have to uproot my life here…"

"Were you not planning on leaving D.C.?" Jasper asked.

"Yes, I was, but to move to England?" She shook her head.

"It's something new, another adventure and with a man who would be waiting to cherish you for the rest of your life," Jasper replied.

"When would we have to get hitched?" Zeva asked.

"I would like to be married to you before I leave, and then I could take the certificate to my solicitor."

Jasper was idly playing with her fingers. "In the three months you are still here we arrange to have your things moved to my home, and when you arrive we announce you to my family and the public."

"I really need to think about this," Zeva said weakly. "It's a lot to ask a girl after knowing her for three days."

"I know, and if you want me to leave I understand that as well." Jasper sighed. "Just know, regardless of whether it's a yes or no to my proposal, I want to see you. I'm not opposed to a long distance relationship until you are ready for a permanent change."

"What about your title?" Zeva asked gently.

"Pardon my French, but fuck it. I was doing it because of my father's wishes and in his memory. I have a cousin that the title would go to, and I also think my mother is trying to marry off Miriam to him thinking that if the title falls to him she would be able to reap the benefits. She's got all her bases covered, apparently. Either way I'd still have my manor house and my business and hopefully have you."

"So, she wants you to get married and bring more money into the family fold, or she wants one of your cousins to marry another second or third cousin, I have no clue, and thus would retain money to help fund her lavish lifestyle?" Zeva asked, finally making sense of the situation.

"In essence yes," Jasper answered.

"That's a fucked up situation, and all you are trying to do is retain the title that has been in your father's family line," Zeva mused. "And you are willing to give up that title to be with me."

"Forgetting all of that, what I really want is you, yes," Jasper confirmed. "And before you ask, yes after three days. I've always been a man who makes decisions rather easily. I know what I want and usually get it."

Zeva gave a husky laugh. "Careful Jasper, your upbringing and title is showing."

"Tell you what, I won't stay for dinner and I'll give you a chance to think." Jasper drained the last of his beer and stood. "Call me tomorrow and let me know your decision. Then I can pick you up and we can go for a nice dinner out. I'd love to see you in that red dress again before I leave."

Zeva stood as well. "Even if I say no."

He pulled her close and kissed her. "Even if you say no, luv."

"At least let me make your plate to go. I made dessert too," Zeva said. "I'll make one for your uncle as well, sounds to me like he needs a good meal to offset the drinking."

"You don't know the half of it," Jasper sighed.

She saw the defeated slump of his shoulders and how much this was affecting him. Not only the business of his title and his mother and cousins, but the fact that he was trying to save his uncle who could possibly not be saved. He carried the weight of his world and she wanted to care for him and love him, yet she had to think. Zeva was always in the habit of keeping containers to take her lunch with her. So she packed two to-go packages for Jasper and his uncle and then filled two of the smaller plastic Tupperware with the tiramisu. She put them in a warming bag and led him to the front door.

"I'll call you tomorrow," she promised and stood on her toes and lifted her head to kiss him.

"Oh no luv, I need more than that to hold me over," Jasper murmured.

He set the bag on the floor and in a deft move turned her so she was pressed against the wall and devoured her lips in a kiss. As his tongue penetrated her mouth, he thrust his hips against her, and she felt the sweet ache of wanting to be naked and entwined with him intimately. Zeva wrapped a long leg around his thigh and rubbed it up and down his jean-covered leg. He groaned as their lips mated and ran his hands up her waist to the underside of her breasts. Zeva wanted more, she wanted him to complete the action and touch her. But he pulled away with one more hard kiss and stepped back.

"Bloody hell, you make me forget the world outside," he said after taking in a ragged breath.

"I can honestly say I have never been kissed like

that." Zeva fanned her face, hoping to dispel the heat. "I keep thinking about us being naked."

Jasper gave a laugh. "You just say exactly what you are thinking, don't you?"

"Easier if people know exactly what I'm thinking," she replied. "This is how you know I'll call you one way or another tomorrow."

He nodded. "I certainly see that, it makes me want you all the more. Goodnight, Zeva."

She opened the door. "G'night, Duke. Oh, I forgot to tell you, you saved me today."

Jasper stepped out and turned. "How so?"

"My commander decided he was going to up the ante. He's getting bolder now that my time is getting short. I told him my boyfriend would make this a diplomatic incident if I wasn't home for dinner." Zeva grinned. "If you saw his face, you would think he was going to pop."

"Glad I was able to help." Jasper grinned. "Night luv."

"Tomorrow, Jasper," Zeva promised and handed him the bag he'd left on the floor.

He nodded and she watched as he went down the steps and hailed a cab. When he got in, he gave a small wave and she watched as the yellow vehicle went down the street before she closed the door. There was a lot to think about and she put together her meal, disappointed that she didn't ask him to stay. The mood would have been tense after his proposal of marriage and the reason why. In the midst of all his family drama he did say two things that caught her attention. One, that he would give up his title just to have the chance to be with her, and two, that he could see forever with her. She wanted the same things in a way, a relationship that would last.

While she ate she broke down the various aspects of her life. What did she have holding her in D.C., or anywhere for that matter? Nothing. The military was all she knew, her family was various foster homes until she had aged out at eighteen and then the military became her family, friends were few to nonexistent, she met people with her various service changes and each new place she was posted. Being alone and raised in foster care made her hesitant of people, whom to trust, whom not to trust. She amended the word from friends to acquaintances, because she was never settled enough in one place to form connections.

It's what made it easy to move from one place to the next. Foster care had made her introverted as well. She learned quickly to squirrel away her things, her precious belongings. To have a space of her own was something she had craved. When she finally had it, she wanted to keep it to herself, to make her apartments her sanctuary, but in the end she was alone in the world no matter where she moved to after D.C. It would be a new start and trying to fit in to a new place with new people. Why not in the United Kingdom? She would have Jasper and they fit in this imperfect world.

Even though they had known each other for such a short time, she had more of a connection with him than with anyone at this point in her life. *Why not?* She mused to herself. Her subconscious answered, *Yeah why the fuck not?* Still she mulled it over while watching the news, while in the shower, and then in her bed. Her mind was basically made up. There was nothing holding her here and the prospect of something new thrilled her. It was going to be yes. *Holy shit, I'm saying yes to marriage and moving to the England!* She picked up her cell to make the call to Jasper, choosing not to wait lest she lose her nerve.

He answered on the second ring and his voice sounded amused. "Checking on me to make sure I made it home okay?"

"I'm assuming you did, and you aren't tied to a kidnapper's chair are you?" Zeva teased.

"Me watching a rousing talk show on the telly may be considered as such," Jasper replied. "The food was delicious, thank you. I got uncle to eat as well with a nice cup of hot tea and he's back in bed. He loved the tiramisu."

"I'll have to make it sometime for him when I'm

at the manor house, maybe he'll come over for dinner," Zeva said.

There was silence for a moment before he spoke. "Does that mean what I think it means?"

"Yes, I'll marry you and become the duchess of Northumberland, blah, blah, blah," she said with a laugh.

"That's absolutely smashing." Jasper's voice held pure happiness. "I'll get with a solicitor friend of mine tomorrow, and we'll get the license and be married. I leave Friday…"

"So we'll be married Thursday. We could do it in the evening, my commander will be an ass to let me out half a day on Thursday," Zeva mused. "I could claim female problems. That always gets him a tizzy then a half hour long spiel about women and their feminine problems. Wait, will your uncle be with us?"

"No, it's best he not know until you're there and we are ready announce," Jasper answered. "He can't seem to keep anything from my mother."

"Okay, just us and your lawyer friend. I'll see if I can get out earlier than five, I know the court house stops doing ceremonies at four."

"You'll be leaving at noon on Thursday and we won't be getting married at the magistrate," Jasper said wickedly. "Just be ready to go and pack a bag. We'll be gone for the night."

"What are you planning?" Zeva asked doubtfully.

"A small diplomatic incident," Jasper admitted.

"I look forward to it," Zeva said with a laugh. "I guess being married to you won't ever be boring."

"I hope not luv, we have fifty years to fill," he teased.

"I honestly like the sound of that," her voice was soft. "I hope this works for us, Jasper."

"It will," Jasper promised. "I'll take care of everything tomorrow and see you Thursday afternoon."

"I look forward to it," Zeva said, and she truly meant it.

He hung up and she lay back in bed and gave a small laugh. Everything in her life since she was a child had been structured, and this was her stepping outside the mold. It felt exhilarating and Thursday would begin a new life. Jasper could turn out to be the best thing that ever happened to her, or if he and his family were the worst he was in for a hell of a fight. *Duchess Zeva McTavish.* She tried out the name and it didn't seem half bad. She hoped they lasted for the next fifty years like he promised, it seemed like they were meant to be.

Chapter Four

Thursday Zeva walked into the offices dressed in her uniform, and as usual she looked crisp and ready to do her job. But in the corner of her small office there was an overnight case, and hooked on the door was a dress bag. Today she was going to become a wife. She tried to put that thought out of her head and focus on work but the seconds ticked by while she performed her duties. While she looked totally together on the outside, on the inside she was a bundle of nerves and excitement.

Today at some point she was marrying a duke. Still, she was worried about how he planned to get her from her chauvinistic boss's clutches. Commander Brighton noticed her hair was down first thing when she took in the morning briefings to him. Of course he didn't notice her exemplary work or the fact that she had his agenda prepped before he walked into the office after her. Strutting like he owned the world and only commenting on just the hair.

"Look at you, dolled up for me, finally." Commander Brighton grinned. "You look exceptional with your hair down, less severe."

"I aim to please," she said through gritted teeth. "Everything is ready for your morning meeting, sir."

"You should sit in personally and take my notes," he said and lowered his voice to provocative creep factor that made her stomach roll.

"I type faster from the recorded notes, sir," Zeva said politely. "If there's nothing else I'll return to my desk."

"Very well, back to your duties." Commander Brighton smiled. "You look lovely today, my dear."

Without a word she'd turned and went back to her office. A mixture of anger and tears clogged her throat. This new administration brought out all the worms from the woodwork, the racists, the homophobes, the sexually corrupt, and the men who thought women were just objects for their pleasure. In her office she looked at her calendar where she marked off the days to her freedom from D.C. in red. *Seventy-two day left,* she repeated to herself and focused on the fact that she would be starting a new life in the U.K. It seemed that Jasper's proposal meant just as much to her as it did to him. By twelve-thirty she began to worry, Jasper still hadn't arrived. She was supposed to be on her lunch break but stayed in her office.

One in the afternoon and she was pissed, thinking that he played her and all this was hype. Commander Brighton wanted her to come into his office for a meeting. *Wonderful,* she thought gathering her notebook. Before she went in she twisted her hair back into a bun. There was no way she was going to have him leering at her while they worked. She stepped into his office and Commander Brighton sat behind his desk with a red face. Two others were there, Jasper and another older man she assumed was his friend the lawyer. Her soon-to-be husband grinned at her and gave her a wink.

"Sergeant Troy, your fiancée told me today is your wedding day and you need to leave early," Commander Brighton's voice was friendly. "Why didn't you tell me you needed to leave early?"

Zeva cocked her head and answered truthfully. "Because if I had, you would have complained about the female gender and other various things… sir."

"Now, now, you know we don't have that kind of relationship," Commander Brighton blustered. "I was teasing, it's the military way, we bust each other's balls."

"Apparently your 'teasing' was making my fiancée uncomfortable." Jasper's wonderfully accented voice was mild but she could hear the deadly seriousness of his tone.

"Especially if she felt she couldn't tell you it was her wedding day or even get the day off for such an event. I hope she won't be reprimanded or made uncomfortable when her husband returns home. Think of the diplomatic incident that could cause if the newspapers got wind of it." Jasper's older friend spoke, and she could hear a hint of British in his own voice. He had to have been living in America for a long time, and she assessed him quickly. Salt and pepper hair, tall, thin and wore a wedding ring and looked distinguished in his black tailored three-piece suit.

"She will be safe and under my protection. Zeva knows she can tell me anything," Commander Brighton said and gave her a look that dared her to say otherwise.

She had time left so she thought it best not to poke the bear too much. "I didn't want to inflict myself on your time sir. I know your major undertaking is your career and this country needs your input. I respect you and your time too much, sir."

It was a load of horseshit, but she saw the old man puff up with pride. Commander Brighton beamed at her as he stood. "And you, my dear, are the best aide I ever had, but today of all days I can do without you for the day. In fact, take the weekend to spend with your new husband. I will see you Monday."

"Are you sure, sir?" Zeva played her role and looked concerned.

"Certainly, you are always days ahead in my schedule and my briefings. Congratulations to you both and enjoy your weekend." Commander Brighton came around his desk and embraced her before shaking Jasper's hand vigorously. "Hopefully one day in the future when I retire me and the missus can visit your home and see our Zeva."

"You are more than welcome," Jasper said in a cordial voice. He escorted Zeva out of the office and to her own where she collected her belongings and the dress bag from behind the door.

"You really didn't mean he was welcome to visit us, right?" Zeva asked as they left the building. "That old man plays the role well, but he is absolutely disgusting and you can be assured I'm not his or his wife's Zeva."

"If he ever comes we can lead him out into the moors and let the muck take him. We will wait here for the limo to arrive," Jasper replied. "By the way, Zeva luv, meet my very close friend, Keith Wharton."

Zeva shook his hand. "Nice to meet you. I like how you subtly told him your intentions if he kept harassing me."

"That's all the lawyering I do," Keith teased. "Jasper asked me to help you finesse your move to Northumberland. With that said, you can contact me anytime if the old fart-bag gives you any more trouble. I've met his type many times throughout my work here in D.C., and I despise the way they treat women, especially in this new political climate."

"You can always move back to North U," Jasper said. "I would be thrilled with it and, as a matter of fact, so would many people."

Keith smiled. "Glad to know it mate, but Lanie loves it here and we've built a life. Besides, the organization needs me, especially now."

"What organization would that be?" Zeva asked.

"I head a group of lawyers who fight for the underdogs in D.C.," Keith explained. "People like you, women who have been sexually harassed, people who have been exploited in politics and basically blackballed for their views. We get them justice if we can and bring to light the black underbelly of this town."

"In this city that probably makes you lots of enemies," Zeva said worriedly.

"We've been threatened, bricks thrown through the window and harassing calls," Keith grinned even as he said it. "Nothing in this life is easy. We could run away and give up, but no one else is and these people have to live with much worse, so we manage."

"Plus you have that security detail you hired," Jasper said. "Mac is not one to be messed with."

"Mac another friend?" Zeva asked.

"Yes, quite British and bad ass as hell," Jasper replied. "He also keeps Keith and his family safe."

Zeva smiled and nudged him with her shoulder. "And here you were making me think you knew no one in this town. You even have a connection with Joan and Ralph. You're practically a native."

Jasper grimaced. "Please, anything but that. By the way, Keith, if Uncle Brewster calls and asks I got snookered with you and ended up staying at your place."

"Understood. I know you have to keep this under wraps until you announce at home to the banshee queen," Keith replied.

"I take it he means your mother," Zeva said dryly. "Can she really be that bad?"

"Think of the worst person you've ever met and up that by one hundred percent," Keith spoke before Jasper could.

"Her evil could make walls bleed," Jasper added. "Don't worry, we don't see her often and you, my dear, can handle the queen of the Morlocks."

She laughed, but she was worried about a woman who could make her own son hate her. She, Jasper, and Keith chatted until a sleek black limo arrived, and when she got inside there was another woman who Keith introduced as his wife. The drive to the Hotel Du Pont was a short one, and Jasper had everything prepared. There was a suite and waiting for them was a justice of the peace who was a friend of Keith. As she changed, Zeva shook her head over the connection they all seemed to have in the small circle of friends. Keith and Lanie would be their witnesses for the wedding, and she felt like she was among friends. Zeva was a part of them now and basically she felt a little less alone in the great big world.

Zeva looked at herself in the full-length mirror of the bedroom in the suite. She had chosen a soft champagne colored dress that ended at her knees with a lacy hem. It was slightly off the shoulder and the fabric clung to her curves. To add a little spice to the ensemble she wore the red heels that she wore the night of the gala where she met Jasper. It matched the lacy bra and panties set she wore beneath, because if this was her wedding night, she was sure as hell going to knock his socks off.

Jasper's voice came through the barrier of the door after a soft knock. "Zeva, are you ready?"

Zeva took a deep breath and moved to the door. "As ready as I'll ever be."

She felt the heat of his gaze as he took in her appearance from top to bottom.

"You look absolutely fantastic, smashing, bloody gorgeous," he said almost reverently.

"Keep that up you may give me a big head," she teased.

"You're lucky I'm not throwing rose petals at your feet." Jasper took her hand. "I feel like the luckiest man in the world right now. You're wearing red shoes, that's fucking hot."

Zeva looked up at him. "You say the nicest things in the most dirty way. Are you sure you're a duke?"

"The most unconventional one you'll find," he promised.

He led her to the center of the living room area of the suite, and waiting for them was Keith and Lanie plus a woman wearing a dark robe. The ceremony was quick and simple, and soon she was Duchess Zeva McTavish. In a way it blew her mind when Keith gave them a small bow and said, "Duke, Duchess, it was an honor to be a part of this."

They shared a small lunch with her new friends before they left early in the evening and they were completely alone. They sat together on the sofa and she kicked off her shoes and tucked her feet under as she leaned against him. It was comfortable, like they had done this every night for years. Zeva could hardly believe they meshed so well so quickly, but it was still very new. She wondered if it would change, especially when she moved and his family got into the mix.

"People aren't going to be bowing and stuff to me when I get to Northumberland, are they?" Zeva asked worriedly.

"I can't say not, people know me and know that I am basically easy going," Jasper explained. "But the older generation still likes to follow the old ways, and women at the shops will call you duchess when you go into town."

"Okay." She blew out a breath. "I'll have to get accustomed to that."

There was a knock on the door, and Jasper jumped up quickly from the sofa and she fell against the cushions

"Hey!" Zeva said with a laugh.

"I'm sorry, but it's the champagne," he said grinning.

"Well then, carry on," Zeva said sitting up.

The room service attendant brought in a cart with a gracious smile. It was filled with champagne, fresh strawberries, desserts, and more. Jasper tipped the man from the wallet in his pocket and then he wheeled the cart in front of the sofa himself.

"A toast," he said as he worked the cork from the bottle. "To our marriage, and years of love, laughter, and children for us."

She watched as he poured them both two glasses. "I like the sound of that."

Jasper gave her a glass before sitting down. "I do too, very much so."

"Does it feel like we've known each other forever, or is it just me?" Zeva asked. "I've never been so comfortable with a man, in all honesty, I've never made such a big decision so quickly in my life. I spend more time debating myself mentally about things that most people take for granted. But this... I'm married and moving, starting a new life all in less than a week."

He turned to her. "I think we saw something in each other we both were looking for. There's so much I have to learn about you, and vice versa, but it feels bloody right and I don't doubt my instincts in the least."

"I'm glad you don't, you may have to remind me to stop over thinking every once in a while," she admitted. "I was raised in foster care and basically took care of myself all my life. Speaking of which, what will your family and the media think of you marrying a woman who doesn't even know who her family is?"

"What people think has never been a concern to me," Jasper replied. "I have to tell you, there will be a dinner at the manor where I introduce you to the family and others in the society of Northumberland."

"Then the news will run with it," Zeva assessed.

"Yes they will, and we will be fine," he answered honestly.

Jasper held up his glass. "To us, Duke and Duchess of Northumberland, and to the beginning of our adventurous marriage."

Zeva touched the rim of her glass with his. "To us."

They took a sip and the bubbles tickled her nose. The champagne was sweet, with a bold, fruity flavor and while they enjoyed it, they tried different desserts on the tray and sampled the fruit.

"This champagne is excellent," Zeva said draining her glass.

"The bottle is gone." Jasper held it up.

"Awww," she said with a pout.

He reached under the cloth of the cart and pulled out another ice bucket with a bottle inside. "But we have another."

"Yay!" She clapped, enjoying the evening immensely.

Jasper popped the cork and poured them another glass. She took a sip, and when he sat down next to her, Zeva kissed him. Jasper plucked the glass from her hand and placed them on the room service cart. He moved and pressed her back into the sofa, covering her body with his own as he kissed her hungrily. Zeva loved the feeling of his body on hers as they kissed. They fit together like two pieces of a puzzle, as he settled at the apex of her thighs. She lifted her hips against him with a soft moan as his tongue slipped deeply into her mouth.

"I think I like this portion of the evening very

much," Zeva murmured when he lifted his head to look at her.

"I'm amazed someone as beautiful as you would be with me right now," he said huskily and caressed her face. "Thank you for being my wife."

She truly felt humbled. "Thank you for choosing me."

He stood and held out his hand to her. "Shall we go to bed?"

Zeva put her hand in his. "Yes, let's."

As they stepped into the bedroom, Jasper pulled her close and she felt her breath catch at their intimate connection. Zeva unbuttoned his shirt slowly and pushed it off his shoulders. The bare expanse of his chest called for her to touch him, and she ran her fingers through the soft thatch of hair over skin and muscles.

"I want to see you," he said huskily.

Zeva suddenly remembered her shoes. "Sit there and I'll be right back."

He laughed. "Just know I'm very aroused, and anything you do may cause me to ravish you."

She gave him a wicked smile from the door. "Here's to hoping that happens."

Zeva grabbed her shoes from the floor and put them back on before heading back to the room. Jasper's eyes followed her as she stood in front of him and slowly slipped the dress from her body. She heard him suck in a harsh breath when she stood in front of him wearing only her panties, bra, and shoes, all in that sexy red.

"Dear God, I may have died and gone to heaven," he murmured. "Your skin takes hints of light and it turns to bronze. You are like a goddess."

"You and those pretty words." A slow smile spread across her face as she stepped between his legs. "Does that mean you like what you see?"

"Very, very much," he murmured. He ran his hand down her waist to her hips. "I want to taste you everywhere."

"Do it," she dared him.

His eyes flashed with desire before he pulled her down to the bed and covered her body with his once more. He took her lips in a fierce kiss that left them both reeling. She moaned under the onslaught of his lips and tongue, trying to get closer, and still it wasn't enough. He lifted his head and stared into her eyes for an instant, as if making sure she was real before swooping in to take more of her lips. Zeva could get drunk off his kisses. His taste was bold and masculine with hints of the dessert and champagne they consumed earlier.

This new sensation was making her heady. She felt almost drunk with the desire she and Jasper created. She gasped as he roamed soft kisses down her neck to the swell of her breasts and cupped the heavy globes through the lacy fabric of her bra. Jasper reached around and with deft fingers unhooked the lingerie easily. She was impatient to have his hands on her skin. She sighed when he cupped her breasts in his hands and massaged them gently before bringing them to his mouth. Then Zeva moaned when he used his tongue to tease her nipples.

"You have the most delicious nipples," Jasper murmured as he moved from one to the next.

"More," she begged, and her head fell back at his touch.

He obliged and took one of the coca bean tips into his mouth. Zeva cried out in agonized delight and trembled in his arms.

"Oh yes, God that feels so good," she encouraged him breathlessly as she held his head to her body. "Take me, Jasper."

"Oh no, not yet luv." His voice was laced with need. "I'm going to learn each and every nuance of your body." Jasper kissed a beeline to her stomach and took the lacy scrap of her panties down her legs and over her heels. He pressed a kiss on the trimmed hair at the apex of her thighs. "I can smell your scent, I want to taste you, luv."

Zeva met his gaze and did as he requested, revealing her already moist sex to his heated gaze. He ran a lone finger down the slit and she felt him graze her clit. The sensation caused her to shiver, and

Zeva parted her legs wider in a silent plea for more. His head bent between her legs and she whimpered at the long, slow lick. Jasper groaned and pressed his face against her pussy. The way he used his tongue to ravish her made Zeva buck as the need speared through her. She arched upward to meet each flick of his hungry tongue. The things he made her feel, Zeva was reeling from the sensations.

Jasper parted her sex and sucked at her clit before he delved between the soft folds of flesh to penetrate her with his tongue. It was driving her to the edge of reason, and she cried out, gripping the sheets of the bed and writhing under his ministrations. Her excitement built with every new thing he did. A small flick of his finger across her clit had her begging for more. He circled around her opening, teasing her with the sensation of almost penetrating and she bit her lip in sweet agony. Finally he gave her what she needed and slid one, then two fingers into the warm caverns of her pussy. The cry that left Zeva's lips she was unable to stop. She undulated her hips, lifting them upwards to meet the repetitive insertion of his fingers.

She closed her eyes as pleasure coursed through her and her breath came in short pants. He fingered her moist entrance with deep penetrating movements that became faster and harder until she was begging for release. Her body tightened and arched with an orgasm that took her breath away, and her mouth opened in a silent scream while she shuddered helplessly. He pressed his mouth against her sex and she heard his guttural groan of need as she came again, bucking wildly.

"Oh luv, that was bloody marvelous, I love how you come," he said huskily. He kept his fingers moving inside her and sent her spiraling into another round of ecstasy.

When she met his gaze his eyes had a wild look of passion that Zeva had never seen before. It aroused her to no end, the primal look on his face, and that she was the one he wanted and needed. He held on to her thighs, pulling her closer to him and burying his mouth against her pussy again. She arched when he burrowed his tongue deep inside, tasting her flavor. Zeva grabbed his head and pulled his face deeper into her soft wetness. He excited her to the point of insanity, and she wondered if anyone just slipped into blissful unconsciousness from pleasure. His tongue was fast flicks and penetration of her sex. She could feel herself losing control as her hips moved furiously against the seeking appendage of his mouth.

"Oh God I need…Oh Jasper, please, I can't stop!" she begged.

He knew just how to make her come again and kept up his passionate ministrations, sliding his fingers into her to match the movements of his tongue on her clit. His name was a keening cry from her lips as her body convulsed and tightened around his fingers before the warm flow of her juices dripped down his hand.

"Now, now, I want you inside me," Zeva said urgently.

"Tell me to take you." Jasper's voice was raw. He moved and knelt between her legs, rubbing the tip of his cock between the lips of her pussy and making her tremble against him.

"Yes Jasper, I want it, I want you baby." Zeva was wanton in her plea.

He groaned as he obliged her request and sank deep inside her. Zeva eagerly wrapped her legs around his waist as their bodies moved instinctively together in unison. She lifted her hips to match the movement of his hips with each deep thrust. Zeva ground toward him, trying to take more and give more all at the same time as they consummated their marriage.

"I love how you feel wrapped about me, you clench around my cock and it feels so damn good." His voice was a harsh whisper by her ear.

His words fueled her need, his accent was thick with desire and it was as if each word was another intimate caress. She knew that with no other man had she ever felt like this. Zeva wanted to be consumed by him, mind body and soul. Their connection was a fire in her blood.

"Only you, oh yes," she said on panting breaths. "Oh baby, I'm going to come. I can't hold back."

The words barely left her mouth when she felt her body begin to tremble and her pussy clenched around his throbbing cock. He pressed his face against her breast before sucking her nipple deep in his mouth. The sensation was like a spear to her core, making her cry out in the midst of her release. She felt Jasper let himself go and fell over the abyss with him. He groaned her name and filled her sex with his seed. They lay panting in the aftermath of their mating with slick bodies twisted and pliant in tangled sheets.

"Well, we know the sexual part of our marriage works," she mumbled.

Jasper chuckled as he trailed his fingers down her arm. "Works, made me see fireworks, possible loss of the use of my extremities…"

She laughed and snuggled closer. "Now if you snore then we need to buy a supply of ear plugs. I can deal with it, if you keep this level of gratification up to par."

Jasper nuzzled her neck until she squirmed. "Willing to live with snoring for my sexual prowess may be the best compliment anyone has ever given me."

"Hey, I know how to treat my man right." Zeva yawned. "I wish you didn't have to leave so soon."

He sighed. "I feel the same way, but we'll be together on only a few weeks and then we have the rest of our lives to live, learn, and love each other."

She turned in his arms and looked at him. "Do you think you'll ever love me?"

Jasper kissed her. "Without a doubt."

"Good, because I care for you already. The next step will be love and I don't want to love anyone who can't love me in return," she said simply. "If this is to be a marriage of convenience with some hanky-panky on the side so be it. But don't make me love you unless you can love me back."

"That won't happen Zeva, I swear it," Jasper promised.

"Then get some rest, because we definitely have to do this again before you leave," she announced.

His laughter echoed in the room. "You are bloody marvelous."

Zeva smiled as he pulled her close and held her tight. She didn't say anything but she thought the same about him. Tomorrow he would be leaving and the countdown would start to when she saw him again and her move would begin.

Chapter Five

Two months and thirteen days was as long as it took for Zeva to arrive in Northumberland. Jasper counted each one as he waited for her to arrive. While they spoke every day by phone or video chat, he still missed her terribly, and the only thing he had to soothe him was the memory of her kisses and the scent of her skin. He'd ushered her home under the cover of darkness because he wanted no one to know about her until the following night.

He looked around the formal dining room of his manor home and saw all the people he invited milling around in their fine dresses and expensive suits. Curiosity etched their faces as to why Duke McTavish was having a formal dinner and announcement. Only his mother and the twins from hell guessed they knew the answers, and all three sat smugly waiting for him to speak and give them what they wanted. They thought he was giving up his title so his cousin could then be Duke and thus seal them all in wealth. There was a big surprise coming, and he was so happy to deal them the blow that would knock them down a peg or three.

He wanted it over and done so he could spend time alone with Zeva. But for now he played the role, and when his mother caught his gaze, he lifted his glass in her direction with a nod. She smiled a saccharine sweet smile that was like poison to his soul. Jasper wondered how he could hate a woman so much, even the one who had given birth to him. He recalled their last conversation before Zeva came and knew exactly how. She came to his house by car, and he only knew it was her when he walked out of his shop wiping the sawdust off his hands and saw her standing in the gravel driveway.

"Mother," he said without even moving to embrace her.

"Jasper darling, why do you always look like one of the common folk." She sighed in disappointment. "I taught you how to dress like the English gentleman you are."

"I made it a rule to forget anything you ever taught me," Jasper answered. "Why are you here?"

"Well darling..." The way she used that word always grated on his nerves. "I was wondering what this lovely invitation was about? You never let anyone come to the manor, let alone for a dinner party and announcement."

"You'll see when it's time," he answered. "There was no need for you to drive from father's home to here."

"My home, darling." Her voice took a cold note. "You're father's been dead and buried a long time."

"Yes he has." Jasper didn't take the bait.

"I can only assume it's to renounce your title so your cousin can be Duke, since you have not met the stipulations of the will..." she began.

"Goodbye mother." Jasper turned and walked back to his workshop.

"You were never good at the Duke thing, darling, you weren't meant for greatness, just to be a woodworker with calloused hands," his mother called out. "Why your cousin couldn't be the son I wanted I'll never know. You are a disappointment, why God did that to me, I guess we all have our burdens."

Jasper pivoted on his heel and came striding toward her so quickly she stepped back. Her driver, a big burly man younger than her and whom no doubt she was sleeping with, stepped from the car.

Jasper pointed at him. "You get your sodding arse back in the car before I punch through you until I burst your spleen." The man got back in and closed the door, and he whirled on his mother. "God has nothing to do with you, mother. I thought you knew the devil was your master. Thank God I was never the son you wanted me to be, but I was the son my father raised. But soon, mommy dearest, you'll know the true extent of what kind of man I am. I'd say don't come to the party but I know the curiosity is killing you. Besides, I want to see your face when I make my announcement, I want to see it crack like porcelain and reveal the witch beneath."

He went back to work after that and funneled all his rage into his woodwork. Jasper pictured Zeva in his mind, smiling and happy, waiting for him, and that made it all the easier. She was his anchor in this swirling storm and soon the entire world would know she was his. In the months that he waited for her to be done with work in D.C. he'd grown to love her. Each and every day, though they were thousands of mile away, she had stolen his heart.

He wondered if it had happened before he even left, while they were in bed making love or at the airport where she held him tight and each kiss was the last but there was one more after it. He stopped caring when, and only knew it was there and he treasured it. One of the people he hired for the night gave an almost imperceptible nod from the door to the formal dining room. It was time. Jasper moved to the door, from there anyone could see who was coming down the staircase that had been polished until it gleamed. He cleared his throat and tapped his glass lightly with a small spoon that had been placed nearby. Everyone turned and his mother stood from where she sat.

"Good evening, everybody looks marvelous

tonight," Jasper said with a smile. "I can see on all your faces you are wondering why Duke McTavish, who basically keeps to himself like a beast in a castle, is having a formal party."

The crowd laughed and he waited for them to be silent before continuing again.

"Well, this beast has an announcement that has brought me so much happiness, and I hope that you will be happy for me and give me your blessings in this new path of my life." Jasper paused and looked around. "As you know, part of my father's wishes when he died was for his only son to get married, and more than that, to be happy with his life. More happy than my father was in his own nuptials."

His mother's face was mask of rage, and he certainly didn't care if the truth was known far and wide about who she really was. "We all know that his marriage was not one he would've chosen for himself. Before he died, Dad pulled me aside and said to me, don't chose who the public wants or the family wants, pick a woman you can find forever with. I work hard for what's mine, I think many of you must have one or two pieces of my work in your home."

The crowd clapped and Jasper waited for it to end once more. "I'm happy to say I have chosen well, and tonight I would like to introduce my wife. I met her when I went to the United States, and we got married soon after in a simple ceremony. I'd like to introduce

Sargent Zeva Troy, and now the new Duchess McTavish of Northumberland."

The crowd gasped in surprise, and his mother's face was pure shock and unadulterated rage. Everyone was looking up the stairs and when Zeva appeared, she left even him breathless. She was wearing a jade green dress that looked like crushed velvet, her shoes were the same color and covered in beads that sparkled between the green.

She wore a simple diamond necklace and earrings, a gift from him, and her dark hair was smooth and slicked back from her face and down her back. His guests cheered while she walked elegantly down the stairs and even when she stood by his side. Jasper pulled her close and kissed her amidst the cheering. There was some rambunctious whistles from a few of his friends who weren't shy about showing their approval. His mother pushed her way to the front of the crowd, and when she spoke her voice was dripping with venom.

"You married a darkie, and an American one at that?" Her hands were fists at her sides. "This wedding isn't valid, your father's will stipulated a time limit."

While people gasped at the racial slur and her anger, Jasper took it in stride. He wanted everyone to see her true colors and when he glanced and Zeva's face it didn't even seem to faze her.

"Please don't use that kind of language around my wife and among my treasured guest, a few who happen to be black," Jasper said calmly. He could see by some of his guest's faces they didn't appreciate her verbiage either. "Secondly, this marriage is around three months old, isn't that right luv."

Zeva laced her fingers with his. "Yes it is, and it's been wonderful."

Jasper kissed her hands. "I'm sure you all remember and know Keith Wharton. The solicitor and his family have been part of this community for years. He was my witness, along with his wife, and our marriage certificate was sent to my father's solicitor who has confirmed and been verified. We sent formal notice to her majesty herself and have received her blessing. It's all very much valid, and my marriage is secure."

"I won't let this stand, you hear me, you rotten… I won't let this stand!" his mother screeched.

"Cornelia, calm down." Uncle Brewster came from out of the crowd and put his hand on her shoulder.

His mother slapped him. "You let this happen, you weak, pathetic man. Get away from me." She raised her hand and called to the twin cousins waiting close by with fear in their eyes. "Girls, come along!"

They scrambled to follow her, and Uncle

Brewster stood there with a red face before moving through the crowd quietly. Jasper knew he was heading to the bar. He couldn't stop him, not now, when Uncle Brewster became upset there was no stopping the drinking.

Jasper put a smile in place. "With that bit of nasty business over, shall we celebrate, my friends?"

Again the room erupted in cheers and he led her into the center of the room and started to introduce her around. The music started up and it played lightly in the background as people interacted. Zeva got to meet many of the residents that she would be seeing when she was in town and the surrounding area. They finally made their way to where Uncle Brewster stood, staring glumly into a tumbler glass of amber liquid.

"Uncle Brewster, I'd like to introduce Zeva, from that night at the Gala," Jasper said gently.

"It's very nice to meet you." Zeva's voice was sweet as she held out her hand.

"Wonderful to know you will be part of the family, my dear. I am sorry I was not able to attend the wedding, I knew nothing about it." Uncle Brewster took it and kissed her knuckles in a very gallant gesture. "I'm sorry for my sister and my daughters' reaction as well."

"None of this is your fault nor should you feel guilty." Zeva's voice was firm. "Everyone is responsible for their own actions, this is not your burden to take on."

"I didn't tell you, Uncle, because I didn't want her to know and you can't keep anything from her," Jasper explained. "I didn't want to put you in an uncomfortable position."

Uncle Brewster downed his drink. "I'm already there, my boy. I am living in a prison of my own making. But don't let that mar your night, enjoy and be happy in your marriage."

Uncle Brewster walked away and they watched him leave.

"I feel sorry for him," Zeva said softly.

"I do too, he needs to be happy." Jasper turned and looked at her. "As much as I am right now."

Zeva gave him a wink and twined her arms around his neck. "Wait till later, you'll be ecstatic."

He threw his head back and laughed, pulling her close, and it drew the attention of their guests once more who began to clap.

"Are they going to do that every time we kiss or hug?" Zeva said close to his ear.

"They're happy their Duke took a wife." Jasper pulled away to look at her. "And you look absolutely amazing tonight."

"You don't look bad yourself, Duke." Zeva kissed him. "Not bad at all."

The party went on until late into the night. It was

after two on Sunday morning when they said goodbye to the last guest. Jasper had already asked two of his closer friends to get Uncle Brewster home after his inebriation started to make him loud and then overly emotional. The caterers and other staff would be back the next day to clean up and put his manor house back to rights. He made sure the house was locked up and took her hand to lead her upstairs.

"I thought it went well," Jasper said.

"All but the part where your mother called me a darkie and acted like the demon queen of the underworld," Zeva replied. "You said she was awful, but I think she is beyond that. Is she dangerous?"

"She is a witch and a wicked one at that, but I don't think she is dangerous," Jasper answered. "Still, be careful around her if you see her and I doubt that will be an issue. Are you worried?"

Zeva laughed as they walked up the stairs. "No, just gauging the enemy. I'm a military woman. I will kick anyone's ass who comes at me wrong."

Jasper put his hand around her waist. "You are so badass, it's hot."

He opened the door to the master bedroom and flicked on the light, bathing the interior with soft light. She had been so tired yesterday that when he picked her up from the airport, the jetlag took her and she crashed almost instantly. She'd slept most of the day while the caterers and party organizers worked downstairs and she'd eaten upstairs while relaxing in his large bed.

"Tomorrow, we can brunch in town and you can explore, maybe take in some shopping. I set up an account for you and there is plenty of money in it so you can do as you please," Jasper said.

"I have my own money, Jasper. I have been very frugal thought the years." Zeva stood in front of the vanity mirror and took off the necklace and earrings. That and the jewelry box that matched it were two of his favorite pieces he created and he put them in bedroom just for her. "I have enough savings that can get me through until I figure out what I want to do here."

He came up behind her and put his hands on her hips. "You don't have to work, Zeva. Between my business and my inheritance, I am very well off. Much to my mother's disappointment and I won't share with her."

She leaned her head against his shoulder. "That's all well and good, but I need to work. I've always worked. I can't while away at home. I'd go batshit crazy."

"At least take a few months to get accustomed to your new life," Jasper encouraged. "You've never really had one, have you?"

"Not really," she admitted and leaned her head

back against his shoulder to look at him. "I missed you. I know we talked every day but I missed the physical you."

"I felt the same way." He kissed her and instantly the arousal stirred within him. "I almost took a red eye a few times but I had so many order deadlines to meet I had to be patient."

Zeva ran her hand down his chest over the crisp fabric of his shirt. "You don't need to be patient anymore."

"Bloody hell yes," he said.

Jasper wrapped his arms around her, leaned back, and pulled her curvaceous body over his. She smelled like heaven—a scent of perfume he only could attribute to her, exotic and heady. Her body molded to his as they kissed, and the passion that built for the time they were apart burst into a heated flame.

Jasper loved when Zeva made a soft sound of pleasure that made his cock ache. Pulling her closer, he deepened the kiss until every nerve ending in his body screamed her name and begged to feel flesh against flesh. Each night while they were apart, he had ached for her and now they were finally together. Jasper broke the kiss and with lips barely a millimeter away from each other it was like he was sharing her sweet breath. He buried his hand in her hair and scraped her scalp, loving the way she purred and arched against him at his touch.

"I want you so damn much, I was going crazy without you," Jasper said the words on a moan. "You feel so right in my arms."

"You and these sweet words." She pressed butterfly kisses onto his face.

Jasper growled and captured her face, kissing her savagely. A primal sound escaped his throat as they both submitted to the desire that raged within them like a wildfire. *I love her.* The thought rushed through his head, and along with the passion he felt a sense of completion. It was all about Zeva, her taste, her smell, the strength and confidence that she exuded was all an addictive package. The soft velvet fabric of her dress crushed beneath his fingers as he undressed her slowly.

He loved the feel of her hands as she did the same to him, leaving them naked to each other. The dim light from the fireplace played like nymphs across her skin. The patterns dared him to follow and trace the shadows with his tongue. He lifted her into his arms and placed her on the bed. Zeva returned his kisses hungrily, and when she slipped her tongue into his mouth he couldn't help the groan of pleasure that escaped him.

Jasper pulled her across his body and loved the feel of her spread out above him. His hands moved from her hips to the curve of her ass. Zeva gasped as his hands roamed and massaged her body, then she spread her legs so they could connect more intimately.

He cupped her breasts as she hovered above him, and he watched her reaction as he plucked at her nipple with his mouth. Her responses pleased him immensely as he re-learned every inch of her body since their wedding night. Jasper was already hard and aching, he could feel the moist heat of her sex against his cock. She moved sensuously above him, teasing his shaft between the soft lips of her sex but never giving him entry. He groaned and pulled her down to devour her lips in a kiss.

He tore his mouth away from her. "Jesus, I've wanted you for months and now you're home with me and I feel like it's a dream."

She looked into his eyes. "I'm real, Jasper, and I'm here. Prove it, touch me everywhere and see I'm real."

Her hands roamed over the strong contours of his shoulders and she buried her fingers in his hair. Her touch inflamed him, as each caress was like a fire that made the ache within him worse.

"Do you know how pleasing this is to me, to have you over me like this?" He moaned as he buried his face between the twin mounds of her breasts. "Do you like how my hands feel on you, the way I touch you?"

"Oh yes, baby, I want more," she whispered.

His cock was already hard when she touched him and ran her finger over the tip of his shaft. Jasper's chest rose and fell with each excited breath when she ran her hand down her chest. He groaned while he watched her in anticipation of what she would do next. She took his cock in her grasp and stroked, and his breath hissed out between his teeth. His hips rose and fell to the rhythm of how she stroked him with her hand in a firm fist around his shaft.

Zeva gave him a wicked, sensual smile before she bent low and wrapped her lips around the head of his shaft and a low, agonized moan left Jasper's lips. She took him deeper into her mouth and he thought he could die from the bliss her lips and hands were creating. The way she flicked her tongue down the length of his shaft was driving him wild.

He couldn't stand any more. Jasper pulled her roughly up his body and against his chest before taking her lips in a hunger-filled kiss. He needed to touch her and slipped his hand between their bodies to her pussy. She was slick and wet. Without hesitation he slid his two fingers deep inside her. Zeva arched and she cried out his name. He fucked her with his fingers, loving how she trembled as the first echoes of her orgasm began.

"That's what I want, I need you to come for me," he growled.

She was amazing and beautiful to watch as she

took his digits deep. Her back was arched in enjoyment, lips parted as she panted and she offered him her breasts as she writhed above him.

"You're like liquid heat around my fingers, take it all luv, that's it," he coaxed her softly.

His thumb circled the sensitive nub of flesh in between the soft folds of her pussy. He gorged himself on every nuance of her reactions. From the way her body rose and fell, to the way her thighs tensed when a new level of sensation peaked within her. With every movement he felt the wetness of her essence drip down and coat his fingers.

"I'm going to come." Her voice was breathless, urgent. "Jasper, oh Jasper."

The way she said his name and how her body shuddered drove him wild. He pressed his digits deeper inside her and pulled her close so he could kiss her and hungrily penetrate her mouth with his tongue. Her second release came with a scream and her body trembled. Jasper was beyond a frenzy to take her. The need to bury his cock inside consumed his being.

She eagerly poised over his erect cock, and Jasper pulled her down on his waiting shaft. The feeling of her hot, slick pussy enclosing around his engorged cock and the muscles clenching around him, tore a guttural cry from his lips. The sheer pleasure of her body undulating above him almost sent Jasper into his own orgasm. He gritted his teeth, restrain and control of their pleasure was an effort to maintain. Slowly their pace increased until a sheen of dampness coated her skin when he ran his hands down the valley of her breasts to cup them. He feasted on the ebony globes, taking the dark areolas into his mouth, deep, until her urgent piston-like motion on his cock took the last of his control.

She leaned over and kissed him fiercely. "Come with me, don't let me go alone."

"Yes." Jasper heard the raw sound in his own voice.

He grabbed her hips and thrust upwards to meet her, and their breathing echoed and became a mirror of each other. His was harsh and primal, while hers were whimpers and soft cries while he pounded inside her. His groan mixed with her cries of bliss as they went over and into the sexual abyss of release. Jasper didn't stop moving until he drove her to a second release.

Zeva fell against his chest and his arms automatically wrapped around her, cocooning her in his loving embrace as he turned to his side so he could lay her on the bed. Jasper couldn't seem to stop kissing or bring himself to release her from his arms, and Zeva didn't seem to want to move. They fell asleep that way, with her pliant body next to him and her chocolate thigh thrown over his thigh.

Chapter Six

It was definitely a culture shock. Zeva looked around as they drove from the manor house into town. Blyth, Northumberland was near the coast, and from her research there was the River Blyth and some moors around the area that led to rocky bluffs that overlooked the sea. It used to be a town built on coal mining and sea trade, specifically salt, and used to be the main trading area for pulp to make newspapers from Scandinavia. The town was re-developed over the years to bring in more industry after the eighteen hundreds to increase the population and to increase investment into the town.

As she looked around, it was like being transported back to early England with quaint two story shops and restaurants. Jasper had explained that many people lived in the apartments over their businesses. But scattered in there were one or two small apartment buildings as well. He had described the manor house where he lived as simple, and the night when she arrived she was too tired to comprehend the magnitude of her new home. It was a mansion made of stone, or a small castle, with at least ten bedrooms and just as many bathrooms, a formal dining room, family room, game room, indoor pool, solarium, and a kitchen that was bigger than her entire apartment.

He didn't keep a staff, and they were alone there so she could putter around and explore. There was also a library, with a window seat and a large stone fireplace. The master bedroom had a woman's sitting room that was all her, with a full claw foot bathtub. Jasper had decked it out with flowers just for her, and in between her complete astonishment and slight fear of her new home the intimate action from her husband made her feel welcome. After sleeping in late, they got up together and made breakfast in the humongous kitchen, and he gave her a guided tour of the manor and his workshop.

She saw pieces of his work in various stages of completion and ran her hand over some of the smooth wood etched with Celtic knot work. *He is more than talented*, she thought as she traced some of the intricate designs. After another round of mind blowing sex in the very large bed she would now share with him, they showered together and took one of the cars into town. The whole marriage thing seemed to be meant for them because they had the newlywed thing down to a science.

"So you know you downplayed the manor and

your work," Zeva commented mildly as they drove slowly through the countryside.

He glanced at her quickly before looked back at the road. "How so?"

She poked him in the shoulder. "You live in a mansion, Duke Jasper McTavish, and your workshop is huge and you are completely an artist with amazing talent." He grinned. "If you keep that up I may start blushing."

"Just stating the facts, darling," she teased and watched him frown. "What's wrong, what did I say?"

"I dislike the word 'darling', it's something my mother says all the time. I cannot stand the word," he explained.

"Duly noted," she murmured and kept silent. It was just a bit hurtful that he would equate something she said in affection to his mother.

He kept one hand on the steering wheel and reached over to take her hand on her lap with the other. "Hey, don't be mad, it's my issue. I'll learn to deal with it."

"I'm not mad, I'm wondering how much I'll have to deal with from not only your mother but from you and the trauma she has put you through," Zeva admitted.

"I'm hoping none," Jasper replied. "But this is years and years of her treachery and abuse I'm trying to navigate, and as soon as she is out of my life it will be perfect."

"We'll see," Zeva said. She was starting to wonder what she actually got herself into. It was as if she was placed as a wedge between the issues of him and his mother.

They finally got into town and pulled up in front of a large pub style restaurant named Haile's Tavern. When they went inside Zeva could see how Joan and Ralph had brought a piece of the U.K back with them in how they decorated their own pub in D.C. The love of polished wood and leather, brass and ornate fixtures seemed to be prevalent among pub owners. As soon as some of the guests saw them come in, the loud whispers of excitement started up. She looked around as they waited for the owner who was Jasper's friend and saw a toddler staring at her in interest. Zeva started up a game of peek-a-boo with the baby who began giggling, much to the mother's delight.

Jasper noticed the interaction and murmured in her ear, "You can go over and say hello."

Zeva glanced at him. "I don't want to interrupt their meal, that's rude. I just love kids."

Jasper squeezed her hand that he was holding. "They are quite friendly here and as Duchess they kind of expect it."

"Are you sure?" she asked hesitantly. "After your

mother's outburst last night, I don't want to offend anyone with my dark skin."

"That was her, luv, she doesn't reflect Northumberland or the people that live here at all. Haile will take a minute, go say hello; you'll be living here after all."

Zeva smiled. "Okay."

She slipped her hand from his and walked over hesitantly to the mother and the toddler in the wooden high chair. The baby, like her mom, had a head full of brunette curls and wide hazel eyes. Her mom had a few tattoos that could be visibly seen and a wide smile on her face as Zeva approached.

"Hi, I'm…"

"The new Duchess, I know," the woman gushed. "Nice to meet you ma'am."

"No, please, just Zeva." She tried not to grimace at the formality of being called ma'am. "And who is this?"

"This is Brittany, my daughter, I'm Tori, her mum," she answered and laughed. "Of course I'm her mum, I'm just nervous about meeting royalty."

"I'm just little old me." Zeva held out her hand to the baby and Brittany slapped her chubby hands against hers happily. "How old is she?"

"She's two," Tori answered and looked down with a red face. "I'm a single mum, you may hear about me around town. I dance in a club one town over to make ends meet." Then she added quickly. "But I also work at the market, too. But you may not want to associate with me or my girl here."

Zeva was shocked. She had more respect for a young woman who was willing to do what she must for her child and to live than just tossing the baby girl into the system to be raised by strangers. Zeva didn't have a clue who her family or parents were. At least Tori was trying her hardest for her baby girl.

"I'm just fine knowing you and your adorable little bit right here," Zeva said firmly. "In fact, if you ever need anything you come to the manor house and find me, and if I'm in town you come on up and we'll grab lunch and have a grand old time. Anyone who doesn't like it can kiss my grits."

Tori grinned. "You certainly are not like the Duke's mum or the rest of the family."

"I hope not." Zeva winked. "It was nice to meet you, Tori… and you, little miss Brittany."

"It was wonderful you came over to speak with us, Duchess, thank you," Tori said gratefully.

"Bye now," Zeva said and touched Brittany's nose with her finger, making the little girl giggle.

Zeva waved and walked back to where Jasper stood waiting with a very large red-headed gentleman with a beard. He was wearing a sweater and a pair of faded jeans and dark boots. He reminded Zeva of the men she read about in books who went out to sea and came back home with a catch of fish to support their family.

"Zeva, this is Haile, my oldest friend in the world," Jasper introduced him. "Haile, this gorgeous lady is my wife."

Haile's smile was wide beneath his beard, revealing pearly white teeth. "You finally got someone to marry your scrawny arse?" He laughed loudly and took her hand, kissing it gently. "It is very nice to finally meet you, Duchess."

"Please… Zeva," she said with a smile of her own. "Everyone here is so nice but formal."

He laughed. "Wait until the weekend pints start flowing and the dart games start up, it can be downright brutal."

"I may have to come into town for that one. I'm pretty proficient in that game," Zeva said.

"Oh, yeah." Haile looked at her with interest and took her hand to lead her to a private booth in the pub. "Jasper, it seems you hit the jackpot with this one. Tell me, Zeva, do you have any sisters, or cousins as fair as you looking for a ginger in their life?"

Zeva laughed. "Unfortunately no, but I will keep an eye out."

"I'll be back with a few pints," Haile promised. She watched his large frame stride over to the bar, eating up the space with only a few steps.

"He seems nice," she commented to Jasper.

Jasper looked over his shoulder at his friend at the bar getting their drinks. Haile promptly threw up his middle finger at his friend and Jasper chuckled. "Haile is a good man. He moved here from London about fifteen years ago and bought this pub, and before that we were mates at school. As you can see, he has no training at all in social graces."

"He doesn't seem to care about your title," Zeva commented.

"He'd piss on my title if it was on paper. Haile was part of the royal army and SAS for years. The man did duty for God and country, he deserves more respect than any title waver should get."

"Well, it seems we have something in common, me and him," Zeva said.

Jasper gave her a mock stern face. "I've already got you, don't try to jump ship for the military man."

"Honey, I don't think he can do for me what you do." Zeva leaned over to kiss him.

"And don't you forget it," he said against her lips.

"If you'll stop trying to suck her face off mate, I have beers," Haile said. He'd managed to grab three pint glasses with his large hands and placed them on the table. "Drink up."

Zeva took a sip of the ice-cold beer and sighed. "This is wonderful."

"I'm glad the duchess is pleased." Haile lifted his glass in a salute and took a large gulp. "When Jasper told me he married an American, and an army girl no less, I was shocked."

"Why?" Zeva asked.

"Not his usual type when it comes to women," Haile answered honestly. "I thought his mum would surely marry him off to some uptight, highbrow twat and we'd never see him again. But he came home raving about you, and you're unlike anyone in his life, or his mother for that matter."

"Lucky for you both he found me," Zeva replied without batting an eye.

Haile laughed loudly. "Cheers to that."

Haile called over one of his waitresses and they ordered their meals. While waiting, they chitchatted back and forth, but most of the conversation was between Jasper and Haile. Zeva listened and silently assessed them both. As they spoke she started to feel less like a new wife and more like a chess piece in a long-going game. She kept silent and focused on her steak with gravy and red potatoes, getting more irritated as each minute passed by.

"Did you happen to find what I was looking for?" Jasper asked.

"Yes I did." Haile looked up from his beef stew and spoke as he broke a wedge of bread off the chunk beside his bowl. "Lillian Edwards lives in

Deal, Kent, a nice cottage that overlooks the coast. I put eyes on her. She seems happy and very much unattached."

"Good, I'll go see her in the next week or two and see if I can get this into the works," Jasper replied. "Any new information on my mother, Patrice or Patricia?"

"They've been quiet, but I'm sure there will be more activity now that you've brought Zeva home and they try to circumvent your marriage."

'They can try, they'll fail. I still have the final piece of ammunition in my cache." Jasper smiled wickedly.

Haile took a sip of his drink. "Good to know."

"And since this has nothing to do with me, I should go. Car keys, please Jasper," Zeva said crisply.

They both looked at her and Jasper said, "What?"

"Oh, you remember I'm here now," Zeva said. "Look, you have family business or plotting to discuss, fine, but why drag me along. I could've well stayed home and made my own dinner."

"You're in trouble mate," Haile said gleefully. Zeva gave him a withering look and he instantly went silent.

"Zeva, it's not like that. I wanted you to meet my friend, see the town," Jasper replied.

"I saw the inside of the pub and listened to you

and Haile hatch plans," Zeva said stiffly. "If you're done I'd like to go."

"The tab is on me. Take your wife home and grovel, lots of groveling," Haile said. "Nice to meet you, Zeva, you saucy thing."

"Nice to meet you," she replied as Jasper slid from the booth so she could get out.

"We'll talk soon, Haile, thanks," Jasper said stiffly.

"Anytime."

She heard his friend respond but was already a few steps ahead of Jasper heading to the door. She stood by the Mercedes, and when Jasper unlocked the door she got inside without waiting for him to hold the door. He walked around and slid into the drivers seat before starting the car and driving away silently back to the manor house.

"So you have nothing to say?" Zeva said finally.

"I do not like arguments." Jasper's voice was firm and held a note of finality. "I've watched too many of them throughout the years."

"So you plan to have none at all?" Zeva said. "We are married, we're going to have arguments. It's when we stop trying to hash things out and go quiet that's the big problem."

"I don't see why you are upset," Jasper said.

"For one, you take me out and spend the evening talking about your mother and family," Zeva pointed out. "I'm started to feel less like your wife and more like a pawn used to piss your mother off in this war you are waging with her."

"I'm sorry if I made you feel that way," Jasper sighed. "That's certainly not the case."

"From my point of view it sure looks that way," Zeva replied. "We got married, had one night together, and were separated for three months until I arrived here. I'm technically on my third day and we should still be in the honeymoon phase learning about each other, hell, drinking champagne off each other's bodies. Instead, we are at a pub strategizing and looking for people and secret weapons."

"That all sounds lovely but I can't give my mother an ounce of space to try to outsmart me," Jasper defended his actions.

"At the expense of us?" Zeva asked unbelievingly. "What if you two are going at each other for years, should I wait until it's all over for us to start a life together, a real one with love and children? Do you want to be like your Uncle Brewster and lose it all? Or am I just a tool to be used in this battle of wits with you and your mother? If that's what you are asking me, then you are selfish and you should have spelled that shit out before we got married."

"That's not what I'm expecting at all," Jasper said in exasperation.

She turned in the car seat and looked at him as he drove. "Jasper, I understand in a way you are fighting for your life. When you asked me to marry you, you said you'd give up the damn title to be with me. You don't have to do that at all. I'm asking that you put as much time and energy into our marriage as you would trying to one up your mother. You need to think of what is more important to you, a life, a good marriage, a home, things we both never really had, or revenge."

He didn't answer and the rest of the car ride home was in silence. At the manor house they walked in, and he locked up. She watched television and found some of her favorite channels through his satellite dish, and he went to work in his workshop. She didn't press. They needed a little bit of space and he definitely needed to think. It got dark and Zeva went upstairs to take a hot shower. She would have to get accustomed to the chilly nights in Northumberland, because while it got cold in Washington, in the U.K it was a damp chill that seemed to get into your bones. By the time she came out, Jasper was in the room and she could see he'd taken a shower in his own bathroom. He had a fire lit in the stone fireplace of the bedroom and was grabbing a pillow and extra blankets from the large carved armoire he had made himself.

"What are you doing?" Zeva asked curiously.

"Going to sleep in one of the other bedrooms, you're mad at me," Jasper said and his voce seemed confused at her question.

"Holy shit, they really fucked you up, didn't they?" Zeva said incredulously. She got into bed and pulled the thick blankets back. "Get into bed, Jasper."

He put the items back and made his way to the bed, where he lay next to her. Zeva snuggled close and pressed a kiss on his lips.

"Just because we argue doesn't mean we need to sleep apart," Zeva explained gently. "I never want to sleep away from my husband, so let's not ever think we can't still hold each other even if we are upset." She laced her fingers with his. "This is how we stay connected, when we are happy or times get difficult, we never sleep apart. Deal?"

Jasper swallowed thickly and nodded. His voice was husky when he spoke. "Deal."

"Now turn off the lights and let's go to sleep," she said.

With only the embers from the fire lighting the room she kissed him again. Zeva made sure she was as close as she could be to him as they settled down for the night. There was no way she would ever let him feel like he was alone, but she surmised she had to reconstruct a lot of the damage that was inflicted on him through his life because of how he saw his parents' marriage. While she was learning how not to think of herself as alone, Zeva would have to teach him how love truly should be.

Chapter Seven

"This man is going to drive me insane," Zeva muttered.

Jasper was away with Haile. They'd gotten a line on some trees trunks or wood that had washed up from the ocean or something of the like. His excitement about firing it and making unique pieces from the wood and how Vikings cast wood into seawater before using it was contagious. Personally, she had no clue what he was talking about, but assured him she would be fine for a day alone working on his books and he went off happily. Zeva was left with a stack of papers and a stack on her lap and then a whole other stack on a second desk.

In the weeks that followed, Jasper had asked her to help him tackle some paperwork he was behind on. He didn't once mention he was notoriously bad with keeping track of his business invoices, purchase orders, delivery schedule—practically all of it was in a disarray. After two days of watching him just make small piles, she took over and made it her mission to sort out the mess. Then one night he offered her a job as his bookkeeper and a hefty paycheck. She accepted immediately, and it led into another plan she was forming in her head.

After speaking with Tori and doing some research, she decided to start a charity to help young mothers get an education and proper jobs. They would be taught everything about how to dress and conduct themselves in an interview and given business clothes. She wanted to offer an on-site day care for these young women to leave their children while they went out to find jobs so they could have a safe place for their kids when they were at work. Jasper was thrilled with her idea, and as Duchess she planned to have charity events to fund the whole thing. It felt rewarding to know she was finding her place in Northumberland with Jasper, and that using her new title she could help the residents she lived alongside.

She heard wheels on the gravel and looked out the window facing the driveway to see a car driving sloppily up the lane to the house. The driver parked in a swerve that kicked up more of the rocks, and Uncle Brewster almost fell out the car. *Oh shit,* she thought and looked at the time on her cell phone. It was only three in the afternoon and Jasper had said wouldn't be back until six or seven.

"Jasper!" His uncle yelled in a drunken voice, and his body was not stable as he teetered while he stood.

Zeva pressed Jasper's cell number in her phone

while she walked to the front of the manor. The textured stained glass of the front door distorted his figure outside as he yelled his nephews name again. Jasper answered the phone and his voice sounded so happy she hated to ruin his mood.

"Hello, luv, miss me already?" Jasper asked.

"I always miss you," Zeva answered and sighed. "But your uncle is drunk outside and he's yelling your name. He drove to the manor drunk. Should I try to get him inside till you get home?"

"Blood fucking hell, he drove drunk!" Jasper's voce rose angrily. "I told him about this. Jesus Christ, he could've killed someone on the sodding road."

"Yes, I know, this is why I think I should get him inside and take those keys until you get home," Zeva said gently.

"He's a pretty big guy, Zeva, can you manage? I think it's about time I call the constables on him, He needs to hit rock bottom and start to work his way back up," Jasper replied.

"I'm an Army girl, I carried a fifty pound pack when I deployed and took down guys twice my size in defense class, I'll manage," she said amused. "Even if I have to drag him across the gravel."

"I made a stop on the way home and I think I've found a solution to Uncle Brewster's situation," Jasper told her. "But first I need to get him sober and on the right track. We'll be home soon luv, I promise."

"I'll get him safe," Zeva promised.

"I appreciate that, thank you." He sighed. "Thank you so much, Zeva. I don't know what I would do without you. See you soon."

She hung up and shoved the cell in her back pocket before stepping outside. Even with the thick sweater she wore, the air was chilly, yet she walked briskly toward where the older man was trying to get back in his car.

"Well hello Uncle Brewster, we didn't expect you." Zeva made her voice bright. "Come on inside for a cup of coffee, I made some dinner."

He pointed a drunken finger at her. "You caused all this, you know. My sister is livid with me and making my life a living hell, all because Jasper married you."

"I'm sorry, Brewster, I really am, but it's not my fault she is the way she is," she said gently. "Come on inside and let's talk about it. I bet you haven't eaten all day. I made some thick soup and we have bread. I know you loved my desserts, there's some of that, too."

"I'll come in for a quick minute and visit, but I'm leaving right after," Uncle Brewster announced. "My sister said you and Jasper are the enemy, I have to side with her. I've always protected her."

Zeva nodded solemnly. "As well you should, you are a good brother. I wish I had one just like you."

He smiled up at her. "Really?"

"You bet," she answered and held out her hand. "Come on, let's get you warm and fed."

"You are such a good woman, I am sorry I have to hate you." Uncle Brewster took her hand and allowed her to lead him inside.

"Yeah, me too," she said softly.

Zeva felt sorry for the old man. He was caught between loyalty to his sister and a love for daughters who didn't regard him as a father to loving Jasper and wanting to be a part of his life. Because of Jasper's mother the man could only find solace in alcohol. She got a hot cup of coffee into him and managed to have him eat some soup before he started to fall asleep. Zeva settled him to the family room on one of the long wide sofas and he was out almost instantly.

She covered him with the thick afghan and stoked the fire, throwing a few more pieces of wood on it before she closed the door and left him to sleep it off. She went back outside, took the keys from the ignition, and closed the car before heading back to the warmth of the manor. She went back to work hoping Jasper would be home before his uncle woke up and tried to drive again. The smell of alcohol coming off him was so strong she doubted he would be sober enough to drive until the next day. She was just about to work when she heard another car and looked out of the window to see a sleek black Mercedes.

"Who the fuck is this now?" she muttered and dropped the file she had just picked up on the table with a hard slap.

By the time she got out the door, Cornelia McTavish was stepping from the car. She wore a tapered elegant pantsuit with a long coat with fur at the cuffs and neck. She gave Zeva a cold look, and Zeva clasped her hand behind her back as she stood at the door and waited. She would not be making the first move, if her mother-in-law wanted to interact Cornelia could walk her happy ass over to where Zeva stood. When she saw Zeva wouldn't move she did just that.

"Hello, Zeva is it?" Her voice was elegant and cold.

"You called me Darkie last time so I thought that was the name you gave me," Zeva replied without batting an eye.

"I'm here to collect my brother," Cornelia said.

"He's asleep and Jasper said he was to stay here," she replied.

Cornelia smiled wide revealing perfect teeth. "Ah, such an obedient wife."

Zeva's smile was stiff. "Not really. I just don't like you and how you treat your brother and your son."

"You think you know, little girl, but you are in a

game that you can't win. When I was young you would've been my maid. This is what happens when people forget their place and lot in life." Cornelia sighed dramatically.

"Exactly when were you young? Fuck, I forgot when you sell your soul to the devil it gains you immortality," Zeva replied. "You should really talk to him about those wrinkles around your eyes. Your face could be a road map with all those lines."

"You little bitch," Cornelia gasped angrily and reached into her purse. Zeva instantly thought "gun" and got in a defensive stance carefully not to draw attention. Instead, Cornelia pulled out a checkbook. "I will give you a million dollars to leave here and divorce Jasper."

Zeva laughed. "As far as I hear you are in no position to write checks that certainly can't be cashed."

"I have the money," her mother-in-law snapped.

"Still, I'll say no." Zeva smiled and waved. "You're not welcome here. Go away now, toodles."

"I could have my driver come in and take him." Cornelia had wicked delight written all over her face. "He could mess up that pretty dark skin of yours."

Zeva's heart jumped but she kept cool. "He could try and I'd give him a run for his money and kick your ass, too."

Cornelia laughed. "You Americans are crass as ever. Don't worry, I'll get you gone when you least expect it, one way or another. I had hoped you would choose the easier way before you don't have any breath left to be so rude."

Zeva didn't hide her defense stance this time. "That sounds like a threat on my life. Cornelia, if or when you try, or in your case pay someone because you are too much of a coward to handle shit yourself, you better hope they drop me and I stay down. If not sweetie... darling, I'm coming for you."

"Tell my brother I was worried and came to check on him." Cornelia stuffed her checkbook into her purse.

"I will tell him no such thing," Zeva replied. "Get the hell off our property."

"This was my mother's land. I have more right here than you do," Cornelia screeched, her hands fisted at her sides.

"And yet she left it to Jasper instead of you. I guess she saw your true colors even though you were her daughter," Zeva shot back at her. "Go home, Cornelia, and try to figure out another way to con money from some unsuspecting man."

Zeva stepped inside, closed the door, and went through to the kitchen. From the large windows she could see Cornelia follow her movements with angry strides. She stood at the wide bay window of the kitchen staring at her mother-in-law in a standoff of wills. Cornelia bent down and picked up a paving stone. Her driver saw the action as well and tried to scramble out of the car to stop her. It was too late, and Cornelia threw it at the window where Zeva stood on the opposite side.

"What the fuck!" Zeva moved quickly as the rock hit the window and shattered the glass, spraying the kitchen with glass shards. "Oh, you fucking crazy bitch!"

She retraced her steps to head out the door, literally ready to beat the snot out of Jasper's mother, but by the time she got to the front door she could only watch as the tires sprayed up gravel with the haste of the car's retreat down the driveway. Zeva was fuming and promised that she would not be forgetting the incident. By the time Jasper had come home she'd managed to clean up the glass. She'd found sheets of plastic in his workshop and covered the window so the cold night air wouldn't get in. Both he and Haile rushed into the kitchen, looking frantic.

"Bloody hell, Zeva what happened?" Jasper asked.

"Oh that?" She used her cup of coffee with a healthy dose of Irish whiskey added to point at the window. "Your mother came by for a visit to pick up her brother, who is still here by the way. Then she threatened me and tried to stone me to death through the window."

Jasper moved quickly and cupped her face. "Are you okay? Haile, call the constables."

"Jasper no, it makes no sense trying to call the police when she's long gone and will probably say I instigated it," Zeva's sigh was tired. "I kinda did with the insulting, but didn't, yet it's her word versus mine and additional chaos. I wasn't letting her take Uncle Brewster out of here, though. Even though she threatened to have her driver mess up my dark skin."

"This is going to fucking end," Jasper snarled. "I'm done with dealing with her."

"Settle down—here, drink this." Zeva handed him her mug.

He took a sip and coughed. "How much whiskey is in there?"

"Enough to keep me from getting her address and going to kick her ass," Zeva replied.

"This is fucking awesome. I need a strong wife." Haile, watching the interaction between them, laughed. "Come on, Jasper, let's get some plywood for the window until we can get it fixed tomorrow."

Jasper kissed her. "I'll be back soon, my love."

"I'll be upstairs lying down for a bit. I have a small headache after my very eventful day," Zeva replied.

She could feel his gaze on her while she left the kitchen, and it was only when she was curled up under the thick blankets did she realize he had called her "my love" not just "luv." Zeva smiled, and the ache in her heart was so sweet she pressed her hand over her chest. This wasn't just an affectionate pet name, it was the actual thing. In essence, Jasper just told her he loved her. She must have dozed off because she stirred when he gently shook her shoulders.

"Hey." She smiled up at him. "I may have napped a bit."

"I'm glad. Is your headache better?" Jasper brushed her hair away from her face.

"It's just a dull throb, is Haile gone?" she asked.

"Yes, just a bit ago. I let you sleep for a while and got Uncle Brewster in a guest room for the night," Jasper explained. "Are you up for a little trip to the workshop? I have something I want you to see."

"Sure, just let me brush my teeth and use the facilities. Irish whiskey and coffee leaves you cotton-mouthed and needing to pee," Zeva said. "I'll meet you downstairs."

He laughed and kissed her forehead. "Okay, see you in five minutes."

Zeva freshened up in a hurry, curious to why he wanted her to go out to the workshop. *If he starts talking about the driftwood again I might fall back asleep in the sawdust*, she thought as she went to find him. He was waiting by the front door and smiled when she walked up to him.

Jasper pulled her into a hug. "Are you okay?"

"Yeah, why?" She pulled back and looked at him.

"I thought my mother had pissed you off so much or scared you that you were mad at me and considering leaving," Jasper admitted.

"I'm no punk, she didn't scare me a bit," Zeva assured him. "What pissed me off more is that I didn't get through the bookkeeping I had planned for the day. Speaking of which, you are an artist, I love your creativity, but you suck at running a business. When I finally make some order in that office, let me handle the paperwork from now on. I mean it. You hired me, you just give me stuff and I'll take care of it. No ruining the system I'm creating."

"Yes, dear," he said solemnly and kissed her nose. "Come on, I have to show you something."

Her curiosity was piqued as they walked through the cool, dark night of Northumberland. She was always amazed at the fog that settled close to the ground from the early evening, giving the area an almost spooky feel. She was still trying to get accustomed to the weather, because while the days could be warm enough to work outside without a coat at night the cold and fog settled in. In his workshop, what Jasper showed her took her breath away. On his work table a large, wooden chest stood. It was stained a light color, and ornately carved leaves went around the lid of the box.

The body had his signature Celtic knot work, but she had never seen this pattern in the multitude of drawings he kept in the office. This was unique, and at the top her name was etched in elegant letters, *Duchess Zeva McTavish*. Beneath it was her rank in the army and the years she spent within the military fold. She traced her fingers over the box, the smooth wood cool beneath her fingers. Its beauty floored her.

"This is beautiful, why?" Zeva looked at him and asked.

"It's your wedding present." He smiled.

"You gave me diamonds as a wedding present," she reminded him.

"No, I gave you a gift to wear to the party that night," Jasper pointed out. "This is made with love, and it will last a lifetime and beyond so you can pass it down to our kids, and they can pass it on through the family we create. It's for the foot of the bed, so you can place anything you treasure in it."

"Or use it as a box for our kinky sexy toys," she teased.

"We don't have any kinky sex toys, but if that's what floats your boat, I'm in." Jasper grinned. "We just won't tell the children what's in there."

Zeva laughed. "You are a nut."

"Yeah, but I'm your nut, remember that," Jasper replied.

She threw her arms around his neck. "You always have the most perfect answers, I love it and I love you."

He put his hands on her shoulders and pulled her away, looking deep into her eyes. "Do you mean that? You love me?"

"Jasper, of course I love you," she laughed. "How could you think I didn't? We are a couple, we face the world together. Honey, anything we go through it will be side by side, balls to the wall, me and you, the dynamic duo."

"I love you and everything you just said." Jasper hugged her tight and lifted her off her feet. "I knew you were the one, I just felt it in my entire being that you were meant for me."

"I can't say the same, but you're the only man I ever showed the secret room to in D.C., and then you worked your way into my heart." Zeva laughed. "And here I was thinking you were bringing me out here to show me more wood."

He kissed her once, then again and grinned devilishly. "I've got some timber I can show you."

She moved her hips against his and felt the hardness of his arousal. "I can see that. Wanna give me a private tour of your workshop, Duke?"

"I have the perfect piece to show you, actually," he murmured.

Jasper led her to a massive chaise lounge that was

wood. When he pulled the plastic off the piece of furniture the soft velvet was olive.

"I don't think this will be for sale anymore," Zeva said as she took her sweater off and began to work on her jeans.

"We can put it in the library if you want, you can use it for reading." Jasper followed her actions and undressed quickly.

"Or other things," she said.

"Bloody hell I love the way you think."

They moved toward each other like two magnets drawn together by an invisible pull. The connection they formed from the beginning was only made stronger with the love they vowed to each other. Their kiss was fueled by heat and the passion Zeva knew she could only find in his arms. He sat her down on the soft fabric of the chair and posed her as if he was about to draw her.

"What are you doing?" Zeva openly stared at his body, his cock hard between his legs.

"Committing you to memory because I plan to carve your form one day," he said calmly. "I want you so much, if you weren't already naked I swear I'd of ripped your clothes off."

Zeva felt the heat at her sex and the moistness pool between the folds. "I should've kept them on."

His eyes darkened and he followed her onto the chaise lounge. "I can't wait to be inside you. Sometimes I'm out here just picturing you naked in bed, wet, waiting for me."

"Like I am now." She ran her hand down his chest and torso then grasped his thick cock in her hand.

Jasper groaned at her touch. "I love you, Zeva, you are my heart and my soul, don't ever forget that."

Zeva met his gaze. "You're mine, I lay claim to you now and forever, Duke McTavish."

"And to think they wanted the duke to take a wife and he was claimed by a wanton American woman." He nuzzled her neck.

She laughed huskily. "You love me just the way I am."

"Yes I do."

He kissed her with a hunger that left her reeling. Zeva bit her lip against the whimper as Jasper's hands slid down her thighs and back up to cup her ass. He slowly ground his hips against hers, watching her face as he did. She could feel his hardness and the need that tensed his muscles. Zeva shuddered in anticipation of what was to come.

Jasper bit her neck before kissing his way upward and whispering in her ear, "I want you to tremble for me, I want to hear you call out my name, and every time I look around this workshop it will be you I'm seeing. You will be my muse."

"Then show me, Duke, give me everything you've got," she answered brazenly.

Jaspers eyes were dark with desire and he silenced her with a kiss. There was no build to intensity, he touched her and she burned. She'd rolled her hair up in a bun and he took the tie out, letting the thick tresses of her hair fall against her naked back. Jasper grabbed fistfuls of the thick tresses, holding her head still so he could devour her mouth. Zeva whimpered at the delicious assault of her senses.

Zeva could barely think, all she wanted to do was feel his tongue taste and take from her. She wanted to give him her all, and with each touch she melted like a candle beneath a flame. Jasper cupped her breasts and took one hard nipple into his mouth. She arched, offering him more of herself and Jasper took the invitation by laving each heavy globe with the same intensity.

He tasted her like a man starving and sucking on sweet fruit, and with each whimper his primal grunt of response made her hot and wet, more aroused than she thought possible. Jasper moved back up her body and took her lips again, plundering her mouth as he moved over her on the soft fabric of the lounge chair.

"I like this, so much room for both of us," she teased.

"I plan to be so close to you that most of this

space isn't necessary." His laugh was husky. "I should rethink this piece."

"Don't you dare, this is perfect." Zeva pressed kisses on his shoulder.

Jasper cupped the mound of her pussy where she was wet and ached for him. Zeva moaned, bit her lip, and arched her hips when his finger slipped between the silky folds of her labia, and all the while his dark gaze was on her. He trailed his lips down her body and she arched off the chaise lounge when his hot mouth touched the lips of her pussy. She gave him more access to her sex and when she felt the first lick of his tongue, pleasure speared through her. Jasper pulled her hips roughly to him with his large hands. She could feel callouses on his hand from his craft, and it only heightened her pleasure.

Zeva reached back on the carved, smooth curved top of the chair, trying to anchor herself. A storm of sensations crashed over her as he sipped eagerly of her sensitive pussy, and Zeva pleaded and begged for release. He licked at her sex with savage flicks of his tongue until Zeva crested in her release. Jasper supped on her with excitement, tasting the essence of her desire as it flowed. She slumped back and a low moan was ripped from her lips when he slipped his finger inside her. Soon Jasper had her begging and pleading for release as he drove her desire to the peak again.

She closed her eyes and let the sensations crash over in heated waves. Zeva gave herself over to him and his lovemaking completely as she succumbed to another orgasm. The pleasure held her, its grasp washing over her until she lost her breath. Zeva never felt anything like it, and as she rode the high of her release, Jasper filled her with his cock. He kissed her, and his groan melded with her cry of pure need.

"More please, take me hard," she whispered urgently against his ear.

"Fuck yes," Jasper muttered.

He pulled her against his thick cock savagely. She held on to his shoulders and lifted her legs high around his waist as he pounded into her. Jasper was past reason and in the midst of his own carnal desire, and a primal need was on his face. It only excited her even more and beneath him she gave him everything. Zeva undulated and took him deep with each thrust until it was Jasper who called out her name.

"I'm going to come," she moaned the words and it ended on a keening cry.

"Ah yes, I'm with you, my luv," he said though clenched teeth.

She pulled his head to hers to share a searing kiss. Zeva drove him to the edge while her body shuddered and her release crashed through her. She felt his cock throb inside her as the first of his hot seed filled her, while his guttural cry echoed in the rafters of the workshop. Jasper cupped her neck as their tongues mingled and let go with each hard thrust. She moaned, coming apart once more because of his frenzied movements. Zeva fell into that abyss that lovers find only in each other, connected intimately until they became one. They lay together entwined on a piece of furniture of his own creation with the smell of sawdust in the air, and Zeva never felt more complete.

"Are you okay?" he asked huskily. "We were a bit rambunctious."

"Rambunctious," Zeva snorted in amusement. "I'm perfectly okay, how about yourself?"

"I feel like I could conquer the world." A laugh rumbled through his chest, and she smiled at the sound. "I have to deal with this thing, my mother and my uncle. I have to end it for us to move on."

"I know," she said gently. "I'm so sorry, Jasper, this is going to be hard for you."

"I've known it for a while. I'm numb to her by now, and being scared for my uncle is an everyday thing. But I know to save him and myself from her for the rest of our lives I have to stop her cold. The letter from Joan can help me with that. I've never felt this way with anyone, never had a woman like you in my life," Jasper explained honestly. "For us to survive, to last and have peace in our lives, marriage, for our children to be safe, I have to make her leave Northumberland forever and stay gone."

"And you think the letter will do that?" Zeva asked.

"That and a few other tricks up my sleeve," he said. "Plus, I think everything in life happens for a reason, and I was meant to go to D.C., so I have to thank her for that."

"I was glad you did, you gave me a family in loving you." She cupped his face. "Thank you."

"While I sound like a mushy love song, your love is all I need," he answered huskily and grinned. "Shall I make you something to eat inside? I think bread with cheese, hot chocolate in bed." "Good idea." She smiled and drew a pattern on his chest with her finger. "We'll deal with tomorrow when it gets here. Till then, tonight is just you and me." They dressed each other with intimate whispers and laughter that only two lovers could share. Hand in hand, they walked back to the manor and true to his word they shared a simple meal in bed. They fell asleep in each other's arms, cocooned in the love they created. Zeva knew that she would fight with him and for him, as long as she lived.

Chapter Eight

Jasper looked at the older woman who sat across from him in the kitchen. When she lifted the saucer with the teacup, her hand trembled so much that the china rattled. He vaguely remembered Lillian McTavish; when she left he was still very young and her black hair reminded him of the ravens that used to come around the property. She was just a little heavier and her hair was now streaked with gray, yet she had it cut in an elegant style to her shoulders and her eyes were filled with despair and fear. Yes, fear, because his mother terrorized her until she fled, leaving the man she loved and her children.

"He's on his way here, then?" her soft voice asked after she took a long sip of the hot tea.

Jasper nodded. "Yes he is. I hope he listens to both of us and finally breaks away from my mother."

Lillian shuddered as if a chill ran through her body. "Your mother is… I don't know how a boy like you managed to turn out so good despite her."

"I never let her break me," Jasper answered honestly.

"But I let her break me, run me away from my children, Brewster." Lillian shook her head. "If I didn't I would've died, you understand. I contemplated taking my own life because of this woman. It took a lot of therapy and years for me to gain the strength to even contemplate coming back to see him, to help him."

"We'll talk with him first, and then go to the mansion to talk to the girls," Jasper said. "Lillian, I have to warn you she has them completely warped."

"My poor girls." A tear slipped down her cheek. "I resigned myself that I had lost them all, even my Brewster, long ago. If I can help save just one of them I know the rest will fall into place. I have faith in that. We'll get him to stop the drinking, and I hope he comes home with me, he needs love and care."

"I hope you are right." Jasper sighed. This was phase one of getting his family chaos solved. Phase two would be confronting his mother with his ultimatum, and Joan's letter revealed a hell of a plot twist in their lives.

Lillian placed her cup gently on the table. "Where is the new Duchess? I hear you caused quite a stir marrying an American, it has been in all the papers. Your mother must of went bonkers when she found out. She is completely beautiful, by the way."

"Zeva is in town, she will be home by six." Jasper smiled, thinking about the woman he loved. "She is setting up a resource center for single mothers in need for Northumberland. She's already had so much positive help for the residents and is setting up a charity event to raise money. They love her around here, she is everything my mother was not as duchess."

Lillian reached over and patted his hand. "I am glad you found happiness, Jasper. I really am…"

The sound of a car pulling up cut off her words. From the bay window Jasper could see Uncle Brewster's car. After the night he showed up drunk while Zeva was home, Jasper laid into him about driving drunk and vowed to call the constables if he ever did it again. His uncle was steady when he got out of the car, and Jasper breathed a sigh of relief. He was sober.

"If you'd like to wait in the family room, I'll bring him in," Jasper said as he stood and helped Lillian to her feet. He squeezed her hand. "It will be okay."

"Thank you Jasper, for everything you have tried to do for him," Lillian said.

Uncle Brewster rang the doorbell a few times while he got Lillian settled, and Jasper hurried to the door.

"I was just going to check the workshop and see if you lost track of time in there," Uncle Brewster said with a smile. "How are you, my boy?"

"I'm good, Uncle." Jasper clapped him on the back. "I've got tea and coffee in the family room."

"Did Zeva make any of her pastries?" Uncle Brewster ran his hand over his trimmed mustache.

Jasper chuckled. "She knew you were coming and made a batch of her cranberry-almond scones last night."

Uncle Brewster laughed. "Wonderful girl."

At the door of the family room, Uncle Brewster stopped short when he saw who was inside. Lillian stood.

"Brewster, you look well," Lillian sad gently.

"What are you doing here?" Uncle Brewster sounded wary. "Jasper, what is this?"

"No, you ask me, Brewster," Lillian said firmly. "I'm here to beg you to get help for your drinking and to come home with me. Leave Northumberland and finally start to live your life."

"You left, Lillian, not I," Uncle Brewster pointed out.

"Because you let your horrid sister terrorize me without consequence!" Lillian cried out. "You let her take our girls and warp them into spoiled little monsters."

"Uncle." Jasper led him into the room and sat him down. "My mother doesn't care about any of us, just about herself. She didn't care that you lost the love of your life, as long as she had what she wanted. You've spent your whole life cleaning up her messes and living for her. When is it time for you? I love you, I want you to find some happiness in this life. Not staring at the bottom of a bottle trying to drink and forget."

"I never stopped loving you, Brewster." Lillian knelt by the chair where Uncle Brewster sat. "I ran because the hold Cornelia had on you was one I couldn't break. But my love never failed, I just had to heal myself, get stronger before I could even dare try to heal you."

"She's my sister..." Uncle Brewster swallowed thickly. "I'm the only one who can protect her."

"Uncle, you've seen my mother operate. Does it seem like she needs protection from anyone?" Jasper asked. "She uses you, and how do you feel that you have to drink to forget? You know everything she does is wrong, it weighs on you, all of it. All these years of her treacherous behavior is like a stone around your neck, dragging you into the bottle."

"I hated how she treated you." Uncle Brewster cupped Lillian's cheek. "I wasn't strong enough to stop her, and then it was too late because you were gone."

"It's never too late." Lillian placed her hand over his. "Come with me, let's start a new life, let's work on your problem together, and for as long as we have left on this earth let's be happy. I have a treatment center close to my home now, there's a spot waiting for you there. After you get a steady, sober foundation we will work on us."

"You'll wait for me?" Uncle Brewster asked huskily. "After all I've done?"

Lillian smiled at him. "Brewster, I was waiting for the opportunity to be with the man I love, the right way. Jasper gave me this chance, let's take it and run."

He nodded and tears fell down his cheeks and slipped into the thick hair of his mustache. "Yes love, I'll go with you. I'll get the help."

"Yes." Jasper gave a fist pump.

Uncle Brewster leaned forward and grabbed him in a hug bear hug. "Thank you, my boy, thank you for everything."

"It's not done yet," Jasper explained. "When Zeva comes home we go to my mother's and we end this once and for all. We try to get my cousins to leave her as well, and I get her to leave Northumberland and never return."

Uncle Brewster furrowed his brow in confusion. "You know she will never leave this place, we don't have any leverage to make her do otherwise."

"I think I can work it out." Jasper looked at his watched and then went to the window to peer outside. "It's getting dark, Zeva should be here. She probably left a few minutes late and will be here soon."

By seven he knew something was wrong and called Haile and asked him to go by the office rental to see if she was still there. Jasper picked up his coat and found the keys to the Land Rover. The warning signals made his stomach clench and his mother had to be at the center of it.

"We're coming with you, son," Uncle Brewster said firmly. "If Cornelia has done something to Zeva she's gone too bloody far."

"She went too far long ago." Jasper's voice was deadly. "If anything has happened to Zeva, there is no place to hide from what I will do my mother."

By the time they got into town Haile was waiting by the car Zeva had taken that morning and the hood was up. His face was grim when Jasper got out of the large vehicle.

"What?" Jasper's voice was terse.

"Someone disabled her car, good job too," Haile replied. "They went under the main part of the engine and pulled the wires. She wouldn't have known where to start to fix it, the plugs, brake lines, and everything looked intact."

"She could've walked to the pub and got you or called," Jasper said and ran his hand through his thick hair.

"Not if she was taken," Haile said grimly.

"Get in the car. Haile you follow us, we are going

to my mother's house," Jasper said. "I'm beating the shite out of everyone until they tell me where Zeva is."

"How could she be so cruel to do this to her own son," Lillian cried out.

"She's pure evil, she feels nothing," Jasper answered. "But when I'm through she will understand she made the biggest mistake by taking my wife."

His words held deadly intent and everyone got silently into the vehicle to go to the mansion where Cornelia McTavish resided. Her day of reckoning had come, and Jasper would be the one who delivered the final judgment.

It had been a good day. Zeva looked around the office space for Northumberland Hope Center and felt a sense of accomplishment. In area where they lived, residents had to go to one of the larger towns for resources. Now she and others would be able to help many when the doors to the center opened. She hired Tori as a full time assistant and the young woman was thrilled. She wouldn't have to dance anymore to support her daughter, and with the day care on-site, the baby had someplace safe to be while her mum worked.

She was still hiring staff but had already received

hefty donations from some of the more wealthy residents. She knew from her job in D.C. how to work a crowd at a charity event. She planned to have the center funded and helping residents by the next month, and by Christmas she wanted to have a domestic abuse shelter open for women and children. The address would be secret, and Haile had already agreed to help her find security for the site. Along with bookkeeping for Jasper her life was full. The fact that she loved her husband and thinking about him made her warm all over only sealed the fact that she was where she was meant to be.

Zeva locked up and went to the car. She had sent Tori and the baby home for supper an hour ago while she finished up a few things. It was time for her to go home and meet Lillian, Uncle Brewster's wife, and hopefully he had agreed to get help. Jasper had it all planned out, and while she would've loved to be there to support him Zeva felt it better they handle Uncle Brewster on their own. She had only been part of this family for a few months, and she knew embarrassment could drive the uncle to refuse just on stubbornness.

Zeva slid behind the wheel of the car and rubbed her hands over her shoulders vigorously. "I'm going to have to wear a thicker coat, it's getting brisk out there."

She turned the key in the ignition and the car

didn't even stir. Zeva frowned and turned the key again. Nothing. "Damn it," she muttered and got out of the car. She was already late, but when she pulled her cell phone from her bag of course she'd forgotten to charge it. It was dead. The phone service wasn't going to be turned on in the center until the next week. The only option she had was to walk to Haile's pub and call Jasper from there, then ask him to take her home. Thunder rumbled in the distance and she felt the first small drop.

Of course, rain, she thought. Zeva had seen how rainstorms developed in the area and hoped by the time she got to the pub she wasn't drowned. She was just about to set off when a car slowed and pulled in next to her. Zeva heard the whir as the automatic window rolled down slowly, revealing the face of one of Jasper's cousins. They were identical twins, and she had never talked to either of them so she didn't know which one was driving.

"Hello, you look a bit put out." The young woman smiled. "I'm Patrice, Jasper's cousin."

"Okay, hello," Zeva said doubtfully.

"Why are you walking? It's about to start pouring any minute." Patrice's voice was friendly.

"The car won't start. I'm going to head to Haile's pub to get a ride home," Zeva replied. "It was nice talking to—"

"Come on, I'll give you a lift," Patrice cut her off.

"Why would you do that? Your aunt would prefer to see me drowned before helping me, and as far as I hear you and your sister are her clones," Zeva said bluntly.

Patrice laughed. "I do have my own mind, and while we may not all get along, I wouldn't see anyone, let alone my cousin's wife, needing help and do nothing. I was actually quite curious about our new ventures. It's all the talk about town and maybe I could volunteer?" Patrice sighed, a little dramatically in Zeva's opinion, but she was British and rich and tended to be good at acting. "To be honest, we can't keep going like we are now, the big divide within our family. I would like to change that, maybe it can start with us. Besides, the pub is two streets over, you'll be soaked before you get there."

Zeva looked at her, trying to gauge her sincerity and finding nothing she could compare it against because the girl had done nothing to her. "Okay, thank you for the ride."

Patrice smiled. "Come on around and hop in, I'll turn the heat up."

Zeva got in on the left side, while Patrice sat in front of the steering wheel on the right. The car was warm, and Zeva sighed gratefully as the heat hit her just as the rain began to fall. "I appreciate this. My cell died, and you are right, the rain came in fast."

"Not a problem at all," Patrice said as she pulled

away slowly. "Mobiles, technology makes it harder sometimes, I swear."

Zeva smiled. "Yes it does."

The drive started out okay, and then Zeva frowned when Patrice didn't take the turn on the road that would lead to the manor house. The rain had stopped but more was still on the way, light drops still hit the windshield of the compact car.

"Um, you missed the turn," Zeva pointed out.

"It's okay love, I have to make a small stop. I'll take you right back," Patrice said. "Besides, I wanted to talk to my cousin about dad's drinking. It's gotten much worse."

"Jasper would appreciate any help in getting him to go into recovery," Zeva said.

The road turned rocky then meandered into nothingness. It was dark all around and she couldn't even make out the wilderness in the pitch black.

Patrice stopped and Zeva looked at her. "What are you doing?"

"I leave a care package here every few weeks for a friend who lives out here near the moors," Patrice said seamlessly. "He doesn't come into town and has become essentially a hermit, an old friend of my father's who went a bit mad after his wife died. I have the things in the boot of the car, I'll pop it open and we can leave them by the post standing in those rocks and he will pick them up."

Zeva was hesitant but anything to get back to civilization. "I'll help but let's move quick. Jasper told me the rain can turn these roads to mud in minutes when it rains."

Patrice nodded. "He is quite right."

They both got out after the young woman leaned over and pressed the button to open the trunk. Zeva grabbed one package and Patrice another to move toward the old wooden sign post that was so old it didn't even have a sign anymore. It was only an old, thick piece of wood standing in the darkness, solitary and alone. She didn't notice Patrice had lagged back until she heard the thump as something fell. Zeva whirled around and saw Patrice running toward the car.

"You bitch, what the fuck!" Zeva yelled and started to chase her down.

Patrice was already in the car and pulling away. Zeva heard her laughter though the open window as she ran behind the car. The rear light was swallowed up by the darkness in seconds as the young woman sped away. Zeva stopped running and heaved out a sigh of exertion just as the skies opened up again and the rain poured down. She could barely see through the sheets of water, and the tire tracks that she planned to follow were quickly washed away. Zeva walked and looked around. She saw nothing, even the packages were swallowed up the night that was like ink in a bottle. She couldn't see through it. Zeva understood they wanted her to die out there from exposure or to walk lost into the moors and be trapped in the mud to sink to her death.

"Not going to happen, bitch." Zeva firmed her shoulders in the rain and started to assess the situation. She would find her way home and then there would be hell to pay.

Chapter Nine

There was no stopping Jasper. When his mother's driver, lover, butler, or whatever he was opened the door, Jasper greeted him with a fist to the face and another to the gut. When he bent over, Jasper kneed him in the face and left him moaning on the ground.

"Haile, beat him to death if necessary to find out where Zeva is." Jasper didn't even glance back. He walked through the foyer, and his voice echoed through the house. "Mother!"

Cornelia came to a stop on the stairs wearing a silky bathrobe and her hair put up in a neat style. The twins came out of a downstairs room, and when they saw Jasper's face, the fear in their eyes was evident as they glanced at each other.

"What is this about, Jasper? How dare you barge into my house?" his mother demanded.

"What have you done with Zeva?" Jasper snarled.

"Jasper, you've lost track of your wife. You should really put a bell on her." His mother laughed at her own joke.

Haile sent her driver boyfriend skidding across the marble tile floor. "I think it's safe to say he knows nothing."

Cornelia took stock of his face and cried out, "You brutes, what did you do to him?"

"We rearranged his face, and trust me you'll wish it was this easy when it comes to what I have planned for you," Jasper replied.

"Cornelia, what have you done this time?" Uncle Brewster shouted. "You have gone too far."

"Shut up, Brewster. What the hell is she doing here?" Cornelia flicked a cold glance over Lillian. "I thought we got rid of the trash years ago."

"Darling Cornelia, you just look into a mirror and deal with those old age lines. I thought you'd age better, I was wrong," Lillian said in a mild voice. "Brewster is going with me and hopefully my daughters are as well, if you haven't poisoned them to the core."

Patrice and Patricia moved next to Cornelia and Patrice lifted her head defiantly. "She is more of a mother to us than you ever were."

"Then you go down with her." Jasper was so angry his yell made them all jump. "Where is my wife!"

"We don't—"

The doorbell rang, and Haile moved to the door since the man of the house was incapacitated. He threw it open and there stood Zeva, soaking wet, her hair dripping from the rain and her eyes flashing fire.

"Oh my God, Zeva!" Jasper moved toward her quickly.

"Honey, I'm home," Zeva muttered and he noticed that she stared past him to the twins. She pointed at them. "I want them. I don't know which one is Patrice, but she left me in the moors. Since I can't tell them apart I plan to kick both their asses." She gave Cornelia a deadly look. "I told you, crone, to make sure you drop me and you didn't. You're next."

She moved with purpose and Jasper let her go. They deserved whatever Zeva doled out, and he had no problem watching her tear them apart.

"It was her!" one of the twins pointed. "She's Patrice and Aunt set her up to it!"

The both tried to hide behind Jasper's mother, and she stepped aside. Zeva grabbed Patrice, and with a right hook to the chin, the woman crumpled to the floor like a rag doll. Zeva turned and slapped Jasper's mother so hard the sound echoed, and her handprint appeared quickly on her alabaster skin.

"I'm calling the constable and filing assault charges!" Cornelia rubbed her cheek.

"You do that, you call the fucking constables and explain to them how you orchestrated them leaving me to die in the moors, oh, and throwing a brick through our window!" Zeva snapped and got in her mother-in-law's face. "You forget one thing... darling. I'm United States Army, I had to survive in heat and cold, learn how to deal with the wilderness and fucking fight insurgents in between rocks. I have battery acid in my blood, and the likes of you would never get the best of me."

Jasper pulled a cashmere blanket off a chair and threw it around her body. "You tell them, sweetheart. Haile, find her a brandy in this house please. Try the piano room. Mother dear always keeps it stocked."

Haile rubbed his hands. "Let's see what I can find."

"Brewster, make them stop this nonsense, you have to help me." Cornelia's voice was pathetic and soft.

"Never again, Cornelia. I'm leaving Northumberland with Lillian and I am living for me now." Uncle Brewster took Lillian's hand. "You made your bed, you lie in it, sister dear. You destroyed my life and turned my daughters against us. No more."

"You can do nothing to me, son of mine," Cornelia said snidely to Jasper. "I have photos of you and that one, in your workshop naked, doing unseemly things. I will release them to the tabloids."

Jasper laughed and looked at Zeva. "She wants to release pictures to the tabloids of the duke making love to his duchess. Go ahead, do it. When the press comes around I'll tell them I love her so much I can't keep my hands off her. I certainly don't care what anyone thinks, unlike you mother. I wonder how they will react when they find you are a fraud and not Lady Edwards after all, but in fact the bastard child of the gardener?"

"How dare you speak of my heritage like that?" Cornelia seethed. "My mother and father had a legitimate marriage."

"Oh it was, but Lord Edwards was cruel to grandmother and she found solace in the arms of the groundskeeper. She sent a letter to her maid, one who was close to her heart and moved to America. She detailed the abuse and the affair, also the pregnancy that came from it. Lord Edwards couldn't get her pregnant, and that made the beatings he gave her worse. When the groundskeeper got her pregnant, Lord Edwards thought the children were his. And to save her true love's life, Gran sent her lover away, knowing the twins she bore were his."

"Lies, lies, lies!" Cornelia screeched. She sat on the steps as her legs gave out. Patricia sat on the floor holding Patrice, who was still unconscious.

"I have the letters and it has been validated by the solicitors as Gran's handwriting matching her will," Jasper explained. He had to admit watching his mother go pale was satisfying. "Which means you are not Lady Edwards, and when you married my father it was under that pretense. You can lose everything your father left, including this house and all my father bequeathed you under the law."

'That means you lose everything as well," she said gleefully. "And Brewster would lose all his assets."

"You've piddled it all away anyway, and a title means nothing to me," Uncle Brewster looked at Lillian. "What truly matters is right beside me."

"And I am the legal son of my father, he was married to you after all and even if you had no title, you still had a son within the marriage," Jasper pointed out. "It also means your assets will now become mine."

"You would not dare leave your mother with nothing in the streets," Cornelia said with pride. "Your father raised you better than that."

"You are right, father raised me, not you." Jasper moved and crouched in front of his mother and his tone became deadly. "But you tried to hurt my wife, and that is worse to me than anything you did in my entire life. So I should take everything from you."

"Jasper, please." His mother's lips trembled and she forced a few tears from her eyes. "Please don't leave me penniless."

"Even now, that's what matters to you, not the fact that you almost made me lose the woman I love or the fact that you made all our lives a living hell. You show no remorse." Jasper shook his head. "Mother, I will not leave you penniless. You will sell me this house at a discount, take whatever stipend is left from father, and you will leave Northumberland. You can live wherever you want but not here, not around me. And budget wisely, mother, because you will never get another penny from me."

"You are putting me into exile?" his mother said angrily. "What about my friends, my duties here?"

"You have no duties, mother. You and the twins do nothing, Zeva has done more in the few months she's been here than you ever did," Jasper pointed out. "Your friends are better off without you. It's either that or I release all this information to the tabloids and I have the proof verified, you lose everything, and I also file charges against you and the twins for assault against the Duchess of Northumberland, my wife. Make your choice."

"I choose exile from my home." Cornelia stood and turned her attention to Zeva. "I hope you're happy, you destroyed my life."

Zeva, who was wrapped in the blanket and now sipping brandy courtesy of Haile, lifted her glass in a cheer. "I am quite happy, the only thing that could make me happier is hitting you again, but I'll let that go."

"What do you plan on doing with my house, Jasper?" his mother asked. "I would like to know that she is not living in my home."

"As if anyone wants to live around this gaudy crap," Zeva muttered.

"I have an even better idea." Jasper grinned wickedly. He took Zeva's hand. "Honey, you wanted a place for people to be safe from domestic violence, women, families who need help. You wanted to give them a place to live until they are back on their feet. I'll donate this mansion to the cause, convert it into small apartments and a safe home for those in need. Mother, you have thirty days to vacate the premises and get the hell out of our lives."

"No!" Cornelia cried out.

Zeva laughed. "That's fucking awesome. I accept this generous donation."

His mother screeched in rage as Zeva wrapped her arms around his neck and gave him a noisy smack on the lips. She was safe, and he felt the rage dissipate in her arms. If she had been hurt, his mother's fate would've been way worse, but it all worked out in the end. Uncle Brewster was leaving and getting help, his mother would be out of their lives, and he could finally live a normal, happy life with his wife. He could already picture the warmth of his home and the amazing things his wife would do for the community he cherished. He'd picked the perfect woman to be his bride, his duchess. Uncaring of his mother or whoever was around them, Jasper kissed her deeply, sealing the promise of the future they would build.

Two days later, Zeva lay in bed wiping her running nose after another bout of sneezing. Her little adventure in the moors in the middle of the rainstorm that hit courtesy of one of the bitch twins had left her with a cold, or the flu or death, she wasn't quite sure. On principle, she wanted to find Patrice and infect her with her cold, but she was too exhausted to move. In between the fever, then the chills, Jasper took excellent care of her, and the doctor had come to the house to see her.

"Wow, doctors make house calls here, cool," she recalled mumbling as he checked her over.

After that the cough syrup the doctor prescribed kept her knocked out, and Jasper woke her for soup and then hot tea with biscuits. He made sure she had a hot bath with eucalyptus oil, and while it made her feel better Zeva was still down and out. He knocked and came into the room looking at her with concern.

"How are you sweetheart?" he asked gently.

"Miserable." She could hear her nasally voice and hated it. "I'm missing work and it's putting the center behind with me sick."

"It will all be fine. Until you get better, I've just been putting invoices on the desk in the office like you said," Jasper said with a smile. "Are you up to eating a bit of soup?"

"I want a steak," she muttered. "With all the trimmings, including the baked potato."

"While I would love to give you that, the last time you threw up after eating a heavy meal. The doctor said keep it light until you make a turn for the better." Jasper caressed her face. "I'm sorry you feel terrible, my love."

"Not your fault, it's the three witches of Northumberland that caused this." Zeva wiped her nose.

"You'll be happy to know that Uncle Brewster left today. He was going to pop around, but I told him you were sick so he sends his regards," Jasper said.

"Haile said that my mother has begun packing up to leave. So very soon you can start reconstruction of the mansion."

"I'm thinking I will name it the Lady Susanna House, after your grandmother," Zeva said. "I came up with the idea in one of my fever hazes."

Jasper grinned. "I love the idea, even with your melodramatic statement."

"Are you saying, Jasper McTavish, that I am not completely miserable right now?" Zeva folded her arms and demanded.

"I'm sure you are, luv, forgive my statement," he said solemnly, but amusement made his lips twitch.

"Meanie," she muttered but smiled at her husband.

"You love me," he retorted.

"Yes I do, very much," she said softly.

"You know I was terrified when you didn't come home, and to find out what they did..." Jasper swallowed thickly. "If I had lost you, I would have been lost forever, nothing in my life would've been right."

"Honey, there was no way I was going to let them keep me from coming home to you," Zeva said gently. "And you forget one thing."

"What's that?" he asked.

"You made one badass, army-strong woman your duchess," she reminded him.

"You're right, and I love you for it." Jasper moved forward to kiss her.

Zeva put her hand on his chest to stop him. "Hey, you'll get sick if you kiss me."

He cupped her cheek. "Through sickness and in health, my love. I'll have my kiss now."

Zeva let him take his kiss, because if he ended up in the bed next to her sick they'd make it work. They'd proven they could maneuver life and the chaos that it could bring together as a couple. The Duke may have taken a wife, but when she met Jasper he'd completely stolen her heart.

The End

Three Times

A Lady

Chapter One

It was always cold in Northumberland. Even in the summer months there was a chill in the air when the evening came in. It was late September, and it was downright cold. Twilight started at four, and it was completely dark by five. The mist hung low down to the roads, some paved with asphalt and the cobblestone from when the town was young. Tonight was no different from any other as Haile drove home. He'd gone to dinner at the manor house, invited by Jasper and Zeva.

Two years into marriage, and they were more in love than ever. Zeva was glowing in the final weeks of her pregnancy while Jasper was frantic. The crib he made was already set up in the nursery, but Jasper was building a set of drawers that he didn't think would be finished in time. Zeva was suffering Braxton Hicks contractions, and every time she made even a small sigh, Jasper was out the chair with a wild look in his eyes. To Haile, it was hilarious to watch, but he felt a tinge of sadness. This would never be a part of his life.

When the mist was like this, stores usually closed early. And combined with the rain that had just started to fall, it was a miserable night. Haile was tempted to drive all the way to his house but knowing it would probably get worse before it got better, he decided to stay in his apartment over the pub.

When he turned the corner, his lights almost missed the small figure standing under the awning of Zeva's charity house, The Northumberland Hope Center. Two bags were next to the person who seemed to try to huddle into the wall when the headlights from his Land Rover hit them. Haile trusted his instincts, and he slowed his vehicle and rolled the window down. It was a she, and she was shivering. Fear rolled off her in waves, and her demeanor reminded him of a scared rabbit, any sudden sounds or movement, she'd be ready to run.

"Good evening, are you okay?" Haile asked gently. "It's getting ready to pour down buckets of rain. You shouldn't be out here."

"I-is there a hotel or motel — cheap — around here?" she asked hesitantly.

American, even stranger, Haile thought before answering.

"Unfortunately, the bed and breakfast is closed up for the winter and any the chain hotels are pretty far away from here," Haile answered. "You're

American." She didn't answer, and her shoulders slumped in defeat. "Listen, you are obviously in trouble. Let's get you loaded up and someplace warm."

"I would be stupid to get into a car with someone I don't know," she answered. "My name is Haile Buchannan. I own the Celtic Cross Pub right up the street," Haile said. "I won't hurt you, I swear it, and tomorrow I can take you to the Duchess. She is American and runs the center where you are standing now."

"The American Duchess, she lives here?" she asked tentatively. She wiped her eyes, confirming the fact that she was crying.

"Not at the center, but she lives on a property outside of town with her husband and my good friend Jasper," Haile explained. "I'll call them, and they can give you my references of being a great guy."

"After the day I've had, if I end up dead in a swamp for trusting you it would be my fault," she muttered. "They say British people are nice, not so much."

"We're not all bad." Haile smiled. "If I wanted to hurt you, I could've grabbed you by now. Look, I swear I'm not going to harm you in any way. We can call the police and have them escort us to my pub if you want."

She pulled her phone out quickly and snapped a picture of him. The light blinded Haile for a moment.

"What was that for?" Haile questioned.

"I sent your picture with a note to the cloud on my phone. If my friend in Texas doesn't hear from me, she can access it, and you'll be the prime suspect," she announced firmly.

Haile grinned and looked up as thunder rolled. "Good idea. This downpour is about to get going. Let me help you get your bags in the boot and we'll go someplace warm."

"Thank you," she said gratefully. "I don't mean to seem like a terrible person, but I've had a hell of a day, and I just got here last night."

"You can tell me all about it over a hot meal, yes?" Haile put her hard cases in the back of the rover and helped her inside the passenger seat before closing the door.

"I appreciate that. I honestly think the last thing I ate was peanuts on the plane," she admitted and held out her hand. "My name is Marisol Elliot, but people call me Mari."

"Nice to meet you Mari. People call me Haile or Red when they're drunk." He grinned and shook her hand.

The sky opened up, and the downpour came down quickly. It was a good thing he'd convinced her to get in his vehicle, because while she was slightly damp standing there for only a little while she would have been soaked in less than a minute with this rain. She pulled the hood of her sweatshirt down, and he was finally able to see her in the dim light. She had a sweet, round face under a short pixie cut. Her nose was a cute button in the center of her face, and her lips were a soft pink with the bottom lip being fuller and delectable.

She wasn't tall—he put her height around five two or three. Compared to Zeva, she was an elf and a cute one at that. He recalled the fear and anxiety in those wide brown eyes as she stood in the rain, and Haile's curiosity was piqued about what had brought her to Northumberland. He parked in front of the pub and rushed to unlock the heavy mahogany and glass door before she got out and rushed inside. He followed her in and closed the barrier against the rain and then turned on the lights.

"You weren't lying, it is a pub," she murmured looking around.

"I'll grab your bags when it lets up out there a bit." Haile smiled. "Sit anywhere you want, and I'll grab us some food. Mrs. Humphrey always leaves something warming after they lock up for the night."

"Is that your mom?" Mari laughed. "Of course not, why would you call her Mrs. Humphrey if she was."

"She could be my mum, she certainly acts like it."

Haile chuckled. "You know what, sit in the booth next to the fireplace. I'll put it on for you."

"Please don't trouble yourself to build a fire for me," she gasped.

"Don't fret at all, it's gas." He laughed.

He flipped a switch, and the flames leapt to life from within the stone hearth. Haile heard Mari sigh as she scooted closer, and without a word he turned and went to the kitchen. "Bless your big heart, Mrs. Humphrey," he murmured. His cook had left mini chicken potpies in the warming oven, expecting him to be hungry or if someone needed a meal. The menu said mini but after eating half of one you were ready to pop. Haile readied the meal and made a large cup of tea. She had the look of someone who needed to be warmed up from the inside out. When he returned to the booth, Mari's feet were tucked up beneath her, and she stared into the fire.

"How about a personal chicken potpie for dinner?" Haile announced and put the plate on the table.

"That's meant for three people," Mari said and eagerly moved forward. She took the spoon, broke into the flaky brown crust, and brought a big bite to her mouth. She closed her eyes as she chewed and sighed. "This is the best thing I ever had."

"Mrs. Humphrey can cook for angels as far as I'm concerned," Haile answered.

"I hear them singing now." Mari ate eagerly.

Haile waited until she was about halfway done and drank some of her tea before asking, "Mari, why were you alone in the rain with your luggage? Northumberland is quite a ways from London to be lost."

"I'm an idiot, that's why. I was telling you I can't get in a car with a stranger and I left America for one," she muttered. "I met a guy online, Jeffery Moermond."

The name made the muscle in Haile's jaw tick, and he clenched his teeth. But he kept his face as impassive as possible. "Moermond is married." Haile didn't elaborate further and waited for her to continue.

"I wasn't under that impression for the six months we were talking on the phone, texting, video chatting. I was catfished," Mari explained.

"What does a fish have to do with this?" Haile asked.

Mari sighed. "It's an American term for being duped. After six months he said, 'move to London,' and since I had nothing in Lumberton, Texas to hold me there, I took a leap of faith and landed on my ass."

"What happened?" Haile asked gently.

"I flew into Heathrow, thinking I was moving to London. He wasn't there," Mari started her story. "I get a text from him saying I need to take the train to Northumberland, he is there on business, and we will be staying at his mansion while we are here. Okay… I buy a ticket and take a car service to this house. Nice house but certainly no mansion."

"I know where he lives," Haile said. "Sorry to say the only mansion around is the Manor house where Jasper and Zeva live."

"The Duke and Duchess," she assessed.

"Jeffery." The name made the bile rise in his throat. "Is from this area and lives on the teat of his wife's money."

"I figured that when I showed up with my suitcases, and she wrote me off as the new nanny for their son," Mari said. "He thought I would live there and pretend to work, and when his wife as asleep he would sneak to my room and…" She took a deep breath but tears seeped out. "I'm sorry, but I'm so mad and hurt because I thought I was so dumb to think this would work and to believe in love and happy endings."

"This is not your fault, Marisol. He deceived you, and I'm sorry to say that's his method in this town." Haile ran his hand through his hair. "I'm sorry to say there is some serious bad blood between me and him, so I'm not a fan of him at all."

"He told his wife I got the wrong impression, and I wanted to sleep with him," Mari said. "Even when I offered to show her the texts where he contacted me first and his profile on the dating app, she refused.

Called me a whore and kicked me out in the rain. Now I'm stuck. There is no way for me to get back home, and hell, there is nothing to go back to. I wanted a new life here, and now I don't know what to do."

"Zeva can help, she can get you home if you want or help you get settled here," Haile tried to soothe her.

"I'm totally unsure of what I want anymore. If I stay, I'll have to hear the gossip about the American girl who tried to ruin a marriage," Mari said. "His wife said as much, that she would tell everyone how much of a trollop I was. I don't even understand what a trollop is."

"Joslyn can hardly say a thing, she isn't a person anyone listens to anyway, only her phony cronies would entertain her words," Haile commented. "Listen, nothing can be solved tonight. I have an extra room upstairs you can sleep in, and tomorrow we will work on this."

"Are you sure I'm not imposing? I have a few bucks I can pay for the night stay," Mari said.

"I'll have none of that. Zeva would kill me if I didn't seem hospitable." Haile stood. "If you're done eating, I'll show you to the apartment and you can get some rest. It seems you went from traveling to a train to standing in the rain with nowhere to go."

"That's essentially it, I spent fourteen hundred

dollars to get here." Mari followed him up the stairs. "Fuck my life."

"Now don't be down on yourself. You were lied to, but we will take care of it." Haile opened a door. "You never can tell when you may have a surprise guest or a regular who has tied one on a bit too much, and we are a hospitable lot here in Northumberland. The place is clean there are extra blankets in the chest by the bed and a bathroom through the door in the hallway on the left."

"Thank you so much, Mr. Haile. I was completely lost and thinking what should I do? Then you show up and give me a place to sleep and food…" Mari's words ended when she impulsively stood on her tiptoes and put her arms around his neck.

"Thank you," she whispered, and he heard the tears in her voice.

He squeezed her, quickly uncomfortable with the closeness and the way his heart tripped. "Not a problem at all. You rest, and we'll talk tomorrow."

Mari closed the door, and he looked at the barrier for a moment before heading back downstairs. He pulled the phone from his pocket and pressed the button to dial Jasper's number.

"Why are you still up?" Jasper asked after answering the phone on the first ring.

"It's ten and I'm not a senior, plus I run a pub," Haile replied. "Why are you up?"

"Trying to finish these drawers for the baby," Jasper answered. "It's a Tuesday and raining. It's well known by now that Mrs. Humphrey closed the door and kicked everyone out to go home at nine."

Haile laughed. "Very true, but on my way home I came upon a situation—an American girl, Marisol Elliot. She was under the awning of the Hope center, crying with her luggage. I brought her to the pub with me."

"What the hell is that about?" Jasper asked curiously.

"Two words: Jeffery Moermond," Haile said grimly.

"Fuck," Jasper spat the words out. "Tell me everything."

Haile recounted the story, including what Joslyn had threatened, and Jasper listened silently until the end.

"She is lucky to be alive," Jasper murmured. "Jeffery is a fucking maniac, and I have no doubt Joslyn's money has helped keep his crimes a secret. Her and Cornelia were hand and glove buddies before she left."

"We could never prove it but if he sees Mari is staying here. He'll try to pick at the scab, and I can't say that I'll be able to restrain myself," Haile said.

"Bring her here. Jeffery won't dare try a thing," Jasper said.

"I'll take care of her. I already plan to offer a job, and she's asleep upstairs," Haile replied. "I'll protect her."

"Haile, it's not the same as before..." Jasper began.

"I understand that, I... she needs my help," Haile answered.

"Hmmmm," Jasper said.

"What?" Haile heard the note of irritation in his own voice.

"Nothing at all," Jasper said. "Still, bring her around tomorrow and let Zeva start some paperwork on her for a work visa and papers to cover all our bases. I'll give her an update tomorrow when she wakes up."

"I don't want to bother her, she is pretty much due any day now," Haile replied.

"It gives her something to do so she doesn't go crazy again and try to clean the entire manor house," Jasper said. "We'll make sure that this doesn't end with a missing person due to Moermond.."

"It won't. I'd kill him first," Haile said bluntly. "See you tomorrow, Jasper."

He hung up and walked behind the bar and poured himself an Irish whiskey neat. He stayed away from Moermond. They lived in the same town and gave each other a wide berth. Jeffery knew what he did and what he got away with, and when Haile came home from deployment, his only thought was to kill the fucker. Jasper saved him that day, and while there was no proof, Jeffery taunted him, hoping he would slip. This would be slow and steady, and his patience seemed to have paid off. Mari would be safe with him and Jeffery wouldn't be able to touch her.

He would make sure of it.

Chapter Two

There was so much more to her story, but one she couldn't quite tell, not yet, maybe never. Mari sat in a lavishly decorated sitting room-slash-office with a fire crackling merrily in the background. A very pregnant Duchess Zeva McTavish sat at the desk typing quickly at her computer while her husband rubbed her shoulders. She smiled as the Duchess slapped at his hand in irritation more than once and it never fazed her husband. He would start right back up again, and she would sigh, letting him continue. It was beautiful to watch.

Haile sat close by, looking in her direction every once in a while as if making sure she was okay. All the while these people were trying to help her, and she bit the inside of her cheek to keep her mouth closed. She had run toward Jeffery Moermond and a new life because nothing held her in Texas, and if she were still there, she'd probably be dead by now. They listened to her story while feeding her scones and tea, Zeva printing the screenshots of the conversations and his profile she saved before he sanitized his life and deleted the accounts. They needed a record in case Jeffery or his wife chose to take the issue any further. God, Mari hoped not, because all she wanted was to find some peace in her life.

"We need a job offer for her Tier 2 Visa," Zeva said. "These get accepted quicker when there is a solid job offer on the table and a salary involved. It wouldn't hurt to have an address where Mari will be living."

"She'll be my new bar manager, and she can take the apartment over the pub," Haile announced.

Mari looked at him in surprise. "You don't have to do that. You don't even know if I have the skills or anything."

"Can you order beer, food, and keep my suppliers in order, sometimes bartend or waitress in a pinch?" Haile asked.

Mari nodded. "Bartended before, waitressed before, I was running the concessions at the bowling alley in Lumberton before I left."

"Then you're perfect for the job." Haile turned his attention to Zeva and Jasper. Mari could tell by their look this was unlike Haile's personality. "She'll be paid three thousand pounds a month, and the apartment is included with the job."

"That's too much. You've been generous enough, Mr. Haile." Mari shook her head. "All of you have gone out of your way to help me…"

"First, let's drop the Mr. Haile, shall we? It's just Haile," he said, cutting her off. "Second, that's the average anyone would make for the job, and the apartment sits empty most of the time. You can utilize it, make it a home if you so wish."

"But where will you live?" Mari questioned.

"I have a house close by off Terrace Place," Haile answered. "I was going to stay at the pub last night because of the rain."

"That's so much more than what I was making in Texas," she admitted. "T-Thank you so much, all of you."

Zeva smiled. "It's okay. Sometimes we need a change, even if it's an entirely new country to make our lives better. I honestly never missed D.C. after I left, and I hope you can make a life here as well. If not, we can always get you back home, if it doesn't work out."

"I never want to go back." Mari heard the intensity of her tone and saw the question in their eyes. It was the perfect time to tell them the truth, but she couldn't bring herself to show them how much more she was damaged.

Haile wasn't as subtle. "What happened to you at home?"

"She'll tell us when she is good and ready," Zeva said firmly. "I don't care if we are helping her or not, we're still three strangers asking her life story."

"You've been more kind to me than most people in my life," Mari said gratefully. "Thank you, from the bottom of my heart."

Zeva smiled. "I'm going to enjoy this. I feel like the only American here, it will be good to see another face."

"Who knows how to chicken fry a steak," Mari pointed out.

"Oooh, I haven't had one of those since Fort Sill," Zeva said excitedly. "With gravy?"

"All the trimmings," Mari confirmed.

"So that's a thing? How does a chicken fried steak work?" Jasper asked curiously.

"You'll just have to taste the magic," Zeva said. "Mari, I'm going to send that packet in today and have it expedited by a lawyer friend of ours who helps us out sometimes. In about four weeks or less you should be good to go."

Mari looked at them gratefully. "Again, thank you all for helping me. I thought I was totally shit out of luck after Jeffery screwed me over. That man is so dishonest and deceitful, he's slicker than a boiled onion, I'll tell you that right now."

"A boiled onion..." Haile mused on the words.

"It's an old Texas saying," Zeva said with a laugh. "One thing I loved about the South was the twang and the quaint sayings. My favorite is 'Bless your heart.'"

"I say that to, Mrs. Humphrey," Haile said.

"When you say it, it's sweet, and you're saying she is a good person," Mari pointed out. "When we say it, it's like you poor silly thing, bless your heart you are so dumb."

"Never tell this to Mrs. Humphrey when you meet her," Haile answered. "Speaking of which, we should go so I can show you the workings of the place before we open up and people start coming in."

He stood and Mari followed suit. Zeva was going to stand but Mari hurried over to her instead.

"Please, you stay here. You are ready to drop that baby any minute now." Mari bent to give her a quick hug. "I appreciate all you have done for me."

"Glad to help." Zeva smiled and rubbed her belly. "Maybe I'll get to come in for some shepherd's pie before the baby comes. I've been craving Mrs. H's and doused with hot sauce."

"She's been eating very strange things in this pregnancy," Jasper said with a smile. "She doesn't like Yorkshire pudding but has been eating it every night."

"My friend was addicted to Rocky Mountain oysters with hot sauce and ketchup when she was pregnant," Mari said with a laugh. "She hated those things before."

"Oysters are yummy fried or raw," Haile commented.

"Rocky Mountain oysters are fried cow testicles," Mari explained and watched Jasper and Haile go pale.

"On that note, we'll take our leave," Haile said and after another round of goodbyes escorted her out.

On the drive back to the pub he glanced at her and asked, "That's not really a thing, is it, to eat fried testicles?"

"It's a delicacy in Texas." Mari laughed. "I'm not kidding."

"Dear God, and they say us Brits are strange," he murmured.

Mari laughed again and for the first time in a long time it was a real laugh, one that had a hint of freedom in its tone. Her life was filled with anxiety, even more so after her failed attempt of love in the world of online dating. For once it seemed like she was taking the right steps even in a new country. *Please, please let this work out,* she sent the message out into the universe hoping that some higher being heard. She was tired of the constant battle to survive, of running, and she wanted to live now, for her and not in fear of anyone else.

By the light of day, Mari took in the comfortable

atmosphere of Haile's pub while he showed her around. She took the time between the tour to study the man who had literally plucked her off the street. He was a full-fledged ginger: his red hair and beard were the same perfect shade. While he kept his beard trimmed neatly, today his hair was tousled and windblown compared to the night before when he had it combed and styled. Haile had deep green eyes pierced through her and when he looked at Mari, she averted her gaze because she swore he could see all her secrets.

He was tall, she liked that, and his chest was broad beneath his sweater. It didn't take being in his life a long time to see that he'd been through some damage of his own but her instincts told her he was kind and could be trusted. Hell, because of him she had a job now and some kind of stability; he didn't want anything in return. Mari was accustomed to that, with him she didn't need to be wary. Mrs. Humphrey bustled out of the kitchen as he showed her around the office and introductions were made.

"Well now, if she can make some kind of dent in this chaos you call an office, she is an angel in my book," Mrs. Humphrey announced. "He can eat, but the boy doesn't have the patience for paperwork."

"It's nice to meet you, and if you ever need help in the kitchen, I'm your girl," Mari said with a smile.

"I'll tell you right now, Miss, the kitchen is my

domain unless I give you permission," Mrs. Humphrey said sternly.

Taken aback Mari nodded. "Yes ma'am."

A sudden smile broke out over the older woman's face. "But I'll be glad for some company sometimes."

"The potpie I had for dinner was delicious," Mari said. "If you don't mind teaching me…"

"So you came in last night then?"

"I picked her up at the station," Haile said quickly.

"No, tell the truth, I won't have lies surrounding how I got to be here then the truth makes me look more ashamed," Mari said firmly and explained how she ended up in Northumberland. "I want my side to be clear if Jeffery Moermond or his wife speaks ill of me. I had no clue he was married, and I certainly did not expect to be where I am now. Luckily, between Haile and the help I received from Duke and Duchess McTavish, I'm getting myself together."

"I thought after Cornelia McTavish left they would too." Mrs. Humphrey made an angry sound in the back of her throat and shook her head. "It is alright, Mari, Jeffery has tried that same scenario with almost every young woman in this area. Some are wise to his actions and others fall into his bed willingly. And you can understand the type of women they are. Joslyn… Well, she would prefer to cut her own down than to accept her husband is a man whore."

"Dollie, such language!" Haile teased.

"I say what I mean and I mean what I say," Mrs. Humphrey said primly. "If anyone says anything to you, Marisol Elliot, you direct them to me, and I'll set them straight. Jeffery Moermond shouldn't be walking free after what he did to Haile's sister is my opinion…"

"That's enough of that," Haile cut off the older women gruffly.

"Now you don't get to snuff my words, Haile Buchannan," Mrs. Humphrey swatted at him with a hand towel. "Just because you're the Lord of the lands doesn't mean you are the boss of me."

"Excuse me?" Mari looked from one to another, and Haile turned beet red under his ginger hair.

"Oh, he didn't tell you, did he?" Mrs. Humphrey's crowed. "Well, he doesn't like people to know, but this is Lord Haile Buchannan of Alnmouth, a lovely seaside town bordering Northumberland, it was once a fishing town. His family started that town centuries ago and showed fealty to the king, earning them the title and it has been passed down to the oldest son since the eighteen hundreds."

"Thank you for giving her the history of my family," Haile said sarcastically and got swatted again for his sass.

"Don't you take a tone with me, boy," Mrs. Humphrey gave him a mock curtsey. "Your welcome, M'Lord, now I shall go back to my kitchen to prepare your meals."

"Whatever," he mumbled as she turned away. "Mrs. Humphrey."

"What, you smart mouthed tadpole?" she answered.

"I love you Dollie." Hailed moved and gave her such a big hug he lifted her right off her feet, and she giggled like a schoolgirl.

"Oh, be off with you," she said, smiling. "Mari, if you need me I'll be in the kitchen."

"Yes ma'am," Mari said.

She watched the exchange between them, stunned at his title and seeing the genuine affection they had for each other. She met Haile's gaze and understood instantly the many questions she wanted to ask him had to wait. His face was guarded, and she saw hurt in his eyes.

"So show me the rest of the place," Mari said with a smile.

"Come on, we'll go meet the waitstaff and update them that they'll be reporting to you," Haile said, and she could hear the relief in his voice.

The wait staff came in for the lunch hour, and soon introductions were made and they welcomed her warmly, even though she could see the questions in their eyes. They just assumed that she was a friend of the Duchess, but if anyone questioned her she would tell them the truth. Later that night, when Haile was gone and the pub was closed, Mari try to settle herself in the apartment that would now be home at least until she got her own place. Yes, she was planning to stay and maybe she could make this place her home. With her laptop in front of her, she sat on the comfortable, worn sofa with a blanket over her legs. It has started rain outside again and the drops beat steadily against the window in a comforting thrum.

"Lord Haile Buchannan's sister," she murmured as she typed the words on the keyboard.

Her eyes scanned the search list, and she clicked the most recent article she found. The picture of a gorgeous young redhead popped up, and the caption she read made her blood run cold.

"Missing twenty-year-old, Lady Angela Buchannan, linked to Jeffery Moermond, a suspect in her disappearance," Mari read aloud.

The article painted a picture of love gone wrong, and Jeffery getting rid of Haile's sister when his wife found out but there was no proof. There were some who believed the liar, and of course his wife stood with him in his denials. Haile had called for him to be arrested, and there was a video from four years prior where Haile grabbed the man, and they had to pry his fingers from around Jeffery's throat.

"Oh hell, what have I gotten myself into?" she said quietly.

Could she have been a victim of Jeffery's, or was there more to the story? It was all a lot to take in, and she closed her computer, deciding to go to bed. Essentially she was caught between Haile who had some kind of royal title and the man who could have caused his sister's disappearance. *Chaos seems to find me wherever I go.*

Chapter Three

Haile understood there was no way he could keep her cooped up in the pub. Jeffery Moermond would never step foot in his place, but by now the gossip would have gotten back to him and his wife that Mari had stayed in Northumberland. From his sources, Joslyn was not pleased while Jeffery seemed almost too interested. If this was the place she chose to live, she would need to get out and learn the area and the people. In the two weeks she was working for him, he saw her skill at management and the easygoing personality she had that made people comfortable.

She laughed with the servers, and if they got slammed, helped out with food or behind the bar. She gained friends in her co-workers quickly, and Mrs. Humphrey developed a fondness for her early on. Haile tried his best to keep his distance and give her a wide birth, but every time she turned in his direction with a smile on her face and laughter in those soft brown eyes his heart sped up just a bit, and he found it harder to resist being around her. Shit, like she needed that in her life—yet another man with secrets and a past hanging around her.

Haile watched from a distance as she started stepping outside to take in the town and explore, buy food or knick-knacks for the apartment. Jeffery would never change how he operated when he thought enough time had passed he would approach her. That day, while she strolled through the market with a bunch of flowers in her hands, Jeffery strolled behind her. Haile got out of his car quickly and crossed the street in the Sunday afternoon crowd. His eyes were ever intent on Mari as she bought a coffee and bun before sitting at one of the outside tables to enjoy the sweet, warm treat. Haile's training kicked in, to remain hidden even with his signature red hair, but by now he was close enough at the fruit stand with his knit hat pulled down over his hair. He could hear their conversation when Jeffery sat down in the second seat at Mari's table.

"Fancy meeting you here," Jeffery drawled. His voice made Haile want to rush over and punch his face in.

"You…" Mari emphasized the word. "Are not meeting me anywhere. I was eating my snack, and you… sat down."

"Don't be that way, love," Jeffery purred. "It was all a mistake, me and the wife, we're getting divorced. That's why I wasn't at the station to pick you up."

"You're kidding me, right?" Mari looked aghast. "Your wife asked me if I was the nanny. You must be out of your damn mind."

"You took up with that drunk bastard, Haile Buchannan," Jeffery sneered. "You seem to have fallen nicely on your back to a lesser man."

Mari laughed and retorted, "Haile is one hundred times the man you are, and trust me, I didn't have to lie down for it. While you, on the other hand, your nose is firmly up your wife's ass. Need to keep mommy happy for an allowance, right?"

"You don't have an inkling about that man, he is dangerous…" Jeffery tried another tactic. "Everyone around here can tell you that."

"Funny, it seems everyone loves him, and for a man so low in character his business is packed every night." Mari nibbled at her bun.

"Lower class," he muttered. "Haile blames me for something that is not my doing, but he's the dangerous one."

"Hmm, I've heard that about you," Mari pointed out. "Goodbye Jeffery. Never talk to me again."

Jeffery put his hand over hers, and Haile could see he squeezed enough that she looked at him in surprise and alarm. "You'd better be careful of me, Marisol. I can make your life very difficult here, and remember you told me everything about your life in Texas. I can use that to my advantage… maybe find

Marcus… But if we meet up and have a little fun now and again…"

He let the words drop, and Mari dragged her hand away. "Go ahead, find him, call him, ask your wife to pay his airfare to Northumberland. He'd hear your pansy-ass voice and hang up instantly. But I'll tell you this: I won't live in fear of him or you ever again. The thought of you disgusts me. I'd rather lie with dogs than with you. Get away from me before I start screaming, and baby, I'm from Texas. I can be loud as a tornado siren if I want to."

Jeffery inclined his head stiffly and got up before walking away from the table. Haile watched her for a moment, and she rubbed her wrist. She said she wasn't scared, but he saw the name Marcus meant something. Plus, when Jeffery grabbed her hand, she had flinched. He was a man who preferred to have all the information so he could make the best decision. While she sat and finished her snack, Haile merged with the crowd and soon had Jeffery in his sight. He loathed and despised that man who was now walking casually and talking on his cell. Haile moved from behind him, and he was so close to Jeffery he could have snatched him around the neck. But he wouldn't do that in a crowd, with witnesses. Instead, Haile rounded a corner on the cobblestone road. There was an alley right along the path that Jeffery would take, and it was conveniently secluded.

Haile waited patiently and heard his voice as he passed by.

"I'll see you later, you nasty bitch. Wear that nasty little leather thing when I show up. I'll bring the money, don't you worry," Jeffery drawled.

Haile's hand reached out as his nemesis pushed the cell in his jacket pocket, and he grabbed the collar of Jeffery's coat. It gave him infinite pleasure to hear the breath whoosh out of Jeffery's lungs when he slammed him against the wall. He pulled him back into the shadows of the opposite building. Haile's forearm was across Jeffery's larynx before he could utter a word.

"Hello, Rat." Haile's voice was soft but deadly.

"Let go of me or I'll have the police after you," Jeffery rasped out.

"Who's going to believe you?" Haile asked calmly. "Everyone who lives around here can see I keep to myself and far away from you. Why would a man who is a decorated part of her majesty's army waste his time on a low life murderer?"

"For the last time, I had nothing to do with your sister going missing." Jeffery could barely breathe, his face was turning red, so Haile eased his hold just a bit.

"You or someone in your employ caused her death. I don't know who or how but someday I will," Haile answered. "This isn't about her right now.

Come anywhere near Mari again, and I'll break your spine."

"Have a thing for that one." Jeffery smiled wide. "Trust me, she is a tasty piece."

Haile slapped him hard across the mouth. "Mind your words, Rat, or I'll rip your tongue out from your head. Joslyn ruined your plan on trying to cheat on her… again, and Mari saw through you."

"You think you got her pegged, you'll soon figure out why she ran to England," Jeffery sneered. "She was coming to me, to do all sorts of nasty things to her. Because that's what she likes…" Haile raised his hand again, and Jeffery flinched before whimpering. "I'm sorry, I'm sorry, please don't hit me again."

"I won't, I forgot you get off on it." Haile looked at the man in disgust. "Even look at her again, and I'll break you in the worst way possible. Joslyn will happen to get a really thick envelope with all sorts of pictures and videos."

"You have nothing on me," Jeffery spat out.

"Try me and find out." Haile was nose to nose with him. "You're a fucking little pervert who can't sit at home too long. I'll be watching, so scurry along, Rat, before I step on your neck."

Haile shoved him away, and Jeffery fixed his coat and tie as he stumbled on the uneven stone. He turned and spoke. "You know, many people have another opinion on your sister's disappearance. For example, you did it yourself because you lusted after her, your very own redheaded pet."

Haile snarled and moved toward him, but Jeffery saw he'd gone too far and ran out of the alley, rounding the corner and gone in an instant. Haile punched the wall, and the pain bloomed through his hand from the brick meeting his knuckles. *Calm down, calm down,* he said to himself as he paced. *Four steps in, look within. Five steps* back *bring down the stack.* He said the mantra that was taught to him when he needed it the most.

When the fury finally settled, he went out the alley the way he came and walked towards the pub while his hand throbbed in his pocket. He thought about what

Jeffery said and pulled his own cell from his pocket. After scrolling through the contacts, he pressed a familiar number.

"Mac, how are you, Mate?" Haile said warmly and listened before giving a small laugh.

"Yeah, yeah, I'll visit eventually, but you know big city D.C. is too much for a small town fisherman," Haile replied. "Listen, do me a favor will you? Can you check out a name for me? Marisol Elliot and someone associated with her named Marcus and no, I don't have a last name." He paused and said, "Thanks mate, I appreciate it, get back with me as soon as you can."

He had learned long ago that information sometimes was better than money and dealt like currency. He'd make sure there were no surprises waiting for him. One way or another, he would see Jeffery punished for his sister. The truth wouldn't stay buried even if he couldn't find her body.

Sunday night ruckus was in full swing. That was what the friendly neighborhood teams named it after the local rugby game. If anyone watched the match, you wouldn't think these men and yes, a few women, worked and lived around each other. Haile had seen most of them and hell, even played in a few. Rain or shine they were out on the field, getting muddy, more often than not bruised and injured. Yet when they got into ye ol' neighborhood pub, pints flowed and egos were soothed.

Tonight was no different, between the fish and chips, beer and mud on the ground. Everyone was loud and cheerful, his people were making good money in tips. He watched Mari work. She was behind the bar at some points or helping bring out food to hungry patrons. Mari wore patchwork jeans that hugged every curve and a top that almost reminded him of a corset with long sleeves. It hugged the underside of her breasts, and hell, every man in the place had their eyes on her luscious chocolate cleavage.

It could get rowdy at the pub, As they got drunk, punches could be thrown, and he was always there to make sure no one got hurt. Car services made money on Sunday nights as well. More often than not, no one was sober enough to drive home. Wives collected husbands or husbands collected wives. It was a toss up on what would be seen on Sunday night. He resisted the urge to let his fist fly more than once with people hitting on Mari. He warned Barney who worked at the fish market about smacking her or any of his servers on the ass twice before kicking him out. Finally, he rang the last call bell with a sigh of relief and watched the panicked faces of Mari and his other bartender as the mad dash to the bar was made.

"Hey pretty lady, wanna come around here and give me something other than a beer?" a voice slurred loudly. "I mean, head on a beer is one thing. I've got a second one you can take care of."

Haile's head swiveled at the crass comment and saw it was one of the ruby players, and his comment was directed at Mari.

"No thank you, the head on Guinness is quite enough for me," Mari answered and slid the beer onto the counter.

Before she could move the man snatched at her

hand and tried to pull her close up to the bar. He leaned over as if to try to kiss her, but Haile was there in an instant with his hand on the man's neck.

"Alex, what the hell did I tell you about trying to kiss my people without permission." Haile slapped him upside the head. "You must be daft… again."

The man called Alex turned and shoved Haile hard. "You just want to keep all the pretties for yourself, especially the brown one. It's all over town you're shagging her."

"That's it, go home, you're drunk," Haile said angrily. "Sleep it off and then come apologize tomorrow."

Alex spat on the floor. "I will do no such thing, fucking pansy. Fight me for her then."

"I will not be fighting anyone. Last chance: walk out on your own or I throw you out," Haile ordered.

"Throw me out, he says," Alex chortled. "You couldn't even protect your own sister from God knows how many men, Jeffery said. Now you want to throw me out. Fuck you, Haile Buchannan, and I'll fuck this pretty little thing too in front of—"

Alex never got to finish his sentence because the punch that Haile landed sent him sprawling across the room. The small crowd that was left let out an "Ooh," and Alex got up with a rage filled snarl and charged Haile. It was a knock down, drag out fight. Drunk or not, Alex gave as good as he got. But soon

Haile had the upper hand and pinned the man to the ground and leveled angry punches at his face.

"Haile Buchannan, get up off him right this instant!" Mrs. Humphrey's voice had the entire pub silent in seconds. "You two idiots should be ashamed of yourselves, brawling as if you were teens in this establishment. Someone help Alex off the floor and call his wife to scrape him from the pavement outside."

"Yes ma'am." Alex's friends crowded around him, and he shoved them away angrily.

"You can't tell me what to do!" he yelled at Mrs. Humphrey.

Mrs. Humphrey tucked her towel into her apron and pushed up the sleeves to her sweater. "Excuse me, you little whelp, I boxed your ears when you were a boy, and I'll do it now. Do you want me to come over there and show you?"

Alex's eyes widened. "No, ma'am."

"Get out of here, all of you," Mrs. Humphrey yelled. "I mean everyone. Don't even finish the damn drinks on that bar or I'll break your fingers."

Money was dropped on the bar quickly, and a mass exodus was made to the front door. Haile stood in the corner quietly because it was a certainty he was next. When he tried to quietly move toward his office, the older woman leveled him with a stare.

"You have a title, and while it may mean nothing

to you, it is a sign of respect for the rest of us," Mrs. Humphrey said slowly, and her voice was intense. "You want to brawl and fight like some gutter raised whelp, then so be it. But don't you ever do it for my eyes to see or my ears to hear. I told your mum I would watch over you as she would. Laura Buchannan wouldn't be having this."

"Yes ma'am." Haile bowed his head in contrition. While his anger still raged, there was an unsaid understanding by everyone. You never dared talk back to Dollie Humphrey.

"Now you help clean this mess, and we close for the night," Mrs. Humphrey muttered and walked away. "I don't know why I don't stay home and mind my grandkids. If the little bugger had any manners I would, but it seems no one here has any either."

The waitresses were pretending to be busy while Mrs. Humphrey chewed him out. But he could see the smiles they and the other bartender, Morgan, were trying to hide. Mari wasn't behind the bar anymore. He frowned but began to sweep and pick up the bigger shards of glass that were broken. It didn't need to be said, but it should be pristine before Mrs. Humphrey came back out there. She hadn't just boxed Alex's ears when he was growing up. At some point, they all could claim that they had faced her wrath and her hands. Finally, she gave her seal of approval as the staff counted tips. Morgan handed over Mari's share to him.

"She ran off when the fighting got really going," Morgan explained. "She looked terrified to tell you the truth."

Haile took the money. "Thanks, I'll give it to her before I leave. You guys get home safely. Remember, buddy up please or call the car service. I'm going to go see Mrs. H off."

They nodded, and he saw Morgan pick up the phone to call the service. He never wanted his people to walk home alone or take a bus late at night. Nor should they have to spend their tips to make it home safely. So he'd set up an account with the local taxi service to take anyone from his staff home, and he covered the tab monthly. It gave him peace of mind to know they made it home without incident. Mrs. H's husband parked out back, and he helped her and kissed her cheek, apologizing once more.

"You scared her senseless, you know," Mrs. Humphrey said. "I came out as she was rushing away, and I saw pure panic in her eyes. I don't think it was the fight. I think it was you. Something went wrong in that child's life, and the violence brought it up in a big way."

"Damn it," he muttered. "I'll take care of it, I promise. Night, Mr. H."

Her husband mumbled something in return from under his old beat up hat.

"You'd better. I like that girl." She smacked him on the cheek before he stepped back and she closed the door.

Haile watched the rear light of the car for a moment before he stepped inside and closed the door. He locked it and threw the main bar across the barrier so no one could try to break in. His face was sore, he'd have a bruised jaw and swollen eye in the morning. He strolled back to the front, turning off lights as he went, and finally he grabbed the stack of bills off the bar and headed upstairs to the apartment. Haile knocked on the door a few times before she even answered. When Mari opened the barrier, she had a thick comforter wrapped around her, and her eyes were wide and afraid.

"You left your tips downstairs," he said gently.

"Thank you." Her words were soft almost a whisper as she took the bills.

He took a step forward, and she stumbled back, terror in her eyes. He suspected before, but her reaction affirmed his suspicions. Haile wanted to kill the man who made her cower in fear. It tore at him knowing this time it was him.

Haile moved back and spoke gently. "Mari, Marisol, I would never hurt you or any woman. I swear it, on my life, on everything I love. I'm not that person."

"You just keep hitting… and hitting… I could hear the sound of your fist hitting skin," she said almost numbly as if caught in her own bad memory. Tears slipped down her cheeks. "I can't stand that sound, I- I had to run… I had to run so fast, and I had to be quiet because if he knew…."

"Oh hell, love."

Unable to help himself, Haile moved forward and pulled her into his arms. She struggled for a moment and the whimpering sounds of fear she made shattered his heart. "It's okay, you're safe, please Mari, no one will hurt you, I won't hurt you," he said the words raggedly in repetition until she stopped and only their breathing could be heard.

Haile used his hand to cup her cheek and lift her head. Mari looked at him with wide brown eyes, filled with doubt and uncertainty. He never wanted her to feel that way about him. it was hard enough for her to trust him to help her that first night, and now, because he couldn't curb his anger, he'd caused this. He bent his head and kissed her tenderly, a soft brush of the lips to show her he was gentle. She gasped, and he caught a taste of her mouth on the tip of his tongue.

She pushed him away. "I didn't come here for this! I don't want to be that girl who runs from man to man looking for something I may never find. I just want peace, Haile! I want to live and work and be happy. Can't I just have that for once in my life?"

"You can." His voice was a soft baritone. "You deserve that and more. You will have it here, I swear on it. I'm sorry I scared you."

He turned on his heels and walked away, even as she called his name softly. Haile didn't dare turn back. He wanted her, and finally admitting it to himself hurt worse than punching a wall or getting his face pummeled. Right now she saw him as one of the many monsters who could hurt her. *You are such a fucking fool,* he thought as he locked up the bar and headed toward his own home.

Chapter Four

Zeva called the next day and asked her to the manor house for lunch. It wasn't only a social call; her visa had come in and since she planned to stay, the first paperwork for her permanent residency in the United Kingdom needed to be completed. Jeffery may have screwed her over, but luck seemed to be on her side. She met the American Duchess who took Mari under her wing. Both she and Jasper offered to be her sponsors. She had never been more blessed than to find friends like them.

In all honesty, she had no one back in Texas. No parents, well they were alive, they just didn't care. No friends, since they all essentially ran away for their own safety. Mari felt more at home in Northumberland than she ever did in Texas, and she needed someone to talk to. Haile had scared her last night, and she didn't know if she should stay in the apartment anymore. Mari came down the stairs tentatively and looked around. It was eleven, and no one was there yet. *Oh thank God, it's Monday,* she thought and sighed.

They weren't open on Mondays, and Haile would be there soon to take care of the books and deliveries. He would sign for them, and she and the staff would put everything away and check the list before they opened tomorrow. Except for the kitchen deliveries, Mrs. H always did that herself Monday afternoon. Mari hurried down the stairs and chose to call the car service from the corner. It was a twenty minute drive to the manor house, and she marveled at the stone structure as the car pulled up in front on the white gravel driveway. The house was at least three stories with a full attic, and it was huge, along with the guesthouse and workshop and the manicured lawns. It was a marvel, and she'd never seen anything that resembled it in Texas.. She paid the driver, walked up to the front door, and rang the door buzzer. Mari waited patiently. Zeva was very pregnant and would be moving slow. She was amazed when the door opened a few seconds later.

"I didn't think you'd move so fast," Mari teased.

"Still an Army girl, this baby weight is a fifty pound pack but on the opposite end," Zeva answered with a smile and embraced her. "How are you?"

"I'm really good," Mari said warmly. "How are you and the lil' bit?"

"I'd be better if he or she stops trying to kick my bladder in." Zeva ushered her in before leading her down the hall into the converted family room/office.

Mari marveled at how elegant Zeva looked in the knit dress and low boots as she moved into the room. She'd seen some pregnant woman who looked exhausted ten times over at this point. But with her high ponytail and royal blue dress, she looked fantastic.

"I ordered us some lunch. It was delivered just before you got here." Zeva pointed at the coffee table. "I promise when this baby gets evicted I'll actually make us some lunch."

"You should've told me to come earlier, I'd have made us something," Mari said.

Zeva waved her hand. "Nah, it's fine, you're my guest. Now, this envelope has your work papers, and the visa is stamped in your passport. You can get an ID and even apply for your license."

"Get out—I can drive here?" Mari asked in excitement as she thought about buying a dependable but cheap car.

Zeva nodded and teased, "Just gotta get accustomed to driving on the wrong side of the road and badly.

"They do drive like maniacs," Mari laughed.

"Let's never tell them that, they'd be offended.," Zeva grinned. "Feel free to dig in. I got the sandwiches from that local deli close to the market."

"Their delivery guy bikes all the way out here?" Mari asked amazed.

"Exactly!" Zeva took a sip of her drink. "In D.C. they seemed to think I committed a crime by asking them to deliver two blocks away. I tip handsomely, by the way, because I appreciate good service."

Mari lifted her cup. "As a good duchess should."

"The gossip got to me already," Zeva hinted. "Haile was in a bar brawl last night?"

"Mrs. H put a halt to it, but it was awful." Mari shuddered. "I never thought… he was a completely different person. It was terrifying."

Zeva gave her a curious look. "You do know he was in the military? From what I've gleaned over the last few years, he's seen some stuff, and then he comes home to his sister being missing."

"And Jeffery Moermond being the main suspect," Mari finished for her. "He tried to sweet talk me at the market yesterday and after that threatened me."

"What does he have to threaten you with?" Zeva was barely nibbling her sandwich and rubbing her lower tummy.

Mari sighed and put down her plate. "I was in a very abusive relationship in Texas. I had to run. This trip was made under the cover of darkness while I knew he or his friends were too drunk to see me slip away. I lived in fear, I lost all of my friends, he and his family basically destroyed my life, and I had to live there because I had no other choice."

"Do you mind telling me how bad it got?" Zeva asked quietly.

"He put me in the hospital a few times. The last time he almost killed me, three broken ribs and a punctured lung." Mari's body began to shake. "His father is the Sheriff and his mother is a complete bitch who came to the hospital and told me in no uncertain terms her son would never get arrested, not in that town. The doctor was furious. She was the one who called the police. Dr. Reid threatened to call the D.A. and got laughed at."

"That makes me furious," Zeva said angrily. "And you started looking for love online?"

"A dating app." Mari shrugged. "It wasn't love per se, I saw it as an escape, and Jeffery had all the right words. Now it seems he's just another version of Marcus or worse. If you haven't noticed I have the worst luck in men." She gave a sarcastic laugh. "The thing is Marcus didn't even want me anymore, he just loved terrorizing me and no one would stand up to him. When I did, I got pummeled for it."

"Nothing about Haile is related to this Marcus or Jeffery," Zeva explained gently. "I can see how that kind of violence leaves a mark on your soul. You probably have PTSD from the trauma and the fact that there was no help in an entire town. Being scared, nothing can compare to it and seeing Haile fight could bring it all back."

Mari nodded. "I could hear each hit echo through my head. I had to run upstairs. I wanted to scream and panic, and I barely made it into the apartment before I fell to the floor."

"Haile is dealing with his own PTSD, and he's never really dealt with the loss of his sister," Zeva revealed. "But I can tell you this: he wouldn't hurt anyone for sport. He is one of the gentlest people I have ever met. He wouldn't hurt you, he'd probably throw himself into the moors before he ever raised a hand to a woman."

"He kissed me when he came to check on me," Mari said tentatively. "I kinda shouted at him and told him I just wanted peace."

"And you deserve that. Men are not good with timing," Zeva said. "Jasper proposed to me the second day we met because he wanted to oust his crazy ass mother in a way. I wanted out of D.C., and we had this attraction."

Mari sat back. "Luckily it worked out for you—me, I'm not so sure."

"Oh honey, if you want this it will, but if you don't, Haile will protect you with his life but never make you feel like you're obligated to him," Zeva explained. "It's all up to you, just take your time, and either way, you have friends and a life here now. It's not dependent on him."

"So if I moved out of the apartment, you or Jasper wouldn't be mad?" Mari asked tentatively.

Zeva snorted. "Of course not. We would help you find a place and a new job. But I have to ask, do you not feel safe with Haile around? Truly, in your heart, do you think he would hurt you?"

"No..." Mari shook her head. "I don't think so but.... Ugh, I don't know how to feel."

"Stop trying to analyze everything now. It's not a race, and it doesn't need to be fixed right this moment. Do what's best for you, Mari, in the long run that's all that matters." Zeva hesitated. "And I think my water just broke."

"You're right I can... Are you kidding me, right now?" Mari stood up quickly. "What the hell should I do?"

"Jasper is in town somewhere with Haile. They had a meeting about something or other..." Zeva blew out a breath. "Oh shit, I think I'm having a contraction."

"You're not telling me what I need to do?" Mari pointed out and felt a bit of panic filter in. "I may be from Texas but I never birthed a baby."

"Birthed a baby?" Zeva laughed, and it ended on a cry of pain and then ended up laughing again.

"You want to tease me about my words now?" Mari asked amazed.

"I'm sorry." Zeva wiped tears from her eyes. "I

think I may be a bit hysterical and possibly terrified. This is really happening."

"Okay, I'm fixin' to call Haile and tell him get Jasper home now," Mari said.

Zeva moved her legs and lay on the sofa. "Yep, that sounds good, do that… fixin'."

She started to laugh again, and Mari looked at her worriedly before feeling around in her purse. Haile's number was one of the few in her new cell phone so she pressed the touch screen and put the phone to her ear. He answered on the second ring.

"Mari?" Haile's deep voice was tentative.

"Hey…. Um, is Jasper with you?" Mari asked.

"Yes, why?" he replied

She took a deep breath and explained. "Can y'all get on over here? Zeva's water broke. She is in labor, and she's laughing at my words."

"Can y'all." Zeva laughed again. "You get all Texan when you're stressed out."

"See what I mean?" Mari muttered into the phone. She heard Haile tell Jasper who yelled. There was a crash of something dropping and then Jasper asked a million questions.

"Shut it mate, give me a minute," Haile said before speaking to her again. "This one isn't too stable himself right now. From where we are it will take us at least an hour to get there."

"You drive her to the hospital," Jasper called out.

"What he said. There is a GPS in the smaller car, take that and you'll be fine," Haile said.

"Okay, I'm on it. I'll get her there safe," Mari promised. "Y'all get there as fast as a prairie fire with a tail wind, you hear me?"

"Um yes, I hear you, and I don't know what you said but we'll get there quickly," Haile answered.

Zeva asked, "Do they really talk like that in Lumberton?"

"Sure as shooting," Mari said firmly. "Now let's get you up and dressed in something dry, and then I'm to drive you to the hospital."

"The address is in the GPS in the sedan," Zeva said.

"Good, one thing at a time." Mari helped her up the stairs.

It took about half an hour and two contractions to get her in comfortable fleece pajamas—Zeva's choice—and her bathrobe. By the time she got them to the car, there was something better than GPS waiting for them. Jasper had called the police, and there were two cars to escort them to the hospital.

One officer scrambled out of the car and took off his hat to Zeva. "Duchess, we'll be your escort."

"Thank you, but you didn't have to," Zeva said.

He nodded with a smile. "Ma'am, this is the first birth of a Duke's child in a very long time for

Northumberland. You'll be in for a surprise when you come home."

"Let's get you in the car," Mari said gently and helped her into the back seat before she got in on the driver's side on the right.

"What do you think he meant surprise?" Zeva asked as she pulled out slowly behind the police car. The second car pulled out behind her and the caravan began its drive.

"I think that means you get a parade or something," Mari answered. "Isn't that what they do for royals and stuff?"

"I don't want that!" Zeva cried out. "These darn Brits and their celebrations."

Mari laughed. "I'm sure tomorrow the beer taps will be dry while they celebrate."

"I hope you stay at the apartment and see Haile is an amazing guy," Zeva said suddenly.

"Maybe I will," Mari murmured and focused on the road.

Right now her attention was on the mom-to-be in the back seat and getting her to their destination safely. The situation with Haile would have to be thought about another day. But she knew from the time she saw his face, her stomach would erupt in butterflies recalling his lips on hers.

By the time Haile and Jasper rounded the corner from the elevator and dashed into the room, Zeva was already in a hospital gown and in bed with the baby monitor on her round stomach picking up the baby's heartbeat. Jasper rushed to her side and picked up her hand, kissing her knuckles before pressing another kiss on Zeva's lips.

"Are you okay, love?" Jasper's words dripped with concern and worry was etched on his face.

"Contractions—don't ever sign up for it, but when I hit four or five centimeters they'll give me the epidural." Zeva's smile was gentle. "I'm okay, Jasper… In a few hours, we'll be a family of three."

Jasper grinned. "I can hardly wait. I love you, wife."

Zeva cupped his cheek. "I love you, husband."

Mari watched them even though she was acutely aware of Haile standing as far away from her in the small room as possible. She still felt somewhat like an outsider, but witnessing the affection of the two people who literally saved her in the midst of all her chaos. It gave her hope and no one could deny they were completely in love with each other.

"I don't know how it got around so quickly, but there is a bit of a royal birth crowd outside," Haile teased. "Someone has a chair and table set up, having a cuppa while they wait."

"You're kidding," Zeva gasped and looked at Jasper. "Tell me he's kidding."

Jasper shook his head. "No such luck, love. We are the closest thing to royal unless you head to London and see the queen and those lot."

"If they think I'm getting prettied up and going outside after pushing a baby out of my vagina, they are going to be sorely disappointed," Zeva snapped.

"I'll go out and say something after, and they'll go on home," Jasper replied. "We'll put a birth announcement and a picture in the paper."

"As long as I don't have to put on make-up." Zeva blew out and grimaced in pain. "Here's another one."

Jasper coaxed her through the contraction, and the nurse came in just at the right moment. Unlike American customs, only the mom and dad were allowed in the delivery room. They were shooed out, and before they left, Haile kissed Zeva goodbye and hugged his friend.

"Congratulations. I love you guys, and you're making me an honorary uncle," Haile said huskily.

"Honorary my ass. You're my brother and family, you are an uncle." Jasper grinned.

Mari was next after a kiss on Jasper's cheek. She bent to do the same to Zeva. "In Texas they say that giving birth is like riding a bull, just hold on tight because it's the ride of your life."

"Thanks?" Zeva said with a teasing smile. "I was half expecting one of those Texan euphemisms you keep handy."

"Not right now, let's see how cute this baby is first." Mari laughed. "The point is, you are bad ass and a rock star, you got this mama. You both do."

Zeva pulled her hand until Mari bent low so she could speak and no one could hear. "You do too, trust me, and you can believe when I say, that man in the corner is one of the best people I know."

Mari looked at Zeva and nodded. "I'll take that into consideration."

The nurse stood at the door with a frown and cleared her throat loudly. It was their cue to leave. Haile stood back so she could leave the room, and the silence stretched between them down the long hall.

"I can take you home, if you're okay with it," Haile said hesitantly. "You'll be safe with me."

Mari stopped. "I don't think you'd hurt me, Haile…. I just… the violence, it scared me, that's all."

"I overreacted. There are usually little skirmishes in the pub, but he talked to you that way and…" Haile shrugged. "I find myself rather protective toward you."

"I don't need you to beat people up for me." Mari sighed and began walking again. "I seem to bring out the worst in people."

"I don't think so." Haile pressed the button to the elevator. "I think you're the best thing…"

The elevator dinged, the doors slid open, and people filed out. She snuck a quick glance at Haile, and he seemed to be relieved that his words were cut off. They entered, and he pressed the button for the lower floor of the hospital.

"Luckily I parked around the corner. The Northumberland press, will be camped outside, and a few other news agencies have picked up the news by now," Haile said.

"We aren't the duke and duchess. We should be fine," Mari said.

Haile chuckled. "Around here, they know Jasper and I are basically brothers. They see me, they'll descend upon us like crows. I'm assuming you didn't want your name in the news or on television so it's best we go out the back way."

"Yeah, you're right." Mari hadn't thought of it that way. She wasn't hiding per se, not anymore, but she didn't want to think how Marcus would react seeing her on television. Nor did she want to find out.

His Land Rover was close to the exit and they got in quickly, heading away from the crowd setting up outside the hospital.

"Wow, it was like on TV," Mari said looking back.

"Honestly, after Jasper most people around here thought he'd be the last of the line," Haile explained. "His mother is a piece of work, and everyone assumed he'd be childless just to spite her."

"I've heard bits and pieces of what happened from the girls when it's slow at the Celtic Cross," Mari replied. "What about you, do they go crazy for Lord Haile Buchannan?"

Haile snorted. "That title is akin to being part of your American congress, no one cares."

"But you have this distinguished military career to go along with it," she teased.

Haile's face turned serious. "A lot of that I'd prefer to forget — not the men or the people I served with. It was just hard, that's all there is to it, but I served my country and did my duty."

"I'm sorry about that and about your sister," Mari said suddenly. "I've heard, and thank you for not letting me go down that path with Jeffery. It has to be so hard not having the truth to what happened to her."

"It is."

That was all he said, and from there the rest of the drive to the pub was silent. At the pub, the news of Zeva's impending birth had already made the rounds. And as Texans would say his words didn't hit the ground because people knew Jasper and Haile's friendship was close. So they filtered in to eat or to grab a pint but mostly they were waiting to hear if the duke and duchess had a boy or girl. She jumped in and worked alongside everyone else because honestly she'd just be sitting upstairs wondering herself. By closing time there was no word, and there were moans of disappointment when Haile rang the bell for closing.

"You could stay open a while longer till we get word," one older man grumbled as he left.

"You mean when I get word, Mr. Moore, and no, I can't stay open. My people have lives and need to go home to their families," Haile answered.

Clean up came and went. Everyone got their coats, and as usual Haile made sure Mrs. H got into the car with her husband.

"Do you want me to turn off the lights down here before I head up?" Mari asked.

"No, I'll be here going through the till and getting the books sorted for the day. I'll get them," Haile answered.

Mari walked to the stairs before turning. "Do you think everything is okay? It's been hours."

"First babies always take a long time." Haile smiled. "I'm sure she's fine, and Jasper is a bloody mess."

Mari laughed. "As any good new father should be. Well night, Haile."

"Goodnight Marisol."

I like how he says my name, Mari thought with a smile as she went upstairs. In the apartment, she looked around and warmth spread over her. It was temporary, but it was still more of a home than she had ever had. She walked over to the window and looked out into the darkened night. The yellow lights that reflected off the streets gave it an old world feeling that she had only read about in books. She closed the thick drapes before moving to the bedroom and stripped down to take a hot shower. By the time she came out wrapped in the plush pink bathrobe and drying her short hair with a towel, there was a frantic knocking on the door. She hurried to the door and opened it to a beaming Haile.

"She had a girl," he announced grandly. "I am Uncle Haile to Abigail Katherine McTavish."

Mari squealed in excitement. "That is the most darling name ever! Did the people outside freak out, is all Northumberland cheering?"

"No clue," Haile answered, grinning. "Jasper was practically crying and laughing on the phone. I heard a baby crying and then he sent me a picture of this scrunched up baby face. And she is the most beautiful baby I've ever seen."

Mari waved her hand. "Well come on, cowboy, let me see the picture."

He pulled out his phone and scrolled through the messages before pressing the screen. Her heart melted when she saw the little face with closed eyes on the phone screen.

Mari looked up at Haile. "She is the prettiest girl in the world. I can't wait to smell her little baby head."

He looked at her in confusion. "Why ever would you do that? Is that some kind of American thing?"

"Babies smell amazing, it's..." She shook her head. "Never mind, you'll see. Thank you for telling me and showing me the picture. It was really nice of you."

"You welcome," he answered. "Your bathrobe has dancing pandas on it."

She laughed. "Isn't it great? I saw it when I was shopping and had to buy it."

"I don't want to be nice, I don't want to be just your friend," Haile said suddenly. "All I've thought about is how your lips tasted since that night and it's killing me not to kiss you again. I get it, I scared you that night, but I'm not a monster, Marisol."

"Kiss me again," Mari said bravely.

A rough noise escaped him. "Don't say that if you don't mean it because..."

She stepped forward. "I want you to kiss me. I don't know where we are going or what tomorrow will bring. But I feel that I'm safe with you, and I want you to hold me in your arms and kiss me as if tonight is the last one on earth."

"I won't ever hurt you, I swear that on my life," Haile said huskily as he pulled her into his arms.

"I'm not glass, Haile, kiss me and mean it," Mari answered.

The groan that escaped him was almost a sound of agony but became a sigh of contentment when his lips met hers. Mari knew exactly what he was experiencing because it was a kiss that felt so right, it was perfect. His lips were firm against her as he languidly tasted her lips, and then he pulled her closer. Haile took it deeper, and she whimpered when he slipped his tongue between her lips. He molded her body against his, and Mari loved the feeling. This was passion, not fear. She didn't feel obligated to fulfill his needs. Yet the dark thoughts that flooded her mind made her press against his chest lightly. Haile sensed the change and stepped back. His green eyes were almost emerald in color with desire.

"I could get used to kissing you," Haile said bluntly.

"It was tantalizing, but I need to move slow. The last two times weren't the greatest choices," Mari admitted.

Haile cupped her cheek and said simply, "I'm not them."

"I know." Mari still stepped back.

"How about this: I take you up to the coast for a

sunset picnic?" Haile said. "Call it our first relaxed outing. There's supposed to be a meteor shower we can see from the beach."

"A date," she surmised.

"You gave it a name, not me," Haile teased. "I hope you understand, I don't give up my sweet buns on the first date."

Mari laughed. "I'll keep that in mind. Yes, I'd like that. A drive and a picnic plus I get to see more than this part of Northumberland."

"Good, how about meeting me out front at five thirty?"

Mari smiled. "Luckily I am off from work tomorrow so that works perfectly."

"May I kiss you again before I leave?" Haile asked formally.

"Yes, you can."

It was a brief yet delicious taste of him before he stepped away and with a small wave jogged back down the stairs. Mari closed the door and went back to the bedroom with a smile. Thank god she never slept with Jeffery. There was an angel looking out for her that night because she found out the truth before anything could happen. Haile was different from any man she'd ever met. He didn't need to boast or use his strength to hurt. He was the strong, silent type, but he had his own demons to face. Zeva's words filtered through her memory, and she would trust her instincts. Maybe fate had set her on the path to the wrong man so she could find the right one. Only time would tell.

Chapter Five

How was one supposed to have a picnic on the coast when it was frigid out? *You improvise, that's how.* Haile grinned. Being from Alnmouth and the descendant of a family of fisherman, he knew exactly what to do. In that town, when people heard his name, they knew exactly who his family was. So when he asked for a dome tent, a heater, and all the other supplies he needed, they were glad to help. He called Mari from the Land Rover around five in the evening, and she came out the side door of the pub bundled up in a thick blue coat with a hood. Haile appreciated the curves of her hips in the pair of thick tights she wore and the fuzzy boots that finished off her outfit.

"Hello there," Haile said as she climbed into the passenger seat. He handed her a lidded cup of hot chocolate.

"Oh bless you," she said gratefully and took the cup. "Good evening, and holy shit it's cold! You can freeze the tits off a tick in this weather."

"Do ticks have tits?" Haile wondered aloud.

"Hell if I know." Mari took a sip and moaned. "Oh, this is so good."

"Wish I was the cup," he murmured to himself.

"What?" she asked.

"Nothing, just commenting on the empty roads," Haile replied.

"Are you sure we should be doing this, a picnic on the beach? I mean, the wind coming off the ocean will freeze us to death."

He glanced at her and gave her a quick grin. "Trust the son of a fisherman, I have this covered."

Mari smiled and settled back in the warm seats. "Okay, let's go on an adventure."

Haile started the car and pulled away from the curb. "And away we go."

From the center of the city to the coast took around an hour drive and then another ten minutes to the spot he had picked out along the beach. It was already dark, but you could make out the high cliff, that was the back drop of the cove he picked out. There was also a large outcropping on the side that would keep most of the salty sea air from chilling them to the core. He loved the Land Rover because it drove easily on the coarse sand, and he parked a short distance away.

"You don't have a basket or anything, what kind of picnic is this?" Mari asked.

Haile stopped and turned her head to the left and pointed. "There."

"Oh," she gasped when she caught sight of the tent.

"Come on, let's go see what's inside," Haile encouraged and took her hand.

At the entrance of the large dome tent, a bonfire was set, ready to be lit. He untied the flaps and ushered her inside. There was a large, thick cover on the sand, and in the center was a picnic basket. The heaters hummed gently in the background, and the warmth cocooned them completely. There was even a bouquet of fresh flowers next to the blanket and a bowl with fresh fruit. *Well thank you Cousin Drew,* Haile thought and knew he'd have to send the man a few bottles of good whiskey for this favor.

"Oh wow, this is amazing and warm," Mari said amazed. "How did you do all of this?"

"Family," he replied. "Look up."

"The top is clear and you can see the sky," she marveled.

"For when the meteors start, if it's too cold and we are sitting inside," he said. "I'm going to light the bonfire and see what's in the basket so we can eat."

"Sure," Mari laughed. "I've never done anything like this in Texas."

Haile looked at her while he tied the flaps to the

tent back. "I'm glad I can provide a new experience for you."

She sat cross-legged at the basket and opened it. "Okay, we have French dip sandwiches, and the *au jus* sauce is still warm."

"That's nice." Haile started the kindling in the bonfire and waited for the fire to spread to the larger logs.

"There's also a thermos and a bottle of wine," Mari added.

"The makings of a good drink." The fire was roaring now, and it lit up the darkness around their tent site.

"What's in the thermos?" she asked curiously.

"Hot chocolate, but don't think the one you get from coffee shops." Haile took the container and opened it. "This is made with real shaved chocolate and cream then we added the red wine."

"No way, you mix them together?" she said, amazed.

"It's a local drink in this area." Haile was busy mixing the concoction in two mugs, and then he passed one to her. "Try it for yourself."

Mari sniffed the mix before she took a hesitant sip. Haile grinned as she took a bigger mouthful. No one could resist the chocolate wine created in Alnmouth. She licked her lips, and Haile almost moaned. That one action settled an ache between his legs and made his cock thicken in response.

"This is really good." She looked over and smiled at him. "Who knew this was a thing."

"Let's grab some food and eat while we watch the stars," Haile said quickly trying to do anything to keep him from thinking about kissing her. It wasn't working.

She wanted to take it slow, and he would respect that. It had been over a month since she arrived in Northumberland, and each day he found himself more and more caught in her web. Haile doubted she even knew she'd spun one around him. She was that type of girl, so innocent to what she could do to a man, and it made her all the more appealing. They moved the blanket closer to the entrance of the tent, and from there they could feel the bonfire while they ate, and the heaters in the tent kept their backs pleasantly warm. They ate and talked about a little of everything from books to television, and when the first shooting star streaked through the night sky, silence reigned. Together they watched the universe showcasing its beauty while they sipped chocolate wine.

"My sister would love this," Haile said suddenly, and his heart hurt in his chest just thinking of her.

"She liked the stars?" Mari's voice was gentle.

Haile smiled up at the sky. "Her room was midnight blue while we were growing up. She painted stars on it and put those little glow in the dark stickers all over the wall. Much to my mother's horror, but it was Angela, no one ever told her no."

"Why?"

He didn't know why he was talking about his sister. It was just happening, and somehow it didn't feel wrong that Mari was listening.

"Angela was a miracle baby. My mom had her at forty-five after the doctors told her she would not have any more." Haile laughed softly. "I was ten, and this little bit of a thing used to scream the house down. How I loved her. She looked like an angel, she grew up, and there was laughter everywhere she went. She danced with ribbons in the yard, and she was a beauty, with red hair that caught the sun. The only times she cried was when others were hurting. Dad died, and then I left for my missions overseas thinking she was safe. She was our angel... I guess she really is one now."

Mari covered his hand with hers. "There's always hope."

He shook his head sadly. "No, I feel it. She's gone. We were that close. I was in a Fob with Americans sleeping after we got a convoy through an enemy line. I just sat up, opened my eyes, and knew something was wrong. I called home, and Ma answered the phone crying—she hadn't seen Angela in two days. She never slept away from home, always checked in with Ma, and would be there anytime I could make contact. I knew it then as sure as my next breath she was dead."

"I am so sorry," Mari whispered.

He shook his head. "It wasn't your fault. We know who did it. There isn't proof, and Joslyn Moermond threw every block in our path she could. Even though she knew her husband and how he lured my sister into thinking he loved her. Angela was so innocent, and now they live like she never existed, and all I want to do is bury my sister. My ma died of a broken heart, literally. This killed her, and I promised her I would find Angela. I'm going to one day, it will happen."

"The universe has a way of working things out, helping us see the truth, get closer and heal. I think it's working overtime on this for you." Mari scooted closer and leaned her head against his shoulder. "I don't see a meteor shower now, I see your sister telling you she's okay and raining stars down to earth just for you."

Haile cleared his throat, hoping that the emotion from her words would be hidden in his voice. "Thank you, that thought makes this all the more special."

"Can we sit inside for a bit? Even with the bonfire the wind is starting to get chilly," Mari said.

"Sure we can. I'll pull the flaps down so the air will be warmer." Haile moved to do just that while she crawled inside. He watched as she lay flat on her back and looked up at the sky through the clear material.

"You can see just as clearly this way too," she pointed out. "They are slowing down though, only one or two every few minutes now."

Haile lay on the opposite side of her. "You're right. Do you want to go?"

She turned her head to look at him. "Not yet, I like this."

He reached down and laced his fingers with hers. "We can stay as long as you want."

"I ran away because my ex was abusing me," Mari said. "I figured you should know that, since we are on a date and all."

"I figured that out from your reaction to the fight," Haile said. He wouldn't push; if that was all she said so be it. Mac had already filled him in extensively but it was her life and story to tell.

"We weren't even together anymore. He just basically held me hostage in the town I lived in." Mari's fingers tightened around his. "His dad is the Sheriff, and he can get drunk, fight, do drugs, whatever, and anytime he's arrested, they just put him right back out. When I begged them to help me, they said it was my fault, and if I stopped antagonizing him he wouldn't hit me. I guess just breathing or going to work pissed him off because I'd get hit for no reason."

"I'll give him someone his own size to pick on if you want," Haile said. His anger burned at her terror, and to think the authorities wouldn't help made him fume.

"It's not worth it, he's far away now." Mari took a deep breath. "He made me give him a key to my apartment. He would come in, and I'd have to do what he wanted."

Haile turned on his side. "Do you mean…?"

She closed her eyes, and tears leaked out from beneath the closed lids. "I never said no, I did it because I was so… so scared, and it was easier than getting hit. I'm so broken, Haile, I'm the last person you want to be around."

He pulled her into his arms. "This wasn't on you, this is a sick fucking bastard who put you in fear for your life. You are not broken. You are a warrior for surviving all of this. You escaped, and by God, he should be happy that he's in Texas and not here." Haile amended his words from what he was thinking. He didn't want to scare her with his rage at what she had gone through. "I would protect you, I promise you that."

She wiped away the tears. "I do, I wanted you to have the truth before this goes any further. I didn't sleep with Jeffery, we never even sexted. Video chats were normal, and I was dressed. Even though he wanted to, I am not that person, and after Marcus I am extremely careful."

"Honey, I didn't need that information, but I believe you." He raised her hand he was holding and kissed it. "Jeffery is a worm, and I want you to be careful. If you see him, go the other direction."

"He approached me in the market last week," Mari admitted. "I shut him down cold, and he tried to say he would use our texts and conversations against me. I told him go ahead. I lived with fear and blackmail for years, I'm not doing it here."

He was amazed she told him what he already knew, but that just reaffirmed that she could be trusted. There were so many times she could have lied to him, to get what she wanted. But everything matched up to what Mac told him, and she worked hard and never asked for more than her paycheck.

"You did the right thing, and thank you for telling me," Haile said gently. "If he ever bothers you again, tell me. I won't hurt him but I can ask Jasper for help in keeping him away from you."

"I'll do that," Mari promised, and she pointed up suddenly. "Look, there's another one."

"That one was bright," Haile said. "I think that is the grand finale."

"No this is," she said and rolled on top of him.

"What are you doing?" The desire he felt for her kicked into high gear immediately.

"Why, I am going to kiss you, Lord Buchannan." She smiled and gently scratched his beard.

"I thought we were taking it slow?" he pointed out.

"And so we are." She kissed him gently. "But I can tell when something feels right, and this does at this very moment."

"I want you—you cannot fathom how much," Haile said huskily. "But after what you've been through, I need for you to see this isn't just sex or my needs. I care about you, Marisol."

"I love how you say my name." She nibbled at his lip, and it was making him hard. "I'm seducing you, Haile, why don't you accept it?"

"Because I don't want you to have doubts about us, I don't want to you regret this," Haile admitted.

"I've spent my life regretting things, situations." Mari looked down at him and caressed his cheek. "The only thing I regret is not meeting you first instead of Jeffery."

"Don't say his name, don't even think about him." Haile's voice became a low husky growl. "Not when I'm about to take your body as mine."

Haile rolled until she was beneath him, and this time the gasp that escaped her was when he pressed his hips against hers. He looked down at her, taking in her ebony skin and wide brown eyes before he kissed her. She whimpered and lifted her hips to find that connection again. There was a slow build to intensity, he didn't want to scare her but for him the burn of desire was immediate. He cupped the back of her neck and felt the ends of her pixie cut against his fingers. Mari moaned, and he took the opportunity to taste her and delve his tongue into the recesses of her mouth. She slipped her hand under his sweater and the contact of her touch made him move against her. Mari spread her legs wider, and God he wished they had no clothes between them.

Haile could barely think. It was all he could do not to tear at her clothes while her tongue dueled with his and he sipped her like a fine wine. If he was made of wax, he would be melted while her hands roamed all over his waist and back beneath his shirt. He moved long enough to help her get her coat off and cupped her breasts though her soft blouse before he pushed the shirt up impatiently just to feel her skin.

"Wait, wait," she whispered.

Lord, he hoped she wasn't changing her mind. He would have to accept it, but damn, he would need to jump into the cold sea to cool off. Luckily it was to take her shirt off, and he followed suit. When their bodies met again, he closed his eyes in pleasure at the sensation that coursed through him. Haile trailed slow kisses down her neck and between the cleavage of her breasts. He buried his face for a moment, inhaling the scent of her skin before taking one nipple in his mouth. The pert nipple beaded hard, and when she cried out in pleasure, he sucked deeply as if he was starved for her taste. Mari arched and slipped her hand around his back to pull him closer and offer him more of her body.

"You taste so good. I can't get enough of you," he whispered harshly between licks and nips.

"Kiss me more," she begged.

He worked his way back to her lips. Haile plundered her mouth, and her hands were at his jeans trying to work at his belt.

"We should be naked," he whispered against her lips.

"That works," she gasped.

Together they worked at her boots, leggings, and panties before Haile moved to the buckle of his belt. Mari stared at him as he discarded the rest of his clothing. *Does she know she licks her lips like she is anticipating tasting me,* he wondered. That thought made his cock throb in response. Haile knelt between her legs and with his hand at her waist he caressed her soft skin, slowly committing each inch of her to his memory. Haile ran his hand down her torso to the apex of her thighs. Her pussy was wet and hot, while he stroked his fingers up and down her slit, he watched her. Mari bit her bottom lip, and she closed her eyes to the sensation of his touch.

"I'm going to taste you." His voice was a low timber of need, and he licked her essence from his finger. "I'm going to until you come and beg me to fuck you."

"Oh my."

He grinned at her words, and her back arched when he blew lightly against her clit. Mari arched, and Haile heard her sexy moan as he lowered his mouth to her core. She cried out and bucked at the first slow lick of his tongue. Her scent and taste consumed him, and he delved his tongue between the soft folds of her labia greedily. She writhed, and the tiny sounds of pleasure she made were driving him mad.

"Oh God, stop, no don't stop." The last word ended on a moan as pleasure coursed through her.

Following her cues and feeding off her response, Haile brought her hips forward with a rough jerk and explored her thoroughly with his mouth. Her hands were in his hair, and she lifted her hips against his mouth, seeking release as he teased her clit.

"I'm going to come," Mari cried out.

She moaned and writhed, and with a final flick of his tongue Haile reaped the reward her body had to offer when Mari came against his mouth and her essence flowed. God, she tasted better than sweet cream and honey. He lapped her with an almost ravenous intent, licking around the entrance of her sex.

Mari lay back gasping, and he watched the rise and fall of her breasts. Haile was not done, not by far, and he meant to have it all from her. He watched her as he slipped one finger inside her, and she moaned in response. Haile added another digit inside, and Mari arched her neck. She spread her legs wider as he created a slow rhythm with his hand. She arched with each deep insertion, panting, and she cupped her breasts while he watched. She was living art, liquid fire, every movement of her body burned into his subconscious.

"Do you like this, Marisol?"

"Yes," she whispered and licked her lips.

"Say my name, tell me you want more," Haile commanded gently as he increased the pace.

"Haile, it's wonderful, oh God, please touch me everywhere," she panted as he pushed deeper inside her wet pussy.

"Just me, Dove, only me who makes you feel this way." Haile wanted her to remember that. God his cock ached to be inside her.

"Only you." Her hips undulated frantically against his hand. "I love how this feels… I'm going to come."

"Yes, darling," he muttered and watched her tremble.

There was no more of a pleasing sight than watching her body draw tight and then release as her orgasm flowed over her. As each sensation rolled through her, Mari begged him to take her between every gasping breath. Watching her come was too much for Haile, he was hard to the point of pain. He covered her with his body and gritted his teeth as he slowly slipped into her wet sex. His groan matched hers as she took every inch of him until he was buried to the hilt. Haile withdrew slowly and thrust deep once more. She cried out, and he knew exactly what she was feeling. The feel of her was pure unadulterated pleasure that danced along the nerve endings of his skin.

"Let me ne on top," she pleaded.

Haile burned hot at her words. Mari was taking control of her sexuality where there was not a choice before. He moved so she could straddle his body, and she took his hard length into her hand and guided him within her wet sex. He groaned as she took him in inch by slow, torturous inch, while her hips undulated gently. Haile clenched his hands into the mat that covered the sand and let her lead their path to fulfillment. Her thighs clenched against his hard ones as she moved, her hands were pressed against his chest, and she bent to kiss him long and deep.

As the tempo of her pace increased, she arched,

and Haile couldn't resist the temptation to run his hands up her body to her breasts. He cupped the rounded mounds and ran his thumbs over her nipples as she moved sensuously above him. Mari took him deeper with every downward thrust, and a tortured moan escaped Haile between his gritted his teeth. He tried to hold on to her, to slow the rhythm before he lost all control. But she was past the point of reason, driven by that primal instinct to find completion.

"I need you, Haile," she cried out.

"Oh, Dove, you have me in every possible way," Haile groaned, and he meant it with everything he had in him.

"I'm going to come," she whimpered.

Haile looked up at her and saw tears on her cheeks. There was a moment of panic until he saw not pain on her face but bliss. Her pussy clenched around his cock. Mari was letting herself go and falling into the abyss of her orgasm, and Haile followed her to the edge and jumped. He held her against him as her body trembled and kissed her with every ounce of emotion that was within him.

The heat coming from the dome's heaters caressed their naked skin. Haile stroked her face and kissed the tears drying on her cheeks and yet more fell. He fit her body against his and looked down as tears slipped from her eyes.

"Why are you crying?" he asked huskily. "Did I hurt you?

"No, not at all." She opened her eyes and looked at him. "I just never felt anything that can compare to this before. It was beautiful, it was... I wanted this, and it was my choice."

"I'm glad you made that choice." Haile smiled.

He pressed his face against her neck and inhaled. Haile thought he would never tire of how she smelled or felt in his arms. The look in her eyes, the trust and the hope, made him feel as if he could conquer the world. He never wanted to see pain or fear in those beautiful chocolate eyes ever again, and Haile vowed he never would.

Chapter Six

There was no denying that she was happier, but Mari kept expecting the other shoe to drop. Jeffery had been quiet, and her mind kept drifting to Marcus. She feared him, even though everyone thought he wouldn't dare come to Northumberland if he found out where she was. They didn't know Marcus. She knew him from high school and he was crazy then, but he was even worse now. She worked and felt she needed to look over her shoulder when she wasn't at the pub or in her apartment. Mari knew she should start looking for her own place soon, but when Haile locked up for the night, even if he didn't stay there, she felt safe.

Haile. Her lips curved in a soft smile just thinking of his name, and her stomach clenched delightfully thinking about what they shared. Since their first date, he had been nothing but sweet, gentle, and kind. When she was naked in his arms, she felt the heat of his desire but she knew he held himself back for her. His hesitancy made her think that he believed any sudden move or too much passion would scare her away, but that was far from the truth.

She trusted him and knew the difference between what they shared and what she was forced into from fear. Was it bad to want all of him, unrestrained and wild? They were both still learning each other, and it was all still new... maybe it took time. Saturday night was busy, but hell, when was Celtic Cross not full? From the time the doors opened it was families, friends, teens, and other groups having fun and eating. Then from around six the evening crowd of people came from work, first dates and regulars came in for the evening.

She had even gotten used to Sunday Night Ruckus after the rugby matches, and since the first incident, Haile and the guy he had fought seemed to be fast friends. She shook her head in bemusement at that fact because she knew rifts between friends in Texas that still hadn't been fixed even though twenty years had passed. It made her happy to see how everyone knew each other, and Haile's pub was the neighborhood hub. But tonight seemed to be different, because at nine that night, Joslyn Moermond walked through the doors with her head held high. She was wearing a crisp blue skirt with a jacket to match. Her white blouse was a mass of ruffles, and she wore the gloves and shoes to match. Joslyn's hair was pinned up in a tight bun of black hair, and her make-up was pristine and flawlessly cold, and so were her eyes.

"What the hell is she doing in here?" Morgan asked.

When Mari looked up and saw her, her heart dropped. Joslyn met her gaze and moved toward the bar with intent clear in her eyes. She was ready to cause a scene.

"I'm going to get Haile from the back office," Morgan said and moved quickly. "I need for you to stop trying to coerce my husband into your bed," Joslyn said loudly.

Even the live band stopped playing and everyone looked toward the bar. Hell, even Mr. Moore the regular scooted closer so he could hear.

"I don't talk to your husband nor do I want to," Mari answered. "Now if I can get you a drink, let me know."

"You Americans think you can come with your whore ways and take our men." Joslyn cast her a cold look. "It won't happen, and if you text him again I will take legal action."

"Listen lady, I do not text your husband," Mari snapped.

"Let's not forget you moved here thinking that you and he would be lovers," Joslyn said loudly. "Now look at you, the barmaid, and still trying to get in his pockets."

"So this is you trying to cause a scene, make gossip, and embarrass me?" Mari asked. "You are making yourself look dumb as fuck, lady."

"Crass, just what this place needs," Joslyn murmured.

"Ice queen bitch, you and Jeffery are perfectly suited," Mari answered sweetly. Haile and Mrs. Humphrey came from the back just at the time.

"Anything I can do for you, Joslyn?" Haile asked casually leaning against the bar.

"It's Mrs. Moermond to you." Joslyn looked him up and down. "Tell your new bar whore to stay away from my husband."

"I haven't, Haile, I swear. Check my phone," Mari stammered. She certainly didn't want the man she was seeing to think she was messing around with someone else.

"I don't need to check anything. I know you're not," Haile said casually. "Joslyn." Mari noted he used her first name on purpose. "I see you live with your head in the clouds, but you do understand he can save anyone's number under her name, right?"

"You would take her side." Joslyn Moermond flicked him a cold glance. "You didn't want to believe what a little slut your sister was. And look how that turned out."

Haile's eye's eyes glittered in anger and his voice was deadly. "What did you say to me?"

"Why are you here trying to cause trouble for that slimy whelp you call a husband?" Mrs. H spoke up and stepped in front of Haile quickly. "You bloody well have it figured out, he has habitually cheated on you for years."

"That is not true," Joslyn said through stiff lips. "We have a loving marriage, and this one is trying to destroy it."

"Oh, piss off with that," Mrs. H snapped. "That boy has dipped his wick in so many different types of wax that it's got more layers that a rainbow lollie by now." People tried to stifle their laughter and failed as Mrs. H continued. "You came in here thinking that you would embarrass this poor girl and you'd feel some gratification and we'd all look at her and cry shame, shame. It's you who should be ashamed, for taking a man's side instead of looking out for your own."

"You should ask Jeffery about those clubs he visits and what goes on there, what he really enjoys… Joslyn," Haile added.

"You stay away from my husband or you will regret this," Joslyn said angrily and pointed a gloved hand at Mari. "I'm warning her, and she'd better heed it before she ends up… well your sister is missing, Haile. You still can't find that red hair."

"Are you threatening her?" Haile roared. "You have information on what your husband did and now you want to come into my place and threaten Mari."

"Get out you stupid... stupid woman before I forget my age and throw you out myself," Mrs. H snapped angrily. "And don't you dare come back."

Joslyn gave a small triumphant smile and a stiff nod before she turned and walked out the door. The silence was deafening, and Haile just turned and walked back to his office without a word.

"Why is it so quiet in here?" Mrs. H demanded. "If you didn't come here to hear a band and enjoy yourselves then get to going home."

No one defied that stern face, and the music queued up quickly as regular conversation slowly filtered back. The waitresses returned to working the tables, and Mrs. H stepped behind the bar.

"Go see him, Mari," Mrs. H said. "I can stand out here for a bit before I head back to the kitchen."

"Yes ma'am," she answered.

Mari took off her apron and set it on the lower shelf before heading toward the door that led to the back of the pub. Guilt gnawed at her because Joslyn had come into the Celtic Cross to embarrass her. Instead, Jeffery's wife hurt Haile using the one thing she knew would be a spear to his psyche. With her hand on the doorknob, she took a deep breath and stepped inside to see him pacing.

"Mari." He looked at her with pleading eyes. "Go

away, Dove, I don't want you to see me angry and frustrated."

"Why?" Mari asked. "She hurt you because of me."

"I don't want my anger to scare you," Haile admitted as he turned to her. "Right now I can feel it seething through me because of those two. He killed her, and that bitch uses it.... They taunt me, and I want to strangle them for it." His voice was harsh and agonized. "He destroyed our lives for his sick pleasure, and she has the gall to throw it in my face."

Mari closed the door and moved to the center of the room where he was. "Haile, you don't scare me. There is a difference — such a big difference — to what you are feeling and what was done to me. You have every damn right to be angry because they took your sister from you." She kissed his large palm. "Marcus hurt me for his sick pleasure and because he could, there is no comparison between you and him. I understand that now. That night I made you feel as if you have to walk on eggshells after the fight. It's obvious, you'd never hurt me and my heart feels that too."

"I'm glad you feel that way." Haile cupped her cheek, and his voice was rough with emotion. "Still this cloud is hanging over my life, and I'm helpless to fix it."

"They're going to make a mistake, and you'll get

your answers, I feel it," Mari promised. "Do you want me to leave? I mean quit working at the pub and move out. They're going to keep trying to pick at me until I break, and you'll be in the middle."

"Hell no, you're the best thing that ever happened to me, and I won't let them make me lose you." Haile hesitated. "I do feel as if you were threatened, though, so I will be keeping an eye on you."

Mari smiled and teased, "How close of an eye?"

He wrapped his arms around her. "Come home with me tonight and find out."

"Okay," she agreed.

Usually they were at the apartment at night, and for him to invite her to his real home was another step in the right direction. She never pushed, but she had started to wonder after the first few times he stayed with her at the pub if he was keeping her separate from his home and maybe a second part of his life.

"This is the first time you'll come to my home," he pointed out.

Mari smiled up at him. "Yes it is, I was starting to wonder."

"I didn't want to push and make you feel it's too serious too quickly," Haile admitted.

"I didn't want to speculate or invade your private space before you were ready," Mari replied.

"We spend so much time dancing around what we think each other wants, let's just talk to each other," Haile suggested. "I want you to see you at my house, in my bed, maybe walking down the stairs nude."

"I see you have been thinking about this," Mari laughed.

"Quite a bit actually." Haile bent to kiss her gently. "I love that you are in my life."

"I'm happy being here," she replied gently. "No, I have to go back to the bar because Mrs. H is in my spot and she may lecture one too many people on drinking."

"Please do, I'd prefer to see a profit tonight." Haile grinned and kissed her again. "Thank you, Mari."

She nudged him with her hip. "I got you babe."

Back at the bar she took over from Mrs. H who was explaining to a young couple why the female half shouldn't give away the milk for free. The girl's face was red and the young man just kept his glass to his lips and looked everywhere but at his date or the old woman behind the bar.

"Thanks Mrs. H, I can take over now," Mari said quickly.

"Remember what I said dear. Make him put a ring on it, listen to the song and get a wedding band before he gets in those knickers," Mrs. H said as her parting words. "Is he okay, Mari?"

"He'll be fine," Mari said. "Thank you for stepping in front of him."

"Joslyn shouldn't worry about Haile. I was getting ready to throttle her," Mrs. H replied as she walked away.

"I have no doubt she would," Mari said and gave the couple a free round of drinks. "That's for the trauma she inflicted loves."

The rest of the night went smoothly. By the time they turned off the lights, Joslyn's presence at the bar was old news. She could still see that Haile was thinking about Joslyn's indirect threat and what happened to his sister. Mari was raised in the church but as she got older, she wasn't that religious. Still, she knew how to pray, and she sent up a silent one for Haile and for the truth to be brought to him, because he deserved peace. They held hands while he drove to his house, and she looked up at the white stone structure on the corner of a cul-de-sac.

His house was at least three stories with a wide garden in the front. The bushes and trees were dead and brown, but she could only imagine how it looked in the spring when they were lush and green. While you could see the history in Zeva and Jasper's house, Haile's was more contemporary. The winding staircase was a polished black wood and curved upwards through soft cream walls with dark beige trim. The living room and dining room boasted a wide-open space with a large fireplace, and he showed her the kitchen and then upstairs. There were two bedrooms on the second floor, and the master bedroom, office, and a separate personal entertainment room was on the third.

"Very impressive and big," Mari said feeling very small and uncomfortable all of a sudden.

"What's wrong?" Haile asked putting his arms around her from behind.

"I feel out of place here," she admitted. "My place was a single wide trailer in Texas. I kept it nice and all but this is… a lot."

"You are exactly perfect right here." Haile turned her in his arms. "This place is walls and emptiness without someone to share it with. I want to hear your laughter echo in these rooms, see you dance and shimmy like you do in the pub to music." Haile grinned. "Watch you nude on the stairs."

Mari laughed. "You keep going back to that."

He tapped his temple. "It seems stuck in here."

"Show me your bedroom and bathroom so I can take a shower," Mari said.

"Yes ma'am." Haile turned, and she smacked him on the ass. "Hey now, don't start something…"

"Oh, I'll finish it sir," she cut him off.

"Come out of the shower naked and show me." His voice was suddenly gruff with desire.

"Why sir, you get me to your house and now it

gets frisky." Mari felt the familiar ache between her legs.

"The thought of having you in my bed has done something to me," he answered. "There are towels in the cupboard, that's the small door on the left as soon as you step in. I don't have any of that flowery body wash that women use, but there is some lavender soap Mrs. H's daughter makes in there." At her curious look he shrugged. "I'm a fool for a new business venture. She was making soaps trying to start a new business, and she wasn't making sales. Mrs. H brought in a basket, and we bought tons of it. I keep in in there to keep the towels smelling nice."

"Sure you weren't using it?" she teased, and he glowered at her. "I'm kidding!"

Mari went into the bathroom and looked around in awe. Black marble, shiny chrome fixtures, and recessed lighting in the ceiling. It was a man's bathroom, that was for sure, and she stared longingly at the tub. She hadn't had a good soak in a long time. Instead she grabbed a towel and a bar of soap from a basket on the top shelf. There had to be at least thirty bars in there and some small bottles of body cream. *That's sweet,* Mari thought, *he bought out Mrs. H to help her daughter.* After undressing and setting the water as hot as she could take it, she stepped under the spray. It felt so good. The heat and the pulsing water were like a massage against her skin.

Mari lathered her body and lingered under the spray until she brought herself out of her reverie and turned off the water. Drying quickly, she wrapped herself in the thick towel and grabbed one of the lotions before heading back out to the bedroom. Haile was sitting up in the bed with the remote in his hand. She noticed the big screen TV on the wall.

"I'm sorry," she said in embarrassment. "I stayed in there way longer than expected."

Haile smiled. "Not to worry, Dove. I took a quick shower in one of the other bathrooms."

"Anything good on TV?" Mari asked as she sat on the bed.

She noted with pleasure how comfortable they were. It felt like this was their life every day. She suddenly felt very at home with him, and for her, that meant something.

"I was looking at the news but so far nothing," Haile answered.

"Can I tell you something?" Mari asked hesitantly.

Haile looked at her. "You can tell me anything, Marisol."

"This feels right," she said hastily and put some lotion in her hand. She smoothed it on her arm and focused on that as she spoke. "No one really understood I never felt at home in Texas. My parents didn't live together, and neither of them seemed to want a child even though they raised me."

He watched her as she spoke. "I was shuttled around from my dad's house where his wife and their children treated me… I was an outsider. To my mother's house with my stepdad, and the kids they shared made me feel the same way. I went off on my own at sixteen and from there it was me trying to survive without anyone in my corner. Then Marcus took away my security, I wasn't safe anywhere and now this. Sitting on the bed, you said there's nothing on TV and we are talking regularly… I'm enjoying this."

"Then stay here with me," he said suddenly.

"I…" Mari couldn't form what to say. "Haile, this wasn't me asking to move in here. I was just telling you how I feel. It's nice how comfortable we are together."

Haile shifted to his side. "And this is me telling you I feel the exact way, and I want to have this every night for the rest of my life. I don't want to push, but think about it—moving in with me that is. I understand we never spoke directly about where this relationship is going. So just know, I'm not with you for sex, I see a future and I, Haile Buchannan, am ready to take steps toward that."

"Let me think about it," she said breathlessly. Her heart fluttered in delight, he saw her in his future and that was thrilling.

"Okay… can I honestly say that right now, I'm

thinking about your skin," he said huskily. "I've been watching you smooth that cream on your body. Let me help."

Her stomach clenched with desire at the thought of his hand on her skin. Mari laid back on the back and handed him the bottle. "I would love that."

He poured a small amount into his hands and rubbed them together, and all the while his eyes never left hers. He started with her legs, massaging the lavender scented cream into her skin and moved downwards. He repeated the action on the other leg, and she stifled a moan when he massaged her feet and toes with firm hands. When Haile was finished there, he worked on her torso and breasts until she couldn't help but call his name in a breathless gasp.

The lotion was left forgotten on the floor as he covered her body with his own. The kiss they shared was filled with promises of the pleasure to come. He tasted so damn good, and his lips ravished her senses. Mari gave as good as she got, making sure he could tell how much she wanted him as well. Kissing Haile would never get old. She could imagine twenty years down the line she would still be eager to feel his lips against hers. Mari shifted beneath him, trying to relieve the ache swirling within her. She wanted more, God, she wanted all of him.

"Damn you taste so good, your body is divine," he muttered against her lips.

"What are you going to do to me?" she asked breathlessly.

"This."

He cupped the back of her neck and exposed the length of her neck to his heated mouth. After a hard kiss, he trailed his lips down her body and took her nipple into his mouth. Mari gasped in pleasure at the sensation of his hot mouth around the pert tip of her breast.

"Do you know how your mouth makes me feel?" she moaned. "It's like electrical currents running through my stomach and making me wet."

He lifted his head and gazed at her. "That is the hottest thing I've ever heard."

"I wish you could feel it from my end," she said breathlessly.

They were a flurry of touching and intimate kisses, and amidst husky laughter, her desire increased. Haile was so hot and hard in all the right places, and he made sure that her pleasure was tantamount. It wasn't just about her body was used and no one caring about her pleasure or…

"Hey come back." Haile cupped her check and looked down at her. "It's just you and me, no one else. The ghosts of the past have no home here, not between us." He gave her lip a quick nip before he kissed his way down to her torso. Haile kissed the mound between her legs before looking up at her. "I want to taste you."

"I'm wet and waiting," she whispered breathlessly, anticipating the feel of his mouth.

"Hallelujah," he muttered.

He buried his face between her legs, and the first flick of his tongue shot pure unadulterated desire through her body. The heated wave washed over him, and a muffled groan escaped. He used his tongue to tease the sensitive bud of her clit before he swirled it around the soft skin at the entrance of her sex. Mari lifted her hips, offering him more, and she couldn't stifle the cry when he slipped a finger inside her. The combination of both the penetration and his mouth assaulted her senses in the most pleasurable of ways. He fucked her with his finger, increasing the pace until she was undulating her hips against his hand. Mari's release built, and she whimpered as heat washed over her in waves, tightening her already aching nipples. She grabbed at the sheets as her body arched off the bed when she sank under the wave of her orgasm. She barely recognized the guttural sounds of satisfaction that Haile made between her legs. She could still feel his tongue lapping at her come.

"I want you inside me, now, Haile, now," she demanded breathlessly.

"I have never been so turned on in my life," he muttered.

Haile covered her body with his, and she loved the feel of him, his strength, the way his body was tense with need. He kissed her, and their tongues dueled and mated from her mouth to his while his cock was poised at the entrance of her sex. He thrust into her and buried himself deep. Haile's body stilled, and she could feel the muscles along his back tremble with restraint. She whimpered into his mouth and teased him with the movement of her hips until he started a fiery rhythm of thrusts that took her breath away. With a primal growl, he pulled one of her legs over his forearm so he could have deeper penetration. He pounded his cock into her and gave a groan of ecstasy. The muscles of her sex contracted around his thrusts as her release tightened in delicious bands through her body.

"God yes, you feel so good," Mari gasped. "I'm going to come."

"Fuck."

The one word left his lips, and Haile kissed her long and deep. His movements took on an urgent pace, driving them both to completion. He pumped himself inside her with long, deep strokes, and Mari accepted each thrust. When she climaxed she arched, her body bow tight.

"Yes now," she cried out.

Her body shook from the intensity of her orgasm. Haile groaned against her neck as he followed her into his release. He kept moving, and the shaft of his cock glided against the sensitive walls of her pussy, sending her into another sweet release. Their bodies heaved as they tried to catch their breaths, and Haile kissed the soft skin at the rise of her breasts.

"Holy mother of pearl, that was fantastic." Mari fanned her face, willing her heart to slow down to its steady beat.

"The best damn thing a man could ever feel or ask for." Haile flopped back on the bed.

"Do you really think we can make this work — I mean like forever work?" Mari asked suddenly. How many times did she think she would find forever only to see that it was a pipe dream?

Haile turned his head to face her and smiled. "Marisol, we already are."

"Give me a few more weeks and if you still feel the same, I'll move in with you." Mari leaned over and kissed him.

"I won't change my mind," he said firmly.

She smiled. "Then a few weeks won't matter. I'll take that leap with you, but I have to be sure."

"I'm a patient man." Haile took her hand. "To be with you is worth the wait."

Mari snuggled closer. "You make me worry sometimes, expecting the other shoe to drop."

He looked at her again. "If it does, you can be sure I'll be right by your side. You aren't alone, Marisol, not anymore."

He wasn't professing his love, but to her this was something better. She had heard, "I love you," after she had been hit and made to think that everything, every bruise and bloodied mouth and injury, was all her fault. But to know he would stand with her no matter what was better than any *I love you*. There would be time for that. Right now, she cocooned herself in the knowledge that she wasn't alone.

Chapter Seven

Haile hoped that he had assuaged Mari's fears, her waiting for the other shoe to drop. He didn't believe in waiting or looking for variables. If something was going to happen, he needed to keep abreast of it. It was coming their way because Mac gave him the heads up. Her ex was on his way, stupid enough to chase her across the pond. He knew exactly where she was, courtesy of Jeffery Moermond who didn't want to lose, especially to him.

Haile would deal with both of them in their own time. He said it once, and it was true in every part of his life: he was a patient man. Jeffery would get his just desserts eventually. Right now, there was another asshole who needed his attention. Would Mari be pissed he didn't tell her about Marcus? Probably, but if he did, she would be a scared cat jumping at every shadow, and hell, maybe she would run away. He couldn't have that. She needed to face him, and as he promised her he would be right by her side. So he kept close, and she began to spend every night at the house instead of the apartment over the bar. Jeffery knew where she stayed and no doubt Marcus would too.

That night after the bar closed, he was at the back door making sure that Mrs. H got to the car safely. Mari ushered the last guest—as usual, Mr. Moore—out, and as he came in, he heard a crash of glasses on the floor. Haile rushed through the kitchen to the door that led to the bar, and Mari was against the wall. The look of terror in her eyes reminded him of a cornered animal. At the door stood the man who had instilled that fear in her. Marcus was at least three inches shorter than he was and wearing a plaid blue shirt tucked into jeans. He was the quintessential cowboy except Haile saw the pleasure that Mari's fear was giving him. Marcus got off on the abuse.

"Well, this is where you got to," Marcus drawled.

"H-how did you find me?" Mari's voice had become small and hearing it so small and diminutive sickened Haile.

"I told you, sweetheart, you can never get away from me," Marcus answered. "Now get your stuff. I've got a ticket, and you're going home with me."

"And who the hell are you?" Haile asked.

"I could ask you the same question," Marcus said casually.

"I own this bar, and Mari—well, I have a vested interest in her," Haile answered.

"Ah, she snowed you too, this girl." Marcus

laughed. "She gives anyone those puppy dog eyes, and they believe anything she says. Did she tell you the spiel about how I abused her and she had to run? This girl is lying and clumsy. She thought she could trap me and my family by using what's between her legs. When I said no, she lied and tried to tarnish my name."

"Haile, I-I..." She shook head and wiped tears away with a trembling hand.

"It's okay, Dove." Haile cupped her cheeks. "This ends today."

"Oh, it's not just her eyes that I believe," Haile replied, turning his attention to Marcus. "I believe my guy in D.C. who told me about you and your family. I believe that you're a sick fucking fool who gets off on pain. I also think you should turn around and go back to good old Texas before I toss you there myself."

"You and that pansy ass voice are going to do what?" Marcus laughed but there was an answer in his eyes. "Mari, get your shit and come on."

When he snapped her name, she literally jumped, and Haile vowed Marcus would pay for it. This had to play out the right way, though. He couldn't save her, Mari had to save herself. She had to reclaim her life.

"Marisol, do you want to go with this man?" Haile asked more calmly than he felt.

"No." She shook her head with vehemence. "I don't."

"Then tell him that, Dove. Forget the fear. He can't hurt you anymore," Haile encouraged.

She stepped away from the wall and took a deep breath. With shaking hands, she ran her fingers over her short hair as she stepped forward.

"Get out, Marcus," Mari said.

"Remember who you're talking to, little girl." Marcus's voice took on a deadly tone, and Haile watched his hand clench into fists.

Not yet, he reminded himself and let Mari continue. He could see the dam breaking within her and this needed to be her time.

"Remember what? How you belittle me, talk down to me, beat me for just breathing?" Mari's accent became thick. "I'm not your little girl, that's not cute, and I belong to myself. I'm not scared of you anymore. I ran away to find me, and I did. I won't have you come to where I work, with people I love, to threaten me. I'm not going anywhere with you, so you can go back to your mama and your daddy. I am sorry for the next woman who believes in your charm."

"Little bitch, you think you're something now. You're the same little black girl living in a trailer underneath it all," Marcus sneered.

"I didn't forget who I am or where I'm from,"

Mari snapped back. "But I will forget you, as soon as you step out that darn door, that's for sure."

Marcus raised his hand, and Mari did something Haile never thought he'd see. She stepped forward and pointed her finger right in his face.

"You don't ever dare raise a hand to me, ever again Marcus!" she yelled. She raised her other hand and made a sound of pure anger. "I swear to God, I will fight you, and trust me, this time I'll win. Why the hell did I let a mama's boy fucked up piece of shit like you put your hands on me, I'll never know. Try it now, try me, and I swear Haile will be mopping up your damn face off this floor. I'll scratch it off and then kick your balls into your chest. How dare you follow me here, how dare you think you were better than me and could beat me into submission. I'm not scared of you anymore, so fuck off and get the fuck gone."

By the end she was screaming, and tears of anger ran down her cheeks. Marcus stood there with his mouth agape, and when she stopped Haile watched his eyes turn cold. They both seemed to forgot he was there, and when Marcus grabbed her Mari was ready to fight him off. This was where he stepped in. Haile pushed Marcus again the wall so hard the memorabilia that hung there shook, and one framed rugby shirt fell to the ground.

"Now, now, don't you touch my woman in an unseemly manner," Haile said casually.

"Your woman," Marcus sneered. "I fucked her in so many different ways."

Haile punched him in the face. "Not by her choice, only by yours. You took a woman by fear and with malice, so trust me, that doesn't count. But this does."

The next hit was to the gut, and he took infinite pleasure in watching Marcus gag. Haile grabbed him by the neck and dragged him to a booth where he sat him to one side and then sat across from him.

Haile looked over and smiled at Mari gently. "Hey Dove, how about you go upstairs and wait for me? Marcus and I are going to have a talk and then we can go home. Have a cup of tea and settle your nerves."

Mari nodded. "Okay. I'll see you in a bit?"

"Definitely, Dove," Haile promised.

He waited until she was completely upstairs and then turned his attention back to Marcus. The smile faded and Haile took the hand that was sitting on the table. He broke one of Marcus's fingers. It was as simple as that. Marcus screamed, but Haile didn't let go of his hand.

"Here's the thing, Marcus," Haile spoke as casually as if they were friends. "I completely get it, you thought that your bad boy act would work for you across the pond. But daddy isn't here to bail you out of jail, and mommy can't speak ill of anyone here to poison their minds."

"I'm going to kill you," Marcus said through gritted teeth.

"Marcus, you're not listening," Haile repeated the action with another finger, and Mari's nightmare ex screamed again. "Now here's what you didn't hear about me, pertinent information and all that. I'm a man who can turn off my empathy when it comes to bullies. People think her majesty's Royal Army isn't up to par to the American military, but it's actually so much... deadlier."

For emphasis, Haile brought his fist down on Marcus's broken fingers. "Here's an example, right now, you're obviously hurting and your fingers are, well, they're not pretty. For what you did to Mari, I could kill you and lose you in the moors. Your parents would never hear from you again, and when the authorities come sniffing around I can be as surprised as anyone else you didn't make it to your hotel after you left. Yes, I'll say you left after threatening Mari."

"I'm going to go," Marcus whimpered.

"Yes, I see that you are grasping the seriousness of my words and you're not going to come back." Haile voice was gentle.

He never forgot his training, and he moved so quickly Marcus wasn't expecting it. He grabbed him by the neck and slammed his face onto the table. "Here's why. No one here cares if your dad is the sheriff of some Podunk town. We don't care who your family is, and when Jeffery Moermond led you here, he really didn't tell you about me. If you are not on a plane tonight, I mean don't even check into the hotel you have booked on Lance Street. Get in that train, head back to London, and go to the airport. Then book a flight and sit there until it's time to board. If I hear you are still in this country by noon tomorrow, I will come find you myself. Understood?"

Marcus nodded. "Yes, I understand."

"Good boy." Haile slapped Marcus's check. "And when you go home, if I hear you said anything untoward about Mari being here in the UK or me, well, I don't mind traveling, and no one will even find out I was there. Are we crystal clear on everything, Marcus?"

"Yes." Tears of pain leaked from his eyes.

"Now you sit here like a good gentleman, and I'll call you a car service," Haile said cheerfully and stood up.

Marcus didn't move. It was typical of a bully. When they were confronted their true colors came through: cowardice. Five minutes later he was in a cab holding his hand, and Haile told the driver to take him to the train station. Marcus looked back as the car pulled away, and Haile gave him a jaunty wave because he was sure he had made a positive impression on the man. He went back inside and up the stairs to the small apartment. Mari was sitting on the loveseat with a cup of tea in her hand. She stared off at nothing until she heard the door and Haile stepped inside.

"Is he gone?" Mari asked.

"Yes, for good." Haile sat beside her and took the cup from her hand before pulling her into his arms.

"I'm sorry, I became a wild animal... there was so much pent up inside me." She turned her face into his shirt. "I couldn't stop it."

"That's because it needed to be said, you need to be free of it," Haile murmured. "Don't be sorry for that."

"I heard screaming," she said.

"Oh, we were having a discussion, and Marcus expressed himself in a manner that certainly wasn't polite," Haile explained. "I subsequently showed him the error of his ways."

"You make beating him up sound so polite." Mari looked at him with a smile. "Thank you for being here with me. I don't think I wouldn't been able to handle this without you."

"I told you, Dove, it's me and you." Haile kissed her gently. "Now let's go home and get some rest."

"And ice cream, there is gelato in the fridge," she teased as she stood up.

"You found my stash." Haile helped her into her coat.

They continued their teasing banter on the way downstairs and in the car. Haile felt the door of the past was firmly closed, and that was all she needed. From there they could move forward and not with fear or apprehension but with hope. If only all things were so easily solved. His thoughts went to his sister. He was starting to lose hope that Angela's disappearance would ever be solved.

"I have never been so excited to go anywhere." Mari literally bounced in the seat.

"I see that," Haile said in dry amusement.

She nudged him with her elbow. "You can sit there and pretend, Mr. Man, but you are just as happy as I am."

"Mmhmm," was the answer she got. Still, he was grinned from ear to ear.

Today they were finally going to see baby Abigail. Zeva had been home for about three weeks, and in that time they were having guests over. Mari understood that the new parents needed time with their baby, and people in and out of the house could bring in any kind of cold or virus. Heck, in Texas no one would be seeing mom or baby until about eight weeks had gone by. They were the only two who were allowed to be there right now, much to everyone's disappointment in Northumberland. There had been no pictures in the paper to go along with the birth announcement. The new parents were still the talk of Celtic Cross with people wondering when Zeva and Jasper would be seen out with their new bundle.

"Since Mrs. H knows where we are going. We are going to be interrogated tonight at the pub," Mari pointed out. "Mr. Moore offered me fifty pounds to get him a picture."

"That old badger, he's the worst out of the lot of them," Haile snorted. "I'm sure Mrs. H told him, and he literally became the town crier."

"Gossip travels no matter where in the world you are, it seems." Mari laughed.

"Trust me, in Northumberland gossip is a certainty," Haile answered. "There is a pool on when we are going to be married and have our first child."

Mari stared at him in shock. "You're kidding."

"Nope, I've got thirty on the end of the year and a boy ten months later," Haile replied with a wide grin on his face.

She folded her arms. "First, that's not fair because you can pad this bet to your benefit. Second, what makes you think it will be so easy, huh?"

"You're moving in soon, and that's the obvious next step," Haile pointed out. "Hell, there is a pool on as to when you're actually going to be completely moved out from over the pub. They bet on everything here."

"That's just weird." Mari had to admit it was disconcerting that so many people seemed so invested in their lives.

"They love you, and they see you as one of us," Haile said as if sensing her thoughts. "If they saw you as an outsider then you would feel it, trust me."

Mari nodded. "I guess I would sense that myself. I felt like an outsider in the place I grew up. Hell, I've been gone for months, and my parents don't even give a damn to call, and trust me, they have my number."

"Did you call them?" Haile asked.

"I told them when I was at the airport getting ready for my flight," she answered. "My mom said okay, and she had to go. Brittany's fiancé was over, and they had to practice for the wedding. I didn't even know my half sister was getting married, and it seems I wasn't invited. My dad's went to voicemail, and he never called back so that tells me where I stand in their world."

"I'm sorry, Dove," Haile said, and she heard the pity in his voice.

"No, don't sound like that," Mari said firmly. "Being the throwaway kid had its perks, no one cared what I did. Now I am making a life in a place where people look out for one another, and I'm included."

"I'm glad you are here. I thank God in a way that Jeffery's behavior brought you to town." He glanced at her. "We were meant to find and heal each other."

Mari smiled. "I think so too."

Finally they pulled into the white gravel driveway that curved in front of the manor house. The excitement to see the baby was back, and she had to play it off casual and wait patiently until Haile escorted her out of the Land Rover. Jasper must have seen them drive up because he opened the large varnished door and stood there with a smile on his face. He was wearing a gray sweater and casual beige slacks. Haile took her hand as they walked up to Jasper and his smile became a grin.

"Well hello you two," Jasper said warmly.

"Hi," Mari said and held out her hand for him to shake.

"Really?" Jasper pulled her into a hug. "We don't do that formality around here, especially when you walk up holding hands with my best mate."

Mari returned the embrace. "Okay, because I really don't want to stop hugging you, you smell like baby."

"I'll need to rub your child all over my clothes to get that kind of hug," Haile teased.

"Oh hush, you get plenty of love and affection," Mari admonished playfully as she stepped away.

Jasper moved aside. "I guess I should let you inside before you run over me."

"That would be nice. I don't think I can control myself much longer," Mari teased. "Where are mama and baby?"

"They are in the family room, Abigail just woke up." As Jasper spoke a baby began to fuss. "Head right on in."

Mari led the way with quick steps while the men trailed behind her talking. She stepped into the family room where the fireplace crackled and the warmth of home and family was in the air. Zeva was sitting on the love seat, and she held a tiny bundle in a pink onesie over her shoulder. She was patting the baby's back, and Mari made a small noise of pure awe and joy before covering her mouth with her hands.

Zeva looked up and smiled. "Come on over and meet her." Mari sat next to Zeva who handed her a blanket to put over her shoulder. "You'll need this, she just had a feeding and may burp up some milk."

"Oh, she can throw up all down my shoulder, that's just baby sugar," Mari cooed.

"Huh, baby sugar," Haile mused. "That's a new way to put it."

"Basically babies are made of sugar and love for Texans," Zeva pointed out.

"They haven't seen her diapers." Jasper wrinkled his nose. "And she only drinks milk."

"Don't listen to them, you are just a sugar lump," Mari said as she took the baby. She looked down at the tiny baby in her arms that stared at her with bright blue eyes. She yawned and lifted a tiny hand to her face, and Mari fell in love. "She is so perfect, oh, I want one."

"You're in trouble now buddy," Jasper said with a chuckle.

"I'm perfectly fine, and it goes directly into the timeline I need," Haile answered.

"Not you and that bet," Zeva said.

Mari looked at her. "You know about it too?"

"Sweetie, everyone knows about it." Zeva laughed. "We have fifty on married by Christmas, baby girl by fall of next year."

"You people are incorrigible," Mari said and looked down at the baby. "I'll comfort myself with her baby smell."

"Come on, Dove, don't Bogart my niece. I want to hold her too," Haile said.

Jasper handed him a burp cloth, and soon he was standing with the baby in his arms. His large hands protected her, and she wondered if he knew that he started an automatic sway from side to side while he held her. Watching Haile, her stomach clenched delightfully. He would make a good father. She was thinking about children when this time last year she had an alarm set on her phone so she didn't forget her pills. A child with Marcus would have bound them together forever, and that wasn't happening. But she could see her life and children with Haile. They left the men talking, and Mari went upstairs with Zeva who needed to change Abigail.

"So I see that you decided to take that leap," Zeva commented casually as she laid the baby gently on the changing table.

"Things just kinda fell into place," Mari answered. "Seems that people were betting on us before we even knew there was an us."

Zeva smiled. "Anyone who saw the two of you together for two minutes knew. It was y'all who were clueless."

"Look at you using y'all," Mari teased.

"I remember my Fort Sill roots," Zeva said. "And the Marcus thing worked out?"

"How did you know? I guess Haile told Jasper, huh?" Mari said.

Zeva looked confused. "We knew the day he got on the plane. Haile didn't tell you?"

Mari frowned. "No, he didn't. He showed up, and I didn't think…"

"Jeffery Moermond slipped him the info about

where you were, the slimy fucking snake," Zeva explained. "When he showed up, Haile didn't know when he would make a move."

"He should've told me," Mari murmured. "I saw him and my knees buckled, but I finally stood up to that bastard. I freed my mind of that fear he instilled in me."

"That's all that matters," Zeva said gently.

"I guess so," Mari answered.

After talking a bit more, they went downstairs and continued their visit. It still bothered her that Haile didn't tell her Marcus had come to Northumberland. Why, and what else was he keeping from her? She tried to keep the atmosphere light, but Haile gave her a curious look, and she averted her eyes from him. She wasn't just irritated, she was mad. It was her life, and she should have been consulted.

"We should get going. Babies need to sleep and mamas need to rest," Mari said after a while. She could see that Zeva needed a rest even as the baby snoozed in a bassinet close to the sofa.

"I'm sorry but when she sleeps I fade quickly. We're still trying to get used to those late night wake-up calls for milk," Zeva apologized.

"No need to explain. Rest, and we'll be back to visit soon," Haile said. As he stood he kissed Zeva's cheek and hugged Jasper. "If you guys need anything, give me a ring."

"And if you need a break, count me as a built-in baby sitter," Mari offered. "It would be my pleasure."

"We'll take you up on that," Jasper answered.

Jasper walked them to the door, and as they drove away, he gave one last wave before closing it against the chilly night wind. Everything was silent within the Land Rover until Haile spoke.

"Zeva told you we knew Marcus was coming," he said.

"It would have been nice if I knew," Mari snapped. "It would have given me time to prepare myself."

"Or to run," Haile replied.

She turned in her seat. "So that's what you thought, I would tuck my tail between my legs and run."

Haile's answer was blunt. "That would have been the gut instinct of a person who had been mistreated for so many years and lived in fear, so yes, I did think that."

"Nice to know what you think of me," she retorted.

"That's bullocks and you realize when you came here you basically were terrified of shadows because of what he did," Haile shot right back. "I did what I had to do to protect you, and I won't apologize for it."

"And I thank you for all you have done, but caring for someone doesn't mean you get to keep them out of the loop," Mari pointed out. "I would've preferred you trust me enough to take my stand with you there as support."

"Understood," Haile said stiffly.

Mari sighed. "No, you don't."

They fell silent for the rest of the drive until they got closer to the pub.

"I need to grab something clean from the apartment," Mari said.

Haile gave a mock salute. "Yes ma'am."

She let out a sigh of frustration as he pulled up to the Celtic Cross. Monday meant they were closed, so no one was around as he unlocked the door and she stepped inside.

"I'll be down in a minute," Mari said as he went around behind the bar.

"At your leisure. I'm just here whenever you need me," he replied.

"Stop being that way. I told you thank you for trying to protect me, but I'd rather have known and be given a choice."

"Seems to me that I'm getting chastised for doing what I'm trained to do best," Haile commented.

"I'm not your job," Mari yelled in frustration. "I'm supposed to be the woman you care for, that you want in your life. I can't go from one man trying to control me by abuse to another man trying to protect and smother me to death with it. Give me choices so I can make them with you. Your problem is you want to go around wearing the cape and saving everyone even from themselves because you lost your sister."

"That was a low bloody blow, Marisol," Haile's voice was harsh, and he turned away from her and went behind the bar.

"But it's true," Mari pointed out following him. "Haile, you found me as Jeffery and his wife screwed up my life. You saw me as another way to find redemption, to heal that open wound of Angela's disappearance."

"I can tell you apart from my sister, trust me," Haile snapped.

"That's not what I mean so don't even go there," Mari said. "I don't need saving, I just need your love, your support and not to be coddled. You have to make peace with Angela being gone but you can't use me to do it. If not, that's not the relationship I want or need."

Haile grabbed her by the shoulders and kissed her savagely. "Does that feel that way? I don't see you as a bandage to any wound I have."

Mari grabbed his neck and pulled him back to kiss her. "I am not glass, you don't have to treat me with kids gloves. I'm not this fragile, scared, broken bird. I'm a woman, your woman if you want me, but you have to let me share the load. You can let go of that staunch reserve you hold on to around me. Let me love you for you and vice versa."

"You want the real me," Haile muttered. His green eyes flittered like emeralds in the dim light. "Then I'll give you what you asked for."

"Is that supposed to scare me?" Mari asked and lifted her head defiantly.

"No." Haile lifted her on the bar. "I hope it makes you so wet that your panties are soaked, and I can lick it all up."

"Oh sweet Jesus," Mari gasped.

"No, no, it's all me." His voice was deep and harsh with need.

Haile whipped her sweater over her head and in seconds had her bra off. He pressed his face between her breasts for a moment before cupping the back of her neck. She felt the kiss to the soles of her feet. Haile speared his tongue into her mouth without teasing or tempting her. This was carnal and primal, the way he devoured her mouth set her soul aflame.

Desire exploded between them hot and fiery when their lips met. They tasted each other like it was their last few seconds on earth, and they wanted their end to come fused together. He cupped her breasts and ran the pad of this thumb over her nipples until they beaded hard, and she whimpered from the friction. They were working hands, he'd pulled ropes and built things with them, and now they caressed her skin leaving fire in their way. Mari pulled his shirt up, struggling to get it over his head before working on his slacks. She struggled out of her thick leggings and boots as best she could, perched on the bar.

Finally, Haile stepped between her legs and the contact of skin to skin made her gasp. He swallowed the sound as he took her lips once more. There was no chill that their bodies didn't consume with the heat they were creating. Haile kissed his way down her neck, to her breast. Mari loved the delicious friction of his beard on her sensitive nipples. He licked and sucked at her nipples, and she whispered his name.

"I can't get enough of your taste." His tone was rough.

Haile continued his downward path with his lips to her torso until he reached the apex of her thighs. Mari tensed when she felt his hot breath against her pussy. She wanted to feel his mouth, and she shuddered in anticipation. He teased her by gently probing between the soft flesh with his tongue. Her breath caught in her throat, and then she gave a soft whimper and shifted restlessly.

"Damn you, Haile give me what I need," she whispered, lifting her hips in invitation.

Haile gave a sexy chuckle as he cupped her ass with his big hands, lifted her hips, and brought her pussy to his eager mouth. Mari threw her head back as pleasure assaulted her and couldn't help the cry that escaped her lips. Haile didn't tantalize her this time, he feasted on her sex, and Mari braced her hands on the bar and held on for dear life. The feeling of his hot mouth and tongue licking and penetrating her pussy almost drowned her in pleasure. She moaned as sucked on her clit, and the guttural sounds he made were primal and erotic. His face was pressed between her thighs, and she came, calling his name and grinding her pussy against his face.

Haile stood, and she could see the hunger in his eyes. His ragged breathing filled the room, and Mari slipped from the bar to her knees and took his cock in her hands. He was so hard, and as she stroked him, Haile threw his head back in pleasure. Teasing the tip of his rod with her tongue caused him to groan. She upped the ante, taking him deep between her lips and stroking him in tandem to her mouth's ministrations. His groan reverberated in her ears, and he slowly pumped in and out of her mouth while her tongue worked greedily at his shaft. Mari looked up at him while she sucked him deeply between her lips. The carnal look of pure need etched on his face made her want him all the more. "Enough," the word grated from between his lips.

He pulled away suddenly, pulled her to her feet, and kissed her with unrestrained desire.

"I need you," she muttered against his lips.

"Not yet," Haile replied.

She shivered when his fingers trailed down her hips then between her legs. He teased her pussy with slow, deliberate movements, and he barely grazed over her clit. Her body shuddered, and she gave in to the need clawing inside her. Mari spread her legs wider in anticipation of feeling his digits inside her.

"Please," Mari whispered. "I want your fingers inside me."

"Look at me, let me see you come," he ordered.

Her eyes opened instinctively on his command, and she got lost in his green gaze. With their gazes connected, Haile slid two fingers into her slick opening until he had it buried, and he used his thumb to slowly circle her clit. He kept the movements a gentle rhythm until she was trembling in his arms.

"You're driving me crazy," she cried out.

"You are so wet," he said. "Damn, you excite me."

He increased his pace and lowered his head to her upturned nipple and plucked it between his lips. Her head fell back in ecstasy at the combination of both sensations. She spread her legs wider, taking more of his fingers. With every breath she moaned as the coil of her orgasm tightened within him.

"Let me see you come for me, Dove." His voice was harsh with need.

Mari bit her lip and pumped against his hands as she reached the pinnacle of her bliss. She screamed as she fell into the pleasurable abyss. His fingers and hand were dripping with her juice, and it ran down her thighs. The sound he made was like the growl of a primal animal, and she trembled. Haile turned her around and bent her over the bar. He ran one hand around her waist and down the flat surface of her tummy to her pussy and teased her clit. Mari was already moaning in excitement as the fire was stoked anew. He used his knees to spread her legs, and she felt the tip of his cock against the entrance of her sex. Haile slowly slipped his cock into her until he was buried to the hilt before he grabbed her curvaceous hips and thrust again. His harsh cry blended with hers, and the gut wrenching need to find fulfillment took over. Mari's arms were braced against the bar, and she pushed back, meeting his penetrating thrusts. The gentleness and reservation that always seemed to be there was gone. This time Haile gave her pure, hot, dirty fucking, and she bloomed with enjoyment at every second of pleasure. The noises they made were raw and guttural, and the sound of their bodies connecting was wet and carnal.

"Oh yes, yes, yes, Haile," Mari chanted as he took her.

The orgasm that took hold of her shook her to her core, and the intensity of it made her knees give out. Haile held on to her tight and continued to fuck her in a rhythm that reminded her of the ocean waves as they hit the beach. Her pleasure continued, and her pussy clenched around his cock.

"Come for me, Haile," Mari gasped. "I want every last drop."

"Oh my God, Marisol," he moaned.

She could hear his breathing behind her, the agonized groan that escaped his lips while he fucked her. Her plea pushed him over the edge, and his hot seed spilled inside her while she undulated against him until they slumped against the bar. They stayed in that position for long minutes until Haile moved just enough to turn her in his arms to kiss her.

"I can never look at this bar the same," Haile teased.

"You? I have to work here every night." Mari smiled. "If Mr. Moore knew what we did here..."

"He'd order another pint and ask if we cleaned up." Haile laughed. "Which we should. Let's go upstairs and grab a hot shower, then come down here and make it spic and span."

"That's a very good plan," Mari said. "We can make hot chocolate when we get home and watch the news."

"Look at us being all homey and domestic." Haile kissed her hard.

"Mmmm, I could get used to this, very much so." She held his hand as they walked up the stairs.

He moved until he was pressed against her back and kissed her shoulder. "Me too."

They'd had their first argument and made up in the most pleasurable way. She'd found her second chance at life and given up the ghosts of her past. Her eyes were set firmly on the future. Good times or bad, she wanted that with Haile. They hadn't said the words yet, but she loved him, and it didn't take a declaration to know he felt the same way.

Chapter Eight

Getting around on her own was definitely easier now that she could drive. Haile took her to their version of a car lot. a.k.a. buying from someone who put a notice in the local paper about selling their car. It put a dent of two thousand pounds out of the savings she was collecting. But there was no need for an apartment now since she was moving in with Haile. Having her own mode of transportation was still as important as her independence. No matter what happened with them in the future, she couldn't give up that part of herself. She made Haile promise she would be able to keep her job or even find a better one without him making a fuss. She knew he'd pull a man thing about being able to provide for them both. It wasn't a matter of that; it was a feeling of self-worth, of earning her own way.

Mari was smiling when she left his house all bundled up for a cold day. She slipped behind the wheel of her new-to-her PT cruiser and headed toward the Celtic Cross. She would be opening with the servers today, and Haile had some work he needed to take care of for a friend. She could tell, he still either worked for the military or did some kind of contract work. There was an air of danger about when he said he was "helping out a friend" or "business to take care of." Eventually they would have to talk about it if they were planning on sharing a life.

But at that moment it wasn't the most important discussion to have. Telling him to be careful was her way of letting him know she understood and to come home safe. She took in the place she now called home. She liked to crack the windows and let a bit of the cool air in, and the scent of fresh bread from the corner deli bakery wafted in as well. The coffee shop had been brewing their dark roast coffee, and the kids in uniforms were walking to school on groups. Mr. Jones was opening the butcher shop, and Mrs. Lovell was sweeping the sidewalk outside of her little antique shop.

Mari sighed in contentment. Everything felt perfect in her world, even when Haile told her Marcus had gotten on a flight back to the United States with a few broken fingers. She certainly didn't feel sorry for the man who had turned her life into chaos for years. Putting that nasty thought aside, she focused on the future as she parked and went inside the pub. Mrs. H was already in the kitchen, making the back smell nice with Irish stew and chopping beef for her shepherd's pie. Elle and Macy were sitting on the bar wrapping utensils.

"Hey guys," Mari called as she hung up her coat. "I'll come out and get the bar set up in a few, I just gotta get the computers on in the office."

"Sure thing," Elle said with a smile.

They were her friends now. Actual friends who wanted to get together and do things like shop and have girl's night. She stepped into the kitchen and kissed Mrs. H on the cheek and gave her a squeeze on her way through as well.

"I do love those hugs of yours," Mrs. H said with a chuckle.

"You've cornered the market on them, you get as many as you want." Mari smiled.

"Now that's a sweet little lie. I'm sure Haile gets more than I," Mrs. Humphrey teased and handed her a paper. "That's my deliveries from yesterday. The raspberries were rotted, I made them take that shite back. They deducted it from the final cost and will replace them today for free."

"I'm sure you gave them hell," Mari said as she left the kitchen.

In the office she sat down and got the computer booted up. Mari checked the invoices from the shipments that had come in and added in Mrs. H's kitchen shipment. She opened a new spreadsheet for the receipts and was ready to head back to the bar when her cell phone rang. It wasn't a number she recognized, but since she was applying for permanent residency in the U.K. she made sure to answer any calls that came in.

"Hello?" She made sure her voice was sweet and pleasant.

"You sound like strawberries and cream." Jeffery's voice made her skin crawl.

"Why are you calling me," Mari snapped. "Wasn't your wife coming in here trying to make a scene enough for you."

"Listen lover…."

"Don't ever call me that." Mari hoped her voice conveyed the disgust she felt.

"Well then." Jeffery's voice changed. "Listen, I may have caused a bit of trouble."

"Only a bit? That's putting it mildly," she answered.

"Will you shut up for just a minute?" His tone took on a hint of panic. "Joslyn, she isn't letting it go. I may have saved another woman's number under your name, and now she is fixated on you."

Mari pulled the phone away from her face to look at it in amazement for a moment. "Well, you better cure her of that notion really quick. I don't want anything to do with you or her."

"It's not so easy. When Joslyn gets this way, she can be dangerous," Jeffery explained.

"I doubt that she is the dangerous one. Stop trying to cover your ass by blaming things on your wife," Mari defended the woman. "She may be a bitch and gullible as hell, but for some reason she loves you. You're a cheat and a liar, and that woman has been out through hell because of you. Be a good husband and not a sickening man."

"Listen, if you see her be careful…"

Mari cut him off. "No, I won't be cruel. She has suffered abuse even though you didn't put your hands on her. If I see her I'm going to talk to her and let her know you have nothing I want."

"Don't be daft, I'm trying to warn you…"

"Bye, Jeffery. Do not call me again, next time I'll tell Haile."

She disconnected the call amidst his jabbering and as she stood, shoved it in the pocket of her jeans. Mari put Jeffery's call out of her mind and went back to her task at hand. She got the bar ready for opening and helped Elle and Macy get tables set and ready for the lunch crowd. Worrying about Joslyn was not one of her concerns. A woman like that would believe her man was the one being chased and not the other way around, and nothing could change their minds. Still, she wouldn't be mean because emotional abuse was just as bad as physical. Eventually

Joslyn would see she was not the threat. There were too much positives in her life to be mired down by anyone else's negativity.

His private work was taking much longer than expected. Jasper knew his life as well as Mac and a few others. When bad things happened, they had a type of network of resources if necessary. Right now, Mac had a client who needed his special brand of services: they needed to disappear and fast. That meant travel papers and a few other necessities and for Mac to travel as well. His friend seemed a little deeper involved with this new client, but it wasn't his place to say a thing. They had each other's back and support.

It was well past two when he finally closed down his private computer network after transferring everything that Mac needed funds wise. A courier sent by Jasper had already picked up the rest and would transport them to the United States directly to Mac's hands. The lunch rush would be over, and there would be a few hours before the evening crowd came in. Maybe he could take Mari down to the market for a bite to eat other than pub food. Not to insult Mrs. H's excellent cooking, but sometimes they needed a bit of pasta or a fresh salad. Haile picked up his keys and was on his way to the pub when a frantic knocking on his front door made him move toward it with purposeful strides. On the other side of the barrier stood a very frazzled Jeffery and every alarm bell in his head went off.

"You've got some nerve showing up at my door," Haile snarled.

Jeffery held up his hand. "Listen mate..."

"I'm not your fucking mate." Haile clenched his hand at his sides. "Get the fuck away from my door."

"Haile, please listen to me, please," Jeffery implored.

Maybe it was the way he said it or the complete fear in his eyes. Or the way he said his name, but Haile decided to listen.

"Say your piece," Haile snapped.

Jeffery looked around. "Not at the door, please let me come in."

Haile stepped back silently, and the man rushed past him. Having the man he blamed for Angela's disappearance in his home was disconcerting, to say the least.

"It's Joslyn. I fear she has gone... Joslyn has never been well," Jeffery tried to explain.

Haile sighed impatiently. "What are you going on about, man?"

"Joslyn—I think she may have gone after Mari," Jeffery said in a rush. "She's had tunnel vision on the girl from the time she showed up on our doorstep. Then, I'm sorry, but I had my mistress's number saved under Mari's name."

"The mistress as in the woman you go to so she can beat you across the balls and all that nonsense," Haile surmised.

Jeffery sighed in frustration. "That is not the point. Joslyn thinks that Mari and I are still involved, and I'm afraid of what she will do. She has the propensity to be rather violent when she... I don't want her to do the same thing she did to..."

"To?" Haile questioned. When Jeffery didn't answer, Haile grabbed him by the shoulders and shook him. "To whom, Jeffery?"

"To Angela," Jeffery whispered the words as if saying them would unleash some kind of horror he couldn't imagine facing. "I can't prove it for sure, I never could, but the things she says... I loved her you know—Angela. That part is true, more than anyone realized. But Joslyn, I never knew that she wouldn't let me go without a fight."

"You're saying that Joslyn is the one who caused Angela's disappearance?" Haile asked sharply. "Why should I believe you?"

Jeffery looked up at him, and tears leaked from his eyes. "Because she was sunshine in my life, and the night she went missing I was waiting for her in Ireland. We were going to run away together, we were going to have children and a family. You can check the Irish Rose bed and breakfast. I was there waiting until the next morning. I thought when she didn't come that she had changed her mind. It was only when I came home I heard she was missing."

"Then why didn't you say that when you were questioned?" Haile asked. "Why did you and your wife taunt me and mine all these years?"

"I told Joslyn I was with my mum, and she confirmed it up to the day she died," Jeffery answered. "If I said where I was, Joslyn would know and my mom was right when she said, that woman would will kill me one of these days. She'd taunt me, sing a little song she made up about the lady with red hair who tried to breathe under water or the claws of death around her neck. Joslyn would sing it as a lullaby to the baby when he was born. Then she would say if daddy ever speaks of it everyone would die, even the baby in the basket. I took it as she would kill us all, and call me anything you want but I wouldn't let her hurt my child."

Haile was trying to wrap his mind around everything Jeffery was saying but still there were more questions. "Then why be on a dating site with Mari and other women? Why the mistress?"

"I wanted to run away to the United States with our son and start a new life," Jeffery admitted. "Mari didn't know any of this, and hell, in my own crazy way I thought her coming here would work, and we could leave with her. Her life in Texas was not the best, but I thought we would move to a different state. I just had to convince her. That went off the rails and the mistress… We all handle our pain in a different way."

Haile ran his hands through his hair. "And now you think Joslyn has gone after Mari?"

"She's not at the house, Haile." Jeffery looked up at him. "I went to the market so I could call Mari to warn her. She told me off, told me if I called again she would tell you and hung up. The baby was home alone when I came home, crying with no one there. I took him to the neighbors and thought about what Mari said, so I came directly to you. You are her protector, the man she loves. You can get through to her and keep Joslyn away."

"Mari is fine. She is at the pub working, and I'm heading there now," Jeffery said. "Go get your son and meet me there. You'll have to repeat all this to the authorities."

"I didn't do anything to hurt Angela, I hope you see this now," Jeffery said hopefully.

"Don't look for redemption from me, she was lost to us because of you," Haile said angrily.

"Can you fault me, fault us, for falling in love?" Jeffery asked. "Look at you and Mari now, would you say the same thing if you were in that position?"

Haile couldn't answer. Instead he pulled his cell from his pocket and found Mari's number in the list before pressing to connect the call. His heart jumped when she didn't answer, but he knew sometimes she left her phone in the office while she worked. He called the phone behind the bar, and Macy answered.

"Hello Macy, is Mari in the office?" Haile tried to keep his tone casual.

"Boss, boss you have to come to the pub," Macy said in a frantic whisper.

"What's going on?" Haile heard the sharpness of his tone.

"That lady from last time, the fancy one." Macy's voice held doubt. "She came in just as the last of the lunch crowd left and asked for Mrs. H and Mari. Ellie went and got them. I was taking dishes back, and I heard a scream. Mr. Haile... I-I peeked, and she has a gun. I came to the office to call the constable, but you called first."

"Macy, stay in the office, lock the door," Haile commanded. His heart began to race and without a doubt his instincts knew from what Jeffery said they were in serious trouble. "I'll call the constables and explain the situation so they know not to rush in. Stay in there and do not come out."

"I won't, I promise, please hurry, she doesn't look right." Macy began to cry.

Macy hung up, and Haile stared at the phone

silently until Jeffery's voice broke through the silence.

"Joslyn is at the pub, isn't she," Jeffery asked.

Haile took his keys. "You come with me. I'll be damned if being associated with you causes a second person I love their life."

The dismay in Jeffery's voice was evident and real. "I didn't mean for any of this to happen."

"It doesn't matter at this point, she has at least three people at gun point." Haile looked at him and asked, "Did she ever say or taunt you on where she took Angela?"

"No, never," Jeffery replied.

"You think about it hard, Jeffery, and even the smallest thing can help." Haile opened the door to usher him out. "I won't be losing Marisol, do you understand? Not ever."

Haile wished he'd told Mari he loved her. He should have said it every day since the day he held her in his arms. From that day he knew that this was the woman who would hold his heart for the rest of his life. Yet he didn't say it. Haile opened the door and strode out with determination, not even looking back to see if the door was locked or not. He was already calling Jasper to tell him everything he learned and next would be the authorities. His new mission was to get them out of harm's way. Marisol was the love of his life, the lady to his lord, and by damn he would fight the devil to keep her.

Chapter Nine

They all sat at one table where Joslyn could watch them. Mari only focused on the gun that Joslyn held in her hand. When Elle came back to get them, she had no clue what Joslyn's agenda was. Macy was passing by with a tray of plates when they walked through to the front of the bar. Macy stayed back there, Mari hoped she saw and was calling for help. Without a word being passed between they never mentioned her name. Mari couldn't even reach for her phone to call Haile. Joslyn watched them silently with cold, shrewd eyes.

"Well Joslyn, are we just going to sit here with a gun pointed at our heads all day?" Mrs. H snapped.

"Don't antagonize her," Mari said softly because she knew that look.

It was a person who had lost all hope, and she'd seen it in the mirror a few times. But there was more behind the dark eyes of Joslyn Moermond. Insanity, and Mari had seen that as well.

"She bloody well either shoot me or let me get back to my work," Mrs. H said with no fear in her voice.

"You've always been a crazy old woman," Joslyn finally said.

Mrs. H snorted. "Well isn't that the pot calling the kettle black."

"Why are you doing this?" Mari asked.

"Because you won't leave my husband alone!" Joslyn screamed at them.

"Okay, calm down," Mari said gently. "Joslyn…"

"Mrs. Moermond to you," she said stiffly.

Mari gritted her teeth, she wanted to slap the woman silly. "Fine, Mrs. Moermond, you can check my phone. I have not received any calls from your husband since our initial meeting. I'm with Haile we are happy and in love."

"You sure are getting around," Joslyn said with disgust. "Did Jeffery tell you there is no way he will leave me? No money to be had and you moved on."

"Jesus Christ," Mari muttered.

"It's like talking to a brick wall," Mrs. H said with frustration. "Listen, Joslyn, and there is no way in this world I'm calling you Mrs. Moermond when I saw you buck naked in your mum's house as a baby. No one wants Jeffery, that spineless twit, and here you are ready to go to jail for him."

"Someone wanted him," Joslyn said gently, the smile was bright. "But I took care of it. That redhead didn't stand a chance and neither will this one."

"Oh my god, say you didn't," Mrs. Humphrey's gasped in dismay.

"Do you mean Angela?" Mari asked, and Joslyn just smiled. "Answer me, damn it, did you hurt Haile's sister?"

The sharpness of Mari's tone seemed to snap Joslyn back to reality. Her hand tightened around the gun she pointed in their direction. Elle clutched Mari's arm, and Mari tried to comfort her by patting her arm gently.

"You don't get to ask me those questions, you little slut," Joslyn snapped.

"Then I do." Mrs. H stood up. "Joslyn, pet... tell me what you did."

"She wouldn't stop, and then I found out the plan—oh there was a plan," Joslyn said and sing-songed, "They were trying to sneak away, like little dormice. Then I would be left in shame, I rather think not. So I sent her a message to meet me, or should I say Jeffery, at the house first."

Mrs. H voice cracked with sadness as she sat down. "Oh no, Joslyn."

"Don't you dare pity me!" Joslyn's back went straight and angry tears fell down her face. "He is mine. How dare she try to break up my marriage? When she came and saw it was me, she almost left... almost. I told her I wanted to talk like women, Jeffery was free to choose her if he so wished. I offered her tea, and after a few sips she got sleepy. Her eyes... she looked at me and knew before she went unconscious. Then it was so easy to put the pillow on her face until there was nothing."

"Dear God," Mari whispered. "You killed her."

"It was the only choice, can you see that," Joslyn implored. "She was going to take my life, my dreams, and make them her own. Not from me, no fisherman's daughter was going to best me."

"Where did you take her?" Mari asked gently. Mrs. H had broken down into tears after Joslyn told them what she did.

"She's at home," Joslyn smiled. "She wanted my life too much. I let her stay in the place where she tried to take my husband. Oh, don't cry Mrs. Humphrey, you soft old bird, she went peacefully."

"She was young and naïve, and you killed her," Mrs. Humphrey cried out. "I knew you were a broken child, but my God, I can't comprehend the extent of your madness."

"So now you plan to kill me, Mrs. H, and Elle?" Mari asked. "We all heard your confession, and we can't tell the police about it?"

"I haven't thought that far ahead yet," Joslyn admitted. "This was just about you, now there is more..."

"No one is getting hurt. Not today." Haile's voice came from the door.

Joslyn whirled, and the gun was pointed at his chest instead of them. Mari was more afraid seeing him in danger than when the weapon was trained on her. Jeffery stepped in front of Haile and held up his hands.

"Joslyn, what are you doing?" he asked.

"Protecting us, protecting my family, the same way I always do because you won't, Jeffery," Joslyn snapped. "Now come over here, be a good boy."

"You need to put the gun down," Jeffery said. "Right now!"

Joslyn laughed. "Look at you trying to be all manly. Try that later maybe."

Mari looked at Haile. "She killed Angela."

The last of the hope in his eyes died away even though he already knew within himself that she was gone. There had been faith that maybe a miracle would happen. That spark of faith left, and the grief was evident on his face.

"I see that now, Dove." Haile's voice was husky.

"You killed her." Jeffery's voice was broken. "Why, damn you, why?"

"Because you loved her!" Joslyn screamed. "Why couldn't you love me like that? I saw all the notes, all the letters. I gave you everything, so it's damn you because it's your fault."

"Normal people fall out of love," Jeffery raged. "But you're not normal, are you, Joslyn? I loved you, and then I was scared of you, and now I'm terrified. You are not right in the head. You killed someone, a person I loved... You should have killed me as well."

"Why would I do that?" Joslyn asked. "It was so much better watching you suffer. She was under your nose all this time, in our house, in that chest in the attic my mum gave me. All this time she has been there wrapped up, tucked in tight, snug as a bug, and you never knew."

Joslyn's laugh was crazed, and with an angry cry, Jeffery rushed at her. That took her by surprise as they wrestled for the gun, and Haile took the advantage to grab her hand and pry her fingers from around it. Joslyn screamed angrily, but she was disarmed, and Jeffery held her as she struggled. Haile went to the door, and soon the pub was flooded with police. They took Joslyn into custody, and while they handcuffed her, she looked at Jeffery.

"Don't let them take me, you love me Jeffery, help me," Joslyn pleaded.

"I'll make sure you get the help you need," Jeffery promised. "But you killed the woman I love... I-I can't help."

"Elle, go back and give Macy the all clear," Haile said to the other waitress and with a nod Elle rushed through the service door. Haile pulled Mari into his arms and hugged her tight before looking over at Mrs. H. "Are you okay Dottie?"

"I'm just fine." Mrs. H patted his shoulder. "At least we have the truth now."

Haile swallowed. "Now we can lay her to rest."

"I'm going behind that bar and make a stiff one." Mrs. H walked away muttering, "Not every day I get held at gun point. The mister is going to love this."

"We're going to close for the rest of the day," Haile said. "Let the girls know. We've got enough of a crowd outside that everyone will have the gossip in an hour why."

"I'm so sorry about Angela, Haile," Mari said gently.

"I blamed the wrong one for all these years." Haile's sigh was heavy. "Can I hold him culpable for loving my sister? I've spent so much time hating him, and now I don't... I have to figure out what to do, how to feel."

"We bury and we mourn her, then you remember her as the person she was before all this." Mari cupped his cheek.

"Can I tell you what scared me the most?" Haile asked.

Mari shook her head. "Yes."

"The thought that I could lose you before I ever said I love you," Haile said huskily.

"I knew," Mari replied. "And I love you too, so much my heart aches."

Haile smiled. "Then we're going to stop the pretense, and you'll move in tonight."

She laughed. "Ah and there's the twist."

"Go on girl, I can win the betting pool if you do," Mrs. H said from behind the bar.

"Good grief, you people." Mari laughed and twined her arms around his neck. "I'll be with you forever so consider me calling this an address change."

"Let's finish this and go home," Haile said. "The hard part is yet to come."

"I'll be right by your side," Mari promised.

She laced her fingers with his, and they walked outside to where a crowd was looking around curiously. Joslyn sat in the back of the police car with her head down, and Jeffery spoke with the police officer.

"We need to go to your house," Haile said bluntly.

Jeffery nodded and fell into step with them. It was completely disconcerting being with the man she loved and the man who initially made him come to Northumberland. Still, they shared something: they both loved Angela. It was time to bring her home. They waited outside Jeffery's house until the police arrived. Jasper came too and again a slew of onlookers. Jeffery led them to the attic where like Joslyn said a large chest sat in the corner near the wall.

The room was cool, and when the chest was

opened, they saw thick blankets and long locks of red hair. Haile turned away and swallowed thickly while Jeffery broke down in tears. Angela had been found. The entire chest was removed, and they found out after the autopsy that because of the atmosphere in the room she was preserved in almost a mummified state. Nothing could stave off the loss that Haile must be feeling but she would be there to help him heal. That was what love did, a balm that soothed even the worst hurt.

Angela was laid to rest one week later beside her parents while they watched. It was a surprisingly warm day with blue skies that belied the season and the morning fog that usually hung low over Northumberland. Everyone who worked at the pub was there. Jasper and Zeva, with baby Abigail, stood beside Mari and Haile. Jeffery, who was also in attendance, was holding his son and tears trickled down his cheeks. Haile was starting to see that the man he hated for so many years had truly loved Angela. And that love caused her death. Haile still held some resentment on that fact but maybe he would learn to cope.

Joslyn was charged with Angela's murder, but because of her declining mental stability she was in a mental hospital. There was no doubt after the trial that was where she would be for the rest of her life. She tried to kill herself and was basically strapped to a bed. This was the end of Joslyn Moermond's public life. He wondered if Joslyn had been given help at an early age if she would be free and Angela would be alive. There were a lot of maybes, but the outcome right now was to move on with life and let Angela's memory be one of the smiling girl with red hair dancing in the sunshine.

That night, after all was said and done, people had come by, eaten, paid their condolences and left, and now it was just him and Mari sitting in front of the fire, watching the flames, and listening to the wood crackle. There was something he had to do, had wanted to do the night Joslyn decided to take the Celtic Cross hostage and Angela's body was finally found. Things had gone in a different direction then, interviews with police, funerals, and reporters coming around. Even making some kind of peace with Jeffery. This was the perfect time. To end the day with some kind of happiness, and he felt in his bones the time was right.

"I'm going to make some hot chocolate, want some?" Mari asked.

"Sounds delicious, add some brandy in mine," Haile replied. "Oh, and some cheese, crackers, and some fruit would also be nice."

"Geez, I thought I only worked at the pub," Mari teased as she bent to kiss him. "I'll get you your snacks, a.k.a. nibbles."

"It's one or the other, sweetheart, not both," Haile called after her.

"Let me live my life!" she shouted from the hall.

"I don't even know what that means, her life has nothing to do with snacks," Haile murmured and shook his head.

He pulled the ring box from his pocket with a grin and dimmed the room lights so the fireplace was the most light, giving it an intimate setting. He waited until he heard her boots on the hardwood floor to get on one knee facing the door. The light of the fireplace danced off the diamond in the ring and when she stepped inside the room, Mari stopped in the tracks. Her face registered surprise, and Mari's gaze settled on him bent on one knee. Her smile was gentle, and the love he saw on her face almost took his breath away. She came inside and set the tray on the coffee table before turning to him.

"What's all this?" Mari asked in a shaky voice.

"Sit down, Dove," Haile said huskily. When she did, he reached out and cupped her cheek. "I love you."

"I love you too," she whispered.

"I think I'll be saying that to you every day for the rest of our lives. I think it was fate that I saw you that night. I was enamored by your beauty, then your strength as I got to know you. Your love and your passion consume me, and I cannot imagine a day in my life without you in it. Marisol, marry me. It's only been a few months, I understand that, but it feels like a lifetime. Share my life with me, and I promise there will not be a day I won't cherish you."

"The answer is yes." Mari grinned. "I'd marry you quicker than a chicken on a June bug."

"A chicken and what?" Haile asked, confused.

"Never mind that." Mari held out her hand. "The answer is yes."

Haile slipped the ring on her finger and kissed her thoroughly.

Mari sighed. "Loving you is sweeter than stolen honey."

"I like that one." Haile laughed. "Are you happy, Dove? Are you sure this is what you want?"

She tugged at his hand. "Get up here, Lord Haile Buchannan." When he sat next to her, she took his hand and kissed his palm. It was a gesture that humbled him, and she placed another kiss on his lips. "You already fill me with a joy that I can't explain. I feel it when I wake up and see you lying next to me and all through the day until we go to bed. I love you, and I am your lady, now, forever, and till death do us part."

"That makes you three times my lady," he teased.

"Ugh, so corny, but I get it." Mari laughed. "Now come on. Our liquored up hot chocolate and snacks, a.k.a. nibbles, await."

"It's one or the other, not both," he pointed out.

"Let me live my life," Mari repeated.

He kissed her again. "As long as you share it with me, you live your life, Dove."

By the light of the fireplace, they shared the food, and he noted more than once that Mari looked at the ring, as if she didn't believe it was real. They'd have to plan a wedding quickly because he wanted her to be his wife as soon as they could find a priest to marry them. Who cares if he didn't win the bet, he'd found a priceless treasure in the love he shared with his Marisol. Besides, Mrs. H probably had the thing lock, stock, and barrel anyway. The thought made him chuckle as he pulled Mari into his arms, and they stared into the flames dancing in the hearth.

The End

The Bride of MacKenzie Black

Chapter One

"Mac! Mac, are you listening to me?" the voice came over the line, causing him to focus.

"Yes, I am," Mac answered even though he was focused on the computer screen in front of him.

"You're bloody well not," Haile said hotly. "Can you get it or not, I want to give Mari a piece of home for Christmas?"

"Uh-huh," Mac said and continued typing. "Home, gotcha."

"Damn it . . ." Haile was starting to get even more irritated.

"It's done, and the package will be at your house well before Christmas Eve," Mac said suddenly.

Haile sighed. "Thanks, mate."

"You should never doubt my powers," Mac said with pride in his voice. "Mari should be married to me, not to you."

"Ha ha, very funny," Haile said. "Are you coming home for Christmas this year?"

Just the thought tied Mac's stomach in knots. "Maybe . . . doubtful . . . no."

Haile sighed. "I'm sure your mum would like to see you."

"She didn't care when I left, so that doesn't sound like her," Mac answered.

"A lot has changed—"

Mac interrupted him. "A lot hasn't."

"Jasper and Zeva would actually like for you to meet their baby," Haile shot back.

"I get videos frequently," Mac answered. "Haile, no one wants me in Northumberland."

"Damn it, we do," Haile said fiercely. "And anyone who says otherwise don't fucking matter."

"Easy for you to say, Lord Haile—and Jasper is a Duke," Mac said. "To everyone I was just your lower-class friend who used his fists instead of his block head."

"That's bullshit, and you know it," Haile said fiercely. "A damn title or lack of one didn't make you any less than us. We love you, man; you're our brother."

"I know that," Mac sighed. "Let me think on it, okay?"

"That's usually a no," Haile grumbled. "You'll do what you want."

"My general disposition," Mac smiled. "Kiss the lovely Lady Marisol for me, and tell her the gift is from me."

"I will do neither," Haile replied teasingly. "Stop trying to steal my wife! Get your own."

"But taking yours would be so much more fun," Mac chuckled.

"Ha ha—ha— and goodbye."

Mac grinned as he hit the disconnect button on his cell, but soon his thoughts grew somber. *Going home to Northumberland?* Hell, he hadn't been there in ten years, and he didn't see a reason to go back. Leaving under a cloud of suspicion and with bruised knuckles. His mother didn't try to stop him, because she wanted him far away from his younger brother. It didn't matter about his truth, only how the residents of Northumberland saw her. Helen Black liked to put on airs where none should be, and because his friends had titles she would parade around the markets and shops with her nose in the air.

So of course, him being in trouble didn't sit right with her plans at all—and then the incident that almost landed him in jail had sent his mother off the deep end. It was easier to relocate to the United States, where he had built his business from scratch. Mac had made a good life for himself in D.C., and the respect his mother craved was now his, away from his home. He was called on to protect everyone from politicians to priests, and his security systems were custom-made. He had installations across the globe. Why should he go back to a place that saw him as some boy in the streets when he was respected for who he was in D.C.? He told his friend maybe, but Mac knew it was more than likely not going to happen. Northumberland held nothing for him, not anymore.

With the fall back in time, the sky darkened quickly, so by the time Mac stepped out of his office to head out into the cold city all sunlight had been extinguished. It had snowed in early November and probably would again before December rolled around. It was D.C. The wind had a bite to it now that winter had truly settled in.

He went home for a quick shower and then went on a date that ended up going nowhere. It wasn't like he wanted to take her home and fuck her, but Leslie had no wit, no fun, no personality whatsoever. She was the type who wanted to be a staunch politician's wife on the camera with a smile that never gave her eyes any warmth. Mac made a mental note to never accept another set-up from any of his associates, by the time the date was over. He considered docking Alex's holiday bonus; why did he think Mac and Leslie were a fit? He actually breathed a sigh of relief when he was in bed and blessedly alone.

Mackenzie Black! Brawler in the streets of Northumberland, come on down. You're next up to play "Is he worthy to leave?"

The dream had him in a man-made ring of old crates and bags of feed down on the docks. He stood in the center of the ring and was already covered in bruises with his knuckles torn, but still he raised his fists ready to fight. He was going to be free of this place one way or the other.

"Once you're in, you can't ever leave, Mac, you know that," Quinn sneered and swung at Mac with a pipe.

He was the one who had brought Mac into the gang at seventeen and who'd vowed to take care of him like he was his son. Mac punched at the thick frame in front of him. He was almost like a brother to Mac, but that changed quickly. Quinn was older and built like a bulldog with a thick middle and a neck that seemed to throw up his bald head. Mac fought for his life, taking every hit of the metal pipe to his ribs, but still he took Quinn down.

Standing over his body, Mac raged thought no more breath was left in his body. "Who's next? I'll fight all of you. I'll take all you fuckers on!"

The dialect he'd tried to hide came out, the smooth, posh, English accent replaced with the harsh gutter talk of a boy who had lived on the wrong side of town. His mother stepped up, and she held out her hands covered with blood as she looked at him with dark, vicious eyes.

"Look what you did, his blood is on your hands!" she screamed at him. *"Donnie . . . is . . . my . . . baby!"*

"Ma, I left," Mac implored. "I left so he wouldn't try to follow me."

"You should've just played with the young Duke and we'd be just fine," she sneered. "He'd take care of us."

"I don't need to live off the charity of others, I made my bloody own," Mac raged. "It's good enough for me to send to you each month, innit Ma?"

"They've got him, they got my baby boy," she fell to her knees and he saw his brother in the corner behind her, broken and bloody.

"I left, Ma, so he could be safe, I . . . LEFT!" Mac raged. "You were supposed to take care of him, not me. It was your job!"

She screamed at him, raged, told him he was never good enough to be her son and that she wished she had another true son. Then, in the dream, Quinn got up and all the demons of Mac's past appeared and surrounded him, trying to beat him down. Yet Mac fought; through the sweat and blood in his eyes, he punched and swung even though no more breath was in his body.

It was then that Mac woke up, gasping for air, fighting the darkness of his bedroom, while in the background, he heard a constant buzzing. He fought the last vestiges of the nightmare and focused on the noise, finally understanding that the sound was his phone. He looked at the readout and saw Jasper's number, and he just knew something was wrong.

"Jasper," he said his name and nothing more.

"Mac, it's your mother, she had a stroke," Jasper said without sugarcoating it. "It's pretty bad."

"Where's Donnie?" Mac asked.

Jasper hesitated. "I don't know. Haile has been trying to find him in the usual places, but so far nothing."

"Okay, I'll be there . . . and Jasper, thanks," Mac hung up and lay back with his forearm across his eyes.

"Shit!"

The word burst out of him, and he felt like someone was squeezing his heart. It seemed regardless of what Mac wanted he was going to Northumberland after all.

He looked out into the world that he wished he could forget but loved more than anything: home. Mac could recall every scent in the drive through the streets of Northumberland from the train station. The rooster hadn't even crowed yet, and the sun was only a sliver of light on the horizon. The window of the Land Rover was cracked, and he could smell the scent of hot cross buns fresh at the bakery, the first hints as they got coffee ready for the early customers who would be in by six-thirty. When you worked on the docks, clocking in could be five am or before. Soon the men and women would be coming out in thick sweaters over the suspenders that held up leather high waders to process fish that had come in on the boats only an hour or so earlier. He was meant to be one of those men, his lot in life his father had said. His mother wanted him to pretend he was like his friends Jasper and Haile. The latter was now driving him home.

Christmas was definitely in the air. The car passed the square where the tree sat in the bowl of the fountain. It boasted the unique ornaments crafted by the local shops and artisans, with fresh garland and poinsettias used like bows and streamers. The lights were made by local glass-blowers and electricians. The wooden star, Mac knew, was carved by Jasper; it was used to cover a light while the star-shaped holes let the light out. It was simple but elegantly beautiful. The streetlamps held the various holiday light fixtures: a candle, the nativity scene, holly, and mistletoe. The shops all had their windows decorated for Christmas. Although it was nothing like New York or D.C., it was more beautiful than he remembered: quaint, cozy. It felt so good to be home, and at the same time, he felt like he was choking and wanted to escape.

"Where's Ma got a bed at?" Mac grimaced and cleared his throat. "I mean which hospital is she a patient of?"

"I know what you meant, been most of the places you grew up, Mac," Haile said gruffly. "She's at Queen Charlotte's, Jasper pulled some strings and got her off the ward into a private room."

"I'll pay for it when I get there," Mac said. "Any word on Donnie?"

"Bouchey's got him," Haile said without hesitation. "We'll have to go get him."

"He'll want money." Mac's voice was flat. "If Bouchey's holding him, Donnie's got a debt."

"You going to pay him off?" Haile asked.

Mac shook his head. "You know he wants money and favors and if he gets it, it won't stop there. I won't be held over a barrel by that man again. No, I go in and get him."

"You mean *we*," Haile corrected. "You've been gone for a long time, Mac. He's changed his operation up big-time, and he's got some muscle who doesn't mind putting a man in the grave."

"He can try," Mac said gruffly. "The apartment over the bar empty so I can sleep after we see Ma?"

Haile cleared his throat. "Um no, Marisol has rented it out to a girl from Barbados who relocated here from London. She's a nurse at the hospital and works at Zeva's center helping the women there as well."

"It's okay, I can get a hotel," Mac answered. "I'll have to find someplace to put Donnie up until I can figure out what to do with him to keep him out of trouble."

"Donnie is an adult. If you get him out of this and he gets back into trouble, then it's on him," Haile's voice was stiff, and Mac could tell he was pissed. "He walks around being a braggart, strutting like some rooster with nothing he's earned. He spends the money you send your Ma and her pension, bringing all types into that flat. I wasn't supposed to tell you, but Zeva said your Ma has come in for food vouchers more than once."

"That little . . . " Mac clenched his fist and took a deep breath. Donnie's main concern shouldn't be Bouchey at that point because Mac was surely thinking about killing his brother for his utter bullshit. "I send more than enough that Ma doesn't need assistance. Dad's pension wasn't a poor man's wage either."

"Gambling in Bouchey's places can get a man in debt in the blink of an eye, those games are rigged," Haile explained. "Your mother wouldn't call and tell you a thing because she still looks at Donnie and sees her baby."

"Plus, she knows I'd come and box him upside the head," Mac said. "Let's get this over with, where's Bouchey holding court lately?"

"That old duplex on Calvary is main office now, the basement is a gambling den, first floor, and he runs the books and lives upstairs." Haile made a sharp turn, and they headed down a dark street. "Let's try to get me home without a bruised face, shall we? Marisol will have my ass and yours if I show up looking like I was in a fight."

"Then fight dainty, Lord Haile," Mac grinned. "I'll go clean up at the hotel when we're done—and there's no one to care what my mug looks like."

"Oh, there is no hotel after this," Haile shot him a grin. "Zeva and Marisol would skin me alive; the cottage house at the manor has been prepared for you."

Mac sighed. "My ma always wanted me to live out there, guess she got what she wanted after all."

Haile grunted. "Listen, we all had a fucked-up life growing up. You know ours, and we know yours. I'll tell you what I learned. We cannot live with the demons they set upon us. Your father had you set for the docks and boxing until you beat your brain to mush. Your mum wanted you to be royalty by default, though we were by far the worst representations of our titles. You are here to make sure she is comfortable and to beat some sense into your brother. Mackenzie Black is who you are."

"Damn, have you opened up a therapy room in the bar?" Mac teased, trying to take the mood lighter. "Being married has changed yous."

"I'm taking you to the moors and leaving you there," Haile threatened.

The rest of the drive was made in comfortable silence, but Mac was mentally gearing up for a fight. Bouchey wouldn't let Donnie go without a fight, and that meant a part of him he'd buried had to be resurrected to get his brother out alive. He hoped he could break their spirit so they wouldn't come after his brother again. The dream was a premonition, and the bruiser was back in Northumberland. At least for now.

Chapter Two

The sloping roof of the duplex sat at the very end of the cul-de-sac of Calvary Road. Which meant there would be no quick exit and they would have to fight their way out and quickly get into the truck. It had to be quick because people would be getting up soon and any trouble would have witnesses. Not that people on Calvary talked to the police anyway, it was one of the streets in Northumberland that was known to have a bad element. Yet good people and families lived there. They didn't have much in the way of income and found a home in places they could afford. No one could fault them for working hard and expecting safety—even on Calvary Road. It was another reason he wanted this sorted out quickly. If he was any good at it, they would have Donnie and be gone before the first person stepped out for work.

Haile made sure to park by the abandoned house on the opposite side of the street. The streetlight had been shattered, which offered them extra protection from being seen. Mac looked up at the sky and saw the first hint of orange was spreading more. The sun would be rising soon. With that in mind, he gave Haile a look and a nod, and Haile reached under the seat to pull out an ancient Billy club. He tested the grip out in his hand. Haile must have felt Mac's gaze; when he looked over, Mac gave him a raised, questioning eyebrow.

"What? Sometimes the old ways work best, it's the only thing some of these guys understand," Haile said. "You need one?"

Mac shook his head. "I always found my fists worked best."

They crossed the street quickly, and instead of using the rusty gate they hopped the fence that was covered in ivy vines. He could still make out the red berries of holly mixed between the wooden slats of the fence in the early morning light. They had the short, long windows of the basement level covered in red tint so the police couldn't look inside. The music pulsed from downstairs, and he could make out the shadows of people still moving around in the room.

"The boys at the door went inside for a little action before they need to clear everyone out," Haile said in a low tone. "We need to get in that door, 'cos Bouchey won't be upstairs until the sun is up and the money is counted."

"Well then, we better knock and see who opens the door," Mac said grimly and bounded up the top steps to the second level entry.

Haile was right behind him as he knocked. "You have no finesse."

Mac smiled. "It was never my style."

The door was opened just a crack, and that was enough for Mac to use his large shoulders to muscle his way in. He cut off any sound the man would've made by clenching his fingers around the man's neck. Haile took the club to the other bodyguard's head and took him to the floor. Three more men came out, and they were dispatched just as quickly. At least two felt Mac's brutal punches, and when he threw them to the floor, they upset the table with stacks of cash. Mac saw a room with the door off its hinges and in the middle of the room his brother was tied to a chair.

Donnie had a swollen face and a few cuts, and his eyes widened when he saw Mac. Bouchey came out of the other room smoking a cigar casually and began watching him and Haile beat the hell out his men. Mac met his gaze and dropped the man nonchalantly as he assessed Bouchey. They'd grown up together, run in the same crowds, and now that Quinn was dead, Bouchey ran the underbelly that was Northumberland. Mac was supposed to be that man, but he had found that cheating and terrorizing innocent people did not suit him. Bouchey had gotten fat in the middle, but it was easy enough to see he still liked to do his own beatings. His knuckles had smears of blood on them; more than likely it was his brother's.

"Never thought I'd see the day Mackenzie Black is back in town," Bouchey's voice had gotten more nasal, more than likely a deviated septum from having his nose broken. "Lord Haile, you back consorting with the lower class again, I see?"

"Well, here I am, I came for Donnie," Mac answered. "Don't worry why Haile is here."

"Your brother owes a debt, you going to pay it?" Bouchey asked.

"No, I'm going to take him home," Mac watched his men groan and try to get up . . . slowly. "You or these idiots will not stop me."

"Oh, I might have some quarrel with that," Bouchey put down his cigar and clenched his fists.

"You really don't want to do that," Mac said in a deadly tone.

Bouchey laughed. "What? You went to America and got soft, while I had to fight my way up from the scraps under the table to take the meat off the plate. Let's see what you got, boy."

With a menacing sound that came from the back of his throat, Mac moved forward and his nemesis swung wide with a huge fist. Mac blocked him easily and delivered two solid punches to his torso that now felt like jelly from too much drinking and high living on other people's money. Mac heard Bouchey retch, but that didn't stop him from embarrassing the man in front of his people. By the time Mac was done, the man who'd held his brother was on the floor bleeding and Mac hadn't even broken a sweat. Mac raised his fist again, but Haile caught his arm.

"He's down, mate," Haile said bluntly.

Mac grabbed Bouchey by the front of his shirt and dragged him up. "I'm taking my brother, and not a penny will leave my pocket to be stuffed in yours. If you come after him again, you'll see how quickly I will respond. You want to see the bruiser come back, fuck with me and mine."

"You ready?" Haile asked as he came out of the room holding Donnie, and Mac let Bouchey fall to the ground in disgust.

"Yeah, let's go." Mac led the way, and when they stepped outside the sun had crested in the morning sky.

"Did Ma call you?" Donnie asked in excited gibberish. "Man, she must be pissed if she called you from America."

"Get in the truck," Mac ordered and shoved him in the back seat while he and Haile got in front.

"Ma must be pissed, I mean . . . I was just going to use the money to make us some more, Mac," Donnie stammered. "I never sent her for the food vouchers. . . . But we had to eat."

As Haile pulled away Mac leaned over and

grabbed Donnie. "You stupid . . . You're almost thirty damn years old and still acting the fool. Ma shouldn't be begging for food. I send enough, but you want to live a high life you don't want to earn."

Donnie looked at him wildly, and his eyes seemed to brighten. "You're the one who left, Mac, and then I had to take care of her. I could never live up to you in this bloody town. I had to strike out on my own . . . you never sent *me* money . . . "

"You struck out with Ma's only means of support, the money I sent, and Dad's pension?" Mac yelled. "I shouldn't have to send a grown man money. You're high right now or coming down off something real damn good. You should be in pain after the beating I know Bouchey put in your arse. But you're acting like you don't feel a thing."

"Mac," Donnie's voice cracked. "I know Ma called you, I'll do better, I won't take from her any-more."

Mac let Donnie go with a heavy sigh and turned to face the road. "Ma didn't call me, Donnie, she's in hospital. Ma had a stroke!"

"Oh God, oh God, it's my fault! I should've made sure she ate. . . . " Donnie's voice held agony, and Mac could see him put his head in his hands from the rearview mirror. Then he reached up suddenly and put his hand on Mac's shoulder. "Tell me she'll be okay, Mac, please!"

Mac never turned around, but he placed his hand on his brother's. "I hope so."

It was two weeks before Christmas, and his homecoming started out with a fight and now he was on the way to Queen Charlotte hospital to see if his mother would survive. The holidays always seemed to bring him trouble, and this was why he preferred to ignore it completely. Haile sped through the streets of Northumberland and the feeling of heaviness seemed to run from where his brother's hand was to his entire body. How could he fix what was broken in Donnie? Mac knew he'd built his career and life in D.C. to portray how he built himself up from nothing. But deep down inside he was just as fucked-up as everyone else.

He hated hospitals, the smell, the oppressive feel of them, and the pristine white walls. Not even the glass arboretum with its warmth and green, lush plants could alleviate the feeling of dread the hospital elicited in Mac. After quickly cleaning up Donnie the best they could in a bathroom, they headed to the third floor. Mac followed Haile's brisk pace while Donnie trailed slowly along, shuffling his feet. Mac had to clench his fist to keep from throwing an annoyed glance behind him. His mother always babied Donnie, and even at almost thirty he still acted like a child.

But Mac's heart skipped a beat for another reason as they drew closer to the main nurses' desk of the third floor. The nurse who looked up at Haile as he approached then smiled and stood. She was exquisite, in his opinion, with skin like a cappuccino whipped-coffee drink and lips so full, with a hint of lipstick, that he wanted to sample them. Her hair was pinned in a bun at the back, but a few long, loose curls framed her face underneath her nurse's cap. Her blue nurse's uniform hugged generous curves, and if you ever had a fantasy about a sexy nurse, it would be her. He knew when they were on the ward they dressed in formal uniforms and in the emergency department they wore scrubs. The nurse came around the desk and gave Haile a hug, which caused Mac to remember their new tenant at the pub.

"Nina Crane, this is Mackenzie Black and his brother Donnie Black. They are Helen's sons," Haile introduced them.

"Nice to meet you both." Her voice was sweet with a soft huskiness to it that only seemed to be accentuated by her accent, as she held out her hand to them both. She eyed Donnie, noting his bruises. "Does he need to be seen?"

"He should be fine," Mac answered. "Donnie got into a scrape."

"Mmm-hmmm," was her answer.

"How is my mother?" Mac asked, changing the subject.

She looked at him sadly. "Barely holding on, I'm sorry. I'll take you to the room and have the doctor come talk to you. We are not allowed to give treatment options or medical information without a physician present."

"No, you tell me," Mac demanded and then added, "Please."

Nina gave a quick nod. "Come with me, please."

They followed her to the room where his mother lay in the dim light looking completely frail in a bed that seemed too big for her. Gone was the bigger-than-life presence that could take over a conversation even if she put on airs. She'd lost so much weight, and he felt guilty knowing she was lying like she was due to Donnie's habits. But he spoke to her even if it was infrequently and she never mentioned . . . It was her pride, he knew it. Helen Black would never let anyone know she wasn't doing well, not even her son.

Nina started to speak. "Mr. Black . . ."

"Call me Mac," he interjected.

"Mac," she amended her words. "Your mother had a massive stroke that prevented oxygen from reaching her brain. We don't know how long she was home before her neighbor found her, so when the doctor administered a drug that could reverse some of the effects, it did not work, because it has to be given intravenously within the first two hours or it has no effect."

"Which means she was alone, on the ground, for hours before anyone found her," Mac surmised and cast an angry glare at his brother, who wouldn't come out of the corner. "So, what's the prognosis?"

"Your mother will not wake up, there is no brain function, no reaction to light or pain stimulation," Nina said.

"You hurt my mother!" Donnie rushed out of the corner, and his reaction caused a cry to escape from Nina, who jumped back startled.

"Sit your stupid ass down," Mac snarled and pushed him in a chair. He turned to Nina. "I'm sorry. He won't hurt you, I swear it, I am so very sorry."

Haile put a comforting hand on her shoulder. "He's just upset, Nina."

She nodded, but Mac saw the fear in her eyes, and it made him angry. After a deep breath she continued. "To alleviate your fears, what I meant by *pain stimuli* is that we basically do a pin prick at the bottom of her feet. If her brain had registered it, it would've caused a reaction, for we all shy away from pain or lights in our eyes. She had no reaction, and brain scans confirmed it."

"So, she's dead," Mac confirmed.

"I'm sorry, but essentially yes," Nina confirmed. "She never regained consciousness."

"But she's breathing," Donnie said weakly.

"The machines are doing that for her," Nina explained gently. "We are required to do that until the family decides what's the best course of action."

"Then let them breathe for her until she wakes up," Donnie had begun to cry.

"Donnie, she's never going to come out of this," Mac explained. "Ma never wanted to live like this."

"But how can I make it up to her if she's dead?" Donnie sat down and wiped his face. "I'll take care of her."

Mac bent down and put his hand on his brother's shoulders. "She's not there anymore, this is her shell being kept alive by machines." He turned his attention to nurse Nina. "Please get the doctor; we will sign the papers to have her removed from life support."

"I'll go get him right away," Nina said and hesitated at the door. "Again, I am so very sorry to have to be the bearer of bad news."

"You didn't do this," Mac said. "Thank you."

"But *I* did this, Mac. I should have been there instead of pissing away our money," Donnie sobbed.

Mac tried to comfort his brother. "She was probably sick and didn't say a word to a soul. Ma wouldn't want you to blame yourself, and neither do I."

Twenty agonizing minutes passed before the doctor finally came in with a stack of papers and a million apologies. He repeated what Nina had said but added his own medical jargon to it. Mac signed the papers, and they watched as he, along with Nina, turned off all the machines that beeped and made whispering sounds as they inhaled and exhaled for his mother. It took another two hours until Helen Black took her last breath and exited the world as Mac held one of her hands and Donnie grasped the other.

Mac kissed her cheek. "Rest easy, Ma. I hope you have more peace in the next life than you did here."

Eleven in the morning arrived before he could leave the hospital to make arrangements for his mother to be cremated and a small service. It all took time. By the time he got Donnie settled in a safe house that Haile had to ensure he didn't get into trouble and got to the cottage where he'd be staying, Mac fell into bed suffering from complete and utter exhaustion. He was grateful for the darkness that surrounded him and no dreams as he slept. He'd had enough reality in the last twenty-four hours and just wanted to sleep.

Chapter Three

"So that's Mac Black," Nina murmured as she took a sip of her gin and tonic at the bar and looked to where he and Haile sat in a booth. "He seems tortured, so alone."

"From what Haile and Jasper have told us, he had a rough go of it growing up and left because of it," Marisol replied.

It was her custom now to get off work and grab a drink or two in her uniform at the bar before heading upstairs. It was her blessing to meet Marisol at a time when living with three room-mates was becoming more uncomfortable because none of them meshed. The offer of the cozy, little apartment over the bar was her lifesaver; it meant she wouldn't end up in the Northumberland prison system. She'd gained a great friend in Marisol, her husband, and their extended friends. Even so, this would be her second Christmas away from Barbados and she loved the holiday. So, her new home away from home was already decorated in November and she had a tree. Plus, she had lent Mari a hand in getting the pub all decked out for the holidays.

"He had to be the rock that entire time I was telling him about his mother's condition," Nina told Mari. "His brother acts like a child and was obviously on drugs. Men don't get to act like that in my culture; I wanted to slap some sense into him."

Mari grinned. "That's usually frowned upon as a nurse."

She took a sip of her drink from the glass tumbler. "I know, but still, it was really hard on Mac, I could tell. I felt sorry for them—him mostly—because it's obvious he had no clue his mother was sickly and his brother wasn't caring for her."

"Yet he made sure Donnie was safe," Mari shook her head. "There's more to him than meets the eye."

"I guess so," Nina murmured.

She focused on the man who sat across from his friend. Mac had dark looks, almost dangerous, with a rugged jaw that sported a neatly trimmed beard. His eyes were an unusual dark gray, like a variation of an onyx gemstone. While he tried to keep them empty, they showed more emotion than he thought. His shoulders were broad and tapered down to lean hips. The small cut over his left eye was hardly noticeable, but as a nurse Nina saw it—and the bruised knuckles. He had literally fought all his life and, judging by the redness and freshly scraped flesh, *recently* to get his brother home.

"Will he be going back to the U.S. after everything is settled with his mother?" Nina asked. Mac looked up and caught her staring, so she looked quickly away.

"I think Jasper and Haile are going to convince him to stay," Mari answered.

"Hope they do, 'cos that boy needs to come home and those three were inseparable when they were boys," Mrs. Humphreys was wiping her hands as she passed behind Mari at the bar.

"How did you hear our conversation from the kitchen with the music on?" Mari demanded.

Mrs. Humphreys winked. "I hear everything, like I know Zeva and Jasper are on the way with Miss Abigail for dinner with you two. Haile requested liver and onions." Mari pressed a hand to her stomach and looked visibly sick as Mrs. Humphreys looked victorious. "I knew it."

Mari feigned ignorance. 'I don't know what you're talking about."

Nina chuckled. "I would know, if I was a nurse or not."

Mrs. Humphreys stepped closer while Mr. Moore, who was in his usual seat at the bar, eyed them. "How far along are you?"

"My assessment from the way she turned green,

I'd say a few weeks," Nina supplied.

Mari nodded. "I haven't told Haile yet, I wanted to wait . . ."

"Oy, Haile, these hens are cackling about you!" Mr. Moore said smugly. "I read lips."

"Obviously not well," Mrs. Humphreys threw a bar towel at him.

Haile and Mack came over to Nina and Mari's table just as Zeva came through the door. She was holding a now one-year-old Abigail as Jasper propped the door open while carrying the baby bag. The baby girl squealed in delight and held her hands out to Haile, who took her and lifted her high in the sky. Nina noted how Mac watched with a small smile on his face, but it never really travelled to his eyes. *You need to stop looking at him,* she warned herself as he caught her staring yet again.

After greetings all around, Nina felt like she was part of a new type of family that was filled with warmth and love. Her family was strict—difficult at best—and chaos usually followed them. When the opportunity to branch out on her own was offered, Nina had jumped at the chance. While she missed her home, she didn't miss the arguments or the family drama. Mac was introduced to Abigail, who was hesitant because she'd never met him but who nevertheless held on to the finger he offered her.

Mrs. Humphreys nudged Mari. "Tell him."

"Not now," Mari answered between a smile and gritted teeth.

"Tell me what?" Haile looked from woman to woman.

"Oh, that thing," Zeva smiled widely.

"Seems a bit unfair all the women knows and we don't," Mac spoke up.

"I tried to read their lips but only got your name," Mr. Moore said mournfully.

Mrs. Humphreys rolled her eyes. "Oh please, the only thing that keeps you on that barstool is years of practice while drunk. You keep out of this."

Mari sighed. "I was going to wait until later when we were alone, but apparently that never happens in this damn town."

"It really doesn't," Mac agreed.

"Haile, you are going to be a father," Mari said primly.

Nina watched his face go blank while his friends clapped him on the back and offered him congratulations.

"What do you mean?" Haile finally said.

"The boy's gone daft," Mrs. Humphreys threw up her hands.

Mari cupped his cheeks and brought him close. "I am with child . . . Pregnant, you have planted a bun in the oven. You're fixin' to be a daddy."

Zeva snorted. "Fixin' . . . "

Mari gave her a look. "Don't you start!"

Haile lifted her against him and swung her around. "Right on schedule, my timeline was perfect."

"Still with the timeline," Mac was smiling.

"Timeline?" Nina asked in confusion.

"It's from his crazy scheme when he was trying to win Mari's heart," Jasper explained with a laugh.

Mrs. Humphreys grabbed another bar towel and dabbed at her eyes. "We're going to have a young one in the Buchanan line. A young honorable son or daughter."

"What does she mean?" Mari asked confused.

"Since you are Lord and Lady Buchanan, your child would be the honorable whatever you decide to name him or her," Nina explained. "Abigail's title is Lady since Zeva and Jasper are the Duke and Duchess, any sons would be Master on either side."

"How do you know all that?" Mac asked.

"Barbados was once part of the British crown until our former prime minister, Errol Barrow, gained us independence in 1966," Nina answered. "Even so, we still have a Governor General who liaisons with the U.K., so your heritage is technically a part of our own."

"I'm going to be someone's dad," Haile said huskily and caressed Mari's cheek.

"Happy?" Mari smiled up at him.

"Ecstatically so." Haile kissed her gently before he turned to the patrons of the Celtic Cross Pub. "Drinks on the house, we're celebrating!"

"Oh huzzah, huzzah!" Mr. Moore cheered loudly. "Blessing to the new baby and all that."

Mrs. Humphreys pointed at the old man. "You get one more pint of Guinness and then you're cut off."

"You're not my wife," he complained.

"Shall I call her then and have your grand come pick you up now?" Mrs. Humphreys threatened.

"No ma'am," he mumbled.

Nina was laughing both at the interaction between the two older people in the bar and the fact that she loved the entire ambiance of the pub. Northumberland felt like home even though she missed the beaches of her island home sometimes. She loved the cool weather, sweaters, and the quaint shops especially now that the windows were decorated for Christmas. There was no one here trying to set her up with a man who wasn't right or calling her prideful for not wanting to settle. *Sue me, I have a type,* she thought irritably and pushed that away quickly. She wasn't going to let bad thoughts ruin her mood or her holiday. Drinks were poured and congratulations passed around, in between conversations with people she was slowly getting to know in the town.

Her eyes kept going back to Mac. Although he

interacted with everyone, there was a distance about him. It was undeniable that he intrigued her, that there was a primal aspect to Mac that thrilled and scared her. *What would happen if . . .* Nina let that thought drop away as she bid everyone good night. She had an early shift the next day and needed her sleep. But as she climbed the stairs to her apartment, she felt Mac's gaze on her. Nina didn't look back even though her heart sped up in her chest. What was it about him that drew her in? She was notoriously excellent at choosing men that weren't good for her. That should have been warning enough.

The hospital was short-staffed, and that meant she worked more than one double shift over the next few days. She missed a German Christmas festival and a play because of the hectic schedule. It was mildly irritating not being able to enjoy decorations and the town festivities, but Nina tried to bring some of the joy to the patients on her floor. She'd hung little trinkets here and there to make them smile as they went from rooms to be tested, and when she could, she put stencils of snowflakes and bells on windows or on walls.

There was a tiny tree at the nurses' desk, and

everyone (including the doctors) liked her spirit—except the head nurse who was called *Chief Nurse* or *Matron* according to English standards. The way she acted, you would think she'd given birth to the Grinch, but she was like that every day to one nurse or sometimes even the doctors. She was known to be cold to patients as well. Their interaction that day played through Nina's mind as she walked home in the brisk, cold wind.

"Nurse Crane, a word, please."

She heard the request come from the stiff lips of the Matron, Mrs. Potter, and she met the gaze of two of her friends on the ward. She turned with a friendly smile on her lips as Nurse Potter walked up to her.

"Yes, Nurse Potter?" Nina said politely.

"I'll thank you not to add any more of this nonsense to the ward, for this is a place of healing not some pub," Nurse Potter said.

Nina knew it was a jab at where she now lived. Her first accommodations had been one of Nurse Potter's rentals, and she was not pleased when Nina left and she concurrently lost that money.

"The patients like it, and it's that time of the season; no one wants to be in hospital around Christmas," Nina pointed out.

"This ward is my charge, and I make the decisions here," Nurse Potter snapped. "You may have fancy friends, but it won't save your position if you undermine my authority."

"I'm to understand that unless I commit an infraction other than decorations, it's the only time my job would be in question and not by you but by administration," Nina smiled stiffly. "Seeing that you are the one no one wants to work with and has gone past her . . . prime. Early retirement may be an option if another complaint goes upstairs against you. And my friends have nothing to do with that."

Nurse Potter's pinched face turned red. "Why, you little chippy . . . how dare you talk to me . . . "

"Problem?"

One of the doctors came up and eyed the two of them. Anyone could sense the tense situation, and other nurses looked on while pretending to work. He was one of the older doctors on staff at the hospital, and Nina knew him to be excellent at his job, not only caring for his patients' physical health but mental as well. There was more than once she'd seen him with families or comforting loved ones. Doctor Kievla was kind and a wonderful physician.

"Not at all, Doctor," Nina answered sweetly and never took her eyes off Nurse Potter. "Matron was just telling me my decorations were a distraction to the patients and threatening my employment if I didn't cease and desist."

"A welcome distraction," the older man said and

frowned at Nurse Potter. "Nancy, you were warned about being heavy- handed with the nursing staff."

"She is disrespectful and does not follow authority, one must wonder why she was sent from Barbados to here," Nurse Potter defended herself.

"She was chosen for the program because she has the best qualifications and scores," Doctor Kievla explained. *"She* chose *us*; she could've stayed in London at Queen Elizabeth Hospital, but she came here."

"I am not disrespectful," Nina argued hotly. "I'm offended at the accusation, ask any doctor or nurse here. I have never been written up, and I offer respect when it is given."

"I want her off my ward," Nurse Potter said angrily. "I have been a long-standing nurse here at Queen Charlotte, and she has been here for a year."

Doctor Kievla shook his head. "That will not be happening. Nurse Crane is an invaluable asset to the hospital."

"Are you sleeping with her, is that why you're taking her side?" Nurse Potter demanded.

A series of gasps went through the nurses, and Nina wished she could slap the older woman silly.

"How dare you say that, what's wrong with you?" Nina cried out. "He's happily married, and his wife works upstairs. He has children and grandchildren!"

"Nurse Crane, please get back to work and you

may continue to add your decorations to the ward." Doctor Kievla's eyes were cold. "I think, Nancy, you and I will be seeing HR later, and this will be solved another way. Please sign out for the evening and meet me upstairs."

With those words he walked down the hall and stepped into a patient's room. Nurse Potter shot daggers at Nina with her eyes before turning on her heels and walking down the hall to where the nurses' lounge was located. The stiff, dark-blue material of her matron uniform barely moved as she walked.

"We'll have to write up statements."

"She was just bitchy, and it finally caught up to her."

"Imagine her accusing Dr. Kievla of that, she is done for sure."

Everyone seemed to be talking at once, and of course no one believed Nurse Potter's accusation. But still it was out there, and it left a bitter taste in Nina's mouth. She went about the rest of her shift with her usual efficiency, but all the while she couldn't wait to clock out. She hated drama of any sort in or out of the workplace, so when it was her time to leave, she did so in a rush. The cold air seemed to cleanse the events from her body while she walked home. Nina was so stuck in her thoughts that she barreled right into a wide chest and strong arms went around her.

She looked up to see Mac's face. "Oh, sorry! I was

not watching where I was going!"

"It's already dark—what are you doing walking alone?" Mac asked without even a hello.

"I just got off shift." She heard the breathlessness of her own voice.

"Take a car service next time," Mac's accent seemed thicker than she remembered when they first talked at the hospital. Being at home seemed to bring it out more. "You shouldn't be walking alone."

"It's just half a street to the shops and the lights, they're open later, and people are out more for shopping," Nina moved away. "You are walking alone."

"Everyone knows better than to fuck with me," Mac said bluntly. "A lot can happen within a short period of time. I'll walk you back."

"You don't have to, you were walking in the opposite direction, don't let me keep you," Nina said hurriedly.

"I was just walking," he said and turned without another word.

There seemed to be no other choice, so Nina fell into step beside him, holding her thick coat around her uniform. It was a long coat, but still she could feel the cold breeze leech through the thick stockings she wore.

"You're a staff nurse," Mac said, breaking the silence.

"Yes, working towards being a senior nurse," she

answered. "I hope to be a matron or get into research after my three years are up."

"Good goals," he said. "You looked upset; did something happen at the hospital?"

"Beastly matron issues," Nina said and went on to tell him the story.

"What an old bitch."

Nina laughed. "I see you're the type to say exactly what you're thinking."

He shrugged his big shoulders. "I don't see a point to being otherwise."

"What do you do in the United States?" Nina asked conversationally.

"I run a security firm for people who are rich enough to pay people to watch their asses."

She pulled her coat tighter. "Sounds dangerous. I guess you're always looking for potential threats. Is that why you were walking tonight?"

"No, I needed to clear my head," he admitted. "It's been a hell of a last few days."

"I can only imagine," Nina said sympathetically. "How was your mother's service?"

He sighed. "Quick, she has one of the mausoleum slots at the church now.

Nina prodded further. "Is your brother okay? He was having a hard time at the hospital."

"I'll get him where he needs to be," Mac answered. "I'm sorry he scared you."

She patted his arm. "I was just startled; I have dealt with upset family before."

"He was high more than anything else," Mac muttered.

Nina offered. "If you ever need help with that, there are resources I can help facilitate for him."

"I may take you up on that," Mac had stopped walking and she noted they were in the middle of town now, where the string Christmas lights were hung from the buildings to the tall fountain statue in the center of the roundabout. "Do you need me to walk to the Celtic Cross?"

Nina shook her head. "No thanks, I'm going to do a bit of shopping and grab a bite of dinner. I have a book in my bag I'm going to read while I eat."

"Sounds relaxing," he said.

Nina hesitated before asking. "Do . . . do you want to join me?"

Mac gave her a small smile. "I wouldn't be the best company right now but enjoy your night."

"Thank you."

"Hey, Mac!" Nina called to him as he walked away, and he turned without a word. Nina sent him a big smile. "Next time I won't take no for an answer."

He nodded. "Good to know, Bajan girl."

She laughed. "You're the first one who actually knows we are called Bajan as well as Barbadians on my island."

"I make it my mission to know a little bit of everything," Mac said, and this time he gave her a wink before walking away.

"If there was ever a man who needed some Christmas cheer it was him," Nina said to herself a little later as she looked into the decorated window of the toy shop.

That wink was the first sign of lightness she had seen from him without his friends present. Maybe she would invite him to dinner again or out for drinks. For now, Nina decided to play it by ear. If they crossed paths again, she would take it as a sign. Being a Bajan girl, she trusted her instincts and they seemed to be sending her directly toward Mackenzie Black.

Chapter Four

Mac couldn't help but be infatuated with Nurse Nina Crane. Those damn curves under that nurse's uniform were begging for his hands to be on them—particularly her hips. Of course, he had to think about the underlying factors: *my brother for one and this damn town for another*. He had no intention of staying even though he longed to. Mac could already feel the stares and hear the whispers. They thought he'd returned to take back a seat at the table, to run numbers and take protection money from people who couldn't afford to say no.

He wanted no part of that; it was his past, a way to take care of his mother and brother after Peter Black ran off with the barmaid from a town over. It didn't matter that he had joined the Royal Army, served alongside Haile, and saw just as much shit as he did. They didn't care that he'd left and made his own way in the United States. The theory was that he ran away because he was about to be arrested and took his bad ways international. He shouldn't care what anyone else thought because those closest to him knew the truth, but it burned him more than anyone realized. He brooded over a pint at the Celtic Cross long after the pub had closed.

Haile had long since gone home with Marisol, who needed to leave early because Mrs. Humphreys' liver and onions made her feel nauseated. Also, everyone had some kind of opinions or home remedy for a healthy pregnancy, and it was working both the Buchanans' nerves. Mac promised to lock up after everyone was gone, including the night's money going into the safe. His friend was going to be a father, go figure. They had all changed throughout the years—and all for the better.

"Hey, what are you doing here?" Nina's voice was soft from the stairs, and it startled him.

"Hi . . . um, locking up for Haile. They left a while ago," Mac answered.

"Looks like Guinness not keys," she teased.

He smiled. "Being a bar manager affords me some perks. I didn't see you come in."

"I worked a sixteen-hour shift from yesterday, so when I came home, they weren't open yet," she explained. "I just crashed, and Marisol texted me to say Mrs. H. had left me some stew in the kitchen. I just woke up, and I'm starving. I did the ward and a shift in the emergency room. Delivered six babies, saw two people pass, and a multitude of other things that could be avoided if people would use their heads."

"I can get it for you, I know where she keeps the warmer," Mac said hurriedly and jumped up. "You have to be exhausted, sit down right there, I'll be back."

He was gone before she could say a word, but he did see her warm smile. *Fuck,* he had to keep his cool. What was it about her that elicited all the dirty thoughts he'd had from fourteen years old onward? By the time he came back with her bowl of thick stew, Nina was sitting at the bar. Mrs. H's stew was the best in Northumberland, with Guinness as part of the base and of course there was her amazing sourdough bread, thickly sliced to go with the meal. When Mac sat the plate in front of her, he went around to the back of the bar and got her a Coke to go with her dinner.

"Thank you," Nina took up the spoon and began to eat. She looked at him standing uncomfortably behind the bar and patted the stool beside her. "Come finish your drink."

Mac took the seat, acutely aware she was in pajamas and a soft bathrobe that rubbed gently against his skin. Her long hair was in two braids, and she had two different-colored scrunchy bands holding them together. Nina looked innocent, a breath of fresh air, and he couldn't help wondering if she tasted as good as she looked.

"Mac?" Her voice infiltrated his thoughts. "I asked if you liked hot cross buns."

"Sure, they are amazing. I haven't had one in forever, though," Mac said.

"If you'd listened . . . " she teased. "I was saying there is a baking competition for them tomorrow, and for once I'm not working all weekend."

Mac looked at her questioningly, wondering where this was going. "That's good. You get to relax, so I guess you'll be going then."

Nina blew out a breath. "Men can be so obtuse. . . ."

"Isn't that a shape?"

She held up her hand. "Hush it and listen. Do you want to go and eat hot cross buns with me? Imagine the taste, warm from the oven with fresh churned butter or maybe some cheese."

"You make that sound almost decadent," Mac murmured.

She smiled wistfully. "It is, and I admit right up-front, I like food. These curves get their exercise because of it."

He winked. "They look great to me."

She leaned her head against her hand. "Well, look at you, being a flirt. I thought that scowl was a permanent fixture on your face."

"I have been known to smile for the right reasons," he told her. "Right now is one of them."

"Consider me flattered that I caused that small rarity," Nina finished her dinner with a sigh. "I have a slice of cake upstairs that will soothe my sweet tooth while I watch some TV."

"Not going back to bed?" He could think of a pleasurable way to pass the time but kept it to himself.

Nina stood. "My work has my sleep schedule all askew; it has been for years. I'll take these dishes to the back and get them washed up."

"No, go enjoy your days off," Mac stopped talking for a moment. "And yes, tomorrow how about I meet you by the bakery and we can go from there?"

"Great," Nina gave a little clap. "They've started setting up tents. I'll meet you at four."

"Night."

Mac lifted his hand in a wave as she trailed her hand around the edge of the bar as she headed upstairs. Nina turned and came back to stand in front of him, and she cupped his cheek. He made a sound of surprise, and then he closed his eyes, succumbing to the sensation of her soft hands against his skin. Mac felt the fullness of her lips pressed against his, and it was exactly how he'd envisioned. Nina tasted like a sip of heaven, and when she tentatively licked his bottom lip, he gave her access so she could have her own taste. When Nina lifted her head, the heavy-lidded sensual expression on her face was even more of a gut punch of arousal.

"Why did you do that?" His voice was husky.

A smile crossed her face. "I said to myself, Nina Crane of Fitts Village St. James, If you run into that man again, you might as well kiss him, so since I am true to myself, I took that leap." She tweaked his nose. "And it was worth it, 'night."

As she walked upstairs, Mac called. "Do you go around pinching grown men's noses?"

Her laugh was the answer, and then he heard the heavy door that led to her apartment slam closed. He grinned. *Why do I feel so light all of a sudden, like I could dance across the hardwood floors?* That was not his nature, and yet as he turned out lights, he did a little slide across the polished wood. Mac regained his composure and finished locking up before leaving the Celtic Cross.

For a moment he worried about her being on the property alone, but there was a great security system—built by him of course. Haile also mentioned that when they took her as a tenant the reinforced door was added at the top of the stairs for added security. With a thick metal strip built into the frame, there was no way anyone was kicking it in. *They'd break a leg first.* Mac got into the rental car and headed toward his home away from home in the guest cottage of his friend. All the while he thought about Nina's supple lips and the simple kiss that had devastated his senses.

One of the reasons he loved Northumberland was the Christmas traditions that had been built from the time it was just a small town with barely thirty houses. As time went by, it had expanded outward from the town square to where it is now, yet the traditions had stayed the same. That included all the festivals they had for Christmas that he remembered growing up. There was more than once when his mother took him and Donnie out to the tree-lighting ceremony or some other event. They'd come home with full stomachs, too much sugar from treats, and she'd clean them up in their small flat and put them to bed. The small tree and lights from the sparsely decorated living room would lull him to sleep.

Mac embraced the fond memories before time and poverty had made them all hard. Before he wanted things she couldn't afford or got upset when he heard her crying at night because they couldn't pay the rent. It was then that he'd decided he would do anything to make her happy, but as time went by it was never enough. She wanted him to take from his friends and use their name for her success as bitterness set in. He pushed the negatives away and focused on good thoughts while he waited with two cups of hot chocolate for Nina to arrive. The square had rows of white tents with heaters blowing warm for those who attended. All the delicious smells wafted around as fresh hot cross buns were baked and the sweet confections or warm soups were offered by vendors not participating.

While the Christmas tunes and the sound of bells filled the air, he spotted her weaving her way through the crowd. The jeans she wore hugged every curve, and the rose suede boots matched the color of her sweater. Nina left her fur-lined coat open even though the evening had turned out to be even more chilly than expected. Her knit was the same rose color and pulled down over her long hair that she left loose. The sun was already going down even though it wasn't quite four, and as people greeted her, she waved. Mac noted that more than one gaze of surprise from the crowd passed in their direction. And then Nina finally stood in front of him.

"Hi," her voice was light and breathless.

"Were you running?" he asked and held out the cup. "Hot chocolate, with whipped cream and caramel drizzle.

"How did you know?" Nina smiled up at him. "And no, I wasn't quite running, just a brisk walk so I wouldn't be late."

"I really didn't, I just picked what sounded good. And I would have waited, there was no need to hurry," Mac moved a stray tendril of hair back from being caught on her coat.

She took a sip of her drink. "I like to be prompt. Have you tried anything yet?"

He gave her a teasing shocked look. "Without you? What kind of man would I be to eat without the person who invited me?"

Nina shook her head in amusement. "Okay, dramatic, where do you want to start?"

Mac rubbed his hands together. "Let's go with what drew us here: hot cross buns,"

"You read my mind," Nina replied.

Soon they were waiting in line for two of the biggest buns he'd ever seen. Although they were traditionally an Easter treat, these pastries had crossed over to various holidays including Christmas. While balancing two of the big buns on a disposable plate that also included a big scoop of butter and cheese, they went to find a bench under the town Christmas tree. Mac prepared his treat the way he liked it, using all the butter and then adding the cheese in the middle after he sliced it. He took a big bite and closed his eyes in pleasure as a groan escaped him. The spiced flavors of the bread combined with the icing and cheese and butter was so good that he chewed greedily, ready for another bite.

"If you'd just heard yourself, I would think you'd agree that this sounded like a porno," Nina teased.

Mac chewed before speaking. "You're lucky my

shirt isn't off and I'm not whispering sweet nothings to this thing."

"I know how to make them," Nina announced. "I'll have to borrow Mrs. H's kitchen—and, trust me, you will want to be alone with my buns." He looked at her with a raised eyebrow, and she grimaced. "Yes, I heard it after I said it."

"All I'm saying is, I don't mind being alone with your buns," Mac teased.

"Hush it."

He noted that was one of her favorite terms to use and while they ate in companionable silence, Zeva and Jasper walked by. The baby was of course bundled up in her stroller, but she smiled and dropped the pacifier out of her mouth when she saw them and squealed.

"Hey guys, fancy meeting you here!" Zeva's voice held warmth, curiosity, and that sound women make when they sniff out a date or new romance. "Jasper, isn't it a *co-inky-dink* that we see them here together?"

Jasper grinned. "She's not subtle at all, is she?"

"And apparently Mari has been teaching her some of her Texas wordage," Nina added. "We decided to come together, so don't go crazy."

"It's friends hanging out," Mac said.

Zeva gave them both an innocent look and smiled. "No one said otherwise."

The baby opened her mouth revealing a few teeth and expecting a bite. Mac looked to her parents for approval. "May I?"

"Of course, just a small bite. She doesn't have molars yet," Zeva advised. "And don't linger at her mouth, those teeth are sharp."

Mac gave Abigail a small piece, and she clapped her hands before going "mmmm" — it was the cutest thing he'd ever seen. *Imagine that,* he thought, noting how lovingly Jasper looked at his wife and daughter. Did he crave this sense of family and home? *Should I even pass on the bad genes to another generation?* He hated where his thoughts went sometimes and focused on the present. Jasper and Zeva were going to walk around so they decided to join them. As a foursome they sampled food and drinks until everyone was completely stuffed and the baby began to complain sleepily. Along the way, they found Haile buying some of the hot cross buns for Mari, who was having morning sickness at night and not feeling up to the festival. Zeva and Jasper decided to take Abigail home while Mac and Nina stood with Haile as he waited for his order.

"I don't know who can win; every bun I sampled is so delicious, I want bite into all of them again," Nina said.

"What you're saying is, you want to bite the buns?" Mac questioned, and Haile chuckled.

She folded her arms. "You know what . . . hush it."

"Well, well, well, isn't it Mackie Black home to roost." The voice made the smile fall from Mac's face, and he turned to see one of the men he used to run the streets with.

"Alec," Mac said the name stiffly. "How've you been?"

"Not better than you it seems," Alec looked like he'd been worked over more than once. Age and time had not been good to him. He took gnarled hands out of his dark-blue wool jacket. He still wore fingerless gloves like the men who used to work on the dock. "Out enjoying the night, I see, with yer fancy friends and some put-together lady."

The comment set Mac's teeth on edge. "Walk away, Alec."

"Why should I? I'm here to enjoy the night like everyone else," Alec said and eyed Nina up and down. "Forget about bread—I like the buns on this one. You always like them thick, Mackie. I figured how could Mackie be back and not visit with his old friends?"

He leered at Nina, and Mac was ready to beat his head open. "We stopped being friends long ago, so go away before it ends badly."

"For whom," Alec sneered. "You are probably more worried about messing up the fancy clothes ya wearing." He grabbed Nina's hand as he said, "Come on, sweets, show me the sights."

Nina dragged her hand away, and her eyes shot fire. "Take your hands off me. . . . "

"Don't fucking touch her!"

Mac had Alec by his collar and within seconds had punched him twice in the head. A small cry went through the crowd drawing attention to them. Mac was in Alec's face, and he was almost rabid to hurt the man for touching Nina.

"Know your place, Alec. It wasn't for me you'd be somewhere dead by now, sank in the mud of the moors and not a bloody person will miss ya," Mac snarled. "Tread lightly, you and your friends. While I'm here cross the street when you see me, *allayuh*! Or I'll crack every one of your damn skulls!"

"Let him go, Mac," Haile ordered gently and then said loudly. "You'd think these guys would learn by now, when women say *no* they mean no. Get going, Alec, before she presses charges."

Mac knew his friend was trying to defuse the situation and help him save face. It only angered him more. He shoved Alec away and watched him stagger down the street through the crowd.

"I don't need you to speak for me, Haile. I can handle myself," Mac snapped.

A spark of anger flashed in Haile's eyes. "Yeah, we all know you can use your fists to solve a problem. Stop letting these assholes bait you; you're better than them and this."

"Am I, Haile? Am I?" Mac's tone was deadly.

"Get the fucking chip off your shoulder," Haile snapped. "Nina, have him walk you home and cool off before he ends up scrapping with his friends."

Nina took his hand and urged him gently. "Mac, come on, walk me home, please. Remember, you don't want me walking by myself in the dark."

Mac allowed himself to be led away while Haile turned back to get his food. He knew he had to apologize for how he'd treated his friend. But right now, he had to cool the rage within him. He walked briskly, and even though Nina kept up, she was practically sprinting. Finally, at the corner before the pub she stopped.

"Okay, thanks for the track meet; we can stop now," she said breathlessly.

"I was trying to get you home," Mac's tone was clipped. "Alec or his boys don't deal with situations like that well."

"Then why hit him?" Nina asked as they started walking again.

"He put hands on you, and if I didn't respond, they'd think I was easy pickings," Mac explained.

She stopped in the shadows by the alley with her hands on her hips. "What do you care? You made your successes, these people shouldn't matter, it's your past. They may not have evolved past being thugs or gorillas, but you are."

"How would you know?" Mac snapped. "You don't know the way of the streets, you're a transplant here. You see the sweet spots, the tourist traps, and the festivals. If you knew the underbelly of Northumberland, you'd be scared in your bed at night."

She pointed at him. "Let me tell you something, I work emergencies more often than not and I see the knife wounds, the gun shots, the beatings people take, so don't tell me about the sordid side of this town I see it *every* day. I've treated Donnie more than once for almost overdosing or being so drunk it took two banana bags of fluid to sober him up."

His head snapped up at her words. "So, you think you know us—or me?"

"I go by instincts," Nina took a deep breath, and her voice gentled. "You're a good man, you strived and succeeded where many couldn't. Be proud of that."

In flash he had her pressed against a wall and was ravaging her with kisses. Where hers had a sweet, tentative taste, Mac's was primal as he speared his tongue into her mouth and molded his body to hers. Her whimper and soft moan only fueled him. His anger was replaced by desire and then internal rage at himself. Mac cupped her breasts through her sweater and kissed his way to her ear.

"Does this feel like a good man?" he whispered raggedly. His erection was hard in his pants. "Are you wondering how many women I fucked in alleys like this coming home from bars and wanting a taste of my cock? Right now, I can tell by those sex noises you're making that Nurse Nina is creaming in her pants. Should I strip them off your hips and pull your panties aside and fuck you from behind? You wanna see what this boy from the wrong side of the docks can do? I can make you explode with my fingers and lick your come off two, maybe three, of them Can you take it?"

He felt her hand on his chest, and then she pushed him away. Although she was breathing hard, her eyes shot fiery daggers of anger in his direction.

"I like dirty talk as much as the next woman, but I won't be fucked in anger, not now, not ever." Nina's voice was stiff, and he could hear the anger and hurt in her tone.

"If you want me to be a tool for you to get your angst out, baby boy, I am *not* the one. All of this comes with stipulations—and assholes don't taste the sweetness of this damn fine treat. You're a grown man, act like it, you are not the first or the last person to go through shit."

Nina poked him in the chest. "We rise above, and like Haile said, we get rid of that chip on our shoulders. Now I'm going to my apartment, and the next time I see you, there had better be an apology on your lips or I will act like you don't exist. You have good people in your corner, your friends and me. By the time you figure that out, you may have pushed everyone away. Good luck with that."

"Nina . . ." His voice was ragged.

She held up her hand and stepped out from between him and the wall. "Not right now. I can get home on my own. But here's the thing, Mac."

"What?"

"If you were anything—and I mean *anything*—like Alec or those other people that know how to press your buttons, you wouldn't have stopped when I pushed you away," Nina said.

She gave him a long, sorrowful stare before walking away, and he was in no position to stop her. She, Haile, anyone who knew him was right: He *was* being a complete and utter jerk. He wasn't a product of his environment; Mac knew he was letting it warp his life—and for too long. Even though she said she could walk alone Mac trailed behind her until he knew she was safely inside. It was his turn to take a walk of shame back to his car. The next day he had a lot of apologies to dole out.

Chapter Five

Nina went about her day as efficiently as she always did when working. But her mood was more subdued compared with her regular personality; one of her patients even noticed the change. But soon enough, she shook that off and donned her reindeer antlers to push away the dark mood, Mackenzie Black had caused. Since the night of the festival, she hadn't seen him. His version of an apology was a text to her phone, and she wasn't having that. He acted the fool in person, so he was going to apologize in the same fashion. The text went unanswered, and over the next few days flowers kept arriving at the nurses' station with her name on them.

"If Matron Potter was still here, she would pitch a fit," one of her co-workers commented, laughing.

After the incident in which Matron Potter accused Dr. Kievla of inappropriate behavior with Nina, Potter had been moved to the hospice part of the hospital where her duties would to be to care for the terminally ill patients and keep them comfortable as they passed on. There was very little interaction among the nursing staff unless they were going off-shift and needed to update each other on the status of each patient. Nina understood why they did it that way, for it eliminated her from bullying the nursing staff and she kept her job.

"You need to forgive this guy before he fills this entire ward with poinsettias, freesia, and candy canes," another nurse passed by and took up a floral arrangement in a white vase.

"Take them with you," Nina encouraged. "I already have some in every patient's room."

Melissa, her friend, smiled. "You better give that guy a second chance or I will; I'm a widow after all, so I will stand in your place," she joked.

"I'm calling him right now, we are running out of places to put flowers," Nina promised.

On her break she walked down to the open glass arboretum that graced the entrance of the hospital. With her coffee cup in hand, she sat on one of the white benches next to the fountain, near the thick leaves of one of the plants growing there. Nina pulled her cell phone out of her pocket and dialed Mac's number. As she dialed she wondered how much teasing he'd had to endure to get her number from Marisol or Zeva.

"Hello, Nina."

The way he said her name made her shiver. *Damn it!* He sounded too sexy with that accent, which could be described as smooth as an aged barrel of rum.

"Mac, stop sending flowers to my place of work," she said firmly.

"Not until you accept my apology," Mac answered.

"I won't be doing that," she replied.

"Why not?"

She pulled the phone away from her ear and looked at it incredulously for a moment before placing it back against her ear and continuing. "You cannot be that daft. You act the fool in public and now want me to forgive you by using text and flowers? No sir, you want to apologize, you do it in person or not at all."

"Luckily, I'm right here to do exactly that," he said as he sat down beside her.

She made a small sound of surprise. "Christ Almighty, are you trying to give me a heart attack?"

Mac smiled. "You said apologize in person."

"And I assumed you were nowhere near here," she pointed out. "What are you doing here, by the way?"

"I was coming to see you when you called," Mac explained. "I get it. I was a complete ass, and I am sorry. I came to throw myself on my sword at the nursing desk. Then as I lay on the ground with my heart in my hand as an offering, I was then going to ask you to allow me to be your escort to Zeva's and Jasper's holiday gala tomorrow night at the manor."

"First, that sounds morbid and dramatic; second, I accept your heartfelt apology," Nina brushed a piece of lint of the lapel of his tweed double-breasted jacket. "Third, I would love you to escort me, and lastly, don't ever do anything you said on my ward or I'll have you carted off to the psych ward."

A rich, deep laugh escaped him, and she was delighted at the sound. "Well then, let's keep me of out a straightjacket, shall we?"

"Sounds good to me," she answered. "I need to get back to work, so I'll see you tomorrow night?"

"How about a kiss then to seal the deal?" Mac said with a wicked grin.

She shook her head. "What did I say about my place of work? No saucy stuff."

"No, you said not to send flowers," he pointed out. "A small kiss, or I feel the urge to fall on my sword again."

Nina rolled her eyes and put her hand on his chest before leaning over to press her lips against his. She could feel the texture of his dark blue jacket under her fingers as she gave him a second kiss — well, just because.

"There, are you happy now?" she asked huskily.

"Not by a long shot, but it will have to do." His eyes were intense with desire. "Get on back to work before I go into cardiac arrest from wanting you."

"That's not how that works," she teased.

"Off with you, woman." He pointed at the stairs leading up to the wards.

With a laugh she got up and impulsively bent over to place a quick peck on his lips once more before running up the stairs. She looked back to see him watching her, and with a small wave he walked out the door. The mood of her day definitely improved after that; she hummed Christmas tunes while she worked with her patients and that in turn caused her to smile. By the end of the day, she'd even decided to take a few of the potted poinsettia and candy cane plants home to her own small apartment.

It was while she pushed her a small cart with her plants home that evening that she met a person who made her uncomfortable. On the streets it was getting darker as time ticked by. Nina walked home with plans to drop off her bags and packages before heading back out to find a dress. Of course, she had been invited by Zeva; the elegant invitation had been delivered by courier that week. But now that she was being escorted by Mac, a new dress was in order rather than using something in her closet. Being budget-conscious she had a little reserve cash she could splurge with. The lights of a car behind her illuminated the concrete path in front of her.

Expecting it to go by, she didn't change her pace

until it slowed, and she heard the sound of an automatic window being rolled down. Turning her head, Nina spied a man in the back seat who made her heart lurch in her chest. If there was anyone who could be considered a predator by features alone, it would be this man. His thick neck and thuggish face had a cold brutality to it even as he smiled. His white teeth were akin to a shark before it attacked, and his face had been in one too many fights. Under the light of the streetlamp, her assessment was proving correct. She could see a purplish bruise on his face that was in the process of healing.

"Why, hello there—fancy a ride?" His voice was smooth, but as her mother always pointed out, so was the belly of a snake.

"I don't make it a habit of taking rides from strangers," Nina answered firmly and continued to walk.

"I'm a friend of Mackie or as you call him Mac, so we know each other by default," he said and held his hand out the window as his driver moved slowly to match her pace. "I'm Trevor Bouchey."

She didn't extend her hand and kept her cool. "Since I hardly know either of you, I guess you are still a stranger."

"You are a saucy bit," he laughed.

Nina sighed. "What do you want?"

"Just being friendly," he answered. "It would be

wise for you to do the same; you may need friends like me when Mackie jets back to the United States."

"I think I'll manage just fine," she replied but quickened her steps.

"Where is old Mackie anyway? Out with the Duke and his Lordship while you walk home alone?" His tone began to display a deadly edge. "That could be dangerous; I could have accidentally swerved and hit you on the sidewalk and no one would know a thing."

"Then it'd be a hit-and-run, and you'd be in jail," Nina refused to show fear even as her insides trembled. "Let's wrap this up, shall we? I don't want your friendship, no earthly idea where your Mackie is, I can walk home alone, and if you try veiled threats with me one more time, I will start screaming so shrilly even dogs will hear me clear across this town. Now run along Mr. Bouchey. I just got off work, and I have no time or inclination to do this with you. Have a good evening."

"I like you a lot, saucy bit," Bouchey inclined his head. "G'night, Nurse Nina."

She watched as the window rolled up and his car pulled away slowly before merging right and going around a corner. It was only then that Nina blew off the breath of fear to inhale a deep, cleansing gulp of air. That man scared her, and it was obvious he was no friend of Mac's. The last person she'd heard call him Mackie had gotten boxed upside the head a few nights ago. She wondered if she should tell Mac or Haile and decided to keep the incident to herself. She understood better now why Mac was the way he was, why the instinct to fight was his first reaction. If he grew up with people like that, then he'd fought for every step he'd taken. Mac had needed to revert to his primal instincts to survive men like Trevor Bouchey. God, she hoped she never had to interact with the man again.

Nina preferred to wait for Mac outside of the pub even though it was chilly. It wasn't like it was open because many people from the town and regulars had been invited to the manor house for the party. There were heated tents set up outside, and one was a fully catered buffet hall—or at least that was the gossip she'd heard. Having Mac in her tiny flat made her a little nervous, not because she was scared of him, but because she didn't think they would leave. She'd had a fierce attraction to the man and if the fantasy-like dreams were anything like reality, then being alone in close quarters would leave her hot, sweaty, and begging for more.

Nina fanned herself just thinking about the sex dream she'd had the night before. Mac's rental car came slowly around the corner and up the cobbled street that was one of the features of the historic part of Northumberland where the pub was situated. The street went from asphalt to stone, and you could hear the change in the texture under the wheels as Mac came to a stop.

When he stepped from the car, Nina had to stop her mouth from falling open, then from licking her lips. Mac looked simply delicious in the black tux he wore. The bow tie was black with gold stripes in the fabric that matched the cuff links that caught the reflection of the streetlight when he lifted his hand. His shoes were polished until they caught the reflection of the streetlight, and his broad shoulders only seemed to enhance the cut and fit of his suit.

"You look amazing in red," he said in approval.

Nina went with an elegant, red long-sleeve dress that ended in a fishtail ruffle just below her knee. The back was cut low, showing off a large expanse of chocolate skin, and she'd pinned her hair up, leaving two thick tendrils to frame her face. There was a simple gold locket on a thin chain at her neck and studded earrings in her pierced ears. The look in Mac's eyes told her that he appreciated how the dress hugged her curves and her overall look.

"You don't look so bad yourself," she replied. "I think I've only seen you in a dark T-shirt, jeans, and that rough tweed jacket."

"Are you speaking ill of my favorite piece of clothing?" Mac teased.

"By no means." She laughed. "You cleaned up well, Mackenzie Black, really well."

"Glad you approve," Mack leaned to whisper in her ear as he opened the passenger door. His breath on her ear made Nina shiver.

Their drive to the manor house was done with him holding her hand. As Mac parked, she focused on and was delighted by the amazing job Zeva had done for her gala. Angel lights hung from bare tree limbs and were twined through bushes and shrubs. There was a canopy leading to the front door of the manor that was made of garland, bells, and lights. Holiday music was being played by a live band on an outdoor stage that graced one corner of the landscaped front yard. Heaters and a metal fire pit were set up so guests could stay warm, and the outside fireplace that Jasper and Haile had built that summer was lit merrily while stockings were hung on the brick mantelpiece. Jasper and Zeva greeted their guests under the canopy.

Zeva smiled and held out her hands to Nina. "You look gorgeous; I would kill for curves like that.

Nina looked at her statuesque friend who was dressed in a champagne-colored dress. Over her shoulder Zeva wore the tartan of Jasper's family name, McTavish, while her husband wore the elegant Scottish dinner coat and kilt ensemble of his family. Nina thought they looked utterly fantastic.

"If you want to give me a few inches in height, we could trade," Nina kissed her cheek and then gave Jasper a hug. "You two put everyone here to shame."

"Hey now, we don't look too shabby either," Mac protested.

"Mari and I are rather dapper, if I do say so myself," Haile's voice came from behind them.

Nina turned, and he was in his own tux that had his family coat of arms embroidered on the lapel. Mari wore a turquoise cocktail dress that matched the colors in Haile's family crest. She was pale but smiled brightly being around her friends.

"Let's just call it and say we are three dashing couples," Mari said. "I almost didn't come tonight, but some hot tea and a few ginger snaps settled this evening's morning sickness. Which is the biggest oxymoron ever."

"I'm sorry, mine was a blessed few short weeks of hell," Zeva rubbed her shoulder sympathetically. "I'm glad you came, but whenever this becomes too much, we won't be offended if you go home early. There's always upstairs if you need to lie down."

"We're playing it by ear," Haile said and kissed his wife's hand.

Nina took Mari's hand and placed her fingers at

her wrist to check her pulse. It was strong and sometimes it had a little miss in step, which in nursing and alternative medicines was called a slippery pulse — common to pregnant women. Nina could only describe it as rolling marbles around in a saucer using your fingertips. It reflects the abundance of blood now that Mari was pregnant, and her body was now the life source for two.

"Nice and strong," Nina said with a smile. "But if this intense nausea keeps up, I need you to come in and see your doctor for medication. You don't have to suffer and be miserable. It won't take all the nausea away, but it will help until you hit the second trimester."

"Thank you, I will definitely be doing that on Monday," Mari said gratefully.

"Hey mate, I'm sorry about the festival," Mac said to Haile and held out his hand.

Haile ignored it and grabbed him in a hug before thumping him on the back a little harder than expected. "Already forgotten, we're brothers . . . all three of us."

"Aren't they sweet," Zeva teased.

"All they need is those school uniforms with the shorts and the knee-high socks. . . ." Mari picked up where Zeva left off.

"They'll probably be playing marbles and talking about football or cricket next," Nina finished.

The three men looked at them for a second before walking away together. On purpose they hooked hands and did a little choreographed kick that had the women laughing. It set the tone for a night filled with fun and laughter. Between the food and the various people around, including kids waiting for gifts and to sit on Santa's lap, it was one of the best nights Nina had ever spent away from Barbados. The sense of community was almost the same except they had the beaches and the warmth.

But people came together with tourists to dance and enjoy the holidays with food and music until the sun went down across the Caribbean Sea and well into the night. Nina found herself swaying lightly next to one of the warmers as a slower Christmas song played. Couples danced, and she laughed out loud when one of the young men put mistletoe on his hand so he could steal a kiss from the teen girl he was dancing with. Of course, she obliged until her mother dragged her away. That didn't deter her from waving at who Nina would assume was her new beau by the looks of it.

"Care to dance?" Mac came up behind her and put his hands on her hips.

Nina leaned against him and began to sway before tilting her head at an angle to look up at him. "Isn't that what we're doing now?"

"Ah," he ran his hand along her midsection and

pulled her closer. "Who knew I had the soul of a dancer all this time?"

"I think that may be a bit of a stretch," she laughed.

Mac kissed the bare skin at the nape of her neck. "You take away my dream—and at the holidays to boot."

Nina shivered, and her voice was husky. "I think your ego will survive."

"I don't know, it feels bruised, so you may need to kiss it and make it better," Mac said in a sorrowful tone.

Nina laughed and turned in his arms. "Did that work with the ladies?"

He shrugged. "Is it working on you?"

She shook her head. "Not in the least, but I could be persuaded."

"How?" A slow grin spread across his face, and her breath caught in her throat. If the man knew how damn gorgeous he was when he smiled, it could be dangerous.

"Snag a bottle of champagne and show me where you're staying," Nina said. "I'd like a tour, please. Maybe there is some exotic art I could see."

Mac laughed huskily. "Aren't I the one that is supposed to be trying to lure you to my house not the other way around?"

"Are you saying no?" Nina asked with her hands on her hips.

He pressed a hard kiss on her lips. "Hell no, don't move, I'll be back in the blink of an eye."

He actually took off in a jog across the lawn, and she had a wide smile on her face as she watched him. He wasn't hard to spot as he casually walked over to the bar and, with the stealth of a man who knew his way around, pilfered food. He had a bottle of champagne and glasses in one hand, but on impulse he took a tray of dessert canapes in the other and made his way back to her.

"In case we get hungry," he explained. "Follow me."

Nina did so without hesitation to the back of the manor where the noise of the party had lessened. She walked gingerly in her heels across the stone path that led to the cottage and took the tray as he pressed the code on the door to unlock it. Nina stepped inside in front of him, and he turned on a small lamp on an accent table to reveal an expertly decorated cottage that gave off a welcoming feeling even with contemporary furniture.

"I have never been in here before," Nina said. "Zeva has an eye for decorating."

"Thank God Jasper changed around that manor house when he first became Duke—and Zeva just en-hanced it," Mac said. "When we were young, walking in there felt like walking into the past, with old thick, dusty drapes and out-of-date large pieces of furniture. It used to give me the willies."

She gave him a teasing look. "The willies?"

"You know, the icky feeling like something is going to jump out and eat your face off," Mac took off his jacket and threw it over the back of a high-backed chair.

"Well, I do know what you mean and that visual was a bit extreme. I think we should never watch scary movies together," Nina kicked off her heels. "Oh, that feels good to get those off my feet."

"Well, blast it all—here I was fantasizing about you wearing those with nothing else on," he murmured as he poured a glass of bubbly and passed it to her.

"You want me standing around naked in red and gold heels?" Nina asked before taking a sip from her glass.

"Trust me, you wouldn't be standing for long," his voice was laced with desire.

"Where do you sleep?" Nina asked as her heart raced in her chest.

"Through there." He inclined his head to the doorway of a darkened room.

Nina walked in that direction, but at the doorway she looked back over her shoulder. "Are you coming, or do you want me to start without you?"

"I don't know which I want, for you to start and I

walk in or to be a part of it from the very beginning," Mac moved toward her, pulling his tie loose with one hand.

"Grab the bottle, I may want to lick champagne off you," Nina explained.

His chest was against her back as they moved into the room together. Mac only put on a small light to change the darkness to a sensual dim glow.

Nina put her glass and the bottle of champagne down on the bedside table. She climbed onto the high bed with the curved mahogany headboard. "To your recent pondered choices, I have a counter-offer. We have all night, why not both?"

"God, I adore you,' Mac said fiercely.

He didn't put his own drink down. Instead he drank the contents with two quick gulps before running his hand around the back of her neck and pulling her into his kiss.

"Lord, you make my knees weak when you kiss me," Nina gasped between the hot way their lips met.

Mac groaned. "If you only knew how many dirty things I've dreamt about you."

"Please show me every one of them," Nina encouraged him and moved away long enough to shimmy her dress down her body until her full breasts were revealed to his intense gaze. "Now where do we start?"

"Take the dress the rest of the way off and then sit with your back against the headboard," Mac coaxed gently. His eyes never left her body. "Leave your panties on."

Nina did as he asked and left only the sexy lace boy-cut short panties against her skin. His eyes followed her hands as she cupped her breasts before running them down her torso.

"What next, Mr. Black?" she asked.

"Spread your legs for me," he commanded. His shirt was open now, and he slipped it from his broad shoulders. "Pull your panties aside and let me see you touch yourself."

She moved her legs slowly apart, loving how his eyes never missed a movement. Nina slipped down only a little so she could lift her hips. And with her left hand she moved her underwear aside to reveal the trimmed mound of her sex. A slow hiss of breath escaped him when she ran two fingers down the slit of her pussy and parted it to reveal the pink inner labia. She lightly grazed her clit and bit her lip as the sensation ran through her like electricity. Mac stepped out of his pants and on to the bed, kneeling between her legs and kissing her while she teased her own sex to wetness.

Mac put his glass down and moved towards her, covering her hand with his own and Nina shifted her hips restlessly. His kisses moved to her neck, and he sucked the soft flesh as he sank a digit within her pussy. A gasp escaped her as heat flooded her core and made Nina cream even more between her legs. Mac's touch was slow and deliberate, and to add to her pleasure he sucked one of the pert tips of her nipple into his mouth down to the areola. Her hips lifted to the rhythm of his penetration of her sex, and Nina could feel herself on the brink of coming.

"Ah, Mac," she gasped and pumped her hips against his hand.

"Not yet," he moved his hand away, and Nina vented her frustration with a not-too-gentle bite on his shoulder. "Woman, I am on the brink of losing control."

"That's a good thing, because right now, I really want you inside me," Nina rubbed the outline of his cock through his boxer briefs. "Oh Lord, you are deliciously thick."

"We are so going to need confession after this." He stripped off the last barrier, and his sex was revealed to her greedy touch.

"I'll confess, I loved every minute of it," she licked her lips in anticipation.

Nina moved further down the bed and bit her lips as she teased him by touching herself once more. He watched her hungry touch as her desire rose, while Nina pinched her cocoa bean nipples, loving how they tightened and ached. Her eyes never left his face while her hands went down the smooth skin of her torso to the apex of her thick thighs. Nina wasn't skinny, but she wasn't considered plump either, she was right in that middle ground that made shopping for the correct size difficult. Jeans enhanced the curve of her ass and small waist while her thighs gave her that hourglass shape. Mac seemed to approve and stilled her hands when she went to finally remove her panties.

"I'm fucking you with them on, and then they are mine to keep," Mac's voice was rough. "Make them wet for me."

That little kinky demand only served to make her more aroused. Nina's fingertips grazed the lips of her pussy and gasped while Mac watched. She rubbed her clit, and her wetness coated her fingers. He moved away until his head was between her legs and she could feel his breath on her wet fingers coated with her own juices. Mac seemed to lose control, and he pulled her to him in one rough jerk. He tasted her while she touched herself and she felt his tongue delve into her sex along with her digits.

Nina's hand fell away as she succumbed to the pleasure coursing through her veins. It was his turn to please her, and Mac went about it with almost greedy intent. He spread the full lips of her sex and sucked at her clit before lashing it with his tongue. She heard a low, guttural sound just before he grabbed her thighs and buried his face into the center of her desire. Nina pulled at his shoulder and cried out while her body undulated against his seeking mouth. She pleaded for release, and Mac would not be denied the bounty from her body. He grabbed her hands and pinned then down by her thighs, anchoring her so she couldn't squirm away from his lips and tongue. Nina came with a cry, and as her body arched off the bed, Mac groaned his satisfaction. But he didn't stop.

"Mac, oh God, I . . ." Nina couldn't formulate words to what she was feeling.

He used his fingers to fuck her now: deep, penetrating thrusts with two thick digits that drove her crazy. He didn't relent—far from it—as he stimulated her pussy, he sampled her breasts and then her lips. She could taste her own essence on his mouth and tongue as a second orgasm rocked through her.

"Ride me," he ordered and lay against the mattress.

Nina straddled him eagerly, and he held his cock while she moved her panties aside and positioned herself over his body. Together they were caught in a pure sexual haze where the need to consummate became the one and only mission. Nina bit her lip as she felt the thickness of his cock slide into her; she took him easily until he throbbed deeply within her. Mac's groan seemed to reverberate through her entire being. Nina braced her hand on the sturdy headboard and began to ride him slowly, letting his rod almost slip out of her sex before taking it deep again. She rolled her hips as a timeless rhythm took hold and his hands gripped her hips tightly before moving to cup her ass.

"Tell me what you want," Mac demanded.

"My nipples in your mouth while we fuck," she begged.

How was it so easy to tell him her desires? The thought flashed thought her head but was quickly replaced with passion when Mac did as she asked. He gave both chocolate-colored mounds the same attention, as the pace of their bodies increased and she was pounding her hips against him and the driving race to the culmination of their passion.

"More, baby, more," Mac said through gritted teeth. She bent lower like a jockey taking her mount to the finish line. Nina could feel her wetness against her thighs and his legs. The sweet slapping sound each time their bodies connected filled the room.

"Tell me I can have it," Mac said harshly. "All of you anytime I want, in the car, an alley, bent over the table in the kitchen. Tell me you'll always be hot and wet for my cock."

"Yes!" Nina cried out. "You're going to make me come talking like that."

"You'll be mine, and I'm yours," he pulled her

head down and kissed her savagely. "God, I've been crazy with wanting you."

Mac moved his hand between then and found her clit as they moved, building her to the brink of ecstasy. Nina was writhing with excitement from his talented fingers and the feel of his penetration. She cried out when she felt his fingers almost slipping inside her with his shaft.

"Don't stop," she moaned. "I'm coming."

"Fuck yes, I can feel it," he kissed her hard and with his hand at the back of her neck he pressed his forehead against hers. "I want to see your eyes when you come."

Nina opened her eyes to meet his dark gaze and focused on the mirror image reflecting back at her. She could feel his breath on her mouth like a kiss, and the heat burned through her, searing her to the very core and branding her as his. It built with every thrust, each breath, and her body trembled. Nina closed her eyes as waves of her release almost drowned her in pleasure. The gooseflesh that covered her skin was a side effect of coming. She came gasping his name as she felt his arms envelop her. Mac's release shuddered through him, and together they were left trembling in the aftermath of what she could positively say was the best sex she'd ever had in her life.

"Do you think this proves we have a spark?" Mac asked after heaving out a contented sigh.

"I would say yes," Nina answered. "I wonder if they're looking for us at the main house?"

"They can look; they won't find us," Mac pulled her closer. "I don't plan on moving from this bed unless it's for sustenance or bathroom breaks."

"I eventually have to go home," she pointed out.

Mac cupped her cheek, caressing the soft skin, and their eyes connected. "How about we work on that tomorrow?"

Nina nodded. "Okay."

She spent the night. While they talked intimately, they heard the sounds of the party being wrapped up. More than once people passed by the little cottage talking while they were inside cocooned in his bed. When she finally left the next morning, her coat was folded neatly in a decorative wagon outside the door. Their absence was indeed noticed, and Zeva or Jasper knew exactly where she was. There was no morning-after walk of shame as they walked to his car to take her home. In fact as they held hands, she felt nothing but contentment.

Chapter Six

Why couldn't things run smoothly just once? Mac thought as he drove through the dark streets of Northumberland. This was how his entire day had been eaten up, instead of spending time with Nina and enjoying her effervescent joy over Christmas. He was searching for Donnie, who had managed to slip out of the safe house and go missing. Mac expected it, but still he hoped that for once Donnie would show an inkling of common sense and do what he was told. Bouchey still would be looking for Donnie to claim his debt regardless of Mac's threat. Bouchey wasn't one to give up easily, even if he feared his adversary. He was biding his time waiting for Mac to go home, but Mac had every intention of getting Donnie out of Northumberland before he returned to D.C.

Or am I even going back to stay? That was a question that swirled around in his head now. Should he ask Nina to move to D.C. with him, or should he finally put down roots where his began? It was something he had to work out on his own; his clients were all over the world and he could keep his offices in D.C. *and* stay here.

Mac put his focus back on searching the seedier parts of Northumberland for his brother. Haile and Jasper were out as well, and between the three of them they hoped to find him somewhere alive—not dead in a ditch. It was around eight in the evening when Mac finally got a call from one of his friends.

"One of my people spotted him trying to get into one of Bouchey's places," Haile said in lieu of a greeting.

"Drug hole?" Mac asked.

"No, he was spotted just before that getting his fix across the street; it's when he went to the whore-house they knew it was Donnie for sure," Haile explained. "He's on Height Road."

"Why don't the cops shut these places down?" Mac muttered, turning the car in the direction he needed to go.

"They do, but then they spring up in another place. Bouchey wants to run girls now and get in bed with the traffickers," Haile commented. "Won't be long before the police find his head in the river."

"Maybe not even that big dumb part," Mac muttered. "I'll be there in five. Call Jasper and tell him we have a line on Donnie and to head home. We don't need the Duke of Northumberland being seen outside a known prostitution house."

"But it's good for me?" Haile teased.

"An old whore knows . . ."

"Fuck you," Haile cut him off by hanging up the phone.

The levity was over, and then it was the grim drive to Height Road. It wasn't an easy task to just drag Donnie out of the place that had a neon sign that read *Homeopathic Massage and Circulative Therapy*.

Yeah right, Mac thought. The only therapy in there was hand jobs and pussy by fifteen-minute increments. If they could afford a whole hour with a girl, that was a treat and the john probably saved a whole month for the service.

"Get your brother out of here before Bouchey shows up," one of the doormen said.

He was another guy Mac had run the streets with; even though he worked for Bouchey, he still seemed to have some semblance of morality.

"Wayne, we'll get square with you when we can," Haile murmured to the man.

Wayne nodded. "I know, just not here, too many eyes. Just go through the back when you grab him."

Mac quickly figured out it was he who had called Haile to let him know where Donnie was.

"We have to make it look good, man," Haile said. "We don't need Bouchey questioning your loyalty."

Wayne flexed his neck and glanced at both of

them "Been hit before; give us two in the ribs, that's my weak spot."

"Mac, you go for the ribs, I'll do the face," Haile said. "That will be extra in the envelope, Wayne, thanks."

It was over in seconds, and Wayne was leaning against the wall holding his side. Mac made sure to knock over a table and bust a few doors on his way through the house that had been converted to one-room massage parlors where Bouchey's girls did their business. Donnie was practically screaming for some girl who worked there and begging to see her just for a minute more.

Mac grabbed him by the neck and shook him. "What the fuck is wrong with you; do you actually have a death wish?"

Donnie's eyes were glassy, and his speech slurred. "I have to see her, Mackie. She's all I got."

"Don't ever call me Mackie," Mac snarled and shoved his brother toward the door. "I'm getting you out of here."

Donnie reared back and hit Mac before banging on the parlor door again. "Britt, don't be scared it's just me, please. Please come out."

"Donnie, who's Britt?" Haile held Mac back from grabbing his brother again.

"She's the only thing that matters in this damn town," Donnie said miserably. "Bouchey owns her, and I was trying to win enough to pay him out, but he keeps raising the prices. . . ."

Mac finally began to understand and took a deep breath. "Donnie, you can't help her, especially not when you're not clean."

"I need to get brave, to come and get her," Donnie's voice broke. "I . . . ain't you, Mac. I never was like you."

Haile tapped lightly on the door. "Britt, this is someone that can help. Open the door."

After a few seconds of hesitation, the barrier was finally opened a crack to reveal a waif of a girl. Mac could see wide blue eyes and a fragile face that was deathly afraid. He knew then with all certainty he wasn't leaving until Bouchey was taken down and in jail.

"How old are you?" Mac asked.

"Twenty-one," she said in a thin, weak voice. "Get him out of here before he gets popped!"

"You can come with us if you want," Haile said. "We know people who can help."

She shook her head. "I can't, he owns my contract, and if I go, he will kill my family,"

"We won't let that happen," Mac said. 'Come with us."

A car door slammed, and they heard the noise of Bouchey and his crew, who were notified Donnie was there.

"Go, please, before he kills all of you," Britt said frantically. "He'll beat me just for talking to Donnie."

"We'll come back for you," Mac said firmly. "Donnie, we have to go; we'll be back, I promise."

"We have to take her, man," Donnie cried out. "Just grab her, and let's run."

"No, I'm not leaving," Britt shook her head in an emphatic *no*.

Haile snapped his fingers. "Last name, what is it?"

"Flagstaff," she said and slammed the door.

Mac hauled a struggling Donnie down the hallway to the back of the house with Haile close on his heels. They got out, and Haile used a loose piece of rebar that was lying in the overgrown backyard to brace against the door. By the time they got around the house, Mac, his brother, and Haile would be long gone. Donnie was starting to shake not from the cold but the shit that was in his veins. Being without at the safe house, he'd gone for a big dose—and God knows how much he'd put up his nose, and in his veins, the entire day he was gone.

"Can you take him to the safe house?" Mac asked. "I'm going to Nina. I don't think this is one we can let him puke out—maybe she can help."

Haile nodded. "I'm on it."

They got him in the car, and Donnie was mumbling to himself in his drug-induced delirium. "Get Britt, she needed help, please . . . Britt . . . Britt."

Mac took his hand. "We'll help her, Donnie, but first we have to save you."

"Go find Nina, we are going to need IV fluids and the like," Haile said.

Mac slammed the car door and jogged to his own vehicle. He made the drive to the hospital in record time and hoped to god she wasn't off her shift yet. He saw her coming down the stairs as he pushed through the glass doors. Her eyes lit up when she saw him, and his heartbeat sped up just a bit faster. No woman had ever looked like that when they'd seen him, and both happiness and affection were written all over her face.

"I didn't expect to see you until later," Nina said and pressed a kiss on his lips.

The sensation was heaven, and although he wanted to sink into it, the more pressing issue of Donnie was at the top of the list.

"Nina, Donnie escaped the safe house and went on a full- day binge," Mac explained.

"Damn it, why would he leave?" Nina asked. "His withdrawal symptoms were managed and everything."

Mac took her hand. "Not anymore, he already has the shakes. Idiot used this as courage to go after some girl."

Nina shook her head. "I don't get that, but meet me at the car, I have to go liberate some supplies."

He laughed softly. "Such a nice way to say *pilfer*."

She slapped at his ass and ran back upstairs while he went back out to the car. In a matter of minutes, she was walking quickly from around the back side of the hospital instead of the front door. She carried a medium, yellow plastic container that looked suspiciously like a bedpan, but he wasn't going to question it. She was doing him a favor by trying to help his brother. She slid the container into the back seat and before he reached over and opened the passenger door.

"I had to take a detour; Matron Potter was snooping around," Nina explained as she got in the car. "I don't know how she ends up on our floor when she works in the palliative care ward now. Anyway, I got banana bags to give him a constant IV, we use it for people who come in fall-out-the-rocker drunk. I have Zofran patches for behind his ear to help with nausea and to dry up some of that mucus he will be making. I don't want him to be miserable so I had a friend in the pharmacy give me something so we can keep him resting."

"Thank you," Mac said gratefully, but he was still worried. "I don't want you in trouble because of me or Donnie."

"I'm not on hospital grounds what I do on my

own time they can't say a thing." She patted his hand. "Besides, they won't know. I have people I can trust."

He nodded. "Okay, well, let's get him back on the right track. The police are looking for him because of things Bouchey had him do. I'm trying to keep him off the radar until that's taken care of."

"You said this was all for a girl?" Nina questioned as he pulled away from the hospital and merged into traffic to drive to the safe house.

Mac explained exactly what had gone on that day and where they'd found Donnie. She was outraged to learn what Bouchey was making the young women do for profit. He also mentioned their plan to shut him down for good.

"We have to get Zeva in on this," Nina said firmly. "They are going to need proper care and resources, so they don't end up back on the streets and being pimped out for a living."

"I agree," Mac answered. "But one thing at a time."

At the safe house he watched as Nina gave Donnie an examination with a gentle but firm hand as he lay on the bed. He was already sweating profusely, and the heroin sickness was making him retch. There was nothing in his stomach to bring up, because junkies feed the high and not their stomachs half the time. But she got an IV into his arm and gave him the medicines she'd brought. Mac saw his brother start to rest more comfortably.

"Can you please fill the pan I brought with warm water? I need a washcloth and some soap to bathe him down," Nina ordered. "There's nothing worse than trying to fight withdrawal in sweaty clothes and sheets."

"I can do that," Mac said instantly.

"It's nothing I've never seen before. You asked for my help, let me do my job," she gave him a curt look. "This is my life every day, Mac, I can be quicker and more efficient, plus I know how to get him undressed without pulling the IV in his arm. Just get me what I need and some clean stuff for him to wear."

"Yes ma'am," Mac said, sufficiently chastised, and left the bedroom.

She did let him help when it came to getting Donnie moved and the bedsheets changed. Together they re-dressed him, and Nina pushed the dark curls away from his face as he slept.

"Poor thing," she murmured. "You'll come out on the good side of this, Donnie. I'm sure of it."

She stood and left the room, and Mac followed. Outside the door he pulled her into his arms and then buried his face in her neck.

"Thank you, love," he said huskily. "He would be suffering right now if it wasn't for you."

Nina wrapped her arms around his waist. "I'm here for you both."

"Get a room," Haile said from the door. In his arms he carried bags. "Mrs. H. sent food, told you both to eat it."

"I won't ever refuse her food," Nina moved away and took the bags.

Nina unpacked the food, and Haile moved closer to speak to Mac. "Jerry said he could come watch him tonight, he's a medic so he knows about the IVs. Since Donnie has proven to be a runner, he will definitely keep an eye on him so you can go sleep."

"What time will he be here?" Mac asked as he looked at his watch.

"Be at least ten-thirty when he gets out of work," Haile explained.

"Mac will be coming back to my flat so he can rest and be close by," Nina said firmly, and her eyes dared him to say no.

Not that he ever would; lying next to her warm body was the only pleasurable thought at the moment.

"I have more surveillance on Bouchey now," Haile also told him. "Wayne won't say shit, but I will give him the head's-up when we bring the hammer down, so he's not caught up. He's a good guy, a bit daft in the intelligence department but dependable. I'll find him new work."

"Sounds good," Mac answered as he moved toward the table. "Are you eating?"

Haile didn't follow; instead he went to the door. "I've got to get home to Mari; I'm worried about this constant morning sickness."

"Isn't her doctor doing anything?" Nina asked.

Haile made a disgusted sound in his throat. "That old idiot keeps telling her she's fine, just power through, women do this all the time. Then he makes it seem like she is being overdramatic because she is my wife and I'm there. We're changing doctors to the midwife center over in Allendale, but we can't get an appointment until next week."

"I'll come by tomorrow and take care of her," Nina said. "One of the female doctors at the hospital won't have any problem getting her a prescription for medicine and an IV filled with yummy vitamins to get her system happy again. She is probably going to end up dehydrated and in the hospital at this rate."

"I basically told Dr. Bryant if anything happens to her or my child, I will take it out on his sixty-year-old ass," Haile said and ran a hand through his hair in frustration. "Mrs. H. has been making her light broth—that stays down—and plenty of ginger ale."

"Stop at the market and get some lemon drops or candied lemon rind," Nina advised. "Also give her a cup of hot tea with lemon, something about the tartness helps with pregnancy nausea."

"I'll stop at the market on the way," Haile promised. "Thank you."

"Send her both our love," Mac said as Haile stepped out the door.

"Will do," he promised and closed the door behind him.

Mac settled at the small table with Nina, and together they ate the fish and chips from the pub. There was also some of the very same broth in the bag for Donnie in case he was able to eat. His brother slept while they were there and continued to slumber when Jerry showed up. They finally left around eleven, and instead of driving out to the cottage at the manor house, Mac did what he was told and climbed the stairs to Nina's apartment over the pub.

Mac looked around, recalling when it was an empty, dusty hideout for him and his friends. Or when he needed a place to lie low after the cops got on his ass. Haile used to bring him food when it was too hot to be on the streets, including the time Mac had beaten his father into unconsciousness for laying hands on his mum. Well, this had been his home for a week where he slept on a dingy, old sleeping bag and listened to the radio to escape the hopelessness and silence that surrounded him.

"Hey, what's wrong?" Nina moved closer to slip her arms around his waist.

"Nothing," he smiled down at her and pressed a soft kiss against her full lips. "Memories."

"Good or bad?" she questioned.

"A little of both," he admitted. "But right now, holding you like this, they seem to melt away."

"You have a very charming mouth," she teased.

"Enough to warrant another kiss?" Mac asked hopefully.

"Better than that," she said with a wink. "How about a shower and a massage? You've been wound so tight, I swear all the muscles of your neck are bunched up to your ears."

"I won't refuse that," he murmured. "I must warn you, it may lead to other kinds of rubbing."

"Oh, I'm hoping," she purred and pushed him toward the bathroom. "There are towels in the small pantry next to the sink."

Mac took a shower in the small bathroom that seemed smaller than he remembered; even the tub made him feel like a large, clumsy oaf. He came out wearing only his boxers, and as she slipped past him to take her turn under the hot spray of a shower Nina smacked his ass. He couldn't help but grin. She made him happy, with her tart mouth and saucy attitude. She didn't take shit from anyone—even him. Nina had no problem calling him on his shit when he tried to be a complete asshole and would accept nothing less than respect. It terrified him that she had become so completely immersed in his life in such a short time that he couldn't think about not being with her. But there was more to discuss, think about, and plan for. He didn't know which way he was going as yet. *Is it fair to ask her to travel an uncertain road with me?*

"You're thinking so hard, you have those lines in your forehead," Nina commented as she walked into the bedroom, drawing his attention to her. She had braided her hair and piled the thick plait on her head before securing it with one of those colorful scrunchie things. She wore short shorts with a hibiscus print and a tank top that allowed a peek at the chocolate skin of her torso. His eyes traveled from the tips of her purple-painted toenails up her legs to thick thighs then to her generous hips and tiny waist. Her full breasts enticed him, and Mac's thoughts were forgotten as desire kicked in for his curvaceous beauty.

"You have my complete attention," the words smoothly left his lips because it was exactly the truth.

"Good," she said and sat on the edge of the bed and opened a drawer. "Turn over and let me work those shoulders."

"Should I ask why you have massage oil in your bedside table?" His voice was partially muffled by a pillow.

Mac felt her straddle his lower back, and he could feel the warmth between her legs as she sat on his ass. Nina bent over and whispered in his ear and spoke in a teasing whisper. "Maybe I like a little extra lubrication when I touch myself."

"Oh wow."

Mack groaned at the mental image, and the little squeeze she gave him with her thighs. There was no doubt his hard cock was pressed into the mattress of the bed as she began to work his shoulders with soft circles using her fists, the oil giving her enough range of motion that she could glide her palm easily over his skin. He closed his eyes in pleasure as her touch not only inflamed him but released the tension that he didn't even notice had tied his muscles in knots. Mac sank into the sensations of her touch as she ran her hands down to his lower back and began to ease the tension there as well.

His mind turned from the sweet pressure of her hands to fucking her until they both couldn't walk afterward. A surprised cry escaped her when he turned, and she toppled off his back. Mac was there to pull her against him before she fell to the mattress, and he was kissing her ravenously. Mac took her hand and slipped it into his loose boxers so she could take his thick phallus into her grasp. Nina wrapped her fingers around him and stroked, causing a guttural noise to rumble from his chest.

"Did I even mention I love your dick," she said and trailed a light touch over the smooth tip.

"Jesus," he muttered. "You keep saying things like that and it will be over before it begins."

"I know your sex game, Mackenzie Black, you never leave me unsatisfied," she said and bit his chin. "You just slip in me nice and slow, and I'm already coming."

"Fuck."

Nina's words drove him to the primal place in his mind where the thought of being buried between her legs consumed him. Her hands roamed over the strong contours of his shoulders while their lips met in short, sweet kisses that soon turned heated and filled with need. Her touch inflamed him as each caress was like fire against his skin. He gathered up the ends of her tank shirt and pulled it overhead, freeing her from the confines of the material. He filled his hands with the smooth globes of her breasts and watched as she arched into his palms.

"You're so bloody responsive; it's like your body craves my touch," Mac murmured with awe and assuredness in his voice. "Do I arouse you, Nina?"

"In every possible way," she whispered.

He chuckled when she squirmed on the bed to get her shorts off. One thing Mac loved about Nina: She never wore panties if she didn't have to. It was an on-going puzzle in his head wondering anytime he saw her if she was going commando under her clothes. And that usually led to a hard-on. Her hands at his shorts brought his attention back to the present, and he helped her remove the last piece of material that separated skin from skin. Nina pressed hot kisses again on his chest and then bit his nipple wickedly.

"You can play now, but you'll be screaming my name later," Mac teased.

Nina winked. "Promise?"

The thought excited him as he watched her with growing desire when she pushed him back on the bed and took his cock in her grasp. He was hard and aching, engorged. Mac held his breath anticipating her next action as she knelt in front of him. Nina looked up at him with sultry, wicked eyes and stroked him, making his hips rise in response. She bent over and licked the tip of his length, and he was unable to hold back a groan as he clenched his fist into the coverlet beneath him. He wanted to feel her lips around his shaft and her tongue as she tried to milk him dry with her mouth.

"How does that feel?" Nina murmured.

"I want more." His thigh muscles flexed as she continued to stroke him. "Taste me."

Nina trailed her mouth along his shaft, and that was almost his undoing. Mac tried to pull her to him and roll her beneath him to fuck her. But Nina slapped his hand away and raised a finger. "Have a little patience, honey bun."

Her mouth was around the smooth head of his

cock, and she used her tongue to swirl around the sensitive tip, teasing him. *Shit!* Mac closed his eyes as his balls tightened, and he forced himself to calm down so he wouldn't release his load on her lips. He arched his head into the pillow and gave himself over to the hot, sucking motion of her mouth, which she combined with the corkscrew action of her hands. Her saliva added lubrication, a sensation that made him burn hot. Mac buried his hands in her hair, thrusting his cock deeper between her lips but pulling away suddenly when he felt the first hints of come building at the base of his cock.

He pulled her eagerly against him and kissed her, and as their lips clung together Nina pushed her undies down her legs in haste. Their lips dueled with greedy abandon, and he tried to control the savageness of his kisses, but it was impossible. The part of him that craved her took over while he slipped his hand between her legs. Nina whimpered into his mouth as he caressed her, and her hips jerked in response. God, she felt so damn good, slick and moist as he teased her clit and when he slid his two fingers deep inside her, she swallowed her cry of pleasure. Mac's own groan echoed from his chest, the hot walls of her sex clenched around his digits as he inserted and retreated from her aroused pussy. He grunted in satisfaction when Nina spread her legs wider, and she undulated on his fingers.

Mac watched her, the kiss ended, and her head was thrown back. Enthralled by the carnal lust on her face, he loved hearing the soft noises of passion that escaped her parted lips. He sat up and anchored her, ceasing her movements by wrapping his free hand around her waist. Mac fucked her with his fingers while he teased and feasted on her nipples. He ached to be buried within her, and she was so fucking wet that it ran down his fingers. Nina was fire, molten lava, a water nymph in the way her body moved, and she had claimed him down to the fabric of his soul.

"Come for me, love," he demanded of her softly. "Give it all to me."

"Yes, oh Lord, now!" Nina cried out.

Her body trembled, and she leaned against his shoulder biting the flesh under her lips. A hiss escaped him, and the sting left by her teeth only seemed to enhance his pleasure as he felt every tremor that rolled through her body. It was all he could take, Mac moved so she was on the mattress and positioned her so he could fuck her from behind. Needing her so deeply was indescribable, he gritted his teeth while he ran the head of his shaft over the wet slit of her sex and she wiggled trying to take him in. A low groan escaped him as he thrust deep. Mac fought against the assault of pleasure coursing through him and trying to take him under too soon.

The only way he could describe it was that she pulsed around his cock, the walls of her pussy seemed to clench around his engorged length each time he drove himself into her depth. She was like liquid satin as she moved her hips, pushing back until his hips collided with her firm ass. With his hands at her waist he let go of the last constraints of his control and fucked her like a man possessed. Nina was on her knees now with her arms around his neck so she wouldn't fall. Mac reached around and cupped her breasts as they raced toward the ultimate end of their coupling.

"I'm so close," he groaned out, his breathing harsh. "I want to . . . make it last . . . ah, fuck!"

Nina was on her knees and elbows, the curve of her body and ass even more accentuated from this position. "Don't you stop, Mackenzie Black, make me come all over your dick!"

"I love when you say things like that," Mac couldn't stop watching her, and he ran his hands down the curve of her back while he pumped into her. It ravaged his senses.

He grabbed her hips and pulled her against him hard, loving the wet slapping sounds their bodies made with each deep connection.

"I'm going to come," she whimpered and arched sensuously.

It was sheer pleasure, primal, a driving force that

raced them toward the end. He vaguely understood that the animalistic grunts and sounds came from him, and when he reached around to tease her clit, Nina's orgasm took hold and he closed his eyes in pleasure.

"Ahhh, fuck!"

The words were almost a shout and torn from his lips. He bared his teeth and threw his head back as his balls tightened to the point of pain before his release. Each thrust sent his come into the recesses of her pussy. He felt her hand stroking the sensitive sacs of his balls while his release rocketed through him.

Mac thrust into her harder, faster, prolonging the sensations and he groaned her name while her cries seemed to echo through him. Nina slumped against the mattress, and he fell against her, his hard body pressing her firmly into the bed. He inhaled her scent, combined with his, and the smell of sex that was unique to them. Time seemed to stand still while he was with her. Nina was all he ever wanted and didn't know existed out there. She shifted and purred, and the feeling of her ass made him think about fucking her all over again. Mac moved until he lay beside her and stared at the ceiling with a satisfied smile on his face.

"Nina I was thinking about us, this is good, what we have here. How do you feel about the United

States?" His voice was husky as he laced fingers with hers.

Nina turned to face him. "I feel like I would be starting from the beginning because the immigration and work visa suck. I'd be a first-year nurse, whereas I'm working toward being in charge of a ward here."

"I have connections, I can work round that," he said, hoping to change her mind.

"That's not fair; for you it was easy, for a black immigrant regardless of if they are from Africa or the Caribbean, it's a struggle to find your career dream there. I'd have to start school all over again to get U.S. accreditation," Nina said gently. "Then, I would feel like a complete fraud, if you'd have to pull strings for me. They're not working against my value, my intelligence, or my experience, it's a favor to you."

"I don't know if I can stay here, after Donnie," Mac said the words and heard the plea in his voice.

"I never asked you to," Nina said bluntly. "And you shouldn't ask me to change my life for you."

"Then where are we in this relationship thing?" Mac asked.

Nina smiled. "At the very beginning, enjoying each other without restrictions or reservations. If you leave, I'll remember you with fond memories because I don't do long-distance. You'll find someone, and so shall I in a case like that."

"I don't want to think of you with any other man." The words were terse when they left his lips.

Nina leaned over and kissed him. "Stop stressing this, whatever is meant to happen will happen."

Mac glanced at Nina. "I don't know if I should be worried that this isn't bothering you."

"You shouldn't," Nina said slowly. "But if this is one of these things where you need an insecure woman to bite her nails down then pull the petals off a flower all the while saying *he loves me, he loves me not*, I am *not* that girl. Don't ruin an amazing night; I think the future will work itself out."

Mac cupped his hand behind her neck and took her lips, tasting slowly and deliberately stoking the fire within them once more. He hoped his kiss spoke volumes about what he wanted to say but couldn't. Could he just walk away and go back to a life in D.C.? Thinking of any other man touching her caused a feral growl to escape him, and he covered her body with his. Mac thrust deep swallowing her cry as she arched against him. He fucked her hard, pushing her legs back so he could see himself sinking into her and then see the ecstasy on her face. He was trying to erase the thought of moving on from his mind and from hers. But even as they raced to the edge of sanity in a sexual storm, it only served to imprint Nina more onto his very being.

Chapter Seven

Nina hummed as she moved around her small kitchen; her Christmas tree was lit, she was baking pound cake, and a small ham was in the oven. There was a glass of Guinness making a wet ring on her table lightly coated with flour, and she was cutting out cookies for the oven. This was her holiday, it reminded her of home, but it was still was way more peaceful. It never really snowed in Northumberland, but she saw some flakes because of a cold snap. And the weather said they may get at least a few inches before or by Christmas. Nina was super- excited for that to happen because she had never seen snow. The fact that there was a man in her life, albeit complicated as it was, only seemed to make it better.

A small frown erased her smile for a little bit. Mac definitely was unlike any man she'd ever met. Him thinking she would blindly follow him to the United States and start all over again kind of pissed Nina off. She'd spent so much time being what everyone else expected her to be, so that when she finally started to live for herself, people couldn't handle it. Moving to Northumberland and taking the opportunities presented to her was the best decision she'd ever made. There was no way she was giving that up to march to someone else's drumbeat. If Mac wanted her or felt this was worth it, he would stay at home where he belonged.

If he got on a plane back to D.C., then it meant she wasn't important enough — and she would move on, too. It would hurt like hell, but Nina had rebuilt her heart, and she could again. Nina already admitted to herself she had come to more than care for Mac, but the ball was in his court. She wasn't going to let that mar her evening — and the party at work would be receiving her baked goods the next day. *Mrs. Claus has nothing on me,* she thought with a smile.

She wasn't even going to think about the strange car that had followed her a few times in the week after her shift. Gossip was already going around that Trevor Bouchey had some kind of beef with Mac and Haile. Jasper's name was never mentioned, but Nina knew he would be somewhere in there behind the scenes because he was part of the trio.

Jasper was more in the spotlight because of his title and his duties as Duke, that didn't mean he wouldn't help Mac or Haile when it came to Bouchey. Anyone could tell they were all as close as brothers. With her music on full blast, she took a sip of her Guinness. The apartment had sound-proofing in the floors and wall, keeping out the Friday night. Nina could enjoy her own music without the pub sounds bleeding into it, so she'd almost missed the loud knocking on her door. Dusting her hands on her apron that boasted red candy canes and snowflakes, she turned down the music and went to answer the door. Mac's handsome face greeted her as he leaned one shoulder against the door frame. He wore the black turtleneck and blue jeans well, but it was the reindeer ears with mistletoe hat that made her laugh.

"What is on your head?" Nina asked.

"Haile has them downstairs on the bar, so I grabbed one," Mac patted the ears. "Why, doesn't it suit me? I hear it's all the rage in the fashion circuits."

"I can dig it," Nina stepped aside. "Come on in; you can help me bake."

Mac walked through the doorway. "Ah, so that's what's on your face and hair! I thought you were a frosted sugar plum just for me."

"Wanna provide the glaze?" Nina asked wickedly.

It took a moment before he figured out what she meant, and his eyes widened before a laugh escaped him. "That is simply perverted."

Nina shimmied in a little dance before smacking a kiss on his lips. "It really is."

"Reggae Christmas music," he commented as he

followed her into the kitchen. "I like it, and it smells good in here."

"Grab some oven mittens and take that tray of cookies out and pop this one in," Nina commanded from her position back at the table. "This is part of Barbadian—well, Caribbean—culture, calypso and reggae can make anything better."

Mac did as he was told before lifting the cloth over a mixing bowl. "Sounds interesting. What's in here? Can I taste it?"

"No, you may not! It's not healthy to eat raw batter," Nina replied. "That's my pound cake, I like to leave it sitting awhile before I put it in the oven."

"Come on, one taste," he begged.

She shook her head and cut more reindeer cookies. "It has raw eggs in it, there is a potential for salmonella, honey bun. You can have a cookie instead."

Mac took a cookie off the tray and bit the head off a snowman. "You called me *honey bun*."

She cast a glance at him. "Did it bother you?"

He shrugged. "It's cute, no one has ever looked at me and thought *well, there's a man I want to give a cute pet name to.*"

Nina sighed. "Well, I see past whatever you or anyone else thinks you are. By the way, why are you here? You and Haile have been playing secret monkey the last few days."

"Squirrel." Mac said.

She frowned. "What?"

He smiled. "It's secret squirrel not monkey."

Nina put her flour-covered hands on her hips. "Monkeys are smarter than squirrels, so they'd have more secrets."

"But squirrels secret away nuts to last them throughout the winter, hence the term," Mac explained.

Nina took a sip of her dark ale. "Look at you, teaching me something new—you deserve another cookie."

He picked another snowman and raised it in a cheer. "Thank you, I think I will. In any case I may need your help with what Haile and I have been doing. The place where we found Donnie, we are going to help facilitate a raid and get those girls out."

"Great!" Nina said. She was worried knowing that there was a place like that around where young women were being exploited. "What do you need from me?"

"Donnie won't leave this town without Britt," Mac said. "So far what we've found is that she's clean just scared shitless of Bouchey and his men. She's like one of his prize possessions, so she hasn't been tricked out unless there is a pretty penny that can be paid for her."

"That's completely horrific, those poor women," Nina murmured.

"I convinced the police to let us take the girls to a safe house," Mac said. "Bouchey isn't in this alone, and his partners will come looking for what they consider their property. We need someone with medical training to assess them. I know you worked trauma and emergency, so you would be the best person to help us. We don't want them at a hospital or anything because that leaves a paper trail."

Nina nodded. "I can do that, but what will happen to them after the safe house?"

Jasper and Zeva are working that end. "We'll find their families if they want to go home or get them set up and relocated somewhere else, away from here."

Nina frowned. "Won't Bouchey's partners find them?"

"The way this works is they usually lure these girls away from home or grab them at a club," Mac explained. "They toss the bags and phones, so they don't have any ID or a way to contact home. They don't care who these women are, they are cattle to make Bouchey and his cohorts' money."

"I wish I could castrate him," Nina said furiously. It amazed her men like that still existed and treated women that way.

"This will castrate his money, and with all the hits the police plan to make, his business will be null and void," Mac said.

"Where are you sending Donnie and Britt?" Nina

felt her heart pick up speed at the next question from her lips. "Are you taking him back to D.C. with you?"

"He could get a fix there better than he does here," Mac muttered. "There's a rehab in Sydney that can treat him, plus therapy for Britt so she can heal. From there I'll help them get back into school and a place to live. They'll be on their feet with a new start in a new place."

"A lot of work from the United States," Nina commented while she worked on her cookies.

"I'll get everything set up before I leave, or I'll stick around," Mac answered casually. "Donnie is doing better now he's over that hump and not thinking crazy since I told him I would get Britt out."

Nina didn't want to say that it thrilled her he might stick around. Everything was still up in the air. "Well, I'll get what supplies I can, and you have my help when the time comes."

"Haile will get the supplies you'll need, and that will be Tuesday. We don't want them spending Christmas in a hell like that," he moved toward the table. "Now put me to work, you sugar-plum fairy."

"Are you sure you don't want to head back downstairs and play darts with the boys and yell obscenities at each other?" Nina teased.

"I would much rather be here looking at the most beautiful woman in Northumberland with flour on her face and in her hair," a slow grin spread across his face. "Hopefully I can leave some handprints in some interesting places later, maybe some glaze."

Nina laughed. "And you call me perverted."

They spent the evening baking and dancing to her music, and he only went downstairs to grab them another pint and some dinner. With her cake and cookies cooling, they slow-danced to a song called "Have a Reggae Christmas," which had a faster beat than how their bodies moved.

"This is not how one dances to this song," Nina told him.

"Then teach me," Mac's hands moved lazily over her hips.

"Ever seen videos of Carnival . . . how the women dance in front of men?" she looked up at him into his piercing eyes.

"Yeah, they grind their asses on the groin area," he answered.

She laughed. "For Barbadians or Bajans, that's called *wukking up*."

His brows furrowed. "Why?"

"Our hips are doing a lot of work or wukking," Nina turned in his arms until her ass was spooned against him. "Now follow my movements."

Nina slowly undulated her hips until he slowly caught the rhythm, and then she took it to a higher level as she let the beat of the music take over. Even with flour in her hair and no make-up on this was one of the best times she'd had with Mac. Home, dancing to her music with a great and very sexy man. She felt his cock harden as she danced against him and the evening took on another tone. Her nipples tightened under the thin T-shirt she wore beneath the apron. He was aroused, and she could feel his length through the leggings she wore. Nina pressed her back against his chest as they moved and reached up to twine one of her arms around his neck.

"Tell me that you have never danced with anyone else like this," he said against her ear.

A soft laugh escaped her. "I am thirty-one, and I lived in Barbados most of my life, so that would be a lie."

He groaned. "I can't complain, it was other men that lived on the island with you."

"Honey bun, I always liked white men, and tourists are always there all year 'round," Nina commented. "I danced with German guys, Americans, and I dated an Australian man for three years. I've dated black men, too, so basically if I have an attraction to someone and they ask me out, I will see where the date goes. Sexuality and love have no color."

The next sound that emanated from him was like a predatory growl. "Don't tell me any more."

"Why?" Nina moved her hips deliberately,

enticing him with her sensual dance. "Does it bother you that other men have touched my body?"

"I would erase them from your memory if I could," he answered truthfully.

She moved his hands up to her breasts so he could cup the heavy globes. "I think you could if you wanted to, how about we give it a try?"

"Hmmm," Mac was busy nuzzling her neck and sending delicious sensations through her.

Nina used a breathless voice. "I'll be the naughty baker's assistant who is working extra-hard to make money for gifts this year. And you're my horny boyfriend who wants to taste my sugar plums and who snuck into my job to see me."

Mac laughed. "That's an image."

Nina untied the top of the apron from around her neck. She slipped her T-shirt over her head exposing her breasts and without taking the rest of the apron off she removed her leggings and panties. She left the material printed with Christmas symbols as her only cover across the apex of her thighs. Mac sucked in a breath, and she felt the heat of his gaze roam over her body.

"I think I'll leave this on to entice you," she purred.

"Baby, that only makes me want to rip it off to get at your pussy," Mac's voice was hoarse with desire.

"Well, follow me to the bedroom and maybe I'll

bend over, so you don't have to," Nina smiled over her shoulder and walked toward the open door to where she slept.

"Jesus, the things you say make me rock hard." He was behind her in seconds, and he pulled her against him. Mac reached around to the front of her body underneath the fabric and slid a finger between the soft lips of her sex. "Fuck, you're already wet."

"All the better for you to taste me, my dear," Nina turned in his arms, and Mac kissed her until she was weak in the knees.

Mac's mouth was relentless and demanded entrance, and she gave it to him willingly. She was in awe at how he knew exactly how to touch her and make her sizzle with need. Nina gave herself over to the passion, because Mac's fierce kisses made her lose all reasonable thoughts except to be connected intimately with him. Standing there, Mac grabbed her hips and molded her against him, and she feel his hard cock heavy against her. The way he played at her full breasts while they kissed only delighted Nina all the more. He cupped one in his large palm, and she could feel the callouses of a man who used his hands for work, rough and still gentle. Using the pad of his thumbs he brought the pert tips to hardness. The heat of his touch and the sweet friction made her moan, and she arched into his hand, silently begging for more.

"Oh, you like my hands on you," Mac asked as he trailed soft kisses to her ear.

"If you have to ask that, then something is so wrong with my reaction," her laugh ended with a moan when he tweaked her nipple. "Maybe this will be clearer: taste me."

He needed no more invitation. Moving his lips downward while his hand was splayed over her neck made her feel wanton. Mac gave her a wicked look just before he captured the first tight cocoa bean tip between his lips. Nina cried out his name as that simple action speared a bolt of heat though her straight to the center of her sex. She parted her thighs with anticipation of his touch, and Mac obliged. Gently, he rubbed her clit, and she moved in his arms, the sensations making her legs weak. Nina writhed against his touch, seeking more from the light flicks of his fingers. She wanted his fingers inside her, to imitate the sexual act until she came against his hand.

"Oh God . . . Mac . . ." She was silenced by his hard kiss, and the pressure against her clit increased.

His whisper was fierce with arousal. "I love how you tremble in my arms, so hold on to me tight, love, I'm going to make you come."

Mac slipped his fingers inside her, and she bit her lip, praying that her legs didn't give out completely. There was no control over her reaction he slid the two digits deeper then slowly withdrew. The muscles of her abdomen clenched and so did the walls of her pussy as she felt the band of her release tighten. Each time Mac's fingers went a little deeper, she undulated her hips wantonly, parting her legs wider under his ministrations.

The wet sound of her sex at each pleasure invasion only heightened her pleasure. Nina came with a frantic moan of his name and a gush of sexual fluid that escaped her core. She slipped her hand inside his pants and rubbed his cock, loving the velvet over steel sensation of his shaft. He sucked her nipple back into his mouth with renewed fervor at her touch. Her moans were wild and frantic, and they blended with the primal sounds at escaped him as he greedily tasted her. Mac's touch played a merciless game with her pussy, spurring her on until she was sent a second time over that pleasurable edge.

"I want you inside me now," Nina demanded with lust filling her voice. "Fuck me hard until I come all over your cock."

"You have such a dirty mouth, I adore it." His voice was deep with desire.

Nina climbed eagerly onto the bed, and as soon as Mac undressed, the apron she wore was trapped between them. She had barely wrapped her legs eagerly around him before he thrust upward and filled her supple, wet sex.

An agonized groan escaped Mac. "Damn, I love how feel wrapped around me—you're so hot and wet."

Delicious sensations ran through her body at the friction created by his every thrust. There was no sweet lovemaking about this act, the rhythm was a fierce pounding as he buried his cock deep into her, grabbing her hips and anchoring her for his penetration.

"Spread your legs, take it all," the words grated out from between his lips, and when Nina looked at him the mask of primal need was on his face.

Nina wrapped her arms around her thighs, holding them apart for Mac. He had more access to move, and the pressure of his cock entering, stretching, and filling her made her bite her lip. Nina cried out when a harsh sound escaped him. It was like he was pulled into the moment and the world around them had fallen away. He bent his head and sucked her nipple deep into his mouth. Nina returned the action by pinching his nipples, and he grunted in satisfaction. The waves of heat started to pulse over her body. The fullness of his cock within her drove Nina to the brink of the abyss. His groans mixed with hers in response to his rhythm that increased and seemed to match the racing beast of her heart in her chest.

Wild with the pleasure of their copulation, she

cried out, "Let go, baby, fuck me like there is no tomorrow."

"Damn Nina, oh my God, fuck!" He made a feverish sound, and it was he who lifted her legs higher over his shoulders before pounding his cock within her sex once more.

"Come with me," she heard the rise in her voice as she chanted the words.

"Ah, fuck, yes!"

She heard his harsh cry as her orgasm took hold—with her leg on his shoulder she was pinned under his onslaught. Nina cried out his name, and Mac's loud, primal groan blended with the low music that was still playing in the apartment. The thickness of his cock pulsed inside her pussy as he let go of his thick come and filled her wet crevice as she felt it run down the crack of her ass. Her leg slipped weakly to the bed, and Mac kept moving, prolonging his release, until he finally heaved out a sigh of pure contentment.

"I'm so dirty," she murmured.

"Yeah, you are," Mac chuckled.

She slapped at his bare shoulders. "I mean I have flour in my hair, and I'm sticky."

"Mmm, me, too," he laughed. "You make this too easy."

"How about a shower, nightcap, and bed?" Nina asked.

Mac kissed her gently. "I can get behind that."

"You were tonight," it was her turn to tease.

Mac didn't end up staying the night because it was his turn to stay with Donnie, and they needed some time alone to work out their issues. With a few more kisses at the door she watched him leave and run down the stairs to the pub that was closed for the night. Nina went back to her baking and decorated her cookies until she was too sleepy to continue. *They can be finished in the morning,* she thought, and walked by the windows in the living room. She noted a dark car parked outside opposite the Celtic Cross.

There was a man leaning up against the car, and he was looking up at her window. Fear leached its way into her heart, and she went quickly to the bedroom to get her phone, turning off the lights on the way. Nina pressed Mac's number and waited for him to answer as she went out of the apartment to check the foyer locks. They were secure, and she went back inside and locked her own door again just as he answered the phone.

"Hey, baby, miss me already?" Mac said sleepily.

Nina was back at the window and looking out, but the car was gone.

"Nina?" His voice was more alert. "What is it?"

Probably someone out for a night walk and a smoke. She took a deep breath and made her voice light as she spoke. "Yes, I did miss you, very much."

There was relief in his tone. "I'll stay tomorrow, or, even better, you come home with me."

"That sounds perfect," Nina answered. "Goodnight, honey bun."

He laughed. "Sweet dreams, sugar plum."

You're probably making something out of nothing, Nina told herself as she made sure the flat was secure again and went to bed. She had very secure doors keeping her safe, and one of Mac's security systems protected both the outside and inside of the Celtic Cross. It was more than likely anxiety because in the next few days they would be dealing with very traumatized women. Nina put the car and the man out of her head and went to sleep with a contented sigh. Her body was deliciously satisfied, and her man was on her mind. Yes, Mackenzie Black was her man—even if he didn't understand that yet. But Nina knew by the way he touched her and looked in her eyes that he considered her as his woman as well. His head just had to catch up to what his heart knew already.

It was horrific. Nina looked at the women sitting on cots covered in thick blankets, and she was disgusted at what they'd been forced to do at the hands of Bouchey. There were ten of then and the tiniest was

Britt, the little blonde waif that Donnie was enamored with. Nina swore the girl had to be a hundred pounds soaking wet, but she had a soft, beautiful face that could only be called *elf-like*. The upstairs of a safe house had been set up quickly to house the women. Haile had done a good job of getting supplies, from clothes to food and medicine.

They were all undernourished, Nina noted. She'd checked each of them out in a separate bedroom after they'd taken hot showers and were clean. She'd gotten one of her nurse friends involved, and together she and Melissa were able to make sure all the girls were in reasonable health and that none needed immediate hospitalization. They all got at least one banana bag or rally pack to give them a boost of vitamins and minerals to correct any chemical imbalances in the body. Nina could tell that more than half of them were using drugs — probably to help numb themselves to what they'd endured. Treatment options would be necessary, and Nina knew Zeva and her charity would be there to help them all. So that was at least some good news there.

Mac and Haile had just dispatched the women to the safe house, leaving two policemen to keep guard before going again. Nina wondered where he was and if he was okay. Bouchey was to be taken down that night as well, so it was safe to assume they were a part of it.

"They'll be coming for us," one of the girls trembled as she sipped hot cocoa. She kept glancing at the door as if she expected her captors to burst in. "Bouchey doesn't let go that easily."

Nina took her hand. "My guy is taking care of that, I promise. You won't ever have to go back."

The girl shrugged her shoulders and faced the wall. Nina saw her quickly swipe at tears on her cheeks. She had been taught not to show weakness, Nina sighed sadly wondering how many more women were out in this world being exploited? It was hours before she and Melissa got all the women settled and resting comfortably. It was only then they were able to enjoy some of the cocoa, which was still hot in the thermos, and sandwiches. Melissa was an older nurse who'd worked the emergency room for the last fifteen years. She was known as no- nonsense and brisk, but with a caring heart. Somehow she'd taken to Nina and they'd become friends.

"This is a bloody mess," Melissa tucked her brown hair behind her ear. "I would never think this was going on in our little area."

Nina sat across from her and chewed a bite of her sandwich. "My mom used to always warn us how men came from Europe and America to steal young women away to sell them. This is all too real for me — man, she could've been right."

Melissa nodded. "The girl in the far corner, she

says her name is Raine. She has to be from the Caribbean, and she's no more than eighteen. She said they had her for two years, so anything is possible. All of the animals that prostituted them should be put in barrels, set on fire, and rolled into the moors."

"I agree completely," Nina looked at the sleeping women, some with IVs still dripping into their arms. "My guess is that Zeva will have to go international to find Raine's parents."

"She has no one," Melissa said. "They took her on the way to school from an orphanage. I'm going to take her in."

Nina gave her friend a surprised look. "Really?"

Melissa shrugged. "I've got no one at the house since Brad passed and the kids are grown and gone. I can mother her and get her some classes and a decent job somewhere until she has finished school. After talking to her . . . she needs someone on her side."

"Look at you and your big heart," Nina gushed.

Melissa narrowed her eyes at her. "Don't make me put you on bedpans for a month."

"Yes ma'am," Nina said, but she saw Melissa was grinning.

"So any more weird things happen?" Melissa asked bluntly.

"I think I was scaring myself," Nina gave a laugh. "Why would anyone be watching me?"

"Your new Mister, maybe," Melissa pointed out. "He had a reputation, and him and Bouchey had no love lost between them."

"Mac won't talk about his past," Nina picked at the remnants of her sandwich.

"Mackenzie was always a good boy, he did what he had to do after his Pa left," Melissa explained. "Working the docks, he would never be able to take care of a brother and his mum. So, he fought in backroom fight, did some dirty work for the men in charge at that time. He had some pride, that he did. Haile's mother tried to take him in, and so did Jasper's family. Cornelia, his aunt, put a nix on that real quick, and Mac would never take a handout."

"So, he and Bouchey were rivals from way back," Nina surmised.

Melissa shook her head. "No, they were friends, joined at the hips until Bouchey got a taste for hurting people and running drugs. Mac fought his way out of that group just like he fought his way in. I should know, Jasper and Haile brought him to emergency all broken up. When he got better, he joined the Royal Army with Haile, and from there he went to America. Bouchey always hated that Mac got out and made something of himself."

Nina finally understood some of the backstory and the past between him and Bouchey. By the time they'd finished their simple meal it was around midnight. Nina encouraged Melissa to go home, but she refused immediately.

"They'll need us when they wake up," Melissa said. "Besides there is nothing to go home to but an empty house. I'll stay."

Mac and Haile showed up around two in the morning, and Zeva and Jasper were with them. Nina led them quietly to the kitchen where she and Melissa could update them on the women's overall health.

"I'll let Nina take the lead," Melissa said and gave her a nod.

"How are they?" Zeva asked looking out into the room. "My God, ten women right under our noses being pimped out."

Nina picked up the legal pad where they were keeping notes and looked it over. "Physically, they are dehydrated from the alcohol and not much else for liquids, malnutritional because they all are way below the recommended weight for their height index. They've got some drug use, we can tell by their noses, thank God none showed heroin tracks."

"Bouchey and his partners would want to keep their skin flawless," Mac said grimly.

Nina continued. "They all are going to need major therapy from being abused this way. Rehab for the girls who were dosed with cocaine. We gave them rally packs to get their metabolism started back on the right track. They all ate because they were literally starving, some threw up because their stomachs couldn't handle a big meal, but then they kept soup down. They're resting comfortably, and Melissa wants to take custody of Raine in the corner. We feel she was taken from the islands and trafficked here."

"Wow, just wow," Zeva sat down at the table. "How could anyone . . ."

"Monsters, they are fucking monsters," Haile's voice held restrained anger.

"What about Bouchey?" Nina asked.

Mac answered. "The police hit all his little haunts at the same time, even the underground fighting down at the docks. He got shot, so I expect he'll show up at a hospital or one of his henchmen will get him to an off-the-books clinic. Either way he'll be found soon."

"Stands to reason there will be a press conference tomorrow and the police will announce they are looking for him," Jasper spoke up. "We wanted to see the women for ourselves. When I speak, I can say they are being cared for and with Zeva's charity and our resources we'll get them the help they need."

"I want to talk to them individually to see what they need, when they wake up," Zeva's voice was somber. "I want everyone involved in this to be prosecuted at the full extent of the law. I have two of my social workers coming in the morning, and I'll be here when they wake up."

"Well, we caught 'the Russian,' " Haile said. "He's small- time trying to be a player at the table, but he undercut his boss, so that won't go over well with them when they see he was arrested and in jail. He has two options: spill his guts and get into protective custody or stay silent and die. The people he works for don't take kindly to being stolen from."

"Who is with Abigail?" Nina asked.

"Mrs. H. came to the manor, she'll babysit gladly until we get back home," Jasper replied with a smile. "It wasn't a chore to get her to come out to the house."

"We should settle in, going to be a long night," Nina said with a sigh.

Melissa held up the thermos. "Cocoa anyone?"

Night turned into day, and they spoke to each woman individually, learning their stories and taking as much information as they could. Jasper left to be a part of the press conference while Zeva and her social workers stayed on. Nina and Melissa kept up the medical care, watching for nausea and other signs of withdrawal in the women.

"Where's Donnie — can I see him?" That was from Britt, and it was the only time she spoke.

Nina smiled at her gently. "Would you like to go see him?"

When she nodded, Nina took her downstairs and witnessed the very sweet and emotional reunion between them. By the time she left with Mac for home, she had been gone for forty-eight hours straight and it was Christmas Eve.

"I am bone-tired," Nina said with a sigh and leaned her head back against the headrest of her seat.

"Zeva has set up for the ladies to have a nice Christmas dinner and some gifts," Mac said.

"Melissa said she'd be staying, her kids are half-away across the world for the holiday and she's kind of got attached to Raine," Nina said. "I'll go back and check on them after I get some sleep."

"Well, not so soon," Mac took her hand in his and kissed her knuckles. "Spend Christmas with me."

Nina smiled even as her eyes were closed. "You have no decorations, so how about my place?"

"As long as you let me make dinner," Mac replied.

She laughed in shock. "You can cook?"

Mac chuckled. "Just you wait and see."

Nina let the gentle way he stroked her lull her into doze as they drove to her flat over the Celtic Cross. It had been so hard to watch women too terrified to even eat until they relaxed and finally understood they were safe. Nina wanted to wipe the fear and the bruises on their bodies out of her mind at least for a little while. She remembered how

Melissa had said if she ever got numb to the horror that they saw, it was time to stop being a nurse. Nina didn't think she could ever get such a thick scar over her psyche. But she wanted to spend Christmas with Mac and pretend the world outside didn't exist for a while. That was how she would heal herself and put some happiness in the midst of such a dark place. Immersing herself in the holiday spirit and the man who seemed to make her world just a bit better.

Chapter Eight

Nina faced Christmas morning with the excitement of a child as they opened gifts that neither of them knew the other had bought. She bought Mac some argyle socks and a silver man's bracelet that had Celtic crosses embedded into onyx.

"Nina, this is beautiful," Mac marveled softly and looked at her. "I didn't expect anything like this."

"Well, socks are socks, even if they are argyle," she teased.

He laughed and kissed her. "Those are wonderful as well. I'll wear them often. Now open mine."

She gently pulled the silver foil open on the small box and inside was a long, velvet box. It held diamond studs and a necklace to match. The jewelry caught the lights of her tree, and she gasped at the beautiful gift.

"Mac, this is too much; I can't accept this," Nina said looking at him.

"Not for you, they don't even compare to how exquisite you are," Mac answered huskily. "Anytime

I see you wearing them, I'll think they would never compare to you."

"That's very sweet, Mac, but you plan on leaving when Donnie is all safe and tucked away," she pointed out gently. "You won't be seeing me to admire these."

"We can video-chat," he said and cupped her cheek. "You can visit, I can visit."

She got to her feet and called as she walked to the kitchen. "I told you I don't do long-distance relationships."

"No, you said you wouldn't move to D.C. So what you're really saying is that if I leave, it's over? If I want to keep what we have, I need to stay in a place that haunts me with bad memories?" Mac asked, following her.

Nina whirled to face him. "I never said that. I am not asking you to choose—I'm not even in the equation. I am telling you what I won't do, and I won't change my own morals to suit your needs. I cannot be happy flying all over God's green earth for any man; I am settled here," Nina narrowed her eyes at him as her anger began to simmer. "I love Northumberland, and while you think that bad memories haunt you, I have seen more people happy to see you home than not. This is your issue; you can try to hide from it or put it to rest, but that's your decision. But don't try to weaponize my words."

"Nina, I don't want to lose you," Mac implored.

"Nor I you, but the fact that you want to go and I want to stay basically says this is the only Christmas we'll spend together," Nina pointed out softly. The thought made her heart ache, and she felt like crying, but it was the truth.

Mac came up behind her and wrapped his arms around her. "I don't want us to spend Christmas mad at each other or worrying about the future."

She turned in his arms. "I know; I'm sorry I brought it up. It's an amazing gift, thank you."

Nina kissed him, and the desire burned hot and quick. It was almost as if there was a desperation between them, words unsaid and neither one willing to give up ground on what they thought was best. He wanted to go, but Nina would stay where she felt happy and at home. As he speared his tongue into her mouth, she whimpered, not only from the need that pooled wetness between her legs, but from the ache of knowing she would lose him soon and she didn't know how life would be after that loss.

It was then she admitted to herself that she had fallen in love with Mac, the man with the scarred knuckles and who rarely smiled. hat thought spurned her on and they slowly moved toward the living room, not willing to break their lips apart. The sun was barely up, but in the dimness of the room the lights of her tree and strung up in the apartment played across their bodies as Mac molded her to him. He groaned and took control of the kiss. His hand was in her thick hair as he sampled her greedily. The passion they had barely contained broke free.

"I need you, Mac. I need you." Nina whimpered feverishly, knowing she meant not only his body. She wanted everything, even the parts that seemed to be out of reach.

She tried to press her body more firmly against his as he roamed his big hands over her body and over the thin material of her pajama shorts and top. The kiss was filled with starved and uncontrolled need, and to Nina at one point it was like they shared one breath.

"I've never wanted someone as much as I want you Nina, you make me ache, you are in my thoughts every minute of every day," his words were a deep growl. He took her hand and pressed it against his thick cock. "Feel what you do to me."

Then why are you leaving? her mind screamed. Instead she wrapped her hands around his shaft through his shorts, and Mac groaned in response. He was so thick; recalling the first time, she'd wondered if he would hurt her when he finally entered her pussy. Now she knew they were a perfect fit. They shared more heated kisses, and he sucked on her neck as they fell to the sofa, making Nina gasp. She bit his shoulder. He thrust his hips against her thighs, the action telling her he liked her possessive, sharp love bites.

Mac pulled away and looked down at Nina, his breathing heavy. "Do you know what you do to me? The thought of not being with you drives me mad."

She slipped her hand behind his neck, pulling him to her. "Then don't think, not right now."

Mac's body pressed her into the soft cushions, and she wrapped her leg around the back of his thighs. There was fire in his kiss, and she was consumed by it. Nina spread her legs farther apart so she could feel his hardness between her legs, hoping to appease the ache. Nina moaned as pleasure infused her body and made her shiver. She could feel the muscles of his back bunch under her fingers through the fabric of his T-shirt. Impatiently she tugged at the hem, and Mac took it off and tossed it aside quickly. Emboldened, Nina used her toes to push at the waist of his pants.

"Take them off," he encouraged her with a laugh. "You got those legs high enough, finish the job."

She continued the action while he nibbled at her lips, and finally Mac completed the job of removing his shorts. His kisses were softer now, loving, and he teased her mouth, causing her pussy to become slick with arousal. He helped get her naked and then stopped to admire her naked form. He pressed his forehead against Nina's and for a moment their eyes connected, and no words were needed.

Nina caressed from his neck to his cheek. "What's wrong?"

"Nothing, I . . .I didn't expect to meet someone like you when I came home," Mac admitted. "I almost expect to wake up back in D.C. and you were just a figment of my imagination."

She kissed him gently. "I'm not a dream."

Nina wanted to say she was his, *but, hell he may be gone before long.* That fact was a jarring wall between them that brought tears to her eyes. She closed them so Mac wouldn't see and focused on the building need within her as he trailed kisses across the smooth surface of her neck to her breasts. She shifted restlessly holding back a moan as the heat of his mouth surrounded her nipple. Her pussy clenched in delight at the sensations he created. As Mac groaned, he gave her second breast the same attention.

The feel of him caused the most decadent and wanton thoughts to course though Nina's mind. They had not even begun to explore the depth of their sexual relationship, and now he was leaving. She'd never gotten to tell him she liked his hand lightly around her neck or that she wanted to be tied up and open to his exploration. They'd not yet made it to drinking champagne off each other's bodies. The thoughts combined with his mouth made her body shudder, and as if sensing her growing arousal, Mac's hands roamed hungrily over her body. Nina lifted her hips against his hand in anticipation when he settled a big palm between her legs. A lone finger slipped between the swollen lips of her labia to caress her slick pussy.

A low moan of need escaped her lips when he rubbed the pad of his finger against her clit. Without hesitation, Mac slid one long finger inside her again, and this time a cry escaped her. She could feel him watching her, memorizing her every reaction as he penetrated her deliberately with his finger. Mac added a second, and Nina's head fell back in pleasure, his name an almost keening sound that escaped her lips.

"You are so fucking tight, even around my finger, it's like you clutch at me," he muttered. "Yes baby, spread those sweet thighs wider, that's it! You want more, don't you? You want to come hard while I watch?"

"Oh yes, please, Mac!"

Everything inside her screamed to be able to come, her hips pumped against his hand until it became almost too much to bear.

"Wait, Mac, wait, let me catch my breath," Nina begged, grabbing his wrist, for she was to the point of losing control.

Nina could feel her own wetness as it ran down to the crease of her ass. He fingered her, moving the digits deeper while his mouth played at her breasts.

Her orgasm was like a tightening band that wrapped tighter and tighter until it snapped, and she closed her eyes, relinquishing herself to the overwhelming sensations.

"I'm going to come, oh fuck, yes!" She dug her heels into the cushions.

"I love how your body responds," Mac muttered.

He used his fingers to manipulate and fuck her until she was drowning in the waves of glorious passion. Nina found her second orgasm with a scream while holding his wrist trying to still his movements. Mac would give her no reprieve while her essence flowed. His lips were on hers, kissing her with a desperate hunger she'd only had a hint of before. The small, sexy sounds she made were muted by his lips. She could feel his hardness probing the entrance to her pussy, and she raised her hips ready to have him inside her. He met her gaze, and she licked her lips, making Mac groan. A low groan emanated from low in his throat as he took her with slow deliberation. The feel of him gliding against the walls of her sex was pure bliss to Nina, and a hiss of gratification escaped her.

"Stop teasing me," Nina demanded. "You know what I like."

Mac kissed her hard. "Yes, I do."

As he said the words, Mac thrust his cock deep inside her and Nina cried out as ecstasy coursed through her. She luxuriated in the feeling of fullness of his engorged rod stretching her. Mac got to his knees on the carpet and turned her so her legs would be around him in that position. He penetrated her again and fucked her with an unrestrained wildness. Sexual sounds escaped them both and combined with the slapping sounds of their lovemaking. He was on his feet again and sat on the sofa and pulled her to him wordlessly. Nina straddled him and moaned when she sank down on his waiting cock. His grip tightened on her hips as she began to move, and Mac only enhanced the pleasure by pulling her down hard against him for deeper penetration.

Nina gave him a saucy smile and then she bent and plucked his nipple between her teeth. Mac groaned her name as she teased and pinched on his cock and she threw her head back with a soft cry. She succumbed to the need that gripped her entire being and built to frenzied heights. It was Mac's turn to take her nipple into his mouth, which sent her swirling into an orgasm that made her clutch at his shoulders. He fucked her with a new kind of ferocity, he heels dug into the carpet as he pumped into her as she straddled him on the sofa. She reached back behind her to cup his balls, while she rode his cock, feeling them tighten under her fingers.

Mac's guttural cry escaped as he arched his head into the back of the cushions. He buried himself to the hilt inside her wet slit and she felt his come fill her hot and thick. Her name was wrung from his lips as he pumped within her to savor the sweet sensations. Nina collapsed against his chest and could hear her own frantic pants slow and ease as her heart slowed. His calloused hands ran down her back to the dip before he cupped her ass. Mac moved so he was lying on the cushions of the chair and her legs were over his thighs. They met each other's gaze and said nothing as if they were searching for answers within their depths.

"I wish we could stay like this forever," Mac said suddenly.

"Naked on my chair covered in sweat and . . . glaze," Nina teased.

She didn't want to think about it, the seriousness of her feelings and the loss that was coming. The man she loved would be leaving his new life for the one he'd created in D.C., leaving her firmly in the past.

"You are a laugh riot," Mac smiled gently. "You know what I mean."

Nina rolled her legs off him and stood, answering brightly. "Let's not think about it. It's Christmas. I'm going to clean up then you promised you would cook today, so I want a huge breakfast."

"I can do that," Mac's tone was soft, and she could feel him watching her and refused to look in case she started to cry.

"Great, see you in five!"

She made her steps perky as she ran to the bathroom and closed the door. After the water got hot and she stepped under the spray for her shower, Nina let her tears flow. They mixed with the water droplets that coursed down her body.

"Merry Christmas, Mac, I love you," she whispered.

Those were the words that she would never say out loud. Her love wouldn't be the thing that made any decisions for him, but it seemed Mac had already chosen to leave Northumberland — and her.

Nina spent the rest of Christmas day pretending that everything was okay as Mac made her meals and they shared the holiday. As they danced to Christmas music, she pressed her face to his shoulders, and he tickled the back of her leg with his argyle covered foot. And then they left; he drove her to work before going to check in at the safe house the next morning. She was completely exhausted, not accustomed to the pretense. Her sleep was troubled, and she had a long shift that day. Boxing Day meant the senior staff got the day off, and nurses like her would be the ones caring for patients in the wards unless some senior staff chose to work. Luckily for her, Melissa chose to work and take the increased pay for a holiday so she would be in the emergency room with someone she knew. Mac dropped her off in front of the hospital fifteen minutes before she was to sign in to work at seven.

"See you later?" he cupped her cheek and kissed her gently.

"Depends on when I get out; I work twelve hours, and I may need to take overtime if someone doesn't come in," Nina replied. She had already decided to distance herself as best she could so when he left, she was broken-hearted.

"Call me when you get out, and I'll pick you up," Mac said.

Nina gave a brisk laugh. "Mac, I've walked home from the hospital for the last two years—even at midnight, sometimes later. I'll be fine, it's not like Jack the Ripper still stalks the streets."

He frowned. "Maybe someone worse; please, just call me."

She sighed as she gathered her bags. "I will, have a fantastic day."

"Why does that sound like eat shit and die," Mac asked. "What's wrong, Nina?"

"Nothing at all," she said in a bright and cheery voice. Nina pasted a wide, fake smile on her face before kissing him quickly. "I've got to run before I get written up for being late."

Nina got out of the car and ran toward the entrance since there was a misting drizzle of rain. "Bye!" she heard him call, and she waved her hand before walking through the hospital doors when they whooshed open not even looking back. Inside, she finally took a breath while the clawing ache in her throat to scream in pain and anger faded. She used the glass crosswalk to get to the emergency department and went to the nurses' lounge to put her things away. Melissa was already there, and Nina used the code of her locker to open the metal door.

"How was your Christmas?" Melissa asked brightly.

"It was a Christmas," Nina's tone was clipped.

Melissa was putting her hair back in a ponytail. "Uh-oh, piss and vinegar. What's wrong?"

Nina bent down to change her shoes. "Nothing, I had a good Christmas. I got Mac a bracelet and socks, and he bought me diamonds."

"Well, bother it all, I wish I could complain about diamonds," her friend closed her locker.

Nina sat down on the bench. "He's leaving, and he gives me diamonds."

"He's going back to the U.S.?" Melissa said sympathetically. "I thought since you two were seeing each other —"

Nina laughed. "You'd think, but he wants me to uproot my life and move to D.C. and start over from scratch in a place where my education and knowledge will not be utilized. And of course, my skin color will make then assume I'm an uneducated immigrant who needs to be micromanaged."

Melissa chuckled. "It's not all like that; we've all heard the stories, but there are some fine institutions that would welcome a nurse with your caliber."

"Melissa, I don't want to go through that. I like my life here, this was my first choice when I decided to apply for the nursing program," Nina explained. "I won't be happy in that city or, hell, the entire country. I like walking to work and smelling the fresh bread, I like stopping in at the pub to get a drink after work and talking with my friends. I don't want to go to a place where the only person I know is Mackenzie Black."

"Then what's the end game?" Melissa asked.

"I'm going to start distancing myself," Nina announced. "When he leaves, I'll give him a cheery wave of my hand and let him get on with his life."

"But you won't be fine, will you," Melissa rubbed Nina's shoulders gently.

Nina's voice broke when she spoke. "No, I love him, but I'll have to manage, won't I?"

"Come on," Melissa pushed her toward the door. "A packed emergency room will take your mind off this relationship scramble."

She gave a watery laugh. "Oh, let the fun begin."

It was nowhere near fun. Boxing Day was a holiday where more often than not people got drunk and stupid. Mostly young men who never seemed to think, *well, this is a bad idea.* Nina triaged a fork stuck in the head, broken arms, one leg from a trick gone wrong in the yard. An assortment of deep cuts, bruises from fights, and, of course, concussions. And that was only the adults; it seemed like every child who came in had the flu or a stomach virus. Nina had no doubt if she didn't take precaution, she would end up sick because children weren't known for following hygiene orders when they felt cruddy. She was coughed on more than once and almost took a projectile vomit straight to the face when she bent down to talk to one tiny patient.

She loved helping people, and her job was her calling, but a day like this made her rethink every decision she made. It was   nine-thirty when she finally left Queen Charlotte hospital and stepped out into the night. Melissa was going to work straight through until seven in the morning, but with the second shift coming on there were more than enough nurses, so after fourteen hours she was relieved to go home. Nina almost took out her cell phone to call Mac, but wondered why she should. *Who will I call when he's gone?* She'd be back to walking home or grabbing a ride with friends if it got too cold or late.

She certainly didn't want him picking her up out of some feeling of obligation. *I can take care of myself,* Nina thought firmly as she pulled her bag over her shoulder and stepped out into the night. She soon found out how wrong she was when lights came around the corner and blinded her as she walked toward the main street of Northumberland. It wasn't a car but a van—and instead of passing her by, it screeched to a stop. Nina felt the instant danger she was in work though her body as pure fear, and she turned to run. Strong arms grabbed her, and when she opened her mouth to scream a thick hand was placed over her mouth.

She struggled in vain against brutal strength that dragged her into the back of the van and threw her against the hard metal floor. Her head hit the wheel well, and she grimaced in pain as the doors were slammed shut and the van pulled away. Nina tried to stay conscious, but darkness enveloped her quickly from the blow to her head. The last thing she heard was the strong engine working to take her away from all she knew, from Mac.

"You broke her, you fucking idiot, we need her of sound mind," a voice cut through the darkness and then smelling salts made her turn her head to escape the strong smell.

"Look, she's fine, she's coming around," another voice said. "Come on, love, show us them eyes."

Nina chose to keep them closed, hoping they would go away, but the voice became hard and cold.

"Open your fucking eyes before I start waking you in other less pleasant ways," the man barked out at her, and Nina's eyes snapped open.

"There she is." She instantly recognized the face that went along with the voice; it was the man from the street fair who'd tried to call Mac out. "I see you remember me."

"I know your face, but for the life of me I can't remember your name," Nina answered and winced as she touched her head.

He inclined his mean face politely. "Alec is what they call me."

"*Ugly* is what they should call you," Nina muttered. "Mac is going to kill you for this, you know."

"I'll deal with Mac when he comes," Alec said mildly. "I've got a little surprise set up for him. But right now, I need you for something completely different."

"Yeah, I'd rather not," Nina said bravely.

The gun being cocked sent a chill straight through her, and Alec's voice was deadly. "I must insist you help my friend, since it's your man that caused him harm."

It was then she looked over from the old sofa she was lying on to the recliner. Bouchey sat there, and there were obvious blood stains on the bandage around his round middle. Bouchey was pale and sweating; she could see he was in obvious pain.

"He needs a hospital, I'm just a nurse," Nina pointed out.

"You work the emergency department. I know you've seen enough to help me," Bouchey was holding a gun in his hand as well and waved her over with it. "Alec got what you'll need, now come here and fix me."

"You're a human, and I'm not a mechanic," Nina said angrily. "Turn yourself in and get the damn care you need before you die."

Bouchey raised the gun and pointed it directly as her. "If I die, then you die, we're not connected so come here and get to work."

Nina cried out as Alec dragged her to her feet and shoved her forward. How much time had passed, did anyone even know she was missing? The thoughts ran through her head as Bouchey reclined the recliner and she slowly pulled down the blood-soaked bandage around his belly. It was obviously infected, she had been at the safe house for forty-eight hours, then Christmas and Boxing Day. He'd gone more than three days with a gunshot to the belly and no medical care. He was clammy and still burning hot, and as she took his pulse it was racing. Bouchey's body was fighting a serious infection.

"There's no exit wound, so the bullet is still in

there," Nina cast a quick glance back at Alec. "Bring me what you have . . . Bouchey . . . Trevor, you need a hospital. I don't know how to treat this, it's not a cut I can stitch up. There has to be internal injuries, and the bullet is making you sick."

"Do what you can, Miss," Bouchey's voice gentled. "If I die, I'm going out on my terms."

Nina shook her head. From the way he looked he was well on his way out—the bullet wound was already severely infected, and she knew the smell of decay all too well.

Nina tried again. "Bouchey, it's more than likely that bullet did a whole lot of damage to your internal organs or nicked your bowel or intestines. You need immediate surgery and a high course of antibiotics for any infection." Nina looked at him helplessly. "I . . . I can't help you, not with this."

He smiled at her and took a bottle of whiskey from the table beside him. "I know, but I wouldn't be Bouchey if I didn't try. It would take Mac to come back and piss my life up and down. I'm good with dying, knowing that he's gonna die, too. Not in the way you think but losing you will kill him."

Nina looked at him in alarm as she tried to clean his wound, and she kept her voice cool. "I wouldn't want to burst your bubble, but Mac is going back to D.C. I was good enough to play with but not to keep."

Bouchey chuckled. "That's what you think. Alec's been watching him. And now I'm at the end of my road, Alec takes over the business. I was much nicer than he will ever be, and it starts with you."

"Killing me won't mean a thing," Nina heard her voice tremble, belying her bravery.

"Oh, he'll have to fight first, then watch you die," Bouchey shrugged and took another swig from the bottle. He grimaced and a groan escaped him. "I'll go to the devil knowing I finally won against Mac 'the Bruiser' Black."

Hours passed, and she could see night turn to daylight through the closed blinds that barely filtered light in. Bouchey got weaker and weaker until he stared off into the distance and died. After one final breath escaped him, she heard Alec laugh from behind her, and that sound chilled her to the bone.

"The king is dead, long live the king," Alec said, and Nina turned to see his grinning face. "Now what shall I do with you?"

Chapter Nine

Hours had passed—hours without Nina—and Mac was fit to be tied. *They should tie me down,* he thought, because he was going to kill Bouchey and anyone who'd had a hand in taking her. He clenched his hands until they were tight fists. *They are all going to pay.*

Haile looked around the Celtic Cross, which had turned into a command center—all in hopes of finding Nina. *Please be alive,* he implored mentally. If they found her body, it would kill him, and Mac knew the guilt would eat him alive. He knew something was wrong from the time he'd left her that morning and she'd seemed distant. In a way he understood why, they were at an impasse and no one was willing to give an inch.

Mac could understand her part, but to him Northumberland was a reminder of his past. He'd spent the day making arrangements for Donnie and Britt. He'd also lent a hand to Zeva and Jasper with the women they had at the safe house. They all needed so much, and one of the main things was to be able to trust people again. It was after eight when he'd finally showed up at the pub for a bite to eat and a cold beer. The day had worn on him, even more so because he knew that if he left, he would lose Nina and his heart couldn't bear it. He looked at the time on his phone and frowned when he noticed it was almost nine and no call from Nina. He assumed that she had been caught up at work in a busy crush and would be getting off late.

"No Nina yet I see," Mari said as she came out of the kitchen and behind the bar.

"If I don't see her by ten, I'll go to the hospital and wait for her," Mac answered. "It had to be a madhouse; she shouldn't have to walk home after being on her feet all day."

"If you're leaving again, who's going to pick her up on these late nights?" Mrs. Humphreys said as she came out of the kitchen and took a pint glass.

"Jesus Christ, woman, is there nothing your ears don't pick up?" Mac asked.

"I stopped trying very early on to understand her sonic hearing," Mari said.

"Stands to reason you shouldn't be worrying about my hearing but by the fact that you're being a stubborn block head of a man by leaving that girl. You know you love Nina, but here you are, still thinking about Northumberland like it's some stain on your life," Mrs. Humphreys filled the glass with

Guinness and gave him a cross look. "This town never did anything to you, it's the choices you made you can't face. But you did it to take care of your Ma and brother. The only person who is holding it against you is you, Mackenzie Black."

He couldn't refute her words, but before he could answer, the phone behind the bar rang and Mari answered. "Celtic Cross, Mari Buchanan speaking."

She listened for a little bit and frowned. "Hey Melissa. No, Nina isn't here. We assumed she was working late."

Mac instantly tuned into the conversation, and he watched Mari's face become worried as she spoke. "Okay, maybe she stopped for dessert somewhere. . . . Yes, I'll have her call you as soon as we see her."

She hung up the phone. "Did Nina come home, and we didn't see her?"

"I'll run upstairs and check," Mac said and slid off the stool.

In a matter of seconds, he was up the stairs. He found the door at the top was locked. He ran back down the steps and directly outside to look up at the apartment. The only dim light she kept in the kitchen was on; if she were home, Nina would have the living room lights on and he would see the glare of the television. When he came back, Mrs. Humphreys was already on the phone calling around.

"She's not here," Mac strode to the bar and his

heart raced with worry. "Mari, what did Melissa say?"

"She said Nina got off around nine and was going to walk home, it's not that far, she always does it," Mari chewed her bottom lip worriedly. "She forgot to sign out for the night, Melissa was going to do it for her but wanted to know about a patient. Nina hasn't answered her phone or the landline upstairs, so she called here thinking she was having her gin and tonic."

"Get Haile on the phone, I'm going to go look for her," Mac said briskly. "Fuck! I told her to call me."

"Why would she if she thinks you're leaving?" Mrs. Humphreys snapped.

Mac pointed at her. "Don't you start with me!"

"I will start with you all I want and box your bloody ears if you take a tone with me!" she replied angrily. "Nina is an independent woman, and if she feels like she can't depend on you, she'll depend on herself. Now you go find her and bring her home and don't think because you're big I won't take a belt to your ass. I did it when you were fifteen, and I will do it now."

"I'm sorry. . . ." Mac blew out a frustrated breath. "I'm going to search."

It went downhill from there, with all the shops closed and no sign of Nina. Mac knew she'd been taken and probably by Bouchey. He didn't go back to the pub, not for a while. Instead he called to tell them he was going to search further in his way.

"Mac, Haile said to wait for him, he'll meet you," Mari said urgently.

He hung up, not waiting for someone to stop him from what he was about to do. Mac drove toward the hospital and then past that into the seedier area of Northumberland. He found the basement gambling house easy enough, and when he walked up to the front door the bouncer put his hand on Mac's shoulder. Mac glanced at the offending touch and with brute force brought his elbow up and hit the bouncer in the face. It satisfied him to hear the nose break and blood flow between the man's thick fingers. It took two more blows and the burly protector of the gambling house was on the ground. Mac stepped over him and opened the door, and from the time he stepped in he began to destroy anything and anyone in his path.

He toppled tables with chips, cards, and money. He grabbed a bottle of scotch, and as people rushed him, he used it as a weapon. Women screamed and cowered away from the fight, but Mac was beyond caring. None of them were Nina, and right now they didn't exist. He took blows and hardly felt them, his eyes were trained on one man smoking a cigar casually and watching the melee. Until it was his turn and then that cocky look turned to pure fear with no more bodies between him and Mac.

"Bouchey," Mac punctuated his words with two quick blows to the face. "Now."

"We don't know!" The small-time ringleader became a frightened mouse. "We haven't seen him since the raid. But it's business as usual."

"You wouldn't be lying to me, would you?" Mac's tone was deadly, and he wrapped his fingers around the man's neck. "Because if you are, I will squeeze and squeeze until I feel your larynx being crushed and you drown in your own blood."

He shook his head frantically. "I swear, I swear! I just collect the money and wait till I get word to take it in!"

"Shut it down," Mac said. "This place is done, and any others like it. Tell them Mac is back in town, and if he sees this shit, there will be hell to pay."

"Yes sir, Mr. Black," the man stammered.

Mac dropped him and walked back out through the devastation he'd caused, and it was par for the course for the rest of the night. He worked his way through the docks and warehouses asking for Bouchey and destroying anyone who got in his way. Mac barely felt the hits because his body hummed with one mission: his Nina . . . his. By God he would burn it all to the ground to find her. Finally, he went back to the Celtic Cross with no answers, feeling the hints of desperation clinging to the corners of his mind.

Haile and Jasper were on him as soon as he stepped through the door. Zeva was there, Mari, Mrs. Humphreys, even Mr. Moore was on the phone making calls. Numerous others he didn't recognize and some he did: Melissa, Nina's friend, looked at him hopefully and the tears that had settled in her eyes almost drove him to his knees when he was alone. Why didn't he tell Nina he loved her when he'd had the chance? His Ma always said his pride would be the death of him—and now it seemed it was her doom as well.

"You bloody fool!" Jasper grabbed him by the shoulders. "Look at you! Christ, you could've been killed going out there by yourself."

"I'm okay," Mac said numbly. "Any word?"

"Nothing," Haile answered. "Mac, you look like hell; what did you do?"

"I went hunting," Mac moved behind the bar and pulled out a single-malt scotch. He threw himself at least four fingers and downed the entire thing. He barely felt it burn its way down his belly, and he felt the worried gazes of everyone looking at him.

"You're favoring your left side, let me check your ribs," Melissa's voice was firm but gentle. "I may need to wrap them."

"No," Mac said the one simple word and dared

anyone to say otherwise. He'd been hurt way worse than this and survived. "Stop staring at me like I'm fucking dying! Bouchey has Nina and has gone underground."

"Not far enough, someone saw a white van pull away from down the street just after Nina left the hospital," Mr. Moore piped up as he hung up the phone. "Sideways Bob said he's seen that van down near the docks. Alec or one of his friends use it for deliveries when they heist extra fish from the catch."

"Sideways Bob?" Zeva said slowly.

"He's been around the dock forever; no one sees him, but he's there," Mr. Moore said and added proudly, "I know these streets just as good or even better than you milk-breathed boys."

"I was down at the docks, no van, no Nina," Mac poured himself another drink.

"You aren't much help to Nina drunk," Haile pointed out.

"You should know it would take more than this to get me drunk," he retorted.

"If Jasper would give me my piece, I would be right beside you busting heads," Zeva spoke up and glared at her husband.

"You are a duchess and cannot be running around this town with a gun," Jasper pointed out.

"I was a soldier long before I was a duchess; trust and believe if I need to use force to find Nina and get her back, I damn well will," Zeva snapped. "After seeing what Bouchey had going on in this town under our noses, we can't just walk around being all regal. We are not just royals, we are protectors—and people need us."

Jasper cupped her cheeks. "We do help. Through the charity, we make sure women and children can be cared for, we offer counseling. Zeva, we have to do things within the constraints of the law some-times."

"And sometimes we need to get hands-on," Zeva pointed out. "Not just when it's one of us, but for everyone."

"I know that, and I'd stand next to Haile and Mac and fight anyone," Jasper pointed out. "Out of the two of us, I'd rather me be in danger."

Zeva lifted her chin. "I walked out of the moors, I sure as hell could take on Bouchey or any of his assholes."

He smiled. "Of that I have no doubt."

He felt his phone buzz in his pocket, and when he pulled it out and looked down at the number, he didn't recognize it. Mac pressed the connect button, and everyone watching him immediately went silent.

"Yes," Mac's tone was brisk.

"I hear you've been looking for me," Alec's voice made him see red instantly, and he gritted his teeth.

"I'm looking for Bouchey," Mac said.

"He's the old monarchy, you're speaking to the new king," Alec said. "I got your nurse. You gonna come get her — or shall I sample that cocoa myself?"

"Eat a bag of dicks."

He heard Nina's voice in the background, and he wanted to scream her name. She'd learned that little term from TV, and Mac kept the grin off his face. It was a mixture of relief at hearing her voice and the fact that Nina was as spirited as ever.

"What do you have?" Mac asked simply.

"Good boy, don't let your little friends know a thing, I have someone watching that pub," Alec said. "Come down to the far end of the docks where the fights used to happen, the old packing plant. We'll be there, and if you want her, you'll fight for her. I get any messages your people left with you and I will slit her throat."

"Thanks," Mac hung up and met all the expectant gazes of his friends and those who loved Nina. The lie slid smoothly from his lips. "I had a connection out looking, he hasn't found anything yet."

The crestfallen look on their faces almost made him tell the truth, but Nina was his priority. His life didn't matter as long as he could get her safe.

"I need to eat something," Mac said, thinking on his feet. He needed to get out of there and fast.

"Go to the kitchen," Mrs. Humphreys said. "Get some of the chicken, or I'll get it for you.

He held up his hand. "No, I can do it, I need a minute by myself anyway."

He pushed the kitchen door and paced for a few minutes in case Haile or Jasper caught on to his lie and followed him. Mac went through the back door and jogged up the alley and in the shadows, he let the air out of Haile's tires before moving to his car. He was parked far enough away they wouldn't see him as he pulled away from the curb. Mac was heading to the showdown of his life, and Nina was the prize. Psyching himself up to beat Alec to death Mac knew exactly where to go, he'd spent more than once in that old packing plant. So, when it loomed in the darkness, he felt the familiar clenching of his gut as he prepared for a punch. Mac parked in the shadows. If there was a way to get Nina out and make a run for it, he would. But it was doubtful, and when he walked into the pitch-black warehouse, he knew it was a trap.

The lights came on and blinded him for a moment until his eyes got used to his surroundings. Mike sat at the far end of the ring made of old sandbags and crates. Handcuffs were on Nina's wrists, and she was sitting on Alec's lap. The fear in her eyes was palpable, and his anger burst to life. They would all pay; Alec was grinning in triumph and to Mac it was almost sad because the man didn't know that he would be dying that night.

"Nina, are you okay, did they hurt you?" Mac asked gently.

"I'm fine, no worse for wear," she answered.

Alec bounced the knee that she sat on. "How could she be anything but okay? She's sitting on Daddy's lap."

"Oh please, like you could be anyone's Daddy," Nina said, repulsed.

There was laughter, and Mac noted there were at least fifteen men around the ring. It was clear that Alec meant he had to fight for Nina. If he had to knock them all to the ground that still smelled of stale old fish, then so be it. His ribs were already bruised, and he didn't know how much he could take before he went down. If this was going to be his last day, then Nina would know his truth.

"I love you, no matter what," Mac gave her a wink and a smile, hoping to abate her fears.

Nina's beaming smile dulled the throbbing pain in his side. "I love you, too, we've got a lot to work out, Mac. But I need you to do one thing for me."

"What's that, sugar plum?" Mac said huskily.

Her eyes blazed fire. "You kick their goddamn asses! You fight because you deserve happiness, you deserve me!"

Mac nodded and flexed his neck. "So, who's first? You ready to fight for Alec? He hasn't proved himself like Bouchey did. I could at least respect him because he kicked my ass more than once in this ring. But Alec, he always hit the concrete hard."

"Shut your fucking mouth!" Alec snarled.

Mac spread his arms wide, taking the gamble. "Truth is the truth. Trevor and I, we made these streets and you followed along like a little puppy looking for scraps. If you want to be king, fight me for the throne. If I hadn't left, that would be my seat anyway."

"The hell it would be, you fucking sod," Alec snarled. "Go through my boys then you can have me."

Mac laughed. "Since when are they your boys? Did you forget the rules we set up years ago: no one ascends to the throne. We have to fight for it! Blood in return for the spoils of the streets. Bouchey lived the code, now you should, too."

"He's right," a voice called out. "Bouchey lived by the code, we all do. Blood for the throne."

"I have your woman, so I call the shots," Alec yelled.

Mac shrugged. And got into a fighting stance. "Trevor would never hide behind a woman's skirt. He took what was his and the world could fuck themselves. Then there's me. In only a few weeks I had already ripped it from his hands. With connections still loyal to me. He's dead and I'm still here, so who should have the throne?"

"One of you get in the ring and fight him!" Alec shouted angrily.

"How about you do it?" It was the calm voice of Wayne from the brothel. "We lived the code for Bouchey, I ain't following no one who is scared to fight."

"Well, somebody step in here!" I'll take all you fuckers on!" Mac sneered the words with growing impatience, and his words gave him a sense of déjà vu, because it was reminiscent of his dream.

"Alec needs to fight," Wayne called out. "Or we walk and anyone who is in his camp who tries to help will deal with me. Blood for the throne."

Every head nodded in agreement, and they all stepped back as all eyes turned to Alec to see what his next move would be. Would he fight or step down? But Mac knew his thirst for any kind of power; being the man below on the totem pole no longer suited him. He wasn't surprised when Alec shoved Nina off his lap and stood to take off his coat. He stepped over the barrier created with whatever was found in the old warehouse and raised meaty fists.

"You're already hurting, Mackie," he sneered. "This will be easy."

A deadly smile crossed Mac's face. "No, it won't."

Alec charged at Mac, swinging wild, hoping that

one of his blows would land. After all the years gone by, he hadn't changed his usual way of attacking his opponent in the ring. Mac used finesse and dodged the swinging arms easily. He moved in and landed two solid punches in Alec's torso, but that left him open and he felt pain bloom like a red-hot dagger in his left side when Alec caught hold of him. Mac grunted in pain but didn't go down; he looked to where Nina was standing and noted that Wayne had moved closer. That gave him less worry because Mac could tell if he went down Wayne would get Nina out. Mac's nemesis brought down an elbow on the back of Mac's head, and that dropped him to his knees. Alec took that as a sign of his defeat and walked around the makeshift ring like a rooster with his arms spread wide.

"Get up, Mac!" Nina cried out. "You don't get to lose now you said you love me! Kick his entire ass to hell and back!"

"Yeah, Mackie, get up and fight," Alec gloated. "Because when I leave you dead in this ring, she gets to taste my meat, all the way back in her throat."

With a roar of rage Mac lunged at Alec and felt utter satisfaction when a punch caught the man in the throat. Alec staggered back holding his neck, and Mac smelled his victory. He fought savagely, landing blows to Alec's middle, head, and face. It was his turn to be on his knees and then laid out on the ground. Mac saw red as he knelt over his opponent's prone form and continued to beat him senseless until someone caught his arm.

"Enough, he's done for," Wayne said calmly. "The throne is yours."

Mac staggered to his feet and spat the blood from his mouth. "I don't want it, this shit is over, this street monarchy is finished! Go find jobs, move, marry a girl, and get some kind of life, I don't care! But if I hear that anyone is trying to reclaim what I dismantled, there will be hell to pay!"

It was then that sirens were heard in the distance and everyone started to scramble. Wayne stayed to hold him up, but Mac shoved him away. "Go, you're already on their radar; they won't believe you helped me. Contact Haile in a few days when this shit dies down."

Wayne nodded and walked away while Mac staggered to the chair Alec had vacated moments earlier. He was the only one left in the middle of the ring, his breaths whistling out through a broken nose. With a sigh Mac sat down heavily and held his side as Nina checked him over.

"Broken ribs for sure," Nina said. "Mac, you need an emergency room and x-rays."

"Okay." He looked at her through an eye that was already swelling. "Marry me."

Nina laughed. "This is how you ask me to be your wife?"

"This is how the bruiser was born; it's only fitting this be the place I put him in the grave," Mac answered. He reached up and cupped her cheek. "I made the decision before I knew they'd taken you. I'm relocating my business here, and I want you to be my wife."

Nina kissed him. "I would love to be your wife, because I love every part of you, Mac, even your past. By the way, your lap feels much nicer than his.

Mac burst out laughing just as Haile and a horde of policemen rushed in. Zeva was with him, Jasper as well, and they both looked like they were ready for a fight. He was grinning like a loon with Nina sitting on his lap. The police moved toward Alec lying on the ground instantly, while his friends came to where he sat.

"Isn't this a sight, you sitting in that beat-up chair, looking like death but laughing your ass off," Haile walked up. "You owe me a set of tires, you bastard. It can mess up my rims and axle doing that shite, man! A Rover is heavy!"

"I don't owe you shit, they can be re-inflated," Mac said.

"Why the hell are you grinning looking like you do?" Zeva asked in exasperation then asked Nina, "Is he concussed?"

"He has broken ribs for sure, a concussion might be in there," Nina laced her fingers with his.

"Meet my wife-to-be," Mac announced. "Haile, we need to find me and my fiancée a home, and I need a set of offices for the relocation of Black Enterprises. It's about time you start returning some of those favors I do for you."

"That I can do," Haile slapped him on the shoulder, and Mac winced.

Jasper chuckled. "Welcome home, Mac, it saves us from tying you into a chair until you saw the light."

Mac looked at Nina and said softly, "I already have."

With the police around them and during a ride in an ambulance, Nina never left his side. He had almost lost her, and now he thanked the heavens that he'd had the chance to save her and tell her how much he loved her. He'd spent so much time running from his past that he'd almost lost his future, his world, and everything he'd found in Nina. Mac vowed never to take that for granted again, for it was time to stop separating the man he used to be and the man he was now. They were one and the same and enabled him to survive. Plus, they had brought Nina into his world. Mackenzie "the Bruiser" Black was home to stay.

Chapter Ten

Nina never knew love like what she felt for Mac. Their New Year's wedding may have seemed rushed to some, but to her it was perfect. Mac did have two broken ribs and while she was okay with waiting for the ceremony, he was dead-set on standing in a tux for his bride. Bandaged ribs or not.

Bouchey's body had been found, and Alec been arrested for kidnapping. His crime ring was officially disbanded, and the women from the underground brothel could breathe a sigh of relief as they healed. Raine already was living with Melissa and slowly settling into her new life. And they had managed to get three of the young women back home to their families. The process to place and find suitable homes for the rest was ongoing—with everyone's help of course.

There was no new home for Mac and Nina yet, and that was okay. There was so much going on, house-hunting was not something she could fit between work and a wedding, plus injured Mac. For right now he was staying with her in the flat above the Celtic Cross, and they were snug and warm there as they made plans for a life together. It would be a small wedding with their friends in attendance. Jasper and Zeva insisted it be at the manor house with a small dinner party afterward. Donnie and Britt would be at the nuptials before they set off on their own adventure of a new life. Nina watched the brothers work through their issues and form a bond again, all the while finding a new start for the young, troubled man.

"Are you sure this is what you want to do?" Mac asked Donnie and Britt.

They looked at each other and smiled before saying in unison, "Yes."

"Well, that sounds pretty much like a done deal to me," Nina laughed.

They had settled on moving to Sydney, Australia; there was a nice rehab facility there, and it was close to the beach. Warm weather and a place for them to heal appealed to them both, so Mac made sure they had the best of everything to start out. There would even be a job waiting for Britt as a barista, and Donnie would be going back to school after his treatment was complete. There seemed to be good news all around, and for that Nina was thankful because it all could have ended badly, including her own abduction by Alec. It was all settled. Alec would be in jail for a very long time, and Mac was staying.

At first, she wondered if he'd change his mind but so far, he seemed solid in his choices. He was working from a temporary office until he relocated his business, offered his employees the option of staying in one of the small offices he had in the United States or to live in Northumberland. Amazingly enough, many of them had decided to cross the pond to the U.K.

It was January fourth and the day they would become man and wife. It was a flurry of activity at the manor house as it was decorated, and she was hidden away in one of the upper bedrooms to get ready. Mari and Zeva would be standing with her, wearing a pink hibiscus print dress as a nod to her favorite flower in Barbados. It was amazing the resources they all had combined because her bouquet held the same flowers, and it was part of the decorations below in the formal dining room of the manor. Melissa fussed and fixed her dress as they got ready while Raine sat quietly, shy and still hesitant around them on the bench seat by the window.

"Are you sure you didn't want family here?" Mari asked. Her baby bump was a little more noticeable under the dress, and the terrible morning sickness was fading.

"It's kind of late now," Zeva laughed.

Nina smiled. "We'll visit, and they'll meet Mac eventually, but my family has some really convoluted views—and I was never one to conform to them. I won't fight that battle at my wedding. We'll deal with it when the time is right."

"This will be a happy day," Zeva agreed. "At least you don't have to worry about them trying to trap you in the moors."

Nina shook her head. "Jasper's family did not know who they were messing with that day."

"It's a folk story around here," Melissa commented as she fussed with the hem of Nina's dress. "The duchess who walked of the moors and punched the hell out of the McTavish ladies. There . . . Nina, you look amazing. Doesn't she look beautiful, Raine?"

Raine nodded shyly. "Yes, very much so."

Nina smiled at the young woman. "Thank you, Raine, I hope you enjoy yourself today."

Raine nodded and looked away, out of the window, still uncomfortable with the attention on her. Nina assessed herself in the mirror, the simple off-the-shoulder white satin dress with a lace-over-satin fabric was a good choice. The hem was at her knees, but behind her was the flowing train that would trail her as she went down the stairs to Mac. Her stomach clenched with excitement and fear all at the same time, and she pressed her hand against her stomach, hoping to quell the butterflies that took flight.

"Do not throw up in this dress!" Melissa ordered and handed her a glass. "Here, take a sip of this."

Nina took the glass and gulped before coughing. "Holy Christ, Melissa, that is straight vodka!"

Melissa nodded in satisfaction. "That's what my mum did for my wedding, and it worked just fine."

"So, you went down the aisle drunk," Zeva laughed.

"I think my mum was more snookered than me," Melissa smiled. "It was the best day of my life and the best marriage, until my man passed. It will be for you, too, Nina."

"I love being married to Jasper," Zeva sighed and took a swig from the same glass.

"What I found with Haile, I couldn't fathom my life without him," Mari agreed. "If I wasn't pregnant, I'd take a sip."

"I'll do it for you," Melissa took a gulp. "One for the team."

There was a knock on the door, and Jasper poked his head in. "Are we ready up here? Mac is ready to chew his leg off and come sweep you away and elope."

"Tell Mac to hold his horses," Zeva ordered and kissed him. "Cue the music in two minutes, and we'll be ready."

"Understood, you look beautiful Nina," Jasper frowned. "Wait, is that vodka on your . . .?"

Zeva closed the door, firmly cutting off his words. "Nina, let's do this thing."

Nina looked to Raine. "Will you help with my train going down the stairs? You're part of this merry band of ladies, too."

Raine smiled brightly and nodded while Melissa mouthed a "thank you" to her friend. As they filed out of the bedroom, the music started, and it was Nina's favorite song: "What a Wonderful World" by Louis Armstrong. Melissa snuck by to take her seat before Zeva was the first down the stairs, then Mari. Finally, Nina took a deep breath and descended the stairs slowly, two steps behind her friends. When her gaze met Mac's, she was breathless at how handsome he was in a black tux with a silver tie. Their eyes never drifted away from each other, and when she stood beside him, he took her hand.

His voice was husky with awe. "You look exquisite, sugar plum."

"You are quite dashing, Mr. Black," Nina smiled up at him.

"Ready to do this?" he asked.

Nina nodded. "I've never wanted anything more."

"Thank goodness, because I got dressed up to marry people today," the priest of the local church announced. That moment of levity made a laugh go through the guests in attendance, and he began the ritual of marriage. "Dearly beloved, we are gathered here today to join this man and this woman in holy matrimony."

The ceremony was simple, without of the pageantry that would keep them from saying I do all the sooner. Mac would have been impatient, and so would she, to say yes and seal their union with a kiss. When that time came and the priest said, "You may kiss the bride," Mac took her lips before the sentence was even complete. The feel of his kiss drowned out the clapping and whistles that surrounded them. It was a perfect evening wedding where the candles and the flowers enhanced the area as guests ate and laughed. For Nina, the smell of tropical flowers filled the air and reminded her of home.

Finally, at the reception, Jasper tapped his glass lightly to get everyone's attention. "I'd like to propose a toast to the happy couple. Mac, we have been friends, well all three of us, from around ten years old. There has never been a bond closer than what me, you, and Haile share. Now Nina joins the fold, and we could not be happier for you. We are honored to call you our brother, and with our wives we wish you both all the blessings and happiness there is to offer in this world. Welcome home, brother, and congratulations. To Mr. and Mrs. Black!"

"You still owe me tires," Haile announced.

The crowd took up the cheer in the midst of laughter, and Mac leaned over to kiss her gently. When the hints of music for the first dance started, he led her to the middle of the room and pulled her gently into his arms.

"Did I mention how handsome you look tonight?" Nina asked, looking up at him.

"Show me later," he murmured against her ear and caused a shiver to run through her.

"Why, Mr. Black, what about your injuries?" Nina asked innocently.

Mac grinned wickedly. "Mrs. Black, we have abstained until our wedding. Now we are married, and I'll go to the hospital after if I have to."

"That will be the way to do it, get married and you end up in the hospital with people saying I shagged you until I broke something," Nina teased. "We should at least shower off the glaze."

Mac burst out laughing, and it carried across the room while he pulled her closer. "You are such a pervert."

"Says you," Nina laid her head against his chest. "I love you."

"And I you, my heart is forever yours, wife," Mac answered with a chuckle. "Perverted mind and all."

"Ah, you appreciate my dirty mind," she teased.

Other guests began to dance, but nothing or no

one around them mattered because she was in the arms of the man who was the perfect fit, the puzzle piece to match hers. She didn't expect to find love in Northumberland, but now that she had it, there was no way she was letting it go. To Nina it only made her life better to be known as the bride of Mackenzie Black.

The End

About the Author

Dahlia Rose is the USA Today best-selling author of contemporary, military romance with a hint of Caribbean spice. She was born and raised on a Caribbean island and now currently lives in Charlotte, North Carolina, with her five kids, who she affectionately nicknamed "The Children of the Corn," and her husband and longtime love who is also a honorable retired Army veteran. She has a love of erotica, dark fantasy, sci-fi, and the things that go bump in the night. With over six dozen books published Dahlia has become a reader favorite. Not only because of her writing but her vivacious attitude in talking to her fans online and at various events. Books and writing are her biggest passions, and she hopes to open your imagination to the unknown between the pages of her books.

Website: www.dahliaroseunscripted.com
Blog: www.dahliaroseunscripted.blogspot.com
Facebook: www.facebook.com/author.dahliarose
Twitter: www.twitter.com/dahliarose1029
Bookbub: https://www.bookbub.com/profile/dahlia-rose

Printed in Great Britain
by Amazon